THE HAPPINESS ILLUSION

The West has never been more affluent yet the use of anti-depressants is on the increase to the extent that the World Health Organisation has declared it a major source of concern. How has this state of affairs come about and what can be done? Television and advertising media seem to know. Wherever we look they offer countless remedies for our current situation – unfortunately none of them seem to work.

The Happiness Illusion explores how the metaphorical insights of fairytales have been literalised and turned into commodities. In so doing, their ability to educate and entertain has largely been lost. Instead advertising and television sell us products that offer to magically transform the way we look, how we age, where we live – both in the city and the countryside, the possibility of new jobs, and so forth. All of these are supposed to make us happy. But despite the allure of 'retail therapy' modern magic has lost its spell.

What then are the sources of happiness in our contemporary society? Through a series of fairytales *The Happiness Illusion: How the media sold us a fairytale* looks at topics such as age, gender, marriage and rom-coms, Nordic Noir and the representations of therapy on television. In doing so it explores alternative ways to relate to the world in a symbolic and less literal manner – it suggests that happiness comes by making sure we don't fall under the spell of the illusionary promises of contemporary television and advertising. Instead, happiness comes from being ourselves – warts and all. This book will be of interest to Jungian academics, film, media and cultural studies academics, social psychologists and their students, as well as reaching out to those interested in fairytale studies, psychotherapists and educated cinema goers.

Luke Hockley PhD is Research Professor of Media Analysis at the University of Bedfordshire, UK. He is a practicing psychotherapist and is registered with the United Kingdom Council for Psychotherapy (UKCP). Luke is joint Editor in Chief of the *International Journal of Jungian Studies* (IJJS) and a member of the Advisory Board for the journal *Spring* and lectures widely. www.lukehockley.com

Nadi Fadina is a media entrepreneur and a managing partner in an international film fund. She is involved in a variety of arts and media related projects, both in profit and non-profit spheres. She teaches Film Business in the University of Bedfordshire, however, her academic interests outreach spheres of business and cover ideology, Russian fairytales, sexuality, politics, anthropology, and cinema. www.nadi-fadina.com

THE HAPPINESS ILLUSION

How the media sold us a fairytale

Edited by Luke Hockley and Nadi Fadina

LONDON AND NEW YORK

First published 2015
by Routledge
27 Church Road, Hove, East Sussex, BN3 2FA

and by Routledge
711 Third Avenue, New York, NY 10017

Routledge is an imprint of the Taylor & Francis Group, an informa business

British Library Cataloguing in Publication Data
A catalogue record for this book is available from the British Library

Library of Congress Cataloging-in-Publication Data
The happiness illusion : how the media sold us a fairytale / edited by
  Luke Hockley and Nadi Fadina.
      pages cm
  1. Fairy tales—Psychological aspects. 2. Happiness—Social
aspects. 3. Mass media and folklore. 4. Mass media—Psychological
aspects. I. Hockley, Luke. II. Fadina, Nadi.
   GR550.H275 2015
   398.2019—dc23
   2014046171

ISBN: 978-0-415-72869-0 (hbk)
ISBN: 978-0-415-72870-6 (pbk)
ISBN: 978-1-315-74036-2 (ebk)

Typeset in Bembo
by Apex CoVantage, LLC

For Mum – Your protecting power of love is always with me, Nadichka.

For Mum – Thank you for taking me on the journey from Indian myths to Cornish legends, Luke.

CONTENTS

CONTRIBUTORS

Heather Brook, Ph.D., according to an on-line quiz called 'Which Fairytale Character Are You?', Heather Brook is Little Red Riding Hood. It makes sense. Heather enjoys visiting Grandma, sampling the excellent local wines of the McLaren Vale and Adelaide Hills regions, and distance running (especially trail-running in national parks and forests). Heather works in the School of Social and Policy Studies at Flinders University in South Australia, where she teaches Gender and Women's Studies. Her publications include *Conjugality* (Palgrave, 2015), *Conjugal Rites* (2007), and a diverse range of articles including most recently 'Zombie Law?' (*Feminist Legal Studies*).

Alec Charles, Ph.D., is Head of Media at the University of Chester. He has previously taught at universities in Britain, Japan and Eastern Europe, and has worked as a newspaper journalist and as a radio documentary programme-maker. He is the author of *Interactivity: New Media, Politics and Society* (2012), the co-editor of *The End of Journalism* (2011) and editor of *Media in the Enlarged Europe* (2009), *Media/Democracy: A Comparative Study* (2013) and *The End of Journalism: Version 2.0* (2014). His recent work also includes contributions to *Utopian Studies, Science Fiction Studies, Science Fiction Film and Television, Journalism Education, Journal of Popular Television* and *British Politics.*

Josephine Dolan, Ph.D., is a Senior Lecturer in Film Studies at UWE, Bristol. An internationally recognised scholar in Aging Studies, she is co-editor (with Estella Tincknell) of *Aging Femininities: Troubling Representations* (2013) and is a founder member of the AHRC Research Network WAM (Women, Ageing and Media): an expert adviser to ENAS (European Network of Aging Studies) and NANAS (North American Network of Aging Studies); and she gave evidence to the Harman parliamentary inquiry, 'Older Women in the Media' (2013). Her main research interests are British cinema, gender and aging, with recent publications including: 'The Queen: The Bio-pic, Ageing Femininity and the Recuperation of the Monarchy' for *Aging Studies in Europe* (2012); 'Firm and Hard: Gender, Old Age and Hollywood's Gaze' in *De-Centring Cultural Studies: Past, Present and Future of Popular Culture* (2012, eds Prieto-Arranz et al.); 'Smoothing the Wrinkles: Hollywood, "Successful Aging" and the New Visibility of Older Female Stars' in *The Routledge Companion to Media and Gender* (2013, eds Carter *et al.*).

Joanna Dovalis, Ph.D., is a Marriage and Family Therapist in private practice in southern California. She sees therapy as grief work, holding an essential role in the individuation process and fully actualizing the self. As a depth psychotherapist, she combines her passions for the natural partnership of film and psyche, and their critical impact on the contemporary culture. Joanna gives the psychological interpretations to narratives written with co-author John Izod on films relating to the grieving process. Their book *Cinema as Therapy: Grief and Transformational Film* was published by Routledge in 2014.

Nadi Fadina, is a media entrepreneur and a managing partner in an international film fund. She is involved in a variety of arts and media related projects, both in profit and non-profit spheres. Nadi holds a master's degree in International Cinema and is currently completing her Ph.D. in Media Arts. She teaches Film Business at the University of Bedfordshire. However, her academic interests outreach spheres of business and cover ideology, Russian fairytales, sexuality, politics, anthropology and cinema. Nadi's current research focuses on how ideologies of totalitarian regimes and democratic societies construct and deconstruct gender through the most 'naturalized' media products – fairytale animated films. www.nadi-fadina.com

Luke Hockley, Ph.D., is Research Professor of Media Analysis at the University of Bedfordshire. His recent publications include *Somatic Cinema* (2014) and the co-editing of *Jung and Film 2 – The Return* (2011) and *House: The Wounded Healer on TV* (2010). He is Joint Editor-in-Chief of the *International Journal of Jungian Studies (IJJS)*. He lectures widely in Europe, America and the UK. Luke also works in private practice as a state registered psychotherapist (UKCP) in London. www.lukehockley.com

Ryan Howes, Ph.D., ABPP, is a board certified clinical psychologist in Pasadena, California. He is a columnist for the *Psychotherapy Networker Magazine*, blogs 'In Therapy: A User's Guide to Psychotherapy' for *Psychology Today* and is Clinical Professor and Supervisor at the Fuller Graduate School of Psychology. He is committed to the demystification and de-stigmatization of psychotherapy for the general public, which compelled him to establish National Psychotherapy Day, 25 September.

Catriona Miller, Ph.D., is Senior Lecturer in Media at Glasgow Caledonian University, where her research interests include the discourses, ideology and archetypal dimensions of science fiction, horror and fantasy. She has published on *House M.D.*, *Twilight* and the slasher film phenomenon.

Greg Singh, Ph.D., is Lecturer in Media and Communications at the University of Stirling. He has published on a number of subjects, including US indie film, reality TV, Web psychology, kitsch, and game studies, and is author of *Film After Jung: Post-Jungian Approaches to film Theory* (Routledge, 2009) and *Feeling Film: Affect and Authenticity in Popular Cinema* (Routledge, 2014). He is currently working on a monograph relating to affordance and psychosocial aspects of the Web.

Terrie Waddell, Ph.D., is an Associate Professor of Media: Screen and Sound Studies at La Trobe University (Australia). She lectures and researches on the relationship between screen media, myth, literature, gender, popular culture and analytical psychology. As well as numerous chapter and journal contributions, she has authored and edited the following books: *Wild/lives: Trickster, Place and Liminality on Screen* (Routledge, 2010), *Mis/takes: Archetype, Myth and Identity in Screen Fiction* (Routledge, 2006), *Lounge Critic: The Couch Theorist's Companion* (co-editor, The Australian Centre for the Moving Image, 2004); and *Cultural Expressions of Evil and Wickedness: Wrath, Sex, Crime* (editor, Rodopi, 2003). Her co-edited book with Dr Lucy Huskinson is titled *Eavesdropping: The Psychotherapist in Film and Television* (Routledge, 2015).

ACKNOWLEDGEMENTS

There are so many people we are grateful to and who have helped us in the preparation of this book. First must come a huge thank you to Kate Hawes, who did indeed make us very happy on commissioning this volume. She was our wise woman encountered at the start of our quest – little did we realise what was in store for us as we embarked on this project. By contrast Kate, ever prescient, was ready in support with steadying and insightful words at our every step and stumble.

In the movie world the names of directors are household commodities; the names of the craftspeople, who do the actual hard graft and who are responsible for turning creative ideas into movie magic, are much less well known. So too in the publishing world, the work of a really good copy editor goes unnoticed, and we were fortunate to have Andy Soutter to help us on this project. So too our indexer Hilary Faulkener knows this book as well as we do and we are grateful and indebted to her. Along with Kirsten Buchan and the marketing team at Routledge, these people have been our faithful companions on the quest to turn our dream into reality.

In fairytales appearances are often deceptive but the cover designer Nigel Turner has created an enchanting image that does a wonderful job of capturing the spirit of this book. The cover image was taken from a fleeting moment of dynamic interactive installation The Wishing Wall (2014) created by Varvara Guljajeva and Mar Canet. It was shown at the exhibition Digital Revolution (2014) at the Barbican Centre, London, UK. Our thanks are extended to the artists for their kind permission to reproduce this image.

Finally, our thanks go to the Research Institute of Media, Art and Performance (RIMAP) at the University of Bedfordshire, who have so generously supported this research.

INTRODUCTION

Once upon a time . . .

Nadi Fadina and Luke Hockley

There are two quotations that have informed our thinking about *The Happiness Illusion: How the Media Sold Us a Fairytale*. The first comes from the analytical psychologist C. G. Jung while the second is from a literary source and is found in the writings of G. K. Chesterton. These two different vectors, the first originating in the psychological and the second in the cultural, intersect in this collection of essays and in so doing they reflect and refract current cultural concerns about happiness. First comes the poignant observation from Jung that, so typically for him, intertwines a romantic and somewhat traditional view of life:

> Happiness, for example, is such a noteworthy reality that there is nobody who does not long for it, and yet there is not a single objective criterion which would prove beyond all doubt that this condition necessarily exists.
>
> *(Jung, 1936: para. 188)*

To this sobering thought we add Chesterton's observation that 'In the fairytale, an incomprehensible happiness rests upon an incomprehensible condition' (Chesterton, 2008, p. 36). As they wrap around each other these quotations provide the two conceptual strands of a double helix – they are the intellectual DNA of our investigation into the very human desire for happiness.

This collection of chapters explores the extent to which an incomprehensible happiness as promoted by contemporary media does indeed rest on an incomprehensible condition. Culturally, we have come to a point where we now treat the symbolic and mythological as though these products of the imagination were physical and material. It is as though psychological insights have been rendered as objects that can be 3D printed via the machinery of conscious intention. What we are suggesting in this observation is that there is a plasticity to the contemporary malaise which affects Western society – it is a condition in which signs are turned into symbols and *vice-versa*. One of the sleights of hand that our culture is so practised at is to take a throwaway commercial object and to imbue it with an apparently magical quality. Everyday artefacts become the modern day counterparts to ancient magic talismans that we hope will enchant our lives and supernaturally turn the mundane realities of life into deeply satisfying states of happiness. Unfortunately for us, but fortunately for the commercial world, we never quite know what product is going to work, as we cannot predict what it is that is going to make us feel better. Of course we are complicit in the deceit as we want so very much to believe that magic is real and that the lumpen products of materialist culture can have life breathed into them – that they can become, as Jung would have it, a *corpus et* anima, a living psychological symbol.

Like all the most enduring psychological projections, it is able to take root because there is an element of truth to the fantasy. The everyday mediated images that saturate our society can indeed be the vehicles of psychological transformation. That said, advertisers would have us believe that in order for us to benefit from these magical products we need to own them – to borrow a fairytale image, this deceit is the contemporary poisoned apple of commercial seduction. As the best fairytales tell us, what matters is not the object itself, but the relationship we have with each other and to the world. Objects cannot change our lives, no matter how much we would like them to, or how much advertisers want us to believe they can. However, what does make a difference is our relationship with ourselves, with others and with our culture more generally. It is through these relationships that the leaden empty vessels of everyday commerce can be transmuted into the alchemical gold of personal transformation. Anyone who thought that the medieval alchemists could actually turn base metals into gold was, and is, a fool – as Ben Jonson's *The Alchemist* (1610) so wonderfully satirises. What alchemy really enshrines is the belief that it is the relationship we have with the world that changes us – while there might not be an actual pot of alchemical gold at the end of the rainbow, it nonetheless symbolises the covenant we have with life, and it is that understanding of our relationship to, and with, the world that is crucial to our well-being.

Illustrating the cultural implications of this psychological process, the chapters in *The Happiness Illusion* explore how traditional fairytales have been reworked into contemporary media myths. In so doing the book looks at happiness from a variety of perspectives. Drawing on recent films and television programmes (mainly from the USA and UK), *The Happiness Illusion* explores how these media offer unrealistic expectations, with their suggestions that 'if only' we were younger, wealthier, more stylish, lived somewhere different and so forth, then each one of us could be truly happy. Taken together, the chapters in this book provide a psychological and social look at the gap between reality and the expectations created by the media. In so doing they offer a number of ways to understand why Western societies are unhappier than ever before, and also what might be done to remedy the situation.

Today we are richer, healthier and live for longer than ever before. As recently as a hundred years ago modern standards of living, especially in developed countries, would have been considered a dream – a fairytale that has been turned into reality. Yet surprisingly we have never been so unhappy either, with depression affecting almost 20 per cent of the worldwide population. According to the World Health Organisation's report *Mental Health: a Call for Action* (2001), by 2020 depression will become the second leading cause of disability throughout the world – and we are three quarters of the way there. Scientists, psychologists and spiritual leaders are all struggling to find the illusory key to living life with a 'fairytale happiness', as do the rest of us in our everyday lives.

Regardless of our efforts, we keep on worrying about growing old, we do not seem to have enough money, our relationships lack lustre and we are obsessed with being either too, or not enough, masculine or feminine. We think we are too soft or that we lack determination and drive. We feel we do not live life, and instead it is something that seems to happen to us. So we take ourselves to therapy, we consume unprecedented levels of anti-depressants, and we buy stuff. Lots of stuff: cosmetics, food supplements, clothes, exercise machines and gym memberships. None of it seems to make much difference to how we feel. Additionally the stories on television, in films and on the internet continue to make the same broken promise – that a fairytale life is somewhere out there, we just need to try harder, buy more and, above all, keep 'believing'. In the past we knew that fairytales were imaginative stories that had either moral or educational purposes. Today fairytales, old and new, maintain our hope that in the end we will finally be happy and content. There is a powerful belief that as humans we ought to be happy, and that if we are not then there must be something intrinsically and deeply wrong with us.

This book looks at a range of situations where films, television and advertising sell modern day fairytales. By identifying them as modern myths, but ancient fantasies, the book deconstructs contemporary cultural discourses around age, gender, money therapy and relationships. In so doing it implicitly provides a means through which to achieve greater contentment in real life. It turns out the trick is not to buy into the seductive world of make-believe. Instead it is better to read the imagery of contemporary media in a more psychologically and socially illuminating manner. Cinema, television and advertising offer us something that they can never deliver – happiness that is culturally packaged as a fairytale – a story with oppositions running right through its narrative. It is the myth of happiness that has driven much of the self-improvement industry, it fuels the new-age movement and it provides much of the motivation for starting therapy or counselling. This is the fairytale *par excellence* of the modern age and it is in nobody's interest to expose it. Understandably, psychotherapists do not state on their websites that therapy is not going make you any happier.

While each chapter is unique and intriguing, all are built on the same foundation, namely that happiness comes from accepting the reality of our lives and not from buying into the fairytales that have been repackaged and sold to us. It transpires that developing a balanced approach to life's difficulties is the way we do stand a chance of living happily ever after. It has become impossible to think or theorise about modern life without considering the media. The prevalence of television and cinema means that few people would want to dispute the suggestion that mediated imagery plays a role in our psychological life, and this is a trend that shows no sign of diminishing. This book uniquely takes stock of how established media such as television, cinema and advertising have mobilised ancient myths, created new fairy-tales and seemingly enriched life. However, the tale of this book is a cautionary one. By putting the psychological, social and philosophical at its core it offers a way of understanding the myth of happiness in all its incarnations, as it continues to circulate in contemporary culture.

Surveying it from differing vantage points *The Happiness Illusion* performs a gradual amplification of the very idea of happiness. During the circumnavigation of this cultural myth we encounter: gender; age; social institutions (for example marriage); and social practices. Our exploration utilises a variety of psychological, cultural, social and media theories and in so doing it enriches existing discourses. As *The Happiness Illusion* unfolds it will become ever clearer how important it is to recognise the ways in which happiness has become a commodity that is sold. Using psychological insights, language and terminology, the book explores how the myth of happiness has permeated our culture, and this includes the culture of therapy itself.

The structure of the book

The Happiness Illusion has three sections, each of which begins with a short vignette that in a thought provoking and sometimes provocative manner introduces some of the concerns of the chapters that follow. These vignettes provide a conceptual map of the general subject, while the chapters themselves highlight specific cultural landmarks that are of particular interest. The vignettes are rather like the descriptions you find in the best tourist guidebooks – they make you want to explore the city for yourself. Suggesting some of the links that underpin the structure of each section, they map the intellectual territory and in so doing they offer a variety of new perspectives – each conceptual viewpoint offering a fresh new vista on the familiar cultural landscape of happiness.

Section I: There was a Prince/ss . . .

The introduction to the first section, '*There was a Prince/ss . . .*', sets the scene with a brief exploration of the centrality of human sexuality to the fairytale of happiness. It looks at how portrayals of sexuality, femininity and masculinity link to our personal, everyday lives and help in understanding who we are and how we want to be in the world. The commentary foregrounds the ways in which adhering to rigid gender stereotypes sets up unrealistic expectations. It shows that these lead to anxiety and psychological distress. Instead the suggestion is that gender and identity are more helpfully thought of as fluid and negotiated. Conceptually this section revisits some of Jung's ideas about contrasexuality and draws on some of the strengths of his insights, while also seeking to avoid some of the pitfalls of reductionism to which Jung was prone.

In the first chapter in this section Terrie Waddell draws on classic films of the 1980s and early 1990s that contribute to a balancing out of masculinity on screen from clichéd ego-driven heroes to what she calls (drawing on Winnicott's work on infant development) *transitional characters*. These male figures are less invested in finding solutions, and more focused on 'living *with* and navigating *through* emotional/physical instability – *being* in the world without seeking to control it while also *doing*: two qualities often reductively ascribed in psychoanalysis to women and men respectively'. Those selected for close analysis in the second half of the chapter, the Terminator (Dir., Cameron, *Terminator 2: Judgment Day*, 1991), Damiel (Dir., Wenders, *Wings of Desire*, 1987), and Dr Malcolm Crowe (Dir., Shyamalan, *The Sixth Sense*, 1999), have been chosen for their liminality and investment as magical objects of transformation by the key characters who depend on them for survival and individuation. In these interpretations, each is theorised to operate as an object of facilitation in the developmental process of separation and consequent identity formation. By evoking the qualities of early parental mother/father figures of nurture and trust, they can also function as fantasies for audiences, with the potential to foster a more inclusive understanding of masculinity: one not reduced to prescriptive heroic images of desire that continue to eat into the heart of Western myth, fairytales and screen storytelling.

Waddell argues that as robot, angel and ghost, the key characters share whimsical fairytale-like qualities that emphasise their transitional nature. They come into being for the benefit of others, guiding the process of self-discovery. As a form of closure to each narrative they achieve independence through separation, leaving the reliant character with a greater sense of agency, understanding of, and ability to pursue, their chosen path. The chapter closes with a plea for the development of more male characters on screen who have the capacity to touch us on a level more affecting than the task-oriented hero. Perhaps here, what we might call 'happiness' can genuinely be felt.

The second chapter in this section, '*Snow White and the Huntsman*: the fairytale of gender and the female warrior', moves the topic from 'princes' to an actual fairytale princess. In it Luke Hockley starts by noting that recently in both the cinema and on television there has been a surfeit of programmes in which the figure of the female warrior takes centre stage. Hockley goes on to explore the rise of the female warrior as an archetype in contemporary media. In doing so he examines how this figure operates as an androgyne, and subsequently becomes a site of tension around discourses of gender identity and the happiness that our engendered sense of self promises. He uses a revised version of Jungian psychology to explore the ways in which tensions in gender identity, as embodied by the female warrior, can actually be psychologically productive and healthy. Hockley is keen to note that he does not use androgyny in the reductive sense that Jung wrote about. Instead he uses it as a means of understanding contrasexuality and the extent to which the full range of human psychological experience is open to everyone. The chapter illustrates this position with a detailed analysis of the recent adaptation of the brothers Grimm's fairytale in the film *Snow White and the Huntsman* (Dir., Sanders, 2012).

He suggests that we can excavate this, and other similar mainstream narratives, to expose a more radical vein of psychological meaning. Hockley contends that such cultural archaeology has the capacity to let us explore our own engendered values and assumptions.

In the third and final chapter in this section, 'The second loss of androgyny: the fairytale of dualism', Nadi Fadina offers a wide-ranging and provocative view of androgyny. Setting her argument on a historical canvas, she looks at the deep tectonic structures of gender and how cultural shifts open up along the fault lines of androgyny. Any such deep movement is disturbing and fiery, and Fadina enjoys the transforming power of the intellectual magma flows, as they engulf media representations of engendered identity.

In her chapter, Fadina explores androgyny as an ideal unity of opposites, in various roles and contexts throughout different civilisations and epochs. She examines the phenomenon as a central concept in the human's quest for happiness, meaning and the divine self. Focusing on multiple manifestations of androgyny in myths, religions and philosophy, its appearance in the Jungian theory of individuation and the animus/anima dichotomy, and in folktales and film, Fadina explores how genders have been constructed and deconstructed in cultural products by gender politics of dominant systems. The chapter deploys a range of interdisciplinary methods in what is a broadly feminist media analysis of a variety of films such as *Prometheus* (Dir., Scott, 2012), *Anatomy of Hell* (*Anatomie de l'enfer*, Dir., Breillat, 2004), *Boys Don't Cry* (Dir., Peirce, 1999), *Albert Nobbs* (Dir., Garcia, 2011), *Eat, Pray, Love* (Dir., Murphy, 2010), *Orlando* (Dir., Potter, 1992), *Dogma* (Dir., Smith, 1999).

By examining the multiple ways in which patriarchy employs seemingly liberating androgyny as a misogynist tool, the chapter debates how androgyny is an incorporation of culturally produced hetero-normativity of femininity and masculinity. It looks at androgyny as a cultural concept that operates to serve specific regimes of gender politics which are aimed at constructing identities and myths of utopian 'wholeness' that are closely correlated with the human quest for the fairytale of gendered happiness.

Section II: The Quest: the Old Wise Helper and the magical object

The second section takes the principal actors we have already met and sets them on their journey, and in so doing it mirrors the reader's own journey through this volume. 'The Quest: the Old Wise Helper and the magical object' starts with a commentary by Hockley and Fadina that looks at that myth of transformation. Psychologising around the Grail myth, they explore how the idea that products or services of any sort can transform our lives turns out to be a type of modern Grail quest. But rather than understanding this as an inner search, the spiritual search for the Grail has taken on a contemporary commercial form. In so doing the Grail quest has taken on a financial narrative in which the ownership of objects will transform our lives – this has given rise to that most pregnant of modern phrases, 'retail therapy'. Nowadays, products are suffused with magical qualities that promise to transform our lives. They also offer a different perspective on the very idea of happiness by exploring how in the UK therapy, and in particular cognitive behavioural therapy, has been promoted as a 'magical cure' that in a small number of sessions can alleviate misery and bring happiness.

The section opens with a chapter by Josephine Dolan, 'Crumbling rejuvenation: archetype, embodiment and the "Aging Beauty myth"'. She takes her bearings from the recent fantasy films *Stardust* (Dir., Vaughn, 2007) and *Snow White and the Huntsman*, and explores the cultural specificity of the crone archetype as realised through Computer Generated Imagery (CGI) technologies and embodied by stars Charlize Theron and Michelle Pfeiffer. After forging links between traditional myth and fairytale, and Roland Barthes' *Mythologies*, the analysis traces the intersection of femininity, 'successful aging' and rejuvenation agendas as they intersect in the constitution of an 'Aging Beauty myth' embodied by the films' stars. Also, a series of ideological contradictions are identified and untangled. These are inscribed in the closure of each film where the archetypal crones, Lamia and Ravenna, are ostensibly punished for the murderous intent of their rejuvenatory practices. This punishment commences when the glamour of youthful artifice literally peels and drips away, exposing the decomposing, abject old bodies concealed beneath its veneer, in ways that, despite Hollywood's new visibility of aging female stars, reinstates its long-standing pathologisation of the older woman's body.

Given that this is mapped onto an archetypal figure that symbolises both conscious and unconscious psychological aspects, Dolan argues that the symbolic violence enacted on the crone is symptomatic of unconscious ruptures to the conscious repression of anxieties about mortality. Similarly, rapid shifts between rejuvenation and old age made via CGI imagery to the bodies of Theron and Pfeiffer destabilise the link between aging and biology, and instead establish a link to culture and discourse. Thus the closures of both films work ideologically to reiterate essentialist discourses of age by repressing the unconscious awareness of their cultural construction.

In 'Finding the golden egg: illusions of happiness in an age of consumer capitalism', Catriona Miller examines the role of money and wealth in contemporary representations of happiness. To do so she uses a Jungian understanding of identity within a contemporary economic context. Miller contends that wealth has long been a central concern in human society, and folktales reiterate endless stories about it, most making the point that whilst 'happily ever after' may be couched in terms of material well-being, seeking money and fortune for their own sake is to be eschewed. Such stories could be interpreted within a Jungian framework to suggest that they are tales of individuation, with money standing as a proxy for other kinds of wealth, such as wisdom, courage or compassion. These stories are still circulating in contemporary culture, often in the form of films, such as Disney's animated fairytales, but also in more coded form, in movies such as *Pretty Woman* (Dir., Marshall, 1990) or *The Pursuit of Happiness* (Dir., Muccino, 2006). Such an approach, whilst interesting, perhaps misses something vital about the contemporary context.

Society is organised around a capitalist structure, in fact a consumer capitalist structure, where the circulation and consumption of commodities, and increasingly their symbolic meaning, has become ever more important and happiness itself has begun to be considered within an economic context. Themes of money and wealth continue to be present in traditional dramatic forms, but far more prevalent in the era of consumer capitalism are the micro-narratives of advertising.

The power of the branded commodity is about not simply consumption of material utility, but increasingly a consumption of symbolism. This symbolism is employed to perform identity, and there is a suspicion that 'the process of becoming oneself' (which Jungians would call individuation) is increasingly framed in terms of the acquisition and display of commodities. Persona performance and commodity acquisition appear to go hand in hand where the nature of consumer capitalist society is such that adaptation to the external world is constant, not a once in a lifetime event (such as becoming an adult) as might have once been the case. The acquisition of material wealth is an underpinning constant in contemporary consumer capitalist society, which requires that very consumption, it tells us, in order to both display and create identity.

The third chapter in this section is by Ryan Howes. In 'The self-knowledge industry and myths of happiness' he explores how the personal and confidential nature of therapy renders it a mystery and an easy target for psychological projections and fantasies. Professionals cannot disclose the contents of their sessions due to professional and ethical constraints, and clients share the very personal and subjective experiences through their own filters and lenses. Add this to the multitude of theories and techniques utilised in the profession, and a coherent, unified description of therapy becomes nearly impossible. People come to therapy seeking clarity, resolution, and ultimately happiness; but how therapy gets there remains a mystery to many.

Howes observes that the media have a rich history of depicting therapy in a sensationalised form and in so doing notices how interesting it is that unwittingly the conscious goal of entertainment produces the unconscious result of illuminating archetypal therapists. Howes looks at several common therapist archetypes depicted in the media, distinguishing reality from artistic licence. Each therapist is founded upon our collective fears and wishes. In order for therapy to produce the happiness and contentment that many clients seek, they need to distinguish fact from fantasy in the self-knowledge industry.

These concerns are focused through a detailed examination of one of the examples that Howes provides. In the fourth and final chapter of this section, 'The shadow of redemption: the Grail and the self-knowledge industry', Joanna Dovalis explores the ways in which that industry is now a rapidly growing, multibillion dollar business – and one which commercialises the desire of individuals in modern society to seek out the pathway to happiness. The quest for the Holy Grail is an ancient tale that parallels this contemporary search for improving our emotional, spiritual, intellectual and physical selves. Dovalis demonstrates that in order for self-knowledge to become happiness, there must be an integration of understanding and insight, versus information that simply remains intellectualised. Rather than reaching contentedness by neglecting the shadow of the psyche, the illusion of happiness requires that one acknowledges and accepts the sorrow of life in a process of self-reflection.

Happiness is often thought to be the purpose of life. However, to know true happiness, we must endeavour to find a depth of meaning that requires expanding to a more inclusive vision of happiness that embraces the reality of the psyche. A reflective mind-set envisions the psyche as real, as valuable, and just as deserving of attention as the external world. This psychological awareness embodies the full spectrum of the self-knowledge industry, providing the space for the alchemical process of transformation to occur. Thus, psychotherapy plays an integral role in the process towards wholeness. Indeed, the ability to bear suffering is tantamount to personal growth and the expulsion of illusions.

The quest of the knowledge seeker as it relates to the psychological process often begins in the therapy room. In this chapter, Dovalis steps inside the psychotherapy sessions of the client Walter in season 2 of the HBO television series *In Treatment* (Dir., Garcia, 2008). Walter's quest for healing and self-awareness is compared to the mythical story of Perceval and his relationship to the Fisher King on his vision quest for the Holy Grail. Their journeys exemplify the developmental conflicts that arise in midlife and lead to a confrontation with the shadow of the unconscious mind. The journey of individuation leads its traveller towards acceptance by way of the narrow path between the opposites – joy and sorrow – as the self-knowledge seeker gains self-awareness in the happiness illusion.

Section III: May all your Wishes come True

In the third and final section, *May all your Wishes come True*, Hockley and Fadina look at how the dream-like language of desire has been used to create unrealistic aspirations and fantasies. This section as a whole focuses on reality television, personal transformation, the fairytale institution of marriage and the 'realism' of 'Nordic noir' television crime series. By stripping away the patina of the mythological, Fadina and Hockley suggest how it is possible to live in a more authentic and contented fashion. The focus here is on two different types of 'reality' television and cinema that actually turn out to promote a set of beliefs and aspirations that are somewhat disconnected from reality. By psychologically and sociologically deconstructing these programmes it becomes possible to see how they, in turn, reconstruct happiness as the outcome of a magical and personal transformation. Of course, this is an illusion and a fairytale, but it is one that is presented as a reality – as 'reality TV'. Instead a more realistic approach to life is suggested by a more stoic philosophy. They suggest the value of modern day stoicism explains some of the appeal of the current vogue for 'Nordic noir' television series.

Opening the chapters in this section, Heather Brook's lively 'Engaging marriage: rom coms and fairy tale endings' explores how romantic comedies, and the wedding movies that comprise a subset of them, draw on myths of happiness in direct and often obvious ways. Cinderella stories are a staple narrative of mainstream romance, as are a number of other fairytales. In a climate of high divorce rates and flexible family formations, wedding movies offer a particularly intriguing source of social pleasure. Indeed, the enduring popularity of wedding movies (across a range of genres, but especially apparent in romantic comedy and similar 'chick flicks') speaks to the wedding as a site of continuing social crisis.

Using broadly interdisciplinary, feminist methods, Brook surveys a number of popular, contemporary wedding movies – including *Bride Wars* (Dir., Winick, 2009); *27 Dresses* (Dir., Fletcher, 2008); *I Love You, Man* (Dir., Hamburg, 2009); and *Bridesmaids* (Dir., Feig, 2011) – to explore the place weddings and feminist critiques of romance occupy in popular culture today. To what extent do wedding movies recast the 'happily ever after', heavily gendered conclusion of fairytales? The movies explored here show that the themes and anxieties running through wedding narratives in popular movies are paradoxical and productive, and offer opportunities to consider how romantic happiness is produced and reflected in twenty-first-century consumer societies.

Broadening the debates around questions of representation and happiness, Greg Singh's 'The myth of authentic self-actualisation: happiness, transformation and reality TV' examines how the psychological effects of a twenty-first-century culture are already moving into an advanced stage of development; tentatively and somewhat provocatively speaking, he identifies this stage as 'postmodern' or, following Marc Augé's *Non-Places* (1995), a transitory state of non-place, which is both alienating and disaffecting, and for which the genre of reality TV plays a key role in both reproducing and deflecting. Clearly there are a number of ways in which this idea is being addressed through both cultural and psychological theory, and depending on whom one is reading this might be considered a nightmarish malady, or otherwise an opportunity for exploration and expression unbounded by the reactionary constraints of the past.

Singh seeks to explore some of the cultural effects of our times as reflected through the watchful lens of reality TV: that curiously always-already hybrid TV genre that seems to take in the aesthetics and concerns of a whole host of cultural phenomena from fashion and celebrity, to self- and home-improvement and all in between. The myth of personal happiness acts at the centre of this genre as a catalyst of transformation through vicarious consumption, almost as if one is incomplete unless abidingly happy, but that transforming one's life from 'unhappy' to 'happy' exacts a cost in both financial and psychological terms. Often derided as trivial or banal, reality TV shows and tells through narratives of sometimes deeply moving 'personal journeys' of authentic self-actualisation. Through these personal journeys of others, viewers are invited to share in the emotions of the protagonists on a level of vicariousness somewhat unprecedented outside religious rites and rituals. Analytical and depth psychology offer tools and methods through which we might explore such phenomena and which link deep-seated meaningful acts with altogether more superficial trending behaviour; and this chapter discusses those links to the psychological and political realities of transformation, as seen on TV.

Closing the book, Alec Charles takes us into the world of Nordic noir, that new and popular genre of television crime programmes. In 'A difficult task: Sarah Lund and the crime of individuated happiness', Charles explores how on the face of it Sarah Lund (from the television crime series by Danmarks Radio, *The Killing*) might not appear the most obvious of heroes. The same might be said of Lisbeth Salander (from Stieg Larsson's *Millennium* trilogy) or Carrie Mathison (from Showtime's *Homeland*) – or, for that matter, *Homeland*'s Nicholas Brody, or Dexter Morgan (from Showtime's *Dexter*). Charles explores the popularity of these profoundly problematised protagonists of contemporary crime thrillers, not only as avatars of a late postmodern zeitgeist of moral incoherence, disruption and exclusion, but specifically in terms of these characters' capacities for an unorthodox and individuated mode of happiness.

Charles suggests that their problematic relationships with the societies they inhabit are caused by those societies' refusal to accept their struggles towards individuation, and proposes that the notion of happiness is (as much as Michel Foucault's notions of power and of sanity) dependent upon definitions imposed by structures of societal power. In Jungian terms, the sickness or the sin is not that of these individuals but of a society that labels these struggles towards individuation as illnesses or crimes. The recognition (but not the acceptance) of the virtual futility of their struggles is what permits them the possibility of happiness: insofar as, in Albert Camus' words, 'we must imagine Sisyphus happy'. They are, like Camus' Meursault, or Nietzsche's Zarathustra, apparently not only unwilling but almost pathologically incapable of compromising their own sense of themselves, even at massive personal cost. It is this absurdly post-Kierkegaardian faith in their own capacity for individuation (and the necessity of that individuation as the only possible path to happiness, regardless of external demands and constraints) which defines their heroism – and which therefore addresses, invokes, attracts and indeed offers an incongruous sense of faith to contemporary audiences. Charles identifies how these figures from crime fictions act as the saviour-scapegoats who perform and suffer the almost irreconcilable existential tensions experienced by their audiences; they console against, and atone for, these impossibilities – as such, they come to resemble those who, as W. H. Auden wrote in his poem *Detective Story*, 'must pay for our loss of happiness, our happiness itself'.

References

Chesterton, G. K. (2008). *The Essential Gilbert K. Chesterton, vol. 1: The Ethics of Elfland*. Radford: Wilder Publications.

Jung, C. G. [1936]. 'Individual Dream Symbolism in Relation to Alchemy'. In C. G. Jung, *The Collected Works*, vol. 12, eds H. Read, M. Fordham and G. Adler, trans. R. F. C. Hull (1953–79). London: Routledge.

SECTION I

. . . There was a Prince/ss . . .

The androgyne

Luke Hockley and Nadi Fadina

Almost the first thing that is known about us is our biological sex. Parents are understandably curious about whether their baby will be a boy or a girl. The desire to know the sex of our unborn children is deeply rooted in us and there's no shortage of ways to go about it. Before the advent of sonograms and amniocentesis those well versed in folklore had a variety of techniques to predict the sex of the baby while it was still in the womb. Tradition has it that if the mother is carrying low it's a boy but if mum's carrying high then it will be a girl. If the baby is midway then craving salty foods means a boy is on his way, whereas wanting something sweet to eat means it is a girl. Failing that, bright yellow urine means a boy and, yes, pale yellow a girl. The markers of sex discrimination are set long before our actual birth. When we are born our weight and our sex are recorded – two factors that biologically and psychologically will continue to be important to us throughout the course of our life.

Since 2004 in the UK it has been possible to revisit the initial decision that was made about our birth-sex and, using the provisions of the Gender Recognition Act, to apply for what is confusingly termed a Gender Recognition Certificate, although a diagnosis of gender dysmorphia is required. This development in UK policy shows the legal recognition that our sex, and more specifically our gender, is not something that is necessarily either fixed or biologically predetermined. That it still requires a diagnosis reveals the lingering idea there is something wrong with people who question their sex and their engendered identity. Actually, each one of us decides for ourselves what it means to be male or female, and what masculine or feminine characteristics we adopt. This is not a question of binary opposition, of either/or; instead it is a continuum. Just as we decide for ourselves where blue turns into purple, so too we decide where we sit on the spectrum of gender. As the French philosopher Jacques Derrida might have put it, the trace we draw on the architecture of the world is personal and unique – when it come to our identity there is always both presence and absence, both female-ness and male-ness.

Unsurprisingly, the concern with gender and biological sex as markers of our identity has a long history. In his fourth book of *Metamorphoses*, the classical poet Ovid describes the story of Hermaphroditus. He recalls how Hermaphroditus (the son of Hermes and Aphrodite) was bathing one day when the nymph Salmacis seduced him and, calling out her wish to the gods that they should never part, both bodies were combined to create a new person of two sexes. (Not that Hermaphroditus was particularly happy about the arrangement.) The story is depicted in Roman paintings at both Pompeii and Herculaneum. Over the years it has inspired numerous paintings and sculptures, including *The Fountain of Salmacis*, and in popular culture the story appears as a track on the album *Nursery Crimes* by the 1970s rock group Genesis. Psychological androgyny and physical bisexuality are things we are both drawn to and yet also look at with a degree of suspicion. It is telling that the Lady Boys of Bangkok undertake frequent UK-wide tours and regularly appear at the Edinburgh Fringe Festival. We are both attracted to the transgressive and also a little wary of it.

Despite this history, we might say, with good reason, that contemporary society is preoccupied with sex and sexuality in ways that are quite different to those of previous generations. With the advent of easily available pornography on the internet and 'lad's mags' being sold in supermarkets, it is apparent that an intense interest in sex is one of the distinguishing characteristics of our age. First appearances suggest that sex roles and images of masculinity and femininity have remained remarkably static over the last hundred years or so, and our ideas about what constitutes masculinity and femininity do not seem to have changed that much. Of course, there have been shifts in fashion, taste and preference. Even so, the objectification of women, and the existence of basic inequalities in terms of cultural opportunities including pay and status, continue to be markers of sex discrimination. The cultural bifurcation of masculine and feminine qualities adds to the maintenance of these divides.

There are some indications that society is beginning to erode these artificial distinctions. In the 1970s pop icons such as David Bowie, Prince, Annie Lennox and Boy George all offered alternatives to mainstream gender norms. Currently, in the UK one of the stars of the scripted-reality television show *Made in Chelsea* (E4 Productions, 2011–present) is Ollie Locke, who is famous for being rich but more significantly for his flowing hair and his obvious use of cosmetics. After appearing in *Big Brother* (Endemol, 2001–2013) he publicly announced that he was bisexual and that he was dating Sam Faiers (a woman) who appears in yet another reality television series, *The Only Way is Essex* (Lime Pictures, 2010). That 'reality' television is now openly exploring questions of gender and sexuality shows how questions of sexual identity resonate in contemporary popular culture. Equally, models including Willy Cartier, Erika Linder, Agyness Deyn, Kirstina Slainovic, Andrej Pejić and David Chiang illustrate how androgyny is currently both stylish and fashionable.

Similar androgynous themes can be found in fairytales, though it is far more common for characters to change into animals than it is for them to change their sex. The story of the frog that turned into a prince once the princess had kissed it was popularised by Disney. (In the version by the Brothers Grimm, *The Frog King or Iron Heinrich*, the princess does not kiss the frog. Rather, after the frog has climbed into bed with her the princess throws it against a wall, at which point the frog turns into a prince.) However, there are some exceptions and there are a handful of stories where women have a somewhat androgynous character. Interestingly, in these stories it is nearly always women who pass themselves off as men, presumably because culturally men had more freedom and power. The title of Giovanni Francesco-Straparola's story *Costanza/Costanzo* encapsulates such an androgynous motif and it is a theme that is repeated in Giambattista Basile's *The Three Crowns* and again in Marie-Catherine D'Aulnoy's *Belle-Belle: Or the Chevalier Fortuné*. In the Russian tale of *Vasilisa the Priest's Daughter*, Vasilisa manages to protect herself from the prying eyes of an inquisitive king by dressing as a man. Many fairytales end in marriage, with the outspoken and feisty qualities of the bride being nullified. However, in this case the happy ending for Vasilisa is that she avoids marriage to the king. Instead she is allowed to retain a rather androgynous character and she is free to explore and roam as she wishes.

One of C. G. Jung's contributions to the psychology of the individual is his insight that contrasexuality is integral to being human. He thought it was mistaken to limit particular ways of thinking, feeling and being in relationship to one sex or the other. In this regard, he would have had little sympathy for the view that *Men Are from Mars and Women Are from Venus* (Grey, 1992). Instead, he suggested every one of us has access to the full range of human experience. How this works out for us as individuals is going to be different; we have our personal psychologies and our specific cultural experiences. It is the interaction of those two elements that results in our sense of self and how we are in the world. The psychological challenge that faces everyone is to work out how this sense of self interacts with the culture more generally. To put it another way, we are inscribed individually but thrown culturally and the work of gathering the world to us as a means to be ourselves is termed by Jung 'individuation'. This metaphor of individuation is helpful in understanding the ways that our own psychology, and the culture, can have an influence on our sense of self-identity. The figure of Hermaphroditus illustrates that this is not a question of exclusion and instead that it is more about accepting difference, as the story embodies how accepting life's tensions is important for our well-being, and even happiness.

Donald Winnicott suggested that the idea of difference was central to the way that children formed their sense of self. He observed how they used objects such as teddy bears and blankets to work out where their bodies ended and their mother's began. He called these 'transitional objects'. The use of such objects is not restricted to childhood. Winnicott thought that cultural products could be considered as transitional objects and that we used them to help us to make complicated decisions concerning our sense of self and society. Our gender identity acts as a sort of transitional object, or more technically as a transitional phenomenon. It is part of our bodily presence in the world and we use it to sift out what is like me and what is not. It follows that our gender and our identity are in flux. The idea that we are fixed in a rigid gendered sense of self – as a 'girly girl' or a 'man's man' – is to remain stuck in what Melanie Klein refers to as the paranoid schizoid position. In that state we invest energy in gender certainty, and reject any sense of otherness. We become paranoid and frightened by difference as we split ourselves off from the realities of the world. Klein suggests that fortunately many people leave that psychological state in childhood, and instead move towards a greater sense of fluidity. This does not necessarily bring happiness, and it is telling that Klein calls this state the depressive position. By this she means to suggest that it is necessary to reject simplistic and pat answers to life's most difficult questions. To be alive is to struggle with life and it requires us to draw our own trace on the psychological landscape of our lives.

In the terrain of the digital world, changing sex or gender does not require complicated operations, legal procedures or a diagnosis of dysmorphia – it just requires a new username. Forming fluid identities and shifting personas has never been easier. On the internet it is impossible to be certain about the sex of the person you are conversing with. He can be a she, or any variation. As Lou Reed put it, it is easy to 'take a walk on the wild side'. Little is known about just how many people choose to experiment with changing their sexual identity on-line but, in theory, the internet provides a domain where gender identity is free from the social constraints of the material world. However, in practice the fairytale of a tolerant society is just that, and the digital realm has its own 'trolls' who, in their anti-social behaviour, are remarkably similar to their fictional counterparts.

In the essay 'Three Contributions to the Theory of Sex' (1920) Sigmund Freud noted that humans undergo a period of hermaphrodism. Based on this, he claimed that our original predisposition to bisexuality was changed only later in life to monosexuality, although it left behind a trace of the original state. This innate bisexuality is something that Freud mentions in his discussion of Dora and also the Wolf Man. Here, however, Freud's concern is with how our original bisexual state has been turned into a neurotic condition. It was left to Jung to rehabilitate Freud's sexual theory and to integrate it with a more general psychology – a project in which Jung was only partially successful. However, if we return to Freud's idea of an innate bisexuality and combine it with Jung's contrasexual theory, it becomes apparent how the paradigm offered by androgyny offers a central way to make sense of both ourselves and our culture, something which Vasilisa and Costanza/Costanzo knew long before any of us.

1

TRANSITIONAL FANTASIES OF MASCULINITY

Terrie Waddell

This chapter draws on screen texts where performative and clichéd displays of male behaviour, so embedded in media culture, myth and fairytales, give way to a more psychologically rich form of masculinity. Figures displaying this kind of sensibility operate in the broader narrative of the story and the interior world (psyche) of key characters who, it will be argued, incorporate them into their lives as *transitional objects*: that is, they exist in liminal/transitional spaces of development, and in this reading, function as replacement objects for early parental attachment (or lack thereof) in the process of separation and individuation. Endowed with qualities beyond the distorting gender tropes of popular culture, they evoke an uncanny echo of both early mothering and fathering. This role frames such characters as rare and deeply affecting presences in a market saturated with fetishized phallic illusions of prowess, corporate acumen, sexual potency, ambition and entitlement. While the transitional objects of early childhood commonly take the form of comforting soft blankets, teddy bears, etc., male fictional characters can serve a similar function for children and adults within the narrative of film, and as projective fantasies for audiences with the potential to expand our understanding of the multidimensional possibilities of masculinity.

Unlike the task oriented hero, transitional characters focus less on solving problems and more on intuiting the value of living *with* and navigating *through* emotional/physical instability – *being* in the world without seeking to control it while also *doing*: two qualities often reductively ascribed in psychoanalysis to women and men respectively. Yet within this synthesis, transitional characters present a form of idealized maleness as a necessary counterpoint to the patriarchally ego-driven hero of Western popular culture. While the 'action figure' aspires to restore order from disorder, these new (and old) transitional images of masculinity acknowledge the inevitability of chaos and their limitations in the face of change. In facilitating the development of the ego through this kind of positive modelling, they emerge as important go-betweens in a culture that, despite pretensions to gender parity, regularly pumps out images of male privilege and female *otherness*.

Joseph Campbell's (1949) monomyth – the hero's archetypal pattern of descent, trial and triumph as a metaphor for the process of psychological development – has been reimagined through various literary, screen and media formats. It is a form of narrative notably championed (and modified) by Christopher Vogler (1996) as a necessary paradigmatic approach to storytelling that he encourages scriptwriters to follow (also see Hockley, 2014 and his critique of this prescriptive process). Constructed in ways that favour male protagonists as triumphant heroes and female characters as enablers, casualties or prizes, hero myths and fairytales are motivated and shaped by the ideological priorities of various cultures and historic periods. In refashioning the traditional hero, contemporary media ensure that this figure remains a staple of popular culture. Whether imaged as male (dominantly) or female, both sexes subscribe to a sensibility of ego gratification through questing – and this despite Campbell's initial conviction that the hero must transcend *his* self-centred attachments and emerge from the journey having 'died to his personal ego' (1993, p. 243).

Gender delineations in more obvious hero plots are just as prescribed in ancient mythology as contemporary screen versions. Acquiescence-to/acceptance-of role ascription is fairly predictable, with relatively few exceptions to counter these culturally imposed behaviours. In cinematic and televisional adaptations, development does not often begin at any genuine point of transition where the maternal is of prime focus emotionally and physically. Although various narratives acknowledge 'the feminine', usually via facilitating female characters, this sensibility is firmly associated with women/girls and is rarely considered as an androgynous component of the psyche. Instead of genuinely incorporating this *other* aspect of awareness, it is often rendered disabling to the subject's questing for, and acquisition of, the object of *his* desire. To provide a respite from this prevailing spin on masculine desirability in cinema, I have selected three representative examples of male transitional objects, each incorporating the qualities of *being* and *doing* in the service of another at the expense of ego-driven questing: from James Cameron's *Terminator 2: Judgment Day* (1991) with its robotic/cybernetic Terminator (Arnold Schwarzenegger); Wim Wenders' angel Damiel (Bruno Ganz) in *Wings of Desire* (1987); and the ghostly Dr Malcolm Crowe (Bruce Willis) of M. Night Shyamalan's *The Sixth Sense* (1999). These classic texts will be explored in the later section of the chapter, but first, in positioning select male characters as transitional objects, it is important to consider the term from the perspective of early 1950s developmental psychologist Donald Winnicott.

Transitional objects and potential space

From an object relations perspective, Winnicott (1953 and 1971) argues that infants and children adopt certain comforting, tactile or sense-stimulating objects that symbolize the transitional state of separation from the maternal, where 'mother' shifts focus from being considered part of the infant to bring a separate entity that exists as a subject in the outer world. Transitional objects, although having a physical presence as maternal replacements, are deeply embedded within the child's fantasy life and symbolize the 'me and not me' stage of a two-fold interior and exterior state of being: that is, they simultaneously become part of, and exterior to, the child in their role as catalysts for its gradual autonomy.

> The object is a symbol of the union of the baby and the mother (or part of the mother). This symbol can be located. It is at the place in space and time where and when the mother is in transition from being (in the baby's mind) merged in with the infant and alternatively being experienced as an object to be perceived rather than conceived.
>
> *(Winnicott, 1971, p. 97)*

The object itself is neutral and remains unaffected by the kinds of endowments placed on it by the child, who animates or creates the object before eventually discarding it when it is no longer psychologically invested with the magical quality of 'me'. At this later stage, it is registered as existing independently in the world and thus 'not me': 'the essential feature in the concept of transitional objects and phenomena . . . is the paradox, and the acceptance of the paradox: the baby creates the object, but the object was there waiting to be created and to become a cathected object' (Winnicott, 1971, p. 89).

Winnicott calls the imaginary zone in which these objects reside and originate a 'sacred' *potential* or transitional space: a liminality between the child and the environment, 'which initially both joins and separates the baby and the mother' and 'where play and creativity begin' (Winnicott, 1971, p. 103). He emphasizes the imperative of potential space for healthy psychological growth and warns of the likely pathology in disavowing or exploiting this interim period and its developmental promise. For Winnicott, playing leads to creativity and this in turn is carried into the cultural experience and negotiations of individuals. In other words, this is where we start to experience life's creative possibilities, develop a sense of symbols as existing externally and in intimate relationship to one's self, begin to exercise the skills for negotiating relationship boundaries, and explore the limits/possibilities of culture: 'playing and cultural experience . . . link the past, the present, and the future; *they take up time and space.* They demand and get our concentrated deliberate attention' (Winnicott, 1971, p. 109).

While early childhood development hinges on a potential space that initially applies to infants and children, Winnicott also acknowledges its viability for adolescents and adults, given his insistence on playing as necessary for culture building. In valuing potential space in this way, transitional objects and transitional phenomena (related behaviours) intrinsic to this hypothetical area must also be considered as having developmental value for adults. Winnicott draws on examples of adult-invested magical objects. These reassuring, and sometimes parentally compensating, possessions (and behaviours) allow individuals to feel protected, safe and comforted while also harking back to a preconscious period of maternal symbiosis: as Steven Tuber notes of the omnipresence of soothing transitional objects/phenomena throughout life, 'When I teach, I'm often struck by how students typically take the same seats for each lecture, as if these seats have become part of their creating a comfort zone in which to take the class' (Tuber, 2008, p. 150). In his analysis of the uncanny nature of 'transformational-object seeking', Christopher Bollas describes this quest as an:

> endless memorial search for something in the future that rests in the past . . . if we investigate many types of object relating we will discover that the subject is seeking the transformational object and aspiring to be matched in symbiotic harmony within a sense of an aesthetic frame that promises to metamorphosise the self.
>
> *(Bollas, 1993, p. 46)*

Leo Schneiderman's (2000) work on nineteenth-century author Willa Cather's use of actual and fictional characters (as well as places, like caves or attics) as soothing creations/memories that compensate for her problematic relationship with a cold and disengaged mother, makes the case that transitional objects can also take the form of people. This way of thinking recalls the concept of *self-objects* that Self Psychology founder and key theorist in narcissistic behaviour Heinz Kohut (1977) sees as serving identity and development throughout life.

> More important than inanimate and non-human transitional objects are people who serve as objects of identification. Either by their physical presence or remembered absence, these parents, siblings, relatives and friends possess the ability to reduce anxiety, not only in children but in adults as well.
>
> *(Schneiderman, 2000, p. 132)*

Using Winnicott's rationale, Schneiderman also draws attention to the way in which human transitional objects are internalized, and in this state carry symbolic projects which individuals are able to identify with 'as the self and sometimes as an external love object' (2000, p. 132), as can be seen in the later discussion of *Wings of Desire*.

In keeping with this notion of people/characters construed as catalysts for transition, Bollas draws on the patient–analyst relationship that, if successful, relies on the concept of transference: a stage that mirrors the Winnicottian idea of projection, separation and development:

> The aesthetic of psychoanalysis strives to place the patient and the analyst in deep subjective rapport with one another, and this aesthetic evokes a state of being which reenacts the infant's relation to mother. So, whether the material of a session is oedipal, for example, with the analyst functioning thematically as the father, or the oedipal mother, the aesthetics of psychoanalysis, induced

by the analytic technique, places the analyst in the position of the transformational object.

(Bollas, 1993, pp. 47–48)

Schneiderman makes a case that the male and female characters Cather creates are invested with compensatory qualities for her mother's inadequacies and psychological neglect. Not only does she endow her female creations with agency and bravery but she also identifies with supportive male figures, actual and imagined, who demonstrate a capacity to nurture and succeed in the cultural world: 'Cather's long-term admiration for the work of Henry James, and her dependence on him as a model well into her years as a successful writer, are consistent with her search for exemplary, sexually non-threatening father-figures – in essence transitional objects' (Schneiderman, 1999/2000, p. 137). Without wanting to venture into an extended analysis, *Saving Mr Banks* (Dir., Hancock, 2013), the film based on writer P. L. Travers' motivations for both the character of Mary Poppins and the father figure Mr Banks in her 1934 children's book, similarly reveals how fictional literary characters can carry transitional object investments for their creators.

The interest here in relation to male transitional figures in cinema, similar to those Cather creates for her own psychic well-being according to Schneiderman, is their alignment with the maternal (archetypally a non-gender specific quality) *and* their independent existence. The distinction of the transitional objects in the analysis of selected screen characters below is their duality as both maternal and paternal sources of comfort: the more shape-shifting the character, such as the angel Damiel, the ghostly presence of child psychologist Malcolm Crowe, or the Terminator machine, the more clearly they can be positioned both within and exterior to the potential space. This allows those who invest them with transitional properties to experience a (an uncanny) sense of symbiosis and separation. The bigger picture, though, is the way that each character can also be understood as a transitional/compensatory object for audiences saturated in a clichéd, unbalanced and possibly alienating onslaught of machismo, particularly in genres that emphasize the hero arc as one of necessary aggression, power, *othering* of the feminine, and egocentric questing.

Claire Kahane acknowledges Winnicott as an influential voice in the area of object relations, psychoanalysis and cultural relations, but argues that his work is frustrated by problematic gender assumptions. For Kahane, Winnicott's understanding of the maternal role in the mother–child dyad is reductively based on a presumed, or 'natural', biological given that views the mother as 'normally' good-enough in her instinctive feel for the infant's developmental needs:

> After having instilled the capacity for illusion, the good-enough mother *naturally* knows when and how to undermine this hallucinatory omnipotence by a gradual failure of adaptation, a weaning from the breast which allows the infant to realize separation and to enter that intermediate area between me and not-me, the potential space that is the matrix of imagination. This

tendency in Winnicott's text to privilege biology as the self-evident ground of truth and to ignore the way in which culture mediates, if not constructs, our perception of the 'natural' has disturbing ramifications for feminists.

(Kahane, 1993, p. 279)

She further acknowledges Winnicott's admission that the 'breast' can be a metaphor for nurturance, yet finds this undermined by his references to the breast as an anatomical, and therefore intrinsically female, passive rather than active object. Because of the mother's/female role of *being* for the infant, who then 'moves from a primary maternal vortex of corporeal needs and pleasures toward an idealizing primary identification with the Other, an imaginary site of power and desire located elsewhere, beyond the mother' (Kahane, 1993, p. 287), Winnicott claims that '"doing" is male and "being" is female' (Kahane, 1993, p. 281). This discussion of a denied female and privileged male subjectivity is relevant in this analysis of male character fantasies/images as a fusion of both *being* and *doing*: that is, their role as objects of succour (metaphorical breasts perhaps) and simultaneously, or at some point in the narrative, their gradual move towards an existence beyond that of a self-object. This synthesis comforts and guides the characters yet to emerge from variously framed potential/transitional spaces dependent on these 'me and not me' male figures for their well-being. Such fantasies can also be theorized to reassure audiences relentlessly subjected to an often aggressive masculinity that disavows any integration of the active and the passive: qualities that intersect and apply to both genders.

Cinematic access to potential spaces and transitional objects

In terms of literature in particular, Bollas talks of an *aesthetic moment* that bonds the reader to a text. This experience can be transformational:

> A spell that holds self and other in symmetry and solitude, time crystallizes into space, providing a rendezvous of self and other (text, composition, painting) that actualizes deep rapport between subject and object. The aesthetic moment constitutes this deep rapport between subject and object, and provides the person with a generative illusion of fitting with an object, evoking an existential memory.

(Bollas, 1993, p. 40)

The aesthetic objects guiding this rapport are transformational – the film or the book itself. But we can also see this moment within a story. To illustrate this point, Bollas takes the example of Ishmael in *Moby Dick*, a character who fixates on whales and whale related objects as though captured by them and so placed 'in a deep spell of the uncanny' (Bollas, 1993, p. 45). Cinema too (some might say perhaps even more intensely) has the ability to cast a spell of capture where audiences are transported back to the potential space and the pleasure/comfort/irresistible connection with the transitional object. Either the film itself, or characters projected for us to 'create', may become incorporated into our individual emotional worlds.

As Andrea Sabbadini (2011) writes, although Winnicott was only moderately interested in cinema, his work on developmental states, objects and phenomena has been important for screen studies, even if this theoretical framework is relatively new to the field given the prolific application of Freudian and Lacanian theory (cf.: Hockley, 2014; Konigsberg, 1996; Kuhn, 2010 and 2013; Sabbadini, 2011; Silverstone, 1994). In 'Cinematic Experience, Film Space, and the Child's World', Annette Kuhn (2010) draws on the potential space to discuss the way cinema engages with the material and psychological. In addressing the specifics of the medium's ability to produce imagery and sound based on various configurations of space and movement, her paper is a significant contribution to examining cinema's 'capacity to express and evoke – at levels of feeling and memory – highly invested objects, spaces, passages, in particular those which have to do with the task of negotiating inner and outer worlds' (Kuhn, 2010, p. 96). This function permits audiences to step back into the world of childhood and once again play creatively with boundaries. Along with others employing Winnicott's transitional space, Kuhn uses the image of a bridge straddling inner and outer worlds as a metaphor for this concept: its crossing conjures a sense of oscillation 'marking the subject's engagement with transitional phenomena' (2010, p. 84). Similarly for Hockley (2014), both film and the experience of spectatorship can be related to the transitional object and the transitional phenomenon respectively with their associated me-and-not-me slippage between cultural and psychic worlds. This bridge-like negotiation that occurs in early childhood and ongoing psychological development can potentially shape the spectator's evolving sense of identity. The simultaneous submersion *into* the fantasy and awareness *of* the fantasy (inner and outer) has the capacity to arouse feelings of 'conflict' and birth insight:

> in the act of recognizing what is me and what is not me on the screen a new psychological image comes into being. Winnicott talks about the transitional object – the object which is invested with affect and which is used to test out boundaries of the self. Thus the object becomes the recipient of unconscious projections and fantasies which in turn are used as a means through which to define the self – the unknown helps us to understand ourselves.
>
> *(Hockley, 2014, p. 46)*

With this understanding of the transitional capacity of film in mind, and the objects of comfort and guidance that it can potentially generate, I would now like to look at specific examples of how male characters operate as transitional objects, within the text and the projective fantasies of audiences. Of course female characters can also function in this way: director Spike Jones' *Her* (2013) for instance, where a symbiotic relationship develops between a computer user and his female operating system ('who' eventually becomes sentient, develops agency and seeks independence) – but this is another discussion. Of interest here is the kind of masculinity that exists in potential spaces as an object of *being* and a subject that *does*. There is a Janus-like quality in this 'me and not me' aspect of such characters. They evoke a symbiosis with 'mother' by acting as a compensatory comfort for 'her' loss, while also symbolizing movement towards a state of subjectivity. The beauty of these characters is that when situated in worlds exterior to those for whom they serve a transitional function, they never lose their dual capacity to *be* and *do*, unlike the traditional hero who largely relinquishes, or lacks, the capacity to *be* for another.

Cybernetic organisms, angels and ghosts

The characters in the three main films discussed below can be most clearly read as transitional objects because of their ability to facilitate individuation. During the stage of cathexis, the external object that the child enfolds inwardly and empowers as a source of well-being and protection belongs 'to the realm of illusion' (Winnicott, 1953, p. 97). Although not technically under 'magical' control like the *internal object* (the illusory image/concept of the breast for instance in Kleinian theory that the infant internalizes and imagines to be an intrinsic part of its being), in the world of screen fantasy, myths, children's fiction and fairytales, external attachment objects can take on magical properties that accentuate their illusory/transitional function (Pinocchio, Peter Pan, the red shoes, Mary Poppins, Paddington, etc.). The selected characters therefore depart from the neutral material object (of the real world) through their construction as other-worldly shape-shifters/psychopomps (related to the bridge or crossing metaphor). We can see the validity of this technique in director Seth McFarlane's *Ted* (2012), where a teddy bear is animated (anthropomorphized) for us to more clearly, and comically, recognize it as a transitional object that inhibits the development of its man–child owner – never having been discarded as a not-me object. Ted the teddy remains magically cathected until the closing sequences of the film. The three characters discussed below are also imagined to have a similar fairytale identity – as robot, angel and ghost. This element of the fantastic highlights their transitional function in the narrative and positions them as objects existing exclusively for the comfort or self-discovery of another before their role is eventually surrendered, forcing the dependent character to acknowledge the inevitability of separation.

I will only talk briefly about *Terminator 2: Judgment Day*, for while this much theorized classic displays the 'me and not me' dynamic of the transitional object/phenomenon, it also illustrates a wider cinematic/televisual trope alluding to the fear of separation that the object portends – the fear that technology, originally designed to *be*, *serve* and/or *pleasure* the creator/s, may develop sentience and so abandon its maker for an independent (often rebellious or vindictive) existence: *I, Robot* (Dir., Proyas, 2004), *Real Humans – Äkta människor* (Dirs, Harald Hamrell and Levan Akin, 2013), *Blade Runner* (Dir., Ridley Scott, 1982), *The X-Files* (various episodes 1993–2002), *Her* (Dir., Spike Jones, 2013) or *2001: A Space Odyssey* (Dir., Stanley Kubrick, 1968), for example.

Terminator 2: Judgment Day

According to Susan Jeffords (1994), the themes and characters of American cinema in the closing decades of the twentieth century reflected the political climate of the time in their swing from *hard bodied* in the 1980s to *new* masculinity in the 1990s. Made in 1991, *Terminator 2* parodies its hard bodied precursor with hysterical displays of machismo and violence. The story-line follows a robot sent from the future by the resistance leader John Connor to protect his childhood self (Edward Furlong), and so ensure his destiny as a figure of human salvation (J. C. in a Christ myth allusion). With Schwarzenegger in the title role as the Terminator, this machine, or cybernetic organism (reproduced from a production line of pre-programmed models) represents the simulacra of cyclically churned out machismo – a cypher, filtering a set of behaviours endlessly reproduced in Hollywood for audience consumption and disposal. While also exposing the performative facade of the hard body as he arrives naked from the future, adorning himself in biker gear and fitting weaponry stolen from his first human encounter, he is also a fantasy object: positioned between worlds (the future and the present), non-human and designed to serve as a replacement or compensation for John's dead father and incarcerated mother. He exists exclusively for the boy's safety/security and inadvertently guides him to greater self-awareness.

Throughout the film John learns that he can manipulate the Terminator's attitudes and behaviours, as if creating him, and playfully revel in the machine's acquiescence to any command. As the equally parodic hard bodied mother, Sarah Connor (Linda Hamilton), famously says in an internal monologue where she reflects on the Terminator as the ideal of fatherhood, 'It would never leave him, and it would never hurt him . . . It would always be there. And it would die, to protect him.' In the machine's pre-programmed *being* and protective *doing* behaviour we are given not the ego-driven/self-serving hero of classical myth and fairytales, but a hyper-imitation of the macho Hollywood hero. As a metallic network of joints wrapped in artificial silicone flesh and excessive muscle, he becomes a vehicle for exposing the facade of such contrived manliness.

At the end of the film, the Terminator does in fact disintegrate, releasing John into the world where he will eventually see *it* as a machine with a separate material (and so fallible) 'not me' existence. The setting of the narrative in a liminal period when humanity is predicted to face extinction through the rise of a warlike artificial intelligence system (Skynet) that has developed its own consciousness and used this to produce an army of anti-human warrior robots metaphorically suggests (as mentioned above) the fear of separation signalled by the transitional object. For in this duality of the Terminator and Skynet, we see both the uncanny nature of the comfort object and the possible irrational panic of (parental) separation signified by the feared self-awareness of computer technology.

Terminator 2, where a male figure exposing the hysteria of heroic machismo by presenting a new form of altruistic and self-sacrificing masculinity – at once maternal and paternal – is a far cry from director Wenders' *Wings of Desire*. There is no necessity here to parody clichés. We are given a self-contained reality, dependent on the suspension of disbelief for us to experience the aesthetic moment of, as Bollas says, 'deep rapport' with both the film and the central object of transition – the angel 'Damiel'.

Wings of Desire

Written by Wenders and Austrian avant-garde literary figure Peter Handke, *Wings of Desire* used a lyrical form of dialogue and monologue to expose the spoken and inner thoughts of its characters. In this version of angelic intervention, influenced by the poetry of Rainer Maria Rilke, a group of largely male angels (only two fleetingly glimpsed female versions), dressed in neck scarves and dark coats, are tasked with watching over a struggling and still war blitzed 1980s Berlin. These all-seeing/hearing spirits often sit on the shoulders of the bronzed goddess Victoria who forms the apex of the city's Siegessäule (Victory Column). But more often they congregate in Berlin's famous state library (*Staatsbibliothek* or *Stabi*), a repository of knowledge that, like the angels themselves, fuses the past and the present. In what many consider Wenders' ode to Berlin, we are exposed to a city in transition. The angels observe human behaviour, access memories, and touch those in distress by releasing a sense of well-being to ease the negativity of their thoughts. A potential space is created within the film through its emphasis, visually and lyrically, on the play, wonder and optimism of childhood: a time, for Wenders and Handke, of unselfconscious creativity and impulse. These children's engagement with each other, the world, and the angels (for only they can see them) provides a sense of optimistic futurity and so acts as a balm to the suffering of past cultural traumas.

The central narrative focuses on the angel Damiel who, in mirroring this evocation of innocence and potential, yearns to renounce the spiritual zone for the sensate pleasures of the material world where he can 'end infinity and be tied to the earth': a desire made more resolute with the intensification of his love for Marion (Solveig Dommartin), a circus trapeze artist. For the greater part of *Wings of Desire*, Damiel acts as a selfless agent/angel of healing. In inspiring others by penetrating their thoughts and emotions, and so becoming part of their imaginary world, he carries the qualities of a transitional object. Through his ethereal encounters with Marion, we see him as part of her inner experiences, and later, when human, a free agent who nevertheless becomes central to her life. The 'me and not me' quality of the transitional object constellates in the poetry of this relationship.

Like all key male characters referenced in this chapter, Damiel has a strong association with children. The introductory voice-over to *Wings of Desire* hints at the centrality of childhood to the greater themes of the film:

> When the child was a child, it walked with its arms swinging. It wanted the stream to be a river, the river a torrent and this puddle to be a sea. When the child was a child, it didn't know it was a child. Everything was full of life, and all life was one.
>
> *Wings of Desire (Dir., Wenders, 1987)*

While peripheral to the main story-line, the various shots of children capture their ready acceptance of, and engagement with, the serene and non-judgmental presence of the angels. This creates an association with the *imaginary friend* – a form of early transitional object creation. Damiel sits amongst the children, smiles as they pass or gaze at him, and takes pleasure in their wonder, joy and openness to discovery. Like the angels, there is a sense of timelessness about these children. Both are held in a potential field, unaffected by the limits of the world. But the angels become for the children, as Winnicott writes of the traditional mother–infant dyad, 'an object to be perceived rather than conceived' and this engagement can metaphorically signify 'the union of two separate things, baby and mother, *at the point in time and space of the initiation of their state of separateness*' (Winnicott, 1971, p. 97). The angels are therefore catalysts of change – psychopomps guiding subjectivity.

In stark contrast, Wenders splices footage of a war-ravaged early 1945 Berlin into the central story: the actual bombing of the city, graphic images of dead babies in the street, and the clearing of wreckage. A second subplot involving the fictional shoot of a World War II film, with cast and extras who look as if they could have been plucked from old newsreels, along with the desolate and yet to be rebuilt 1980s Berlin setting, captures the liminality of the city and its people still caught in the past. The extreme contrast between this suffering and the fearlessness of Damiel and the children who revel in the pleasures of the material world with no sense of foreboding is Wenders' homage to both human resilience and perhaps the potential space as a site where one can become lost in discovery and rediscovery, and by so doing endure the destructiveness of a heroic/phallic will to power. This space, of possible renewal after crisis, is not unrelated to Victor Turner's understanding of cultural liminality, where society is cyclically able to regenerate itself through a tension of what he terms structure and anti-structure. Here a transitional 'frame' is created, allowing society to 'cut out a piece of itself for inspection' (Turner, 1969, 1979, p. 468) and so, through play, experimentation and creative endeavour, re-evaluate future directions (Turner, 1969, 1979).

Potsdamer Platz, where the more reflective scenes were shot, reads as an apt metaphor for Turner's concept of cyclic regeneration via liminal submersion, and the transitional or potential zone in Winnicottian theory. Now the thriving hub of central Berlin, this public square, bombed during the 1940s and divided in the political aftermath of Germany's defeat, remained an echo of the war until reunification in 1990. Wenders positions Damiel and his co-angel Cassiel (Otto Sander) in this in-between space, walking around or moving seamlessly between the eastern and western fringes of the dividing Berlin Wall, as if to accentuate their unquestioned acceptance of the collective essence of human experience and the futility of politically imposed segregation. Notions of maternal separation, the necessity of transitional objects to ease this release and a sense of bereavement, are also acutely felt in the imagery of Potsdamer Platz. While it is bleak and in a state of decay, the angelic visitations to this no-man's land hint at its transitional symbolism. The sequence where Damiel becomes human begins with Cassiel carrying him through the eastern side of the wall. Black and white film is used throughout *Wings of Desire* to indicate that the world is being perceived through the eyes of angels. Damiel's emergence into the cultural, as he lies on the western boundary in the next shot, is therefore filmed in colour to signify his now human perspective. Although the sequence pointedly reflects Wenders' political view of socialism, it can also be related to the acquisition of selfhood and ongoing personal discovery where hard and fast boundaries dissipate into a more nuanced understanding of the external, its psychological impact, and the way it changes/colours our (inner and outer) experiences.

A circus matinee scene, set in an enclosed tent, also provides us with another metaphorical transitional zone. Here performers, children and angels merge in a state of acceptance, creativity and possibility. The concepts of potential space and transitional object crystallize as a child seated in the audience beside Damiel tries to engage him in animated conversation. While not verbally responding, he accepts his role in the little girl's reality as an object that *is* – existing for her well-being. But as he watches Marion perform, Damiel becomes more certain of his need to leave this state of *being* for an existence that involves *doing*/agency. At this point we know the circus will be closing for the season so that the 'containing' tent, which we later see stripped by riggers, serves as a threshold space: a metaphor for the magical, temporal period of play prior to entry into the cultural *and* a space that can be revisited/resurrected, for the children, Damiel and Marion herself, who, while mourning her limited time of play on the trapeze, welcomes the freedom to, as she later says sitting on the vacant circus grounds, 'imagine anything. It's all possible. I only have to raise my eyes, and once again I become the world'.

Through the developing spiritual-to-material relationship of Marion and Damiel, we witness the *becoming* of the transitional object (Damiel) from mere *being*, to *being-and-doing* through the acquisition of subjectivity. This is a creative metaphor for not only the process of individuation, but also the motivating driver of the film – a faith in the viability of the child-like potential space for collective/individual rebirth. Rather than a trajectory of egocentric heroism, this return, play and giving of one's self to another, allows us to recognize a form of masculine strength so rarely celebrated, let alone acknowledged, in cinema and popular culture.

From Marion and Damiel's first meeting, Wenders makes allusions to a destined unity between them: as if they were part of each other. We first see Marion as a winged angel on the trapeze and as the ever watchful (invisible) Damiel later exits the tent behind her, a circus colleague jokes 'an angel passes by', causing Damiel to turn in shock as if he rather than Marion was being addressed. In the final key scenes, after his many visits and observations of Marion's behaviour and thoughts, even trying to touch her but never able to permeate the divide between their worlds, she has a dream that awakens her to his presence and guides Damiel's resolve to make this now mutual, if intangible, awareness of each other a reality. It is as if she is calling *and* creating him as a child might its comfort toy. The calming and receptive energy of his company and the idea that he is part of her is visualized in the dream through a slow fade from Marion's sleeping image to his, so that at one stage their bodies are superimposed one over the other, constituting an entity – the 'me', before the realization of the 'not me'. When the sequence comes to an end Marion curls up in a fetal position, holding like an infant the memory/feeling of her transitional object.

When he has renounced his spiritual existence, Damiel and Marion meet. She seems to instantly sense that his was the presence in her dream. Together as a couple, Damiel is seen holding secure the rope that Marion manipulates as she practises her aerial performance. His monologue expresses the oceanic intimacy they now share. Possibly alluding to their previous roles as transitional object and dependant, he says 'I was in her and she was around me', and to the longed for acquisition of an external, material existence where he and Marion meet as equals, 'she came to take me home and I found home . . . I know now what no angel knows'. It is easy to read Damiel as a conduit for the (re)imagining of a perfect, uncanny union: a sensuality that borrows from the unconscious memory of, or desire for, symbiosis with a more than good-enough, ideal form of 'mother' – a source of emotional succour that in this instance *is* (for and in us) and *does* (independently maintains the connection when active in the cultural world).

The Sixth Sense

Here we have a similar image of masculinity to *Wings of Desire* but the central character of interest, Dr Malcolm Crowe, takes a backward route through the developmental paradigm. We first see him clearly established in the cultural, from which he moves to the potential space to fulfil his role as a transitional object for the troubled child 'Cole' (Haley Joel Osment), and after a necessary separation, shifts to yet another dimension. For a ghost, this is of course possible. Malcolm and Damiel share the combined attraction of *being* and *doing* – with one or the other quality enacted separately *and* at the same time, as we see when Damiel falls to earth yet maintains his former angelic capacity to *be* for another.

Malcolm is introduced as a successful child psychologist, recently awarded the mayor's citation for professional excellence. As he and his wife celebrate at home after the ceremony, she reminds him of the sacrifices he has made for families in the community – confirmed by a panning shot of handmade thank-you cards from children. In the bedroom they notice that the house has been broken into, and a disturbed young man, one of Malcolm's former patients, Vincent Grey (Donnie Wahlberg), appears in the *en suite* yelling at Malcolm, 'you failed me'. Vincent shoots him in the stomach, before turning the gun on himself. A year later Malcolm appears at the home of the nine-year-old Cole, reported as suffering from extreme mood disorder. We learn at the end of the film that Cole and Vincent have always lived in a constant state of fear and anxiety. Both are able to see ghosts: often terrifying images of murder victims or those who have died prematurely in traumatic accidents – all bearing their physical and emotional wounds. It falls to Malcolm to discover Cole's secret and link it to Vincent's distress, which he was previously unable to diagnose. But what Malcolm also discovers is that he himself is a ghost, and, like the others who confront Cole, doesn't know he's dead. We are shown this in the concluding sequence of the bedroom shooting, kept from us for the body of the film. Previously it appeared as though Malcolm had survived the shot – no blood was evident on his torso as he fell into the bed from the impact. We now see his wife turn him on his side to reveal a thick pool of red pouring from his back and his slippage into death with the final whispered line, 'it doesn't hurt anymore'.

In the context of male characters as transitional objects, *The Sixth Sense* gives us a version of this phenomenon that links very closely with the qualities written into Damiel and (maybe a little uncomfortably) the Terminator. Each persona sits in an in-between/liminal world that can be imagined as an allegory for the potential space. All exist for a significant other (Cole, Marion, John), who stitch this 'man', or messenger/psychopomp, into their being as an object that signals entry into a new phase of psychological development: a fusion (substitute) of early parental nurture under the child's control, and an entity in its own right. Malcolm exists exclusively for Cole. Their relationship has the dual purpose of making the child aware that ghosts come to him for help as a way of moving into the dimension of death, and triggering Malcolm's awareness that he too is one of these tragic figures caught in limbo. Shyamalan cleverly orchestrates the action so that, until Malcolm's status is revealed, we are unaware that he is invisible to all except Cole. Like Damiel's relationship to the children he comes in contact with, Malcolm becomes Cole's invisible friend. Perhaps he failed Vincent because at the time of their meeting he could not function outside the cultural, and so could not be created, controlled or factored into Vincent's internal world: the child's situation therefore reads as a metaphor of entrapment in a fearful liminality with no object of transition to provide a route of escape.

Like John Connor, Cole has no father figure in his life. He wears compensatory objects – his father's broken watch and the large frames of his father's eyeglasses. He keeps toy soldiers for comfort and steals a small statue of Christ as another form of protection. While Cole's relationship with his mother is extremely positive, his collection of male images and adornments suggests a need to invent, possess, and be soothed by a sense of omnipresent fathering (which might also be imagined as maternal). It therefore follows that Malcolm will be added to this collection of transitional objects. When Malcolm has served his purpose for Cole, after acting as a catalyst for the child's emotional and psychological shift into a more knowing sense of self, Cole's reaction to his departure swings from panic to acceptance. He even purposefully releases Malcolm by suggesting he communicate with his grieving wife as she sleeps: an act that enables Malcolm to recognize his death, and with this acknowledgment, more completely transition into the afterlife.

Conclusion

I have discussed shape-shifting characters in this chapter to more clearly demonstrate their transitional object qualities. There are many others on screen, outside this category, that could equally be theorized to have similar significance – evocations of active participation in the world and receptivity. These embodiments of a form of masculinity that is not entirely driven by the aggressive desires of the ego and the *othering* of the (non-gendered) feminine or maternal are, in the scheme of our media, distinctive. They are often seen as idealized fantasies or a form of weakness and/or humiliation. What is argued here is that these characters are central to developing an appreciation of masculine strength through compassion. When thought of as transitional, they carry an added potency. As Schneiderman argues, such attachments, whether in the form of things or characters, are 'not synonymous with regression. On the contrary, such attachment is consistent with a strong drive for achievement and may even provide the psychic energy for such achievement' (Schneiderman, 2000, p. 142).

Shyamalan used the colour red in *The Sixth Sense* to signal a slippage, or collision between the world of the living and the dead. The cloak of the Christ figure that Cole steals from a church and places amongst his protective ornaments and toys is bright red – so here, we have another image of masculinity serving a transitional function. Arguably, Christ/God in the Christian tradition is in many circumstances enfolded in the imagination as an entirely 'me' object: 'created' by believers as an inner source of affirmation, reassurance and guide to a more enlightened selfhood. There is a similar promise with the other images of masculinity discussed in this chapter. With their transitional qualities, these figures, like Christ, can become imaginary friends for audiences to hold close, take into their worlds, and reshape as objects of unconditional comfort. Is this a version of masculinity that we need to see, not exclusively of course, but more often – one with the capacity to touch us more deeply than an idealized action/task-oriented hero? Bruno Ganz's comment on playing Damiel is a fitting summation of the potency of male transitional objects in cinema – an apparent source of *happiness* for the *ménage à trois* of film, spectator and actor that he conjures:

> But what touched me the most deeply was that for several months after the film came out, when people – especially women – recognized me, in Berlin or elsewhere, their eyes opened wide and they said: 'It's the guardian angel' . . . as though they actually took me for an angel. And people in planes said: 'Ah, no need to be afraid, because with you here, nothing can happen. Now we are safe.' Or a mother said to her child: 'Look, there's your guardian angel.' They weren't joking. Of course they knew we are real men and women, but somehow . . . It's strange. I don't know what really happened. That was an amazing feeling. I loved that. Because that means much more than people saying, 'You are a very good actor,' or 'I love your work.' If they say, 'Oh, you are an angel,' it's like a miracle. In some way I *became* an angel . . .
>
> *(Raskin, 1999)*

References

Bollas, C. (1993). The Aesthetic Moment and the Search for Transformation. In P. L. Rudnytsky (ed.), *Transitional Objects and Potential Spaces: Literary uses of D. W. Winnicottt* (pp. 40–49). New York: Columbia University Press.

Campbell, J. (1993/1949). *The Hero with a Thousand Faces*. London: HarperCollins.

Hockley, L. (2014). *Somatic Cinema: The relationship between body and screen, a Jungian perspective*. London: Routledge.

Jeffords, S. (1994). *Hard Bodies: Hollywood, masculinity in the Reagan era*. New Brunswick, NJ: Rutgers University Press.

Kahane, C. (1993). Gender and Voice in Transitional Phenomena. In P. L. Rudnytsky (ed.), *Transitional Objects and Potential Spaces: Literary uses of D. W. Winnicottt* (pp. 278–91). New York: Columbia University Press.

Kohut, H. (1997). *Restoration of the Self*. London: University of Chicago Press.

Konigsberg, I. (1996). Transitional Phenomena, Transitional Space: Creativity and Spectatorship in Film. *The Psychoanalytic Review*, 83(6), 865–89.

Kuhn, A. (2010). Cinematic Experience, Film Space, and the Child's World. *Canadian Journal of Film Studies*, 19(2), 83–98.

Kuhn, A. (ed.) (2013). *Winnicott, Transitional Phenomena, and Cultural Experience*. London and New York: I. B. Tauris.

Raskin, R. (1999). Wim Invents the Film While Shooting. An Interview with Bruno Ganz on *Wings of Desire*. *P.O.V filmtidsskrift: a Danish journal of film studies*, 8. Retrieved from http://pov.imv.au.dk/Issue_08/POV_8cnt.html.

Sabbadini, A. (2011). Cameras, Mirrors, and the Bridge Space: A Winnicottian Lens on Cinema. *Projections*, 5(1), 17–30.

Schneiderman, L. (1999/2000). Willa Cather: Transitional Objects and Creativity. *Imagination, Cognition and Personality*, 19(2), 131–47.

Silverstone, R. (1994). *Television and Everyday Life*. London: Routledge.

Tuber, S. (2008). *Attachment, Play, and Authenticity: A Winnicott primer*. Lanham, MD: Rowman and Littlefield.

Turner, V. W. (1969). *The Ritual Process: Structure and anti-structure*. London: Cornell University Press.

Turner, V. W. (1979). Frame, Flow and Reflection: Ritual and Drama as Public Liminality. *Japanese Journal of Religious Studies*, 6(4), 465–99.

Vogler, C. (1996). *The Writer's Journey: Mythic structure for writers*. London: Boxtree.

Winnicott, D. W. (1953). Transitional Objects and Transitional Phenomena: A Study of the First Not-me Possession. *The International Journal of Psycho-analysis*, 34, 89–97.

Winnicott, D. W. (1971). *Playing and Reality*. London: Routledge.

2

SNOW WHITE AND THE HUNTSMAN

The fairytale of gender and the female warrior

Luke Hockley

Introduction

Recently in both the cinema and on television there has been a surge of programmes in which the female warrior takes centre stage. Television series from the 1970s, 1980s and 1990s such as *The Bionic Woman* (NBC, 1976–78) and *Zena Warrior Princess* (Renaissance Pictures, 1995–2001) show this is not a new development. The emergence of more recent series such as *Hunted* (BBC, 2012), *Tru Calling* (Fox, 2003–6), *Doll House* (Fox, 2009–10), *True Blood* (HBO, 2008–14) and numerous others demonstrate how the cultural interest in this figure is both continuing and current. Examples include the remake of *Battlestar Galactica* (2004–9) which features numerous warrior women, and the actors from that, such as Katee Sackoff, who make notable cameos in series such as the remake of the *Bionic Woman* (NBC, 2007). In the cinema both *Elektra* (Dir., Bowman, 2005) and *Hanna* (Dir., Wright, 2011) once again have a female warrior as a central figure. In both cases the narrative of each film is clothed in either mythological imagery (as is the case for *Elektra*) or in a fairy story in the case of *Hanna*, which in its cinematic style is also reminiscent of *Run Lola Run* (Dir., Tykwer, 1998).

The film this chapter explores, *Snow White and the Huntsman* (Dir., Sanders, 2012), is at face value a fairly typical mainstream narrative film, albeit one that is an adaptation of a well-known fairy story. Illustrating the continuing appeal of this particular fairytale, there were no less than three adaptations of *Snow White* released during 2012. A companion piece to *Snow White and the Huntsman* was provided by the comedic and self-reflexive *Mirror, Mirror* (Dir., Singh, 2012), while by way of variety *Grimm's Snow White* (Dir., Goldenburg, 2012) offered a more whimsical direct-to-DVD release. *Snow White and the Huntsman* retains many of the elements of the version by the brothers Grimm: an evil Queen named Ravenna (Charlize Theron); 'Prince Charming', now Prince William (Sam Claflin); a magic mirror;

seven dwarfs (including Bob Hoskins, Ray Winston and Ian McShane); and the Huntsman (Chris Hemsworth), charged by Snow White's stepmother to bring her stepdaughter back (not just the liver and lungs as in the Grimm version) – even if the ending will remain the same, as the Queen rather gruesomely intends to tear out Snow White's heart. The film also introduces some interesting set pieces that are not in the Grimm version. Of particular interest is an encounter with a magical white stag in 'Sanctuary', which is the home of the fairies and which, we will discover, has mythological and spiritual significance; a misty isle reminiscent of Arthurian legend that is inhabited only by scarred women; and a final battle scene that leads to the death of the Queen.

Snow White is played by Kristen Stewart, who is well known for her role as Bella Swan in the vampire films of the *Twilight Saga* (1998–2012). During the making of *Snow White and the Huntsman* Stewart's personal life hit the tabloids as news of her affair with the film's director Rupert Sanders became public. As we will see, this piece of salacious gossip is actually of psychological interest too, as it encapsulates one of the many splits and dualities that run throughout the film between the innocent virginal purity of Snow White (cf. Bella Swan) and the more lusty realities of Kristen Stewart's actual life. It shows how fantasy and reality intertwine, and also how audiences never watch a sealed-off text. Instead they bring to the experience of viewing a film their expectation as well as their knowledge of the actors and performers involved.

This chapter argues that through the introduction of new elements, *Snow White and the Huntsman* succeeds, albeit unwittingly, in presenting a psychological rather than a narrative drama. In this tale what appear to be inconsistencies and lapses in the logic of the film actually turn out to represent a series of psychological contradictions, differences and tensions. To be specific, the chapter will suggest that the character of Snow White is both feminine and masculine and that the film depicts her psychological development into a semi-androgynous sense of engendered identity. While the film has a tendency to resort to cultural gender stereotypes, *Snow White and the Huntsman* also offers some more progressive qualities. Not least of these is the way in which the different characters in the film represent different parts of the same person. For example, the Huntsman embodies some of the physical and psychological qualities that are underdeveloped in Snow White's personality. There are others who do the same: The scar-faced women of the forest lake, her childhood friend Prince William and the mysterious encounter with the White Stag all move Snow White ever closer to the more integrated character she is by the end of the film. In these ways questions of difference, otherness and relationship permeate the film.

Symbolically, and also in mythological terms, Snow White embraces otherness and difference and in so doing she follows her own path through life. Eschewing marriage and men, she embodies a sense of purpose as she ascends the throne – she is not a wife or girlfriend but a warrior and a queen. As C. G. Jung might have put it, to live life in this manner is to respond to the psychological call of individuation. It is his contention that learning to hold life's contradictions, that finding a personal way of being in the world, and accepting how to exist in a psychological arena that is immersed in cultural and environmental pressures, gives the best possible chance of living life in a contented and authentic manner. The opportunity for this diminishes when such images are literalized, as this turns what is metaphorical and symbolic into something material.[1] In semiotic terms, it reduces symbols to signs.

Snow White and the Huntsman is both conservative and progressive in the mixed messages that it contains. While a psychological approach cannot resolve the contradictions in the film, it can reframe them and by so doing it de-literalizes their interpretation. The result is that narrative inconsistencies, illogical images and unexplained events become moments that offer psychological insights. Such a reframing encapsulates the Jungian view that if we are to understand ourselves psychologically then the intellect alone will always prove insufficient. While thinking is clearly crucial for understanding who we are, it is also the case that emotion, intuition and the capacity to symbolize are no less indispensable. Adopting such an orientation facilitates the emergence of difference and contradiction.

Sexuality and contrasexuality

It is not often that people start therapy with a view to exploring questions about their gender identities. Of course, it does happen but in my experience it is somewhat unusual. What is much more commonplace is that during the course of long-term psychotherapy people come to wonder how their bodies and their sexuality affect their understanding of how they are in the world. In other words, the question of what the lived experience of 'being' a man or a woman means psychologically is much more commonplace. Given the plethora of media images that actively set out to promote particular ways of being and which overtly embody sets of engendered cultural practices, it is not at all surprising that such issues also crop up in therapy. Therapy offers a space in which it is possible to reflect on how our cultures and their mediated images 'affect' us. Contemporary media images strongly suggest that aspiring to highly specific cultural norms is a way in which we can achieve contentment in our lives, and that beauty and happiness are intertwined with a certainty about ourselves and our sexuality. As will be seen, it is interesting that the film of *Snow White and the Huntsman* explores some of the complex ambiguities that are concerned with human identity and particularly sexuality. Further, it does so in ways that are at odds with current cultural norms. These tend to be relatively conscious and often involve material and physical concerns about sexuality, appearance, age and so forth. By contrast, the film adopts a more contradictory approach and a less clear-cut position.

Psychologically, physical anxieties about appearance and age, for example, are matched by a more unconscious inner movement that prompts us to come to terms with a more personal and unique view of how we, as individuals, are in the world. This inner psychological work involves forging a view of ourselves which reflects our inner state and which also encapsulates how our fantasies can influence our everyday behaviour and consequently our sense of selfhood. The suggestion is that the unconscious part of ourselves is in relationship with the material cultural images that surround us. Recognizing the existence and importance of this psycho-cultural interrelationship is a central part of the process of growth. When positioned in this way, somewhere between the unconscious and consciousness, actually it is not quite so remarkable that a film such as *Snow White and the Huntsman* turns out to be intimately concerned with the process of gender identity. In so doing, the film engages with these images of self and sexuality in ways that are both normative, fixed and conservative, and yet which also allow for the possibility of far more fluid and radical interpretations.

Analytical psychology and androgyny

It might at first seem with this talk of fluid gender identity that what is being alluded to is a type of androgyny. Indeed the idea that gender fluidity might correspond to androgyny has occurred to some writers, and in particular those who are drawn to the adoption of a fairly classical Jungian orientation. One such writer is June Singer (1976) who suggests that androgyny as an unconscious state is threatening and disorientating precisely because it places one outside cultural norms. Yet Singer also suggests that there is safety in the idea that it is possible to gain a meaningful sense of ourselves by paying attention to our inner unconscious lives.

> The androgyne will not be discovered by turning outward into the world, but by turning inward into ourselves. It is a subtle body, that is to say 'non-material,' buried in the deep unconscious realm all humans collectively share [. . .] androgyny is a state of consciousness that is far from ordinary, and therefore it threatens many people's state of equilibrium [. . .] androgyny threatens many presuppositions about individuals' identity as men or women.
>
> *(Singer, 1976, pp. 8–9)*

There is something rather appealing in Singer's injunction to accept these inner non-material figures, not least because to give them a non-corporeal existence means that at least to some extent they are nullified. This type of androgyny is reductive, in that it subscribes to a rather absolutist view of both identity and sexuality, and it is also anti-materialist as it reduces the composition of the psyche to that of a subtle body. Here films exist in a rather interesting territory. On the one hand they clearly show actual bodies of real people but these bodies are also rendered as two-dimensional phantoms that exist only fleetingly as part of the unfolding pre-scripted narrative on the cinema screen, embodied by real actors playing fictional characters. This seems to correspond rather neatly to the psychological process of projection, in which our own inner experiences are projected onto the world, and consequently we behave as though the outer world has been moulded into a replica of our own personal psychological experiences. In both the cinema and beyond its walls, the division between the psychological and the material is not as clear as common sense would have us believe.

Of course, fairytales are imaginative worlds where changes to shape, gender, sex and identity are commonplace. Indeed one of the themes of *Snow White and the Huntsman* is that the attempt by Queen Ravenna to maintain an eternally youthful appearance is bound to be unsuccessful. That this is an unrealistic quest is expressed in the film's repeated statement that, 'By fairest blood was it done, and only by fairest blood can it be undone.' In this sense, the fairytale is ahead of the psychology. Rather than fixing gender, albeit in relation to a 'non material body', the film attempts to see identity as something that is both static and in a state of flux, where bodies can be both material and 'subtle', and in Ravenna's case where the same body can be young and old at the same time. (An analogue of the magic mirrors we all own which we hope will reflect a younger face each time we look into them – at least if cosmetics are to magically do their job. So too we hope the mirror might reflect the age we feel we are, our inner sense of our age if you will, rather than our actual age.) In a similar vein, it is important to the film that Snow White herself is both 'fairest of the them all' and can also be a masculine avenging warrior capable of leading an army of men into battle against her evil stepmother. There is a very real sense in which Snow White is also the Huntsman of the film's title, in which two separate characters are converged into one: the implicit message is that difference and otherness need not actually be different and other.

A sense of fluidity comes from the way that the psychological sense of who we are is composited from notions of otherness. In this respect fairytales are an ideal form as they encapsulate a state of otherness in their representation of different worlds and alternative possibilities. In doing so they offer a fertile territory in which to explore how what is me and what is not me can be built up by understanding and holding in our conscious awareness questions not of likeness and recognition, but rather of difference. Andrew Samuels (1985) locates this general psychological step in our psychological development in terms of human sexuality and sees it as a central structuring metaphor, noting:

> This is because a man will, quite naturally, image what is 'other' to him in the symbolic form of a woman – a being with an-other anatomy. A woman will symbolize what is foreign or mysterious to her in terms of the kind of body she does not herself have. The contrasexuality is truly something 'contrapsychological'; sexuality is a metaphor for this.
>
> *(Samuels, 1985, p. 212)*

What Samuels articulates so adroitly in his development of an idea which was originally articulated by C. G. Jung is the way in which contrasexuality should not be literalized and instead needs to be treated as metaphor. Actually there is nothing mysterious about the workings of either male or female bodies. What Samuels encourages is the adoption of the structuring metaphor of otherness. In doing so he helpfully encourages us to de-literalize the images of sexuality which contemporary media insist on rendering as explicit and fixed. From this new perspective, sexuality becomes a means through which to reflect on bodily difference rather than the more contemporary and normative narrative that encourages an aspiration to bodily perfection. Significantly, it is the acceptance of a sense of difference that psychologically is so important. What matters is the realization that while the other is different, at the same time as being 'other' it is also the same – to put it simply, it is just another. Contradictions are a common quality of psychologically rich imagery. Just as dreams represent other worlds that are somewhat like our waking world but which in other regards are quite unlike it, so too films depict worlds that are familiar but which at the same time are also different. When images are positioned as both inner and outer, it is possible to see how they act as a type of amalgam that bonds together unconscious aspects with a conscious awareness. In this way the meaning of images is transient and shifting as they oscillate between conscious perception and unconscious affectivity.

Developing this point further, this chapter will explore some post-Jungian ideas about sexuality and the role of images in bridging the inner world of the psyche and the outer world of materiality. It will show how fairytales take us into a liminal territory. In particular we will see how *Snow White and the Huntsman* both literalizes fantasies about sexuality and yet at the same time offers the opportunity for a more radical model that moves towards an inclusive view of human sexuality that is psychological and material – spirit and body.

Post-Jungian theory and contrasexuality

Jung's thinking about the contrasexual archetype is found in volume 6 his Collected Works, *Psychological Types*. (A detailed account of the development of his ideas can be found in Kast, 2006.) Initially Jung identified two separate archetypes: the anima and the animus. Put briefly, the anima represents what Jung described as the feminine potential in men while the animus represents the masculine equivalent in women. In this division Jung was attempting to make a distinction between an innate biological identity and the cultural identity that is subsequently grafted on to it. There is a rich and useful idea here but it is not one that Jung developed. Instead his view of the psychological value of becoming aware of this duality was that it would assist men and women to become 'fully' men and 'fully' women, even if the culture was trying to pull them away from these roles. This did not entail for Jung embracing much by way of contrasexual qualities. In fact quite the opposite is true, as is clear from the way he wrote about how men and women could be 'possessed' by their anima and animus. (A turn of phrase that betrays something of the conservative attitude that continues in some aspects of Jungian orientated theory.) Jung's earlier followers tended to support this reductive understanding of gender, as typified by Esther Harding's 1933 book *The Way of All Women* (republished 1970) which offers a rather traditional and prescriptive view of sexuality, noting that:

> [A woman] follows the pattern laid down by Eve. She is maid, wife, mother or widow, which are aspects of life that suffice for her. She hardly knows of any other possibilities. Life in relation to her man and to society is fulfilled for her in the living of her feminine functions. She lives as a *woman*. But if she

is to become an independent personality, instead of being only the feminine counterpart of a man, she must bring up to consciousness her own masculine qualities.

(Harding, 1935, p. 69)

These outmoded aspects of the contrasexual theory need to be left well and truly behind. Jung's own writing at this time is riddled with contradictions as he works on refining his theory of individuation. For him, sexuality is part of the primary material that has to be worked on psychologically, and accepting such work involves undertaking the psychological work of becoming who we actually are, and recognizing the dissatisfaction with who life has turned us into. That is what Jung terms the process of 'individuation'. Jung sets great store by the psychological needs of individuals and how these are articulated in relationship with their cultures at large. Contrasexual theory has the potential to offer an inclusive model of human sexuality that regards our biological and psychological identities as states that are fluid and changing; they change as our awareness of the roles that our various cultures play (personal and societal) in shaping our understanding of ourselves becomes increasingly clear. It suggests that instead of regarding anima and animus as masculine and feminine other, both are in fact cultural images of sexuality that are available and meaningful for men and women alike – in other words, everyone has both an anima and an animus and to be human is to be contrasexual and contra-cultural.

Jung glimpsed this insight but he seemed rather too afraid of it to follow it up in any meaningful way. Instead he ends up with a rather reactionary view of human sexuality that seems to fly in the face of his underlying theory of individuation. His view of men and women is rather biologically driven and culturally determined. The revisions made by post-Jungian thinking push matters on and take Jung's insights much further than he himself was prepared to go. The distinction outlined above, between body and culture, means that it is now possible to talk about the father (cultural image) of whatever sex (biology) or the mother of whatever sex. To do so is to acknowledge difference and diversity, but not to reduce such difference to either cultural or biological determinants. As Samuels (1985) comments:

Each person remains a 'man' or a 'woman' but what that *means* becomes relative. The picture is of fluidity within a structure of otherness. This shifts the concept of bisexuality from being something undifferentiated (polymorphous or polyvalent) into a vision of there being available to all a variety of positions in relations to sex, gender differences and divisions. I would add that these positions may stay divided or united – and all the time the issue of 'masculine' and 'feminine' is in suspension.

(Samuels, 1985, p. 223, original emphasis)

Snow White and the Huntsman

It might seem odd to suggest that a popular film such as *Snow White and the Huntsman* could have any role to play in this somewhat complicated and theoretical approach to the psychology of engendered identities. Yet Jungians have long held that mythology and folk tales are the repository of culturally clothed archetypal images, and they contend that such imagery and characters contain psychological insights that are not directly available to the more rational and cognitive parts of ourselves.

The opening of the film sets the scene and leaves viewers in no doubt that they are in a rather traditional fairytale world. Snow White's mother is walking through the snow-covered grounds of her castle and sees a rose that is in flower. She goes to pick it and as she does so she pricks herself on its thorns and three drops of bright red blood fall on the pure white snow, and she thinks to herself, 'If only I had a child as white as snow, lips as red as blood, hair as black as a raven's wings and with the strength of that rose.' Shortly afterwards, Snow White is born. The film moves on apace and quickly explains how Snow White's mother died of cold in winter, that the King remarried and that on the first night of their marriage his new wife, Queen Ravenna, murdered him.

As a character Queen Ravenna has divided cultural commentators. Some find in her an anti-feminist figure, while others take the opposite point of view and regard her as a pro-feminist character who is offering a timely message about current cultural myths of beauty, aging and women's power. Of course, she is both and it is this type of contradiction that suggests a psychological reading of her character is appropriate. Ravenna's character is defined through otherness and in a paradoxical manner also through her non-acceptance of that difference. As a character she is partly a descendant of the familiar Evil Witch/Stepmother found in the Grimm version of the fairytale. In both the film and in the Grimm story the explicit message of the narrative is that old and vain women should step aside to let younger, 'fairer' women take their place. At least at face value, such a message is unlikely to make Ravenna a feminist icon. Add to that Ravenna's vocal hatred of men and that too means she is unlikely to be of much help with the problem of stereotyping feminism as anti-male.

However, one of the more interesting aspects of the film is the way it paints a very different portrait of the Queen to either the familiar version from the brothers Grimm, or the way that Disney portrays her in the film of *Snow White and the Seven Dwarfs* (1937). In both those versions of the story the Queen's character is motivated by a murderous envy of Snow White's youthful beauty. By contrast in *Snow White and the Huntsman* it is the beauty of the Queen that imbues her with power and ultimately military strength. The catch is that this power is only an illusion for it is the result of her glamour (an old Scottish word originally meaning magic or enchantment) but it lasts only a short time before it has to be topped up. To keep the magic alive Ravenna has to literally suck the life out of young women and so the illusion of her youth and beauty comes at the cost of the destruction of other women.[2] Of course there are means of protection against the Queen's power, and disturbingly the women of the lake village cover their faces in an Islamic-like hijab, not out of religious conviction but as an aesthetic decision, as they have deliberately scarred their faces, and by so doing have made sure they are of no value or interest to the Queen.

There are plenty of good reasons to dislike the cold-hearted, murderous and vainglorious qualities of Ravenna, yet her character is also somewhat more nuanced than this caricature suggests. Viewers are able to form a more complete picture of Ravenna as a result of two brief insights into her childhood. The first occurs in the film's opening minutes as Ravenna tells Snow White that just like her she lost her mother when she was very young – this is also one of the first suggestions that Snow White and Ravenna have more in common than might be immediately apparent. (The very first suggestion of this connection is that, echoing Ravenna's name, Snow White has hair as black as ravens' wings.) Ravenna comments, 'I feel that you and I are bound. I feel it there – your heart' and the sinister overtones of that comment will become clear as the film unfolds. Later, viewers learn that as a child Ravenna was placed under an enchantment that gave her power, but only so long as she remained the 'fairest one of all'. If for a moment this fairytale curse is transferred into the real world then it is all too evident that if a child is brought up with the belief that the only way she can have power and agency in the world is by being the most beautiful woman alive, then it is going to lead to a pretty disastrous life. This does not militate against the current cultural myth that beauty equals power. By contrast, Snow White's power comes not from her appearance but instead from her courage and bravery in acts such as escaping the castle, calming a troll, and defending the dwarfs. Indeed, early in the film the Huntsman as narrator informs viewers that Snow White was loved, 'as much for her defiant spirit as her beauty'.

The illusion of beauty and power driven by destruction and desire is central to the Queen's relationship with Snow White. In fairytales there is generally a way for spells to be undone. In the case of Ravenna's beauty enchantment, the illusion can be broken by 'fairest blood'. As the film puts it, 'By fairest blood the spell is done, by fairest blood it can be undone.' The significant point here is that it is purity of blood that will eventually prove to be Ravenna's downfall, and not the physical beauty of youth that the Queen goes to such lengths to preserve for herself. As the spell is cast the sequence visually reprises the opening of the film by repeating the motif of drops of red blood, though this time rather than falling on snow they drop into a milky white liquid as the magical potion is conjured. On the one hand the film denigrates Ravenna's attempts to preserve her youth as it repeatedly stresses how it is that Snow White's beauty comes from her heart and from her blood. Actually she is able to conquer the castle and ascend the throne partly because she *is* young and beautiful and also because, unlike Ravenna's cold but ravenous sexual appetite, Snow White's sexuality has yet to emerge. By contrast, Ravenna is overtly sexualized with dramatic make-up and scenes that prominently feature her high fashion model-like figure, while Snow White remains an adolescent.[3]

As suggested, blood is one of the central visual metaphors that ties together Snow White and Ravenna. As an image, it returns repeatedly throughout the film and in so doing it strengthens the links between the two characters. In a reprise of the imagery that opened the film, and also during the casting of the beauty potion, when Ravenna dies she too sheds three drops of blood as, by fairest blood, the enchantment is undone by Snow White. In case the point is missed, Ravenna comments, 'We're not that different, you and I', to which Snow White retorts, 'I'm everything that you are not.' Of course, Snow White is mistaken.

While the dialogue of the film might deal in stark oppositions, the imagery of the film does not. Unlike the script, the film's images hold together contradictions and tensions, as in the way that blood represents life, death and also power in the film. It was the blood of Snow White's mother as it fell on snow that awoke in her the desire to have a child. But by contrast, Ravenna's blood marks not the desire for life, but the imminence of her own death. As for Snow White, and as the Magic Mirror makes clear to Ravenna, it is only after Snow White has her first period, or as the film rather coyly puts it, her 'coming of age', that her beauty is now greater than Ravenna's. In other words, it is her menstrual blood that symbolizes her new power over Ravenna, and it is this power that will eventually give her the strength to kill her stepmother. In a similar manner there is a dual symbolism to the colour white in the film, where it stands as both an inspiration for life (as in the snow), while the milky coloured liquid in which Ravenna bathes (presumably to help keep her looking young, a beauty treatment with a longstanding history, as shown by the ancient Egyptian queen Cleopatra) represents the illusion of youth.[4] White is then an image of new life and also of aging and death. Further, it is the colour of the horse that carries Snow White to safety after she has escaped from Ravenna; it is the colour of the stag that she will meet in the forest which initiates her transformation into a leader and warrior; and as life and death are once again interwoven it is also the colour of Snow White's funeral dress. The significance of this is that the film does not give us closed readings of its symbolic imagery. Consequently, as viewers we are often uncertain about what is happening and why, and meanings of scenes and even individual images are often not an integral part of the narrative structure. In short, the film requires us to mirror its narrative by holding contradiction and tension – by being unknowing and uncomprehending and by accepting otherness and difference.

Snow White, trolls and dwarfs

One of the interesting additions the film makes to the Grimm version of the story concerns Snow White's journey into the Dark Forest and her encounter at the Troll Bridge. The film's Dark Forest is a dangerous and primeval underworld that provides a home for primitive creatures. It is filled with deadly hallucinogenic gases and it is little wonder that trees appear to turn into snakes. In symbolic and psychological terms, the forest stands for the darker side of the human psyche.[5] The Dark Forest presents another interesting contradiction, as Ravenna, who is the film's darkest character, has no power there. The sequence at the Troll Bridge precedes Snow White's arrival in the village of women, her encounter with the dwarfs and also her arrival in Sanctuary. In the scene a bridge comes to life, revealing that it is a giant, angry troll. While the Huntsman attempts to kill the troll, it is Snow White who simply by looking at the creature is able to calm it down.

It is an interesting sequence for several reasons. First, it shows the relative inability of the Huntsman to do his job and protect Snow White (a failure of traditional masculinity or animus if you will). Second, it shows Snow White's empathy with nature and how everyone recognizes the beauty of her spirit (her anima-istic qualities). However, as will become clear, what Snow White actually needs is in fact something quite different to these cultural stereotypes. While the Huntsman might not be able to defeat the troll through force, when that type of assertive and aggressive behaviour is assumed by Snow White then she is able to lead her army into the battle whose outcome will be the death of Ravenna, and Snow White's subsequent coronation as Queen. It is also tempting to see the bridge as marking something of transition for Snow White as she moves from childhood into adolescence – it is the 'monstrous' and seemingly frightening side of her sexuality which she needs to integrate.

It is important to flag a point here that will be returned to later as it is a significant one, namely that Snow White will become Queen in and of her own right. While her stepmother became Queen through marriage and ruler by murdering her husband, Snow White needs no such patriarchal endorsement or rite of passage. Instead Snow White's journey will take an altogether different route as her own sense of independent psychological self-identity will give her the internal strength to hold state, nature and indeed the very land itself together. So this is a fairytale, to be sure. But if we psychologize around this fantasy for a moment it becomes possible to see how Snow White has not moved into some sort of idealized state of human existence. Instead what she offers is a fantasy of wholeness and, agreed, this is of course an illusion, a fairytale of sorts, but nonetheless it offers the prospect of finding happiness in one's own path through life, however difficult it might appear. We might think of this depiction of the myth of self-actualization that is taking place as a cultural approximation of the processes of individuation.

As Snow White embodies in the film, what she needs is the ability to live a whole and integrated life which accepts that the way we understand ourselves and the world is of necessity composed in metaphors and symbols – to literalize the symbolic and treat it as though it were real ends in disaster. The conservative elements of the film equate Snow White and her female qualities with a girl-like feminine nature that has to be relinquished if she is to turn into that other male fantasy of the Female Warrior. Culturally it appears that in our current discourses around the image of women the tendency is to present either hyper-feminized images or (as suggested in the introduction to this chapter) overly masculinized images. However, the more progressive aspects of the film can be seen in its ability to show how the path to success (or 'happiness') in life is not through aspiring to psychological norms but comes through the recognition that otherness is a metaphor for the psychological condition of the inner state, and hence also of our relationship to the world. By accepting that a sense of otherness belongs as much to ourselves as to those around us (be they a Huntsman, an Evil Queen, or the diminutive dwarfs of the otherworld) it is possible to become more fully the people we are and enter more fully into relationships with others. In short, while it might not be a guarantee of happiness, the acceptance of 'other' at least promotes a sense of fidelity to the inner world. Hence Snow White is in some quality both good and bad, warrior and peacemaker, female and male.

The dwarfs in this film offer a particularly interesting and curious set of figures, as in many ways they are more fully human than many of the human characters. These dwarfs are a long way from the nameless cyphers found in the Grimm version of the story. Nor do they bear much resemblance to the childlike comic characters devised by Walt Disney and his team. For example, the dwarf Beith, while climbing up a sewer during the final assault on Queen Ravenna's castle, chimes, 'Hi-ho lads, it's off to work', to which another dwarf, Quert, quips, 'If he starts whistling, I'll smash his face in.' These dwarfs are quick-witted, intelligent, and insightful. They are also spiritually attuned. As such the dwarfs are more integrated and whole characters than any of the humans in the film. However, unlike their human counterparts they are not individual characters. Instead they work as a team, one with the other, to understand what is happening and to puzzle out their best course of action. As a group they are central to the plot of the film, first leading Snow White into Sanctuary and then spearheading the assault on the castle.

The dwarfs are also quick to recognize Snow White's royal lineage and to treat her with respect. Though, like the Huntsman, they only follow her once she has demonstrated her courage. Indeed, Snow White is welcomed into their company and is included in both their celebrations of life and the rituals that mark its passing, as in the death and mourning of the dwarf Gus. The dwarfs symbolize and embody for Snow White the ability to live life in a manner that is attuned to its realities and which also recognizes the importance of ritual and symbol. As such, they are figures of neither solely good nor evil, and while they are unemployed royal gold miners they are also robbers. These are characters that socially belong to the old realm and not the new period overseen by Queen Ravenna, and significantly it is Gus who saves Snow White's life by putting himself in the path of an arrow intended for her. He dies as a result, but it is his sword that Snow White will use to kill her stepmother.

As mentioned, it is the dwarfs who lead Snow White into Sanctuary, the homeland of the fairies. In the film this is a world set within another world. In terms of filmic style, Sanctuary is given a heavy dusting of Disney's fairytale magic – mushrooms with eyes, animated badgers and rabbits who give rides to fairies sit side by side with a variety of other enchanting digitally rendered animals. Eventually, the fairies lead Snow White to one of the film's more puzzling encounters. In a clearing in the forest stands a White Stag. As the dwarf Beith remarks, 'No one's ever seen this before.' Which leads to the following exchange:

Duir: The White Hart bows before the Princess, Father.
Muir: He is blessing her. You have eyes Huntsman but you do not see. You, who have
    been with her the longest. She is life itself. She will heal the land. She is the
    one.

(Snow White and the Huntsman Dir., Sanders, 2012)

The image of healing the land has many mythological overtones, including sources as diverse as the Arthurian legend and the epic of Gilgamesh. Like many of the film's images, symbols and narrative developments, the appearance of the White Hart goes unexplained. Doubtless some viewers will find this type of narrative reticence frustrating or, more prosaically, an example of bad filmmaking. Yet at the same time it is the very ambiguity of these lapses in logic which gives the film a certain mythological life and which keeps its symbols vibrant. My suggestion is that this is more than a stylistic appropriation of fairytale tropes in which the entropy of over-determined signs ends up with the dissipation of meaning. Instead, when rational logic fails the film shifts into a mythic dimension that relies much more on intuitive and non-rational apperceptions. In so doing it evokes emotions and mobilizes affect that carries an important part of the film's meaning. Tellingly, in describing the contrasexual archetype Jung (1934/1954) uses exactly the same words as the film does when Muir talks about Snow White – for Jung the anima is *'the archetype of life itself'* (emphasis in original), and this suggests that with this imagery we are indeed in archetypal and contrasexual territory.

Of course, it is possible to deconstruct the image of the Stag in other ways. Historically the White Hart was the personal symbol and livery of Richard II of England (AD 1367–1400). But of more relevance to the film is the somewhat archaic meaning of the White Stag as a symbol of Christ, as in French Vulgate cycle of the Holy Grail (AD 1215–35). Perhaps due to its ability to grow new antlers the stag also represents renewal and is a common medieval allegory of Christ. Finally, maintaining its supernatural qualities in Celtic mythology, the White Stag is regarded as an envoy from the otherworld. In more contemporary popular culture the unicorn (a mythological relative of the stag) appears in the Harry Potter films where interestingly its blood sustains life, albeit at a cost. At the end of the White Stag sequence in *Snow White and the Huntsman*, one of Ravenna's band of men looses an arrow and kills the stag, who disappears in a cloud of white flying butterflies with a digital special effect that exactly mirrors the way Ravenna turns into a flock of ravens. The point I want to make here is that in this film emotional qualities are not seen as absolute – even the Christ-like stag and the evil Ravenna are not binary opposites. Nor is it the case that the Huntsman's aggression is good, or that Snow White's connection with nature is pure (she murders her stepmother). Instead what matters is that Snow White can become herself as symbolized by her ascendancy to the throne. Importantly, as Queen she is not part of a royal marriage – she does not need a king to make her regal. By the end of the film she is able to cross stereotypical gender divides and integrate the qualities she needs. She is both King and Queen. Or to put it more psychologically, she is both the King and Queen of whatever sex; she is both child and woman; male and female; and in these ways she embodies contrasexual difference and otherness.

The return of the duke's son, William

Each of the characters in the film is interlocked with the others and it is in this sense that difference comes to represent a specific sort of psychological unity. As in

Snow White's contrasexuality, the apparent contradiction between otherness and unity gives another illustration of the psychological principle that opposites run together. One of the insights of Jung's analytical psychology is that opposites are not limited to those that form a binary division. In fact, Jung adopts a broadly relativist approach in which the meaning of an image is not fixed but rather changes depending on our relationship with it. In this formulation Jung was influenced by the philosophy of Heraclitus and his view that the way up and the way down were the same, and that it was impossible to step into the same river twice, as the river had flowed on and so too you had changed from one moment to the next. The character of William, who the film suggests is a childhood friend of Snow White (although there is also more than a suggestion that he might be Snow White's brother), provides a particular example of this conjunction of opposites. In a scene close to the end of the film William apologizes to Snow White for having abandoned her as a child, as in voice-over a plaintive folk melody comments 'What brings us together is what pulls us apart.' At which point and for no apparent reason the location shifts from an overcast, rainy mountain to a snow covered forest. As with so many of the elements in this film there is no rational reason for the change of location or season. For those with a logical frame of mind, or viewers with a strong narrative sense, this type of disjunction is problematic. However, when seen as a psychological image, what has been effected is a shift into an inner landscape, and one that is waiting for the renewal of spring. It offers a physical framing which encourages a psychological repositioning of their relationship. It might therefore be reasonable to expect something that is psychologically significant to take place, and indeed it does.

This marks the film's *dénouement*, and here there is a swiftness to the narrative movement as it accelerates to its climax. In what is the first of three significant kisses, Snow White meets William in the forest and kisses him on the lips. William gives Snow White an apple and as she starts to eat it she falls to the ground, realizing it is poisoned. Next, William unexpectedly turns into Ravenna. This rather dramatic transformation means that the only romantic scene in the film turns out to have been between two women. Taken literally, what we have is either the suggestion of a 'poisonous' lesbian relationship, or alternatively what we have is a fantasy about seeing Kristen Stewart and Charlize Theron kissing. While not wanting to lose either of these possibilities, psychologically what is also being suggested is that Snow White and Ravenna are different elements of the same being – they have as much in common as they do in difference. It is almost as though the kiss transfers some of Ravenna's dark inner strength to Snow White. Unlike her stepmother, she is able to contain and hold the pull to evil and instead turn it into good. As symbolized by her unconscious state, this is at some personal cost. Of course it is important that Snow White's only vaguely romantic moment turns out to be with her stepmother. But unlike the real world, what matters more in the realm of the fairytale is the psychological and mythological insight that this symbolic gesture offers – after all, in mythology apples are redolent with psychological meanings connected to sexuality and psychological awareness. While at first it seems that the apple has killed Snow White, it transpires that it has just rendered her unconscious and in fact it is from this sleeping state that the stronger Snow White who will become the Warrior Queen eventually awakes. This is the psychological motif of the combining of opposites, which as mentioned above is intrinsic to the process of psychological change.

Believing that Snow White has died, the real Prince William kisses Snow White on the lips. This is the second of the three kisses, and following it her apparently dead body is brought to the castle by the dwarfs and laid out in state. Finally, talking to her body, the Huntsman explains how Snow White reminds him of his dead wife, 'Her heart. Her Spirit.' This leads to the third of the three kisses as the Huntsman kisses Snow White and in true fairytale fashion, with tears streaming down her cheeks, she wakes. Now dressed in a full-length white dress, she has returned to life, albeit looking somewhat ghost-like and otherworldly.

Snow White and the final battle

Snow White's speech to the assembled crowds is the final indication to viewers that, despite what remains as a somewhat childlike appearance, she has internalized an inner strength that can transform itself. It also stands as an image of her internal transformation in which she comes to embody the energies, the power and the strength that had previously existed in Ravenna. The speech is Shakespearian in quality and tone, and it suggests a certain kingly, masculine bearing in her approach that is an integral part of her identity.

> We have rested long enough . . . [The following sentence only *sotto voce* – like an incantation] Frost to fire and fire to frost. Iron will melt. But it will writhe inside of itself. All these years, all I've known is darkness. But I have never seen a brighter light than when my eyes just opened. And I know that light burns in all of you! Those embers must turn to flame. Iron into sword. I will become your weapon! Forged by the fierce fire that I know is in your hearts! For I have seen what she sees. I know what she knows. I can kill her. And I'd rather die today than live another day of this death! And who will ride with me? Who will be my brother?
>
> *(Snow White and the Huntsman, Dir., Sanders, 2012)*

The armour that Snow White wears going into battle is a type of composite of styles that the film's costume designer Colleen Atwood has tellingly described as the 'armour of the people' (www.hollywoodreporter.com/heat-vision/snow-white-huntsman-colleen-atwood-costumes-kristen-stewart-charlize-theron-331107, accessed 3 January 2014). Iconically, she also bears a strong resemblance to Joan of Arc in Luc Besson's film *Joan of Arc: The Messenger* (1999). While Snow White is the people's princess, by visually encapsulating her contrasexuality (her masculine and female qualities) the armour represents how her sexuality also serves to mark her out as different and in so doing protects her – a type of character armour, if you will. Underlining the point the Huntsman quips to her, 'So you're back from the dead and instigating the masses. You look very fetching in mail', and the pun is obvious.

The assault on the castle leads to the penultimate sequence of the film, which is also drenched in mythological imagery. Ravenna has somehow regained her youthful appearance. Bathed in fire like the central character from Rider Haggard's (1886) *She*, it appears both to age her and to restore her youth. In any event, it is no defence against Gus's dagger with which Snow White kills her stepmother. As Snow White comments both literally and symbolically, 'You can't have my heart.' Symbolically, spring arrives as Snow White is crowned and the doors to the coronation chamber close, like the final pages of a storybook.

Conclusion

This chapter has argued that Snow White manages to find and follow her own path and that in ascending the throne she is symbolically becoming the ruler of her own life. Despite this claim, in many ways the character of Snow White is also remarkably conservative and traditional in her psychological outlook. She was born to become Queen and by the end of the film she has indeed fulfilled that destiny. But along the way her adult sexuality has begun to emerge. As it does so she starts to embody a sense of otherness and difference and this is made explicit through her contrasexual encounters. While admittedly it is the kiss of a man that wakes her up from her deep sleep, that kiss does not simply propel her into a normative heterosexual relationship. This film is no ordinary tale in which a Prince Charming ensures that his Snow White lives a predictable and normative life. Instead, by the end of the film Snow White has kissed her stepmother, and murdered her, been clothed in armour, encountered the Christ-like figure of the White Stag, and restored law, order and happiness to her kingdom.

Of course this is a fantasy. Indeed, the idea of individuation itself is something of a fairytale. Nonetheless, Jung suggested it gave the best chance of living life in a manner that is authentic and personally meaningful. In accepting this challenge, like Snow White, it becomes possible to step outside those accepted cultural norms and expectations that stop us from being who we are, while at the same time also adopting those cultural roles we need. There is no right or wrong here. What matters is finding the path through life for each person. This is the central myth of many fairytales – the quest to become fully the people we are and not just reflections of the culture we live in. Does this lead to happiness? Perhaps not, but the direction of travel is away from projection and neurosis, away from depression and anxiety and towards a sense of contentment and acceptance that life's difficulties can be coped with in a state of equanimity and calm. While of course a fantasy, like all the best fairytales *Snow White and the Huntsman* holds a kernel of truth, which is that while happiness is an illusion the struggle to be yourself is the sustaining narrative by which it is possible to lead a psychologically meaningful life.

Notes

1 This is one of the tricks of contemporary advertising – it literalizes the symbolic message from fairytales, as a commodification of what should be viewed in symbolic and

metaphorical terms. Cf. L. Hockley, 'Narcissism and the Alchemy of Advertising', in Hockley (2007).

2 There is more than a hint of the vampire about her desire to extract the life force of others, and in an inter-fictional sense, at least, it gives her a certain proximity to Kristen Stewart's role in the *Twilight* series of films. It is also reminiscent of Ingrid Pitt's roles in *Countess Dracula* (Dir., Sasdy, 1971) and *The Vampire Lovers* (Dir., Baker, 1970).

3 The similarities and differences between Snow White and Ravenna extend to the costumes they wear. The wedding dress worn by Ravenna with its distinctive high shoulder pieces is shaped rather like a bony or skeletal structure and it suggests her continuous proximity to death, even as she ascends the throne. The sinister overtones of the dress contrast with the regal simplicity of Snow White's coronation robes worn during the final sequences of the film.

4 The association between milk and youthfulness clearly finds its origins in a baby's first food, and perhaps a desire to return to that childlike state. Contemporary cosmetics advertising promotes 'bath milk' as a means to achieve 'baby soft skin'.

5 There are numerous parallels between this film and the *Star Wars* movies, of which the primeval swamp in *The Empire Strikes Back* (Dir., Kershner, 1980) where Luke Skywalker encounters his dark side is one; that Snow White and William are attracted to each other and could be brother and sister like Luke Skywalker and Princess Leia is another, and there are also similarities between the roguish Han Solo and the Huntsman.

References

Early, F. and Kennedy, K. (eds) (2003). *Athena's daughters: television's new women warriors.* Syracuse, NY: Syracuse University Press.

Haggard, H. R. (1886–87). *She: a history of adventure.* London: The Graphic/Illustrated Newspapers Limited.

Harding, M. E. (1933/1970). *The way of all women.* New York: Putnam.

Harding, M. E. (1939). *Der Weg der Frau: eine psychologische Deutung* (Translation of Harding 1933). Zurich: Rhein.

Heinecken, D. (2003). *The warrior women of television: a feminist cultural analysis of the new female body in popular media.* New York: Peter Lang.

Hockley, L. (2007). *Frames of mind: a post-Jungian look at cinema, television and technology.* Bristol: Intellect Books.

Jung, C. G. (1934/1954). *The archetypes of the collective unconscious.* In *The collected works of C. G. Jung*, eds H. Read, M. Fordham and G. Adler, vol. 9i (pp. 3–41). London: Routledge.

Jung, C. G. (1953–79). *The collected works of C. G. Jung*, eds H. Read, M. Fordham and G. Adler, trans. R. F. C. Hull. London: Routledge.

Kast, V. (2006). 'Anima/animus'. In R. Papadopoulos (ed.) *The handbook of Jungian psychology* (pp. 113–129). London: Routledge.

Matarasso, P. (trans.) (1969). *The quest of the Holy Grail.* Harmondsworth: Penguin Books.

Pullman, P. (2012). *Grimm tales for young and old.* London: Penguin Books.

Samuels, A. (1985). *Jung and the post-Jungians.* London: Routledge and Kegan Paul.

Singer, J. (1976). *Androgyny: the opposites within.* New York: Doubleday.

http://collider.com/colleen-atwood-snow-white-huntsman-thin-man-interview/ (accessed 3 January 2014).

http://msmagazine.com/blog/2012/06/05/10-reasons-not-to-see-snow-white-and-the-huntsman/ (accessed 4 January 2014).

www.hollywoodreporter.com/heat-vision/snow-white-huntsman-colleen-atwood-costumes-kristen-stewart-charlize-theron-331107 (accessed 3 January 2014).

3

THE SECOND LOSS OF ANDROGYNY

The fairytale of dualism

Nadi Fadina

Introduction

Since the Enlightenment there have been some rather turbulent changes to western society. Although with what is now appearing as historical stumbling and stops, many of the spheres and traditions of public and private life have been challenged, transformed and/or reshaped. However, at least one thing has been constant and stable under the moon for some time – men were men and women were women. Finally the realm of gender certainty has been challenged and changed through the intervention of first suffragists, and later feminists, who questioned the status quo of the patriarchal system and its underpinning of beliefs. Along with debates about civil rights and duties, the very dichotomy of differences between male and female was under reconsideration.

Thus, in the second part of the twentieth century the discourse switched from a two-gender mode to a more three dimensional system. An uncomfortable but intriguing ambiguity of the third sex – androgyny – started its way to the light in both academic and popular social discourses. Who was the daring pioneer who implanted the concept into our culture? Do we owe it to Carl Jung with his theory of unconscious androgyny? Perhaps it was Sandra Bem with her Gender Schema? Or could David Bowie be the catalyst behind this change?

While not minimizing the contributions of any of the above, androgyny is as old as the world itself. Derived from the Greek words ἀνδρ᾽ (*anér, andr,* meaning man) and γυνή (gyné, meaning woman), this core of idealistic unity of both sexes appears in various roles and contexts: from gods to pariahs; from Plato's mythical progenitors of humanity to modern science fiction heroes of Ursula K. Le Guin; from the works of Honoré de Balzac and Virginia Woolf to cinema, fashion and the Japanese manga comics of the twenty-first century.

The precursor to our contemporary search for what is an illusory androgynous wholeness in a world of strict differentiation and binary oppositions was present in a range of mythologies from different civilizations and epochs: be it Ancient Egypt, with androgyny as 'the aim of [. . .] initiation ceremonies' (Zolla, 1981, p. 94) and the Pharaoh 'especially androgyne' (ibid.) or Vedic India with the divine unity of Shiva and Pārvatī – Ardhanārīśvara; or images of bearded Aphrodite or Aphrodite with a penis in Hellenic Greece, or Chinese immortal androgyne Lan Caihe. We can find the androgyne as 'the symbol of supreme identity in most religious systems' (Zolla, 1981, p. 5).

Like many of the other ideas that have been borrowed and adapted from older religions, reproductions of androgyny can also be found in the Judaeo-Christian tradition: be it the Gnostic *Gospel of Philip* or non-canonical *Gospel of Thomas* which comments 'make the male and the female be one and the same, so that the male might not be male nor the female be female [. . .] then you enter [the kingdom]' (*Gospel of Thomas*, saying 22). Whether it is Adam Kadmon of the Kabbalah, 'the unfallen androgyne in the cosmic inscape of an anthropomorphic unity independent of natural settings' (Maiorino, 1992, p. 96), or Gnostic Christ, androgyny is a key figure in the contexts of unity with God.

Androgyny traces are also present in another type of narrative – fairytales. However, classical literary fairytales, and their modern cinematic adaptations, are less likely to depict androgynous characters than folk ones, as both male and female characters of classical literary tales must comply with strict gender canons prescribed by dominant classes and the patriarchal system of beliefs, as argued by Rowe, Lieberman, and Gilbert and Gubar. Jack Zipes notes:

> Almost all critics who have studied the emergence of the literary fairy tale in Europe agree that educated writers purposely appropriated the oral folktale and converted it into a type of literary discourse about mores, values, and manners so that children and adults would become civilized according to the social code of that time.
>
> *(Zipes, 2006, p. 3)*

Meanwhile, some folktales give us a different perspective. Being considered as a paradoxical amalgam of naïve 'depthless' (Lüthi, 1986) characters, repetitive structures (Propp, 1968), universal psychological motifs (Bettelheim, 1976) and esoteric spiritual quests (Jung, 1981), folklore fairytales contain gender role inversion. Of course, taking into account that these narrations might be stories about sex-conditioned initiation ceremonies, folktales are full of traditional gendered stories. However, there are some notable exceptions: for example, in the Russian folktales *Danilo the Luckless, Maria Morevna, The Maiden Tsar,* and *The Wise Maiden* female heroines exercise both social, military and intellectual power traditionally considered to be male prerogatives. A similar inversion is present in regard to male characters of Russian folktales. Russian 'princes charming' – Ivan the Fool/Emelya/Ivan Tsarevich – often express qualities and behaviours considered 'traditionally female': heroes are close to nature, and preserve life rather than kill it; they cry, express emotions, and are praised (or at least not punished) for being passive.

As we have seen, androgyny appears in so many cultures, cults, ceremonies, images and symbols that it seems there must be a reason for it. This chapter will analyse the apparently inextinguishable interest and 'fatal attraction' of the image of androgyny, and explore whether, and why, it continues to inspire, scare, fascinate and repulse us. Using interdisciplinary methods and a broadly feminist media analysis, the chapter will range over androgyny and its manifestations in film, mythology, religious and philosophical thought, its appearance in the Jungian theory of individuation and the animus/anima dichotomy. It will conclude by examining the phenomenon of androgyny as a central concept in humans' fairytale quest for happiness, meaning and the divine self.

The chapter is divided into two parts. The first part explores how androgyny operates within systems of socio-cultural gender conceptualizations, biological determinism and binary oppositions. The second part of the chapter draws on media texts as a means of debating the possibilities of 'genderless' psychological plurality in what remains, even today, a rigid patriarchal ideology of binary oppositions within prescribed modes of being.

Androgyny: defining unity through opposites

Defining androgyny is not as simple as it might seem though. There have been numerous attempts to do it.[1] Historically it has been often confused with notions of biological hermaphroditism or of intersex (reproductive organs of both sexes in one being). The chapter will not debate the biological nature of the phenomenon as instead it is looking at androgyny as a culturally constructed concept that operates to serve specific regimes of gender politics.

Another sphere in which androgyny is often debated is transsexuality and queer theory. Although I shall briefly touch on the transgendered aspect of the phenomenon and sexuality (bisexuality, homosexuality, and cross-sexuality) the main focus will be on heterosexuality, as a part of traditional/'natural'/prescribed identity that is propagated by patriarchy. This chapter will position androgyny as an ideological tool of cultural production and will, in a way, follow Weil in her argument that androgyny 'is not only sexist but heterosexist, focusing on the complementarity of genital differences' (Weil, 1992, p. 151).

For the sake of terminological clarity, I will be using A. J. L. Busst's definition in which he defines the androgyne as 'a person who unites certain of the essential characteristics of both sexes and who, consequently, may be considered as both a man and a woman or as neither a man nor a woman, as bisexual or asexual' (Busst, 1967, p. 1). More thorough definitions could certainly be found. However, all of them would contain references to gender, sex and sexuality. Such references are highly problematic, as both 'social sex' (gender) and biological sex are laden with highly controversial stereotypes and particular attributions that are deeply rooted in a system of gender differentiation in our society, culture and minds. It is in and through that matrix of socio-cultural relations that constructing androgyny is constituted in terms of gender dualism.

At least two problems arise in regard to gender differentiation and its dualistic practice in our society: most non-gender-related phenomena (nature/culture, spirit/matter, to name two) are identified in male/masculine and female/feminine terms; such identification creates an inequality and an implicit hierarchy in which power relations between masculinity and femininity are established and maintained by gender politics in an unequal manner. This differentiation is a part of our patriarchal paradigm of consciousness. Our perception of what constitutes 'male' and 'female' is constructed in similar ways to the differentiated nature of the world in general. From this perspective the world is seen as some kind of a structure containing polar elements: object–subject, sky–earth, top–bottom, dark–light, etc. These pairs are seen as clearly differentiated opposites and, in accordance with cultural values, are often attributed with hierarchical qualities.

While we (both men and women alike) continue to wander in deserts of binary oppositions we take gendered attributions as axiomatic. It is paradoxical in the twenty-first century to continue the traditions of Hellenic philosophy and identify the maleness element (even if implicitly or symbolically) with spirit, logos, activity, strength, rationality, light, etc.; and to associate the female principle with matter, chaos, nature, passivity, weakness, emotion and darkness. There is nothing wrong in preserving and valuing Hellenic achievements and philosophical thought. However, does this practice mean we should praise ancient Greeks in their atavistic understanding of the world and follow them in, let us say, considering brain as an organ made of phlegm? If no, then why do we keep fanatically adhering to their gendered paradigms of differentiation, which cannot be objectively evaluated and could easily be contested?[2] This principle of differentiation and ascription does not make any sense if we look, even briefly, at an elaborated evolution of such attributions. In order to find the roots of our persistent gendered understanding of the world we shall refer to several examples of the dual matrix development and the place of androgyny in this system.

A great while ago, when the world was full of wonders . . .

Palaeolithic H. Sapiens was the struggling child of a hostile environment. From an evolutionary standpoint – being a collective, life-bearing species with a prolonged period of parental dependency – the need for unity in humans might come as no surprise. It is highly possible that ideas on non-dual androgyny formed in the earliest period of humanity's development when systems of religious beliefs were forming.

No gender, no separation, and more importantly no m/others . . . yet. The Great Mother Goddess of Gimbutas is yet to come. Now it is all about a sexless/genderless deity – an incorporation of all alive – androgynous Zoe, 'eternal and infinite life' (Baring and Cashford, 1991, p. 148). The way to find a potential trace of this primal 'unity' and unpolarized vision of the world is to address world mythologies. Good examples include 'creator gods – that is, those who create alone and *ex nihilo*' who are 'by definition, androgynous' (Leeming, 2005, p. 17). However, this is not androgyny in our 'modern' understanding of the phenomenon. Paradoxically, primordial androgyny could have been closer to modern cosmo-chemistry rather than to the later idealistic unity of opposites, as objects in our universe, including (*all*) humans, indeed made of the same elements and particles. We are the one and the same; the unity it is.

However, eventually humanity's beliefs gradually evolve into ideas about binary opposition in the world. As we transferred our species' biological two-sex reproductive system onto deities, our gods had to become male and female in order to give birth. If we utilize more poetic language, 'for the spark of creation to be engendered, the male and the female must come together in all their sexual maleness and femaleness' (Singer, 1976, p. 21). Thus Leeming argues that myths involving the separation of earth and sky are examples of myths in which the universe itself is androgynous and then must be differentiated into male and female in order for life to evolve (Leeming, 2005). As a result we have wholeness comprised of two elements: male and female, eventually replacing the 'ungendered' and non-binary eternal life. The androgynous creator, life itself – Zoe – gradually gets shaped into gods and goddesses. And this is the beginning of our androgyny – androgyny as a unity of opposites.

However, these opposites and their attributions have not always been the same as we now know them.[3] For example, let us look at the tradition in which women are associated with water and earth, and men with sky. That this is a culturally specific image and not a universal one can be seen by the way that in Bronze Age Egypt the primordial waters – Nun – were imagined as 'father rather than mother' (Baring and Cashford, 1991, p. 153) and water was, therefore, viewed as a male element. In Egypt 'earth was male and sky was female' (ibid.). As we know, later traditions ascribed sky with a male principle and the earth with a female one in order to preserve the dynamics of power. Another example contradicts a well-established association of male with order. Thus Egyptian Tefnut (female deity) was initially associated with moisture but later became associated with 'order' (ibid.). Notorious father-order might well not be a universal structure at the end of the day.

Talking about evolution of gendered gods, an inclination to certain cognitive processes, such as analogy, an urge to escape the existential despair of mortality and a need to adapt to certain environments in humans might have resulted in the emergence of certain systems of beliefs. One of the elements of these beliefs was seeing humans as a part of nature, and later, possibly, seeing nature as a female deity (an analogy with life-giving).

Goddess feminists might sing 'alleluia'.

However, the modern practice of praising the wild/true/primordial female principle does not equate to arguing women's contribution to society and providing a new perspective on women's position in history. The practice of glorifying so called 'femaleness' continues with the categorization of male and female nature, psychology, behaviour and social roles which lie at the core of gender inequality. The 'natural' differentiation of male and female, as well as usage of notions of 'femininity' and 'masculinity' in contexts outside cultural constructions, maintain socio-political gendered hierarchy.

If we, nevertheless, assume that the Great Goddess hypothesis is at least partially correct, and the worshipping of a female goddess took place in the Palaeolithic and Neolithic periods, then one might argue it as a starting point of ideological inequality – worshipping one quality over the other. If we were to apply *our* hierarchical views to, for example, a society which praises life-giving earth above other elements we would see that this hierarchy raises the social value of subjects/ objects and their functions associated with divine earth (for example, life-giving and women as life-givers). We must realize, though, that this hierarchy does not make female human beings 'divine' *per se*, nor would they be more 'divine' than men, and any associations and attributions of such qualities are merely constructions of our minds, beliefs and cultures. We also need to keep in mind that in any hierarchical society specific differentiation must be maintained. In patriarchy characteristics defined as male must be regarded as positive and dominant; feminine ones must be labelled as negative and subordinate. Not surprisingly, it is believed to be vice versa in a matriarchy. However, some academics reasonably argue this conception to be a projection of our patriarchal views of domination on different (egalitarian) societal structures.[4] Therefore, if we define the goddess theory in contemporary hierarchical terms it should be considered as product of patriarchal hierarchical thinking as well and, therefore, cannot assist productively in comparing mechanisms of social control.

Leaving goddess feminists to 'run with the wolves' and returning to the evolution of duality – which turned out to be the world-bearing turtle – binary opposition in our culture supports systems of beliefs in which energy channels (yin/yang), unconscious archetypes (animus/anima), body parts, activities and professions, qualities and behaviours, and, paradoxically, happiness, are strictly regulated and comply with the prescribed nature of dualities. Nowadays, even the unconscious is seen as polarized: 'in a society in which the modes of consciousness tend to be polarized, one would expect to find polarization in the unconscious as well' (Singer, 1976, p. 46).

However, we should remember that it is crucial for the homeostasis of a hierarchical system in a differentiated society that dualism is taken for granted as 'natural'. As Chandler argues:

> It is a feature of culture that the binary oppositions come to seem 'natural' to members of a culture. [. . .] Whilst there are no opposites in 'nature', the binary oppositions which we employ in our cultural practices help to generate order out of the dynamic complexity of experience.
>
> *(Chandler, 2007, pp. 93–94)*

Now and always, an enormous existential fear in the face of a world without order unveils itself: gods and individualism, dichotomies and, not surprisingly, divine wholeness – whatever it takes to overcome this deepest despair of mortality and insignificance of one's own being.

'Chaos reigns.'[5]

In constant attempts to give order(s) to experiences, lives and subordinates, patriarchal ideology had to shape gods' duality into male-god monotheism. Again we can find examples in mythological material – for example Yahweh (similar to Greek Zeus), who started on his career ladder as one of several gods, later graduated into the superior male god, allowing the ruling elite to establish a society in which it could 'conveniently shape the relationship of man to woman as one of owner to thing owned' (Dijkstra, 1974, p. 64) or, in Irigaray's terms, of owner and 'commodity' (Irigaray, 1977). In order to preserve this power a certain dynamic of duality must be maintained. From a patriarchal religious perspective this domination of man over woman is natural and is a consequence of both the biblical myth of the Creation and the Fall.

Once upon a time, the still androgynous ideal of immortal Adam loses his immortality, androgyny and god-like image when Eve is made out of his rib (which marks the fall into sexuality) and then, as if that is not enough, he is expelled from Paradise because of her. Mythological Eve, of course, does nothing but tell the truth, and it is intolerance of Eve's disobedience that reveals the underlying dynamics of power in the narrative.

However, in order to find the *lost* androgynous image of immortality, patriarchy can sacrifice everything on its way, including, but not only, sexuality and libido (mainly female, though) as in Judaeo-Christian tradition, or on the contrary as in Taoism – 'intercourse can be used to [. . .] balance [. . .] energies and "immortalize"' human beings (Zolla, 1981, p. 15). In its attempts to restore and/or impose the male divine image, patriarchy can simply praise spirit, defining it as a pure male element, and deny women a soul. It can ground God's image in an intellect and prohibit female intellectual development by law, including the right to education and work. However, all these attempts of patriarchy somehow keep man searching for the lost divine self and happiness, making him believe that someday when he finds IT he will become complete again. He will become once more a divine, immortal god!

And we blame Disney and communism for constructing utopias!

In this 'fairytale' structure men and women alike are to be controlled by a certain punishment/reward system. In any hierarchical society a ruling elite must encourage those qualities and values that are required to maintain its substantiality. In order to do so it must deploy specific systems of beliefs that would preserve its status quo. In a patriarchal, hierarchical, militaristic society the ideological core of its stability must be based on differentiation (binary opposition) between nations, ethnicities, classes, sexes – us–them, west–east, white–black, goodness–evil, man–woman. This along with other means and cultural products, be they from the *Iliad* or Disney cartoons, are employed by such hierarchy to tell a certain story which 'writes identity in a binary separation of its external circumstance from the internal "self" [. . .] This binary both requires and is reinforced by constructed ("Natural") oppositions between child and adult, black and white, women and men' (Miller and Rode, 1995, p. 100).

Not surprisingly female dark forces (devils, witches, stepmothers) are the axis of evil in this system of binary splitting between opposites: black–white, men–women, whore–virgin, bad mother–good mother, etc. Therefore, the bad m/others are to be positioned at the top of the punishment pyramid. Ideas about the demonic (wild/unknown/different) nature of women and its punishment are one of the most significant manifestations of patriarchal thinking, surprisingly maintained by seemingly opposite political forces, for example radical feminism. '*Vaginae dentatae*', be they mythical succubae or their modern cinematic versions (Hitchcock's *femmes fatales* or Lars von Trier's nymphomaniac female antichrist(s)), are manifestations of the phenomenon which serves a crucial role in maintaining gender politics. These images reinforce the established association of female with darkness, sexuality, chaos, evil and punishment. This is often explicit, as in *The Devils* (Dir., Russell, 1971), *The Exorcist* (Dir., Fiedkin, 1973), *Jennifer's Body* (Dir., Kusama, 2009), or implicit as in the film *The Passion of the Christ* (Dir., Gibson, 2004) in which Satan is portrayed as an androgyne, though played by a female actress – Rosalinda Celentano.

The Devil is in the detail.

Paradoxically, but it is exactly the image of the witch that could be so liberating in its ungendered and, therefore, *uncontrolled androgyny*. I am referring to Baba Yaga – a famous witch of Russian folktales who is androgynous, with androgyny defined outside the system of cultural dualism. Here I will focus on magical fairytales (*volshebnie skazki*) and their film adaptations only, as magical fairytales are considered to be the most ancient form of narrative, and therefore to be less affected by later-developed Christian ideology.

Baba Yaga's image is hugely complex and contradictory. Baba Yaga is an anchorite and lives in the deep woods. She is a mistress of all nature and elements, time of day, life and death (Propp, 2004). She lives on the border between this and that world (or, as Jungians might argue, on the border between consciousness and unconsciousness). She lives in a house on chicken legs, lies on a stove, has sharp teeth (most likely relating her to animals), a huge nose rooted in the ceiling (which Freudians interpret as a phallic symbol), and huge breasts (a possible relation to Palaeolithic goddesses). She flies in a mortar, steering it with a pestle and sweeping her traces with a broom (the mortar and pestle in Russian mythology were associated with sexual intercourse). She can turn herself and others into animals and objects. Baba Yaga puts people into a stove, as if to bake them, but I would argue that rather than being a cremation or initiation ceremony (Propp, 2004), initially it could be a healing and immortalizing ritual, similar to the one performed by the Egyptian goddess Isis, and later Demeter, who 'put children to stove to make them immortal' (Baring and Cashford, 1991). Baba Yaga is both a donor and villain (Propp, 2004), she both rewards and punishes (Becker, 1990, cited in Johns, 2004, p. 30). Depending on schools and approaches, academics trace Baba Yaga to multiple origins (to name several): the Indian goddess of death, Kali (Leeming, 2005); 'the ancient figure of Fate' (Zipes, 2000, p. 33); The great mother goddess (Kravchenko, 1987; Hubbs,

1988); the Indo-European goddess of death and winter (Potebnya, 1865; cited in Johns, 2004, p. 20); a dead person and an anthropomorphized animal (Propp, 2004); the Great Mother archetype (von Franz, 1993).

That Baba Yaga is a figure with ultimate power we can understand not only from the original texts, but from a Soviet cinematic tradition in which Baba Yaga is often played and voiced-over by *men*: *Morozko* (Dir., Rou, 1964), *Vasilisa Prekrasnaya* (Dir., Rou, 1939), *Zolotye Roga* (Dir., Rou, 1972), *Ivashko i Baba Yaga* (Dir., Brumberg and Brumberg, 1938). I will cover in more detail this practice of men playing female characters later in the chapter. I would also note that post-Soviet gender politics stressed 'female' features of Baba Yaga's image, portraying her as an envious, ridiculous woman obsessed with her power (*Tri Bogatyria na Dal'nikh Beregakh* (Dir., Feoktistov, 2012)) and appearance (*Pro Fedota-Streltsa, Udalogo Molodtsa* (Dir., Steblyanko, 2008)).

Some scholars argue Baba Yaga is a symbolical representation of a female and male unity – an androgyne (Johns, 2004). However, I would argue that Baba Yaga outreaches rigid gendered forms and systems of binary opposition. Shapiro (1983) supports this point by saying that she might have been an ancient undifferentiated character who was later built into the gendered paradigm. She is an '"urobic" entity' (Goscilo, 2005, p. 13) above all, and returns us to the ideas of primordial absolute, the eternal, the receptacle of all possible variations and beings.

Even her cinematic representation in ideologically infused Soviet cinema supports, in a sense, this ungendered androgyny: Baba Yaga was always portrayed as an asexual and asocial character. This image corresponds well with a concept of androgyny as 'a way out of biological reproduction' (Maiorino, 1992, p. 98). Indeed, Baba Yaga does not comply with femininity and masculinity canons. She is the androgyne positioned outside dualism, the punishment/reward system of social control, gender functioning, and prescribed modes of being.

Happiness: da tales doses[6]

Arguing punishment in regard to gender, I would note that along with other means of maintaining the status quo of a present gendered dichotomy, media (any form) as a system of punishment and reward are very effective by promising a fairytale happy ending for all those who comply with canons, and a 'burning in hell' for those who do not. Images of a Real Man and a Real Woman circulate in mass media, arts, literature, film, etc. In our media-driven world these images contribute to the construction of self-values, self-identity and sexuality. Here we are dealing with not only ideological tools of cultural production, used by dominant systems, but also with the apparatus of the human psyche as 'the depth of psychological significance of images in general, and cinema in particular, exists in the way they provide a personal and unique bridge between inner and outer worlds' (Hockley, 2011, p. 135). This is particularly significant in regard to gender construction in film, as film 'reflects and generates our experience of gender (over and above our recognition and observation of it)' (Pomerance, 2001, p. 11).

The reward/punishment system of gender politics works in all kinds of products. Thus a woman with power 'must be represented as a castrating bitch' (Sells, 1995, p. 181) and, therefore, must be destroyed/killed: for example, Disney's stepmothers/witches, Meredith Vickers in *Prometheus* (Dir., Scott, 2012) or Dr Julia Harris in *Horrible Bosses* (Dir., Gordon, 2011). A corresponding rewarded behaviour might be found in fairytale stories about beautiful romantic princesses and their contemporary personifications, for example, Elle Woods in *Legally Blonde* (Dir., Luketic, 2001). Be they all-powerful robotic porn stars or lap dancers, all of the above-mentioned media products and images continue socializing women into a particular type of prescribed female behaviour which, it is promised, will bring women happiness/liberation/empowerment or punishment/sanctions/death.

The tradition of punishment in patriarchy is especially relevant in relation to any 'other' identities, but especially when 'these others' dare to invade its territory. Here I am referring to female transgendered characters in film. Thus in films where women transfer to the male domain – *Boys Don't Cry* (Dir., Peirce, 1999) or *Albert Nobbs* (Dir., García, 2011) (in both films female protagonists identify themselves as male and live their lives as men) – media texts carry messages of punishment, suffering and unhappiness.

Meanwhile the androgynous nature of women, if they do not invade the male realm or invade it playfully, is more acceptable in western culture. However, it is not that the asexual nature of women is being praised, but rather a male fantasy of women's bisexuality that is implanted in public consciousness, be it bisexual sex symbol of the 1930s Marlene Dietrich or Sharon Stone in *Basic Instinct* (Dir., Verhoeven, 1992). Generally, female bisexuality is more acceptable in western society than that of men, whose androgynous images are associated with homosexuality rather than bisexuality, making them 'others' in the realm of 'real masculinity'.

The moment woman loses the allure of bisexuality she must either get back to heterosexuality (as if she were Sleeping Beauty awakened by the kiss of Prince Charming): *Sylvia Scarlett* (Dir., Cukor, 1935), *Just One of the Guys* (Dir., Gottlieb, 1985), and even a feminist drama-comedy *Yentl* (Dir., Streisand, 1983); or lose man's desire: *The Messenger: The Story of Joan of Arc* (Dir., Besson, 1999), *G.I. Jane* (Dir., Scott, 1997)[7] and so be doomed to be portrayed as an unfeminine object which threatens the hierarchy by transgressing as a subject with an independent status.

Androgynous, asexual female heroines can be found in some sci-fi films. These media texts are publicly praised for their challenge to gender roles. However, I would argue that Ellen Ripley of the *Alien* film series (1979–1997) or her contemporary version, for example Elizabeth Shaw of *Prometheus* (2012), are imaged as divine, androgynous Sophia(s). Theosophical Sophia,[8] as well as media images of seemingly inspiring androgynous female heroines, might be androgynous in relation to humans, but is definitely female in relation to God. These supposedly liberating images of female androgynes are masterfully built into the male discourse (past and present) aimed at preserving patriarchy; be it Bacon's nature/scientist–god/scientist dichotomy[9] or sci-fi guru Ridley Scott's progenitor of humanity in *Prometheus* (2012).

In the opening sequence of *Prometheus* an explicitly male (gendered) alien gives life to all alive. The alien resembles Arnold Schwarzenegger (in his best days) consuming an energy drink which, instead of giving a boost, gets him disintegrated into DNA molecules which will inseminate the planet.

'All things came into being through him, and apart from him not even one thing that has come into being came into being' (*The Gospel of John*, cited in Bruce, 1983, p. 32).

Returning to gendered happiness and androgynous divinity, a discourse on the matter can be found in religious texts of the past and present, and also in some contemporary cinematic products. Generally, religions do not appeal that much to entertainment producers, as such topics touch upon sensitive issues and the box office depends on the rating system and wider target audiences. However, some dare to bare – as did director Kevin Smith in his movie *Dogma* (1999).

With his branded irony and sarcasm Smith features sexless angels, which in their earthly life are all male (gendered). Following a long established dichotomy of muse/anima/soul/female and poet/animus/logos/male, Smith 'dilutes' his man-only club of angels with a muse who in earthly life works in a strip club and is female (gendered) but anatomically neuter as well.

Androgyny does not stop there. Above all, Smith's god is androgynous. However, although it is supposed to be ungendered we know it is *she*, as the god is played by the famous female singer Alanis Morissette. Besides, it wears feminine outfits, evokes sexual desire in men and generally looks like an earthly (and silent!) woman.

'The lady is aflame. And silent. Perfect!'[10]

In accord with religious images in Christian tradition, God has been mainly portrayed on screen as a white male. Even in films challenging this practice, for example *Bruce Almighty* (Dir., Shadyac, 2003) in which God is played by African-American actor Morgan Freeman, the male God has not been silenced. Moreover, portrayals of God have been carrying messages of wisdom and authority. What was the director's intention in regard to God's female voice in *Dogma*? Why when she opens her mouth does the sound she makes literally blow heads off? Regardless of the answer, Smith masterfully shows us our misconceptions and stereotypes, androgyny, misogyny, racism and sexism. Moreover, the end of the movie is celebrated with the melodramatic pregnancy of the main heroine (Bethany), reminding us of the world-old theme of fertility as the ultimate female destination and prescribed mode of gendered happiness.

Regarding male transgendered happiness, a different perspective comes from films in which men transgress and cross-dress. In a society in which being called a sissy (heterosexual and homosexual alike) is one of the most pejorative words for a man, somehow films in which men enter the 'female realm' are mostly comedies (at least the Hollywood mass products): *Some Like it Hot* (Dir., Wilder, 1959), *Tootsie* (Dir., Pollack, 1982), *Mrs. Doubtfire* (Dir., Columbus, 1993), *Big Momma's House* (Dir., Gosnell, 2000).

One might argue that laughter could be used as a defence mechanism or, again, it could be a manifestation of the patriarchal practice of undervaluing the female principle. But there could be a different explanation. Similar to the Taoist technique 'aimed at developing the female spirit' (Zolla, 1981, p. 15), men of different civilizations have attempted to evoke or get access to the 'elusive' female element: cross-dressing in shamanism, Indian Kerala dance, Italian carnivals in which men impersonate pregnant women, and some forms of psychosexual disorders (Ruitenbeek, 1966). Be it Jung's paradise closely related to mother or Boehme's resurrection as restoration of male sin, which in its final stage will be marked by domination of female over male (Koole, 1986), it is a quest for the female as a part of an androgynous dual nature. Societies that despise the constructed 'female' consider the wholeness as female in male. Almost all male discourses on completeness are manifestations of the search for female, rather than an unpolarized being. Could the roots of this tendency go back many thousand years and again to the possible cults of the divine female and their traces in contemporary culture in a form of womb or vagina envy? Could the overall search for that wholeness be a patriarchal desire to reunite with the ideologically invented 'm/other'? For androgyny, as debated by most philosophical thought (be it Aristotle, Philo of Alexandria, Eriugena, Boehme, Gunning, Soloviev or Jung), presents us with artefacts of patriarchal thinking on the matter.

Do women's discourses on gender dualism and their androgynous self give us a different perspective? Is female androgyny a thirst for a *male-self*? A bisexual *male fantasy*? *Ungendered being*? *No thirst at all*? However, such analysis might appear next to impossible as, 'for women [. . .] the concept of androgyny itself has a problematical history, since most of its proponents have been male' (Annas, 1978, p. 10).

Wholeness or hollowness

An interesting reflection on the gender dichotomy is present in the next two films. The first one is director Breillat's *Anatomy of Hell* (*Anatomie de l'enfer*, 2004). Generally, the film could be considered as a female fantasy of female power: the fantasy of waking up the prince with a kiss – making a homosexual man heterosexual, which surprisingly resembles an inverted fantasy on lesbianism in patriarchy. Breillat fantasizes on male fantasies about female. 'Like an ocean, woman could engulf you and make you vanish into its loins'. In four nights Breillat shows the way woman sees images of man's attempts to cognize god-nature-woman: to be god (night one), to kill god (night two), to unite with god (night three), to love god (night four).

As a post-feminist text the film reflects on the gendered nature of women and men and debates a well-established duality of culturally constructed masculinity and femininity dichotomies, one of which is woman-life/man-death: hollowness as opposition to wholeness; hollow (non-pregnant, non-life-giving) man as an opposite of whole (pregnant, life-giving) woman. Moreover, Breillat constructs a Christian dichotomy comparing man with inert faeces and woman's menstrual blood with life, positioning men as killers of life and, therefore, givers of eternal life.

How about the androgyne's image in women's art? The film that is almost always cited in works on the cinematic portrayal of androgyny and gender politics is *Orlando* (Dir., Potter, 1992). The film is based on Virginia Woolf's novel *Orlando: A Biography*, and stars Tilda Swinton. The film's narrative concerns a person called Orlando, who lives through four centuries and changes sex from male to female. The final sequence shows Orlando as an androgynous woman, who has given birth to a daughter. Encountering experiences of different genders in one being, the protagonist debates questions of identity and its fluidity, subjectivity and strict differentiation of binary gendered opposites.

'Same person – no difference at all. Just a different sex.'[11]

The film has received much critical attention both in academic and public spheres. Inevitably some have focused on feminist analysis (Enciso, 1995), as both the film and the novel form strong arguments around misogyny. Others have proposed to examine the film not as 'a commentary on social and economic consequences of tendentious gender fixities' (Humm, 1997, p. 144), but as a 'postmodern consumer spectacle' (ibid.) from which we derive satisfaction. Regardless of the approach, Potter's films in general 'are charged with gender transitivity as well as left wing politics' (ibid., p. 168).

Following Woolf in her attempts to portray ambivalence of gender, Potter underlines its fluidity and our misconceptions. It is not only through the eventual androgyny that we appreciate the ambiguity of the traditional gender dichotomy and heterosexuality, but through our knowledge of the sex of Swinton and her hero/ine. We do know the actress is female, thus in her relationship with the queen, played by Quentin Crisp, we encounter both heterosexuality and homosexuality; with Sasha we sense bisexuality and heterosexuality, in her relationship with Marmaduke, heterosexuality only. Albeit paradoxically, the first 'glimpse' of happiness Orlando experiences is in the later heterosexual relationship. Even the poster of the film portrays Orlando in bed with Marmaduke. Watching the film and each transformation Orlando undergoes, we are surprised to recognize stereotypes deeply ingrained in our own beliefs.

Through debates on the rules, restrictions and notions of what makes a man and a woman, comfortably androgynous Orlando is shown as neither male nor female, although being of a definite sex in each particular period. The end of the film could be one of a very few examples of cinematic attempts to express personal female experience of what it means to be herself – ungendered woman – just a *human being* who combines, experiences and finally accepts multiple selves.

'She is no longer trapped by destiny and ever since she let go of the past she found her life was beginning'.[12]

Wholeness as a must-have

Conversations about androgyny in western media culture would be incomplete without two other manifestations of this (as we have seen) fairytale unity which is directly linked to gender politics and dualism. Two thousand years ago when Plato was writing his *Symposium*, his ideas on creation myths about the struggle between androgynous Titans as the progenitors of humanity and the gods may have put a spell on the polis. But do we still buy into stories of super-powerful androgynes, whose combined male and female characteristics made them a threat to gods? Of course not, we say: at a time when polytheism, as well as monotheism, is a faux pas among intellectuals, it is difficult to imagine contemporary philosophers debating how gods cursed humanity by splitting it into two halves. As a result androgyny has had to reinvent itself and has shifted from discussions of lofty matters to a mass-culture domain. A lucrative modern interpretation of Plato's love mythology starts with an eternal quest either for an other half or for a true self.

The first kind of quest masterfully maintains a utopian myth of romantic duality that can never be reached, be it via dating sites that electronically find your ideal match or through films and literature full of faint hopes of meeting Mr/Miss Right. One does not need to be Bridget Jones to cry a river when a touching psychotherapist in *Good Will Hunting* (Dir., Van Sant, 1997) tells us how imperfect we all are and the only thing that matters is whether or not we are 'perfect for each other'. We keep searching for the perfect one, both on and off-screen.

The myth of a lost other-half is not the only one maintained by our perfectionistic culture of troubled (indivi)dualism. Another dimension of the androgyny-trend is the search for a 'wholeness within' – a new must-have of the season. Although in this chapter I generally analyse cinematic product, here I would like to refer briefly to a different type of media publication, as it may enable me to build the next film example into a cultural snapshot. In Samantha Smithstein's article 'Our Thirst for Wholeness' (*Psychology Today*, 3 February 2012) the author underlines her belief in spiritual wholeness as a remedy for all the evils of our civilization, be it depression, anxiety or addictions. Throughout her piece she refers to Dr Slaymaker, who measured spirituality levels that were in direct relation to 'life satisfaction' and happiness. 'And find it we must', exclaims Smithstein in finishing her argument for finding our way to the whole divine self.

Such *obligatory* searches for the 'inner balance' that is androgynous in its nature (Zolla, 1981) often mixes spirituality, organized religion undertones, pop psychology and gendered happiness in a similar way to the film *Eat, Pray, Love* (2010). The film is based on an autobiography by Elizabeth Gilbert, who travelled the world in order to find 'herself'. Many do forget, though, that the original title of the book is *Eat, Pray, Love: One Woman's Search for* Everything *Across Italy, India and Indonesia* (emphasis added). Although the film, as well as the book, might give us some guilty pleasures (allowed to women these days by post-feminism), several questions arise in its regard. What is this 'Everything' made of? What are the ingredients of the secret formula? According to the film all it takes for a female fairytale happiness and 'total rebirth of the individual' (Jung, 1940/50: para. 204) is to forgive yourself for two things: eating as much as you wish and leaving a boring husband for Javier Bardem.

'Women do get bored with their husbands, your majesty . . .'[13]

The fairytale of individuation

The debate in regard to a wholeness within that one can and must reach is similar to Jungian individuation theory which, like many other grand theories (in Jung's own terminology), have meant well but . . .

L'enfer est plein de bonnes volontés et désirs ('The road to hell is paved with good intentions' – lit., 'Hell is full of good intentions and desires').

It might seem like a digression from the main topic of this chapter, but Jung's individuation theory has had more (often implicit) influence on contemporary society than the public realizes, while his individuation is inseparable from dualism. In his progressive attempts to accept and live with paradox and the multiple self, Jung stumbles over two major points. The first one is the 'true self'. Although some post-Jungians rightly consider individuation as a metaphor,[14] this is not the case with Jung himself, regardless of intentions ascribed to him by his followers. Moreover, some Jungians, especially those with a clinical background, continue to argue that individuation is 'becoming the person you were always intended to be' (Hauke, 2011, p. 186). Intended by whom? How much 'true us' is in us? How should we define this 'truthiness' in our 'unreal' copy of a copy world? Asking such uncomfortable questions might lead to a long-overdue shift in post-Jungian terminology; however, the commodification of the harmonious wholeness helps therapists to encourage their clientele to stay in therapy.

The second stumbling block, and a deeply troubled area, relates to Jung's thoughts on notorious aspects of feminine and masculine, incorporated in his individuation theory. Thus, along with his 'personal myth' (Jung's terminology), his animus/anima theory was heavily influenced by Victorian romanticism, religion (both the Protestantism he was born into and the exotic ones he was researching), and archaic notions of gender differentiation and ideal androgyny. If we were to make a traditional attempt to challenge the myth of gender in prevailing Freudian/ Lacanian academic phallocentrism we might have addressed Jung, as some of his ideas could be a breath of fresh air, since he 'makes room for many potential myths of being' (Rowland, 2011, p. 149). Indeed we cannot blame his writing for being characteristically of its time and ideologically influenced. 'Let any one of you who is without sin be the first to throw a stone.'

However, we cannot and should not leave without attention the fact that Jung emphasized the rightness of reinforcing culturally constructed notions of masculinity and femininity in both sexes on their way to individuation by means of accepting the unconscious true inner selves – animus and anima. In accord with the classicist tradition, Jung's ascribed anima/animus with traditional gender attributions debated earlier in the chapter, thus categorizing the female anima as that which 'produces *moods*', while the male animus is that which 'produces *opinions*' (Jung, 1928, para. 331, original italics). Jung's views on feminine and masculine, along with the whole concept of animus/anima dichotomy, were neither new nor original. Meanwhile, the classicist dichotomy he followed contradicts and undermines Jung's own attempts to overcome restrictions of oppositions. Paradoxically,

Jung denied humans access to a continuum of genderless choice in the individuation process. As Hauke notes:

> in a society dominated by masculinist values and ways of seeing, Jung saw how the repressed unconscious came to be expressed in terms of repressed 'feminine' values within all of us – men and women alike – overshadowed within our dominant patriarchal society.
>
> *(Hauke, 2011, p. 185)*

However, as I have argued earlier, these dichotomies were not always present in the state that we know them now. Moreover, the differentiation itself is an ideological construct. Therefore, we might reconsider our feminine/masculine attributions (and the anima/animus as a part of them) and eliminate them all together or define them as cultural constructs only and stop viewing them as innate structures.

Jungians have developed further Jung's original ideas on unconscious androgyny. Although some (Harding, 1955; von Franz, 1970, 1972, 1996) followed Jung in his misogyny, as Jung believed women's unconscious to be 'essentially different from those found in man' (Jung, 1928, para. 331) and women's psychology to be 'very dissimilar' to men's, other post-Jungians (Singer, Rowland, Wehr) have attempted to apply a feminist critique to his theories. Thus June Singer in her book *Androgyny: Toward a New Theory of Sexuality* (1976) makes an extensive analysis of androgyny and its manifestation in history, religion and therapy. Although Singer recognizes androgyny as an undifferentiated unity and criticizes Jung's patriarchal thinking, she still bases most of her argument on an animus/anima dichotomy. Moreover, when she insists on androgyny as an undifferentiated unity, she qualifies it as an archetypal and innate structure rather than a cultural construct.

Absolutism of 'archetypeness' and innateness of specific images or symbols, so popular with Jungians, poses a problem. We are in the very early stages of understanding how the human brain functions. Therefore, such fundamental and abstract theories as the collective unconscious and archetypes or deep myths are highly speculative indeed. Attributing universal meaning to certain images and experiences dismisses the constantly moving psycho-social dynamics of human existence which are integrated into ideological matrices of dominant systems of particular societies in particular historical periods.

I would apply a similar approach to another grand theory – that of biologically determined gender – which is maintained by and maintains a dual system of polarity. In the twenty-first century with its sweeping changes 'the societal need for continuity and transmission of dominant values may be particularly acute' (Tuchman, 2012, p. 41), giving a boost to seemingly forgotten misogyny in science. Thus in their trendy attempts to investigate the biologically determined nature of gendered psychology, Hulbert and Ling (2007) argue for women's predisposition to choose pink, basing this 'innate/natural' choice on prehistoric labour differentiation – women as gatherers were looking for reddish berries. The research does not consider the historical and cultural factors of this so called 'natural predisposition', which is in fact conditioned by gender politics in each particular historical period, society and culture. Thus less than a hundred years ago pink, as a shade of red, was considered in western culture to be a male colour (Paoletti, 2012). Parents dressed their boys in pink dresses as it was associated with power, action . . . you name it. Little girls were supposed to wear blue instead as this was seen to be the colour of calmness, water, etc. Before the First World War (when the present colour dichotomy began to be established) a hypothesis such as Hulbert and Ling's would have been highly unpopular, as it simply did not accord with the ideologically produced gender associations of the time − unlike the contemporary and commercially lucrative myths of blue Marses and pink Venuses.

Conclusion

The quest for a lost primordial androgyny that is embodied as an ideal divine unity of male and female opposites has stretched out across the ages into all mediated and non-media forms alike. This chapter has discussed the ways in which we continue to adhere to both Abrahamic and late Hellenic traditions, and continue to differentiate between a culturally constructed male and female, with androgyny at the paradigm's core.

Focusing on multiple manifestations of androgyny in myths, religion, philosophy and film, this chapter has shown how genders have been constructed and deconstructed in cultural products by gender politics of dominant systems. By looking at these constructions of humans' attempts to understand the ever-so-changing world around and within, the chapter examined many of the ways that patriarchy has employed a seemingly liberating androgyny as a misogynist tool. One might disagree with many aspects of Luce Irigaray's writings, but it is undeniable that sexual difference is 'the major philosophical issue of our age' (Irigaray, 1993, p. 7), and the feminist debate on essentialism versus constructivism that started in the twentieth century is far from over.

This chapter debated how androgyny is an incorporation of culturally produced heteronormativity of femininity and masculinity and male and female identities. The myth of the essential divine unity was suggested to be considered as supportive of the system of beliefs based on dualism. This fairytale of dualism was argued to hinder society in overcoming the differentiated nature of things. In its attempts to trace androgyny as a myth of an ideal ultimate unity (with gods, m/others, self) in male discourse, the chapter positioned androgyny as a product of ideological hierarchy and proposed that we view androgyny, defined as a unity of opposites, as a manifestation of patriarchy. Briefly the chapter showed how cultures evolve and change and how a hierarchy of prescribed qualities changes accordingly.

The chapter highlighted some folk material that provides us with examples of a full range of experiences available to any human being regardless of their sex, and positions androgyny outside the dualistic matrix of beliefs. It also showed how the utopian nature of wholeness myths correlates with the quest for fairytale happiness.

I have underlined the changing nature of prescribed modes of being and proposed that we not consider such cultural phenomena as essentialist axioms. A gendered differentiation of opposites, with androgyny at its core; prescribed modes of gendered happiness; and femininity and masculinity, are proposed to be approached as psycho-social constructs reinforced by their media representation in modern mythologies, rather than be regarded as innate psychological traits.

This chapter does not deny the right of women and men to feel liberated by accepting their 'natural' femaleness/maleness or on the contrary their 'soul counterparts' (Jung's animus/anima respectively). However, by emphasizing and elaborating on the evolution of culturally produced femininity and masculinity, this work suggests that the comfort that might come with such an acceptance should be seen as a psychological solace which allows us to experience and manifest a wide spectrum of universal human emotions, feelings, and modes of being which are prescribed to an opposite gender or prohibited by prescriptive discourses (including feminism).

The chapter underlined that 'an acknowledgement of the historical specificity of current dominant beliefs about women and men, opens up new ways of conceptualizing gender, not as universally given, but as socially constructed' (Zooner, 2012, p. 31). We, as products and producers of our culture, are socialized into traditional stereotypes in early childhood long before we exercise any critical points of view.[15] Recognizing the unchanging and unchallenged 'pressure to be defined, in social terms, as either male or female' (Kuhn, 1994, p. 235), the work invited the reader to question why we consider gender and sex one way and not the other; what we feel about different identities and our own; why we stereotype this way and not the other; and how we can accept different ways of being.

Such revision of the foundations of stereotyping and dominant beliefs encourages more freedom of choice, and greater understanding and acceptance of our ungendered human nature, thus assisting a redefinition of gendered constructs. However, the chapter does not promise that by asking these questions we might get closer to some sort of fairytale happiness. No, we won't reach the totality of spiritual insight; and we won't be reborn, become perfect or become the true us. Nevertheless, what we can possibly obtain by asking these questions is something more trivial but in the contemporary world still paradoxically inaccessible – *the right to be human* with a whole continuum of choices, qualities, emotions, feelings, behaviours, thoughts and identities regardless of our sex, ethnicity, age, nationality or religion.

Notes

1 See Elena Mancini, *Magnus Hirschfeld and the Quest for Sexual Freedom: A History of the First International Sexual Freedom Movement*, New York: Palgrave Macmillan, 1992. Also Marie Delcourt, *Hermaphrodite. Mythes et Rites de la Bisexualité dans l'Antiquité classique*, Paris: Presses Universitaires de France, 1958; Kathleen P. Long, *Hermaphrodites in Renaissance Europe*, Aldershot: Ashgate, 2006.
2 For works that challenge research on 'objectively' measured, biologically determined differences between male and female psychology, performance and our 'hardwired gendered brains' see Fine (2011); Kimmel (2004).

3 Tracing gendered symbolism in mythology could be speculative though, as subjectivity, cultural influence and academic schools all interfere with its interpretation. Thus Zolla (1981) considers 'Isis-Osiris' as androgyne, 'the same and the other, the mirror and the mirrored' (p. 8), while Baring and Cashford (1991) analyse Isis and Osiris in the 'mother goddess and son consort' system.

4 See works by Heide Göttner-Abendroth arguing matriarchies as non-hierarchical, egalitarian societies of matrilineal kinship, sharing power equally between women and men.

5 Citation from film *Antichrist* (Dir., Von Trier, 2009).

6 D. t. d. no. – 'Da tales doses' in medical prescription (instruction for preparing and dispensing medicines to a certain patient) means 'dispense such doses . . . in number'.

7 Neither film was successful at the box office.

8 See works by Soloviev, Koole, and Zolla on Androgynous Sophia.

9 For Bacon, 'when nature becomes divine' it is no longer female but male (Fox Keller, 1985, p. 21) and the scientist becomes 'more female' in relation to it; and vice versa: the moment nature becomes an object to be conquered, it becomes female in relation to the male master – the scientist (ibid., 39). Female subordination is preserved.

10 Citation from film *Orlando* (Dir., Potter, 1992).

11 Citation from film *Orlando* (Dir., Potter, 1992).

12 Citation from film *Orlando* (Dir., Potter, 1992).

13 Citation from *The Master and Margarita*, a novel by Mikhail Bulgakov, London: Penguin, 1997.

14 See works by L. Hockley for a post-Jungian view on individuation as a metaphor.

15 See works by S. Bem, C. Fine, M. Bennet and F. Sani for examples of the early development of culturally conditioned gender identity.

References

Annas, P. (1978). 'New worlds, new words: androgyny in feminist science fiction'. *Science Fiction Studies* 5(2) (July): 143–156.

Baring, A. and Cashford, J. (1991). *The myth of the goddess: evolution of an image.* London: Arkana/Penguin Books.

Becker, R. (1990). Die weibliche Initiation im ostslawischen zaubermärchen. Ein Beitzag zur Funktion und Symbolik des weißlichen Aspektes im Märchen unter besonderer Berücksichtigung der Figur der Baba-Saga. Veröffentlichungen der Abteilung Für Slavische Spachen und Literaturen des Osteuropa-Instituts (Slavishes Seminar) an der Freien Universität Berlin, Band 71. Weisbaden: Otto Harrassowitz.

Bem, S. (1983). 'Gender schema theory and its implications for child development: raising gender-aschematic society'. *SIGNS: Journal of Women in Culture and Society* 8(4): 598–616.

Bettelheim, B. (1976). *The uses of enchantment: the meaning and importance of fairy tales.* New York: Knopf.

Bruce, F. F. (1983). *The Gospel of John.* Cambridge: Pickering and Inglis.

Busst, A. J. L. (1967). 'The image of the androgyne in the nineteenth century'. In I. Fletcher (ed.), *Romantic mythologies* (pp. 1–95). London: Routledge and Kegan Paul,

Chandler, D. (2007). *Semiotics: the basics.* London: Routledge.

Dijkstra, B. (1974). 'The androgyne in the nineteenth century art and literature'. *Comparative Literature* 26(1): 62–73.

Fine, C. (2011). *The real science behind sex differences: delusions of gender.* London: Icon Books.

Fox Keller, E. (1985). *Reflections on gender and science.* New Haven CT: Yale University Press.

Franz, M. L. von (1970). *An introduction to the psychology of fairy tales.* New York: Spring.

Franz, M. L. von (1972). *Problems of the feminine in fairytales.* Dallas TX: Spring Publications.

Franz, M. L. von (1993). *The feminine in fairy tales.* Boston: Shambhala.

Franz, M. L. von (1996). *The interpretation of fairy tales.* Revised edn. Boston: Shambhala.

Gilbert, E. (2006). *Eat, pray, love: one woman's search for everything across Italy, India and Indonesia.* New York: Viking.

Gilbert, S. and Gubar, S. (1979). *The madwoman in the attic: the woman writer and the nineteenth-century literary imagination.* New Haven CT: Yale University Press.

Gimbutas, M. (1974/2007). *The goddesses and gods of old Europe: 6500–3500 B.C.* London: Thames & Hudson.

Goscilo, H. (2005). 'Folkloric fairy tales: introduction'. In M. Balina, H. Goscilo and M. Lipovetsky (eds), *Politicizing magic: an anthology of Russian and Soviet fairy tales* (pp. 5–21). Evanston IL: Northwestern University Press.

Harding, E. (1955). *Woman's mysteries (ancient and modern: a psychological interpretation of the feminine principle as portrayed in myth, story, and dreams).* New York: Pantheon.

Hauke, C. (2011). 'What makes Jung, Jung?' *International Journal of Jungian Studies* 3(2): 184–186.

Hockley, L. (2011). 'The third image: depth psychology and the cinematic experience'. In C. Hauke and L. Hockley (eds), *Jung and film II: the return* (pp. 132–147). London: Routledge.

Hubbs, J. (1988). *Mother Russia: the feminine myth in Russian culture.* Bloomington and Indianapolis: Indiana University Press.

Humm, M. (1997). *Feminism and film.* Bloomington: Indiana University Press.

Irigaray, L. (1977). *The sex which is not one.* Ithaca NY: Cornell University Press.

Irigaray, L. (1993). *An ethics of sexual difference.* Ithaca NY: Cornell University Press.

Johns, A. (2004). *Baba Yaga: the ambiguous mother witch of the Russian folk tale.* New York: Peter Lang.

Jung, C. G. (1928). 'The relations between the ego and the unconscious'. In *The collected works of C. G. Jung,* eds H. Read, M. Fordham and G. Adler, trans. R. F. C. Hull (vol. 7) (pp. 188–211). London: Routledge.

Jung, C. G. (1940/50). 'Concerning rebirth'. In *The collected works of C. G. Jung,* eds H. Read, M. Fordham and G. Adler, trans. R. F. C. Hull (vol. 9i) (pp. 113–150). London: Routledge.

Jung, C. G. (1981). *The archetypes and the collective unconscious.* 2nd edn. Princeton NJ: Princeton University Press.

Kimmel, M. (2004). *The gendered society.* 2nd edn. Oxford: Oxford University Press.

Koole, B. (1986). 'Man en vrouw zijn een: de androgynie in het Christendom'. In *het bijzonder bij Jacob Boehme.* Utrecht: Hes.

Kravchenko, M. (1987). *The world of the Russian fairy tale.* European University Studies, series XVI, vol. 34. Bern, Frankfurt, New York, Paris: Peter Lang.

Kuhn, A. (1994). *Women's pictures: feminism and cinema.* London: Routledge and Kegan Paul.

Leeming, D. (2005). *The Oxford companion to world mythology.* Oxford: Oxford University Press.

Lieberman, M. (1972). '*Some day my prince will come*: female acculturation through the fairy tale'. *College English* 34(3): 383–395.

Lüthi, M. (1986). *Once upon a time. On the nature of fairy tales.* Bloomington: Indiana University Press.

Maiorino, G. (1992). *Leonardo da Vinci: the Daedalian mythmaker.* Philadelphia: Pennsylvania State University Press.

Miller, S. and Rode, G. (1995). 'The movie you see, the movie you don't: how Disney does that old time derision'. In Elizabeth Bell, Lynda Haas and Laura Sells (eds), *From mouse to mermaid: the politics of film, gender and culture* (pp. 86–106). Bloomington: Indiana University Press.

Paoletti, J. (2012). *Pink and blue: telling the boys from the girls in America.* Bloomington: Indiana University Press.

Pomerance, M. (ed.) (2001). *Ladies and gentlemen, boys and girls: gender in film at the end of the twentieth century.* Albany: State University of New York Press.

Propp, V. (1968). *Morfologia skazki/Morphology of the folk tale.* Austin: University of Texas.

Propp, V. (1946/2004). *Istoricheskie korni volshebnoi skazki.* Moscow: Labirint.

Rowe, K. (1979). 'Feminism and fairy tales'. *Women's Studies: An Interdisciplinary Journal* 6: 237--257.

Rowland, S. (2002). *Jung: a feminist revision.* Oxford: Blackwell.

Rowland, S. (2011). 'The nature of adaptation: myth and the feminine gaze in Ang Lee's *Sense and Sensibility*'. In C. Hauke and L. Hockley (eds), *Jung and film 2: the return* (pp. 148–162). London: Routledge.

Ruitenbeek, H. (1966). *Psychoanalysis and male sexuality.* New Haven CT: College and University Press Services.

Sells, L. (1995). 'Where do the mermaids stand? Voice and body in the *Little Mermaid*'. In Elizabeth Bell, Lynda Haas and Laura Sells (eds), *From mouse to mermaid: the politics of film, gender and culture* (pp. 175–192). Bloomington: Indiana University Press.

Shapiro, M. (1983). 'Baba-Jaga: a search for mythopoeic origins and affinities'. *International Journal of Slavic Linguistics and Poetics* 28: 109–135.

Singer, J. (1976). *Androgyny: toward a new theory of sexuality.* New York: Anchor Press.

Tuchman, G. (2012). 'The symbolic annihilation of women by mass media'. In M. C. Kearney (ed.), *The Gender and Media Reader* (pp. 41–58). New York and London: Routledge.

Wehr, D. (1987). *Jung and feminism: liberating archetypes.* Boston: Beacon Press.

Weil, K. (1992). *Androgyny and the denial of difference.* Charlottesville: University Press of Virginia.

Zipes, J. (ed.) (2000). *The Oxford companion to fairy tales: the western tradition from medieval to modern.* Oxford: Oxford University Press.

Zipes, J. (2006). *Fairy tales and the art of subversion.* New York: Routledge.

Zolla, E. (1981). *The androgyne: reconciliation of male and female.* London: Thames and Hudson.

Zooner, L. van (2012). 'Feminist perspectives on the media'. In M. C. Kearney, *The gender and media reader* (pp. 25–40). Hove: Routledge.

Internet sources

Enciso, N. (1995). 'Turning the gaze around and Orlando'. www.collectionscanada.gc.ca/eppp-archive/100/202/300/mediatribe/mtribe95/orlando.html (accessed 3 February 2014).

Hulbert, A. C. and Ling, Y. (2007). 'Biological components of sex differences in color preference'. *Current Biology* 17(16), 21 August 2007. www.cell.com/current-biology/fulltext/S0960-9822(07)01559-X (accessed 11 February 2014).

Smithstein, S. (2012). 'Our thirst for wholeness'. *Psychology Today*, 3 February 2012. www.psychologytoday.com/blog/what-the-wild-things-are/201202/our-thirst-wholeness (accessed 11 February 2014).

The Gospel of Thomas www.sacred-texts.com/chr/thomas.htm (accessed 1 February 2014).

SECTION II

The Quest

The Old Wise Helper and the Magical Object

Luke Hockley and Nadi Fadina

The idea of personal transformation is of course appealing and understandably so. Who would not be drawn to the idea that our lives can be transformed without effort, overnight and completely? It is the fairytale of winning the lottery. Yet even in the highly unlikely event of winning a fortune, we give little thought, if any, to what will stay the same, or to the problems that a sudden change in lifestyle might bring. Sometimes we forget that fairytales are just that. We also forget those aspects of the fairytale that contain less than positive messages, where characters are punished for their vain and deceitful behaviour.

In today's bookshops the numerous shelves of new-age books that once offered the prospect of a more fulfilling life through immersion in and connection to the unseen powers of the universe are dwindling. They have been replaced by no lesser quantity of self-help books. Replacing crystals, astrology, tarot cards and new forms of spiritualty are books that offer to improve our self-confidence, make us compelling public speakers, and help us to overcome our fears and let us be truly happy. Some tie new-age ideas with self-help together with revelation of an esoteric secret that will change our very personalities, our personal wealth, and our bodies too. Nearly all these guides to personal change suggest that it can be quick, dramatic and permanent. This is one of the fairytales of our age, and the considerable treasures amassed in the modern day castles of industry are used to ensure that the contemporary minstrels of the mass media tell the story in the furthest reaches of the kingdom.

Generically we refer to these books as part of the self-help industry: what they are not is part of a self-acceptance industry – tellingly, there is no such industry. Self-help (sometimes referred to by bookstores as 'shelf help') feeds an almost desperate desire for transformation. The number of diet books, guides on how to sleep well, or on how to succeed financially is astounding – there is no shortage of spells in the modern world. Like Cú Chulainn, the warrior of Irish myth, we undergo a frenzied transformation as we battle against our bodies as they grow old and visibly age, and we take up arms against our minds as we persuade ourselves that both body and brain stop us from being truly happy.

The idea that change, and indeed the less commercially lucrative idea of self-acceptance, has to be worked at is not as appealing as the more magical prospect of instantaneous transformation. However, the insight that change requires effort is found in fairytales and myths, where such change is represented in the metaphor of a long and arduous quest. The narrative device of a lengthy journey across a varied but always hazardous terrain symbolizes the effort and perils involved in the psychological task of coming to understand and accept both who we are and our relationship to the world we live in. In psychological terms, what these stories offer is a depiction of the work of self-understanding. For some, the road to such insight is through psychotherapy, which like its fairytale counterpart is a demanding and testing process. Others will take a different path. Nearly always, however, such work happens not in isolation but in relationship with someone else, and it is rarely quick. Of course we would like it to be so: hence the appeal of therapies such as cognitive behaviour therapy (CBT) as contemporary magical techniques that purport to quickly turn our neurosis and difficulties into something of psychological value. However, it remains a fairytale and one that is reminiscent of Rumpelstiltskin, who spun the straw of everyday mental turmoil into strands of precious gold. However, as a result of Rumpelstiltskin's trickery he ends up tearing himself in two with rage – it is doubtful that CBT would have been of much help with his anger management.

The search for ways to change ourselves is something of a contemporary quest. Indeed, one of the enduring myths of Western Europe is the search for the Holy Grail as a source of enlightenment and contentment with life. It is difficult to know exactly where the story originated, though it has a considerable history and traces of it can be found in Geoffrey of Monmouth's *Historia Regum Britanniae* (circa AD 1100); in both Wace's (circa AD 1155) and Layamon's accounts (circa AD 1190) and also in the medieval Welsh tales of the *Mabinogion*. The great popularizer of the stories of Arthur was Chrétien de Troyes, who gave the tales their now familiar chivalric gloss. He also introduced to *The Matter of Britain* both the figure of Lancelot and that most mystical of objects, the Holy Grail. In Chrétien's version the Grail was a silver platter that was used for serving food on feast days. In later developments it became the chalice that was used by Jesus during the Last Supper and also a cup that caught the drops of Jesus' blood while he was being crucified.

The stories retain a contemporary resonance. Since their revival in the Victorian era they have been retold by poets such as Tennyson, turned into numerous novels, been the source of inspiration for artists such as Edward Burne-Jones (*The Last Sleep of Arthur in Avalon*) and been remade as films and television series. (Bert Olton's book from 2000, *Arthurian Legends on Film and Television*, is a catalogue of these programmes and runs to over 300 pages.) The idea of a quest for something that is unobtainable and that yet offers to transform our lives remains appealing to us.

In particular, Lancelot seems a strikingly modern figure. In an attempt to escape from an unsatisfying life he seeks sexual solace in an affair with King Arthur's wife Guinevere – it was never going to have a happy ending. Indeed, in some versions of the legend it causes nature itself to wither. Equally, the Grail as an object of salvation that is elusive and ethereal has some modern resonances too. The irony of the Grail myth is that even once it is seen by Perceval, he fails to behave in the correct way, as when the Grail finally appears he remains silent. In fact he should have asked the right questions which would have then healed the Grail's guardian, the Fisher King. Even when the object of our quest is under our very noses we fail to grasp its true significance. The reason for this is that the reality of life is only made apparent through questioning.

The idea that we can change our lives through the acquisition of magical objects, or the application of magical potions, is a myth that underpins the contemporary cosmetics industry. It is an idea that we are familiar with through its appearance in fairytales. In *Snow White* the evil stepmother uses her magical power to maintain her youthful appearance. Her vanity is so powerful that it fuels her murderous desire to kill Snow White. While we remember that Snow White wins out because she is the fairest of them all, what we forget is that in the version told by the brothers Grimm the stepmother is punished for her vanity and made to dance to her death wearing red-hot iron shoes. This is not to deride the pleasure we gain in our own appearance and that of others; rather it cautions against an excessive belief in the magical power of objects to make us happy. The story of Snow White is not actually about change; instead it shows how contentment comes from being who we are, and that trying to transform ourselves into something we are not will not make us happy.

Even so we persist in wanting to change ourselves, and such change is not cheap. Cosmetic surgery, high fashion, luxurious holidays, personal transformation DVDs and books, coaching, counselling and psychotherapy are all expensive – though as cosmetics company L'Oreal reminds us, we're 'worth it'. There is something magical about money. In one English fairytale Jack trades his cow for a handful of magic beans. His furious mother throws them away, but overnight the beans grow into a huge beanstalk that leads to a giant's castle full of riches. After several dangerous escapades the giant is killed and Jack and his mother live a happy and rich life. Money is a form of symbolic exchange – coins and paper, and these days ephemeral digital data, are turned into material objects, just as cows are sold for beans, and beans are magically transformed into beanstalks that lead to undreamed of riches and happiness.

We invest money with a supernatural quality. That is why we throw coins into water. Not any sort of water, but fountains and shallow pools. Throwing money into a puddle would be pointless. But bodies of water that resemble in shape either magic cauldrons, or the mystical waters they contain, are altogether different. We make our incantations in sacred spaces, and with our right hand over our left shoulder we cast a spell as we throw our money into the Trevi fountain in Rome, and wish. Respighi wrote classical music about it (*Fontane di Roma*), Fellini featured it in *La Dolce Vita* (1960) and the old song 'Three Coins in a Fountain' celebrates it.

Our desire for a sweet life free from the ogres of depression and anxiety is worth spending a little money on. This is something we wish for, and it is a fairytale that we desperately want to believe in.

The idea that money can bring transformation and happiness through the objects we purchase is a powerful one. Today, there is no need to go on a lengthy Grail quest – we can buy countless versions of the Grail from Amazon without leaving our home. (Some of them, appropriately, by Monty Python.) There is an endless supply of books, DVDs, online courses and social networks that offer to change our lives for the better. The problem is that the illusion of change that is easily won fades equally quickly. Yet we are driven still further by the belief that our objects of desire will instantaneously change us for the better. Understandably, the contemporary giants of consumerism intend to take much better care of their wealth than the dim-witted one in *Jack and the Beanstalk*. Yet the belief that the Holy Grail of happiness can be achieved through the quest of self-transformation is becoming ever more prevalent and trenchant. This is the fairytale that lies at the heart of our modern belief in therapy.

4

CRUMBLING REJUVENATION

Archetype, embodiment and the 'Aging Beauty myth'

Josephine Dolan

Within the space of five years, two big budget fantasy films, *Stardust* (Dir., Vaughn, 2007) and *Snow White and the Huntsman* (Dir., Sanders, 2012), exploit the archetypal figure of the aging crone that has its roots in myth and fairytale, and is best known through the Grimm brothers' *Snow White* and its Disney mediation *Snow White and the Seven Dwarfs*. *Stardust* is an adaptation of Neil Gaiman's novel that weaves together three stories: first, the search for a ruby whose ownership will determine the right to the throne of the magical kingdom of Stormhold by the princes Primus (Jason Flemyng) and Secundus (Rupert Everett); second, the adventures of a forlorn Tristan, who crosses from the earthly village of Wall to the magical world of Stormhold, where he seeks the star that he had witnessed falling from the sky – he believes this star to be a token that will gain the heart of Victoria (Sienna Miller), the object of his unrequited love; and third, that of an earthbound and humanized star, Yvaine (Claire Danes), who is pursued for the rejuvenating energy of her heart by three ancient witches, the sisters Lamia (Michelle Pfeiffer), Empusa (Sarah Alexander) and Mormo (Joanna Scanlan). Like *Stardust*, *Snow White and the Huntsman* interleaves stories of intersecting power struggles for rulership and for everlasting youth and beauty. The film tells the story of Snow White (Kristen Stewart), the daughter of a king, motherless from an early age, whose father remarries before being murdered by her stepmother, Ravenna (Charlize Theron), who then exiles and imprisons her. Ravenna has extraordinary powers of bodily regeneration and rejuvenation that are derived from her ability to inhale the youth force of other women, leaving them dried-up husks of abjected femininity. However, Ravenna's sense of power is disturbed when her magic mirror predicts that Snow White will eventually outstrip her in both power and beauty unless she consumes the heart of the princess. She orders Eric the Huntsman (Chris Hemsworth) to find and kill her rival, and to secure her heart as a trophy. At first compliant, Eric subsequently turns against Ravenna when he learns the true identity of Snow White. After gaining the support of various underworld tribes, including eight dwarfs, Snow White leads an attack on Ravenna's palace, where in hand-to-hand combat she kills her. Like *Stardust*, *Snow White and the Huntsman* depicts the death of the evil, rejuvenated woman as a revelation of the ancient crone that lies beneath her veneer of rejuvenation.

With their references to wicked stepmothers, magical mirrors and rejuvenated crones, both of these films draw on the Snow White story, though neither claims to be a 'faithful' adaptation. (Adaptation scholars quite rightly point out the impossibility of such a claim.) Rather, the references made by these films to the Grimm brothers' story and to Disney's animated films are highly allusive, designed to mobilize memories of previous versions via familiar tropes, whilst also staking claims to originality by foregrounding departures, deviations and additions. Indeed, with *Stardust*, any connection to either the Grimm or the Disney version of *Snow White* is more dependent on cultural associations with the tropes of the 'wicked stepmother', such as the magic mirror and the pursuit of rejuvenation, than to any overt gesture made by the producers. Whilst the eponymous titling of *Snow White and the Huntsman* does explicitly invite inter-textual associations with other versions of the Snow White tale, it is similarly allusive in its deployment of dwarfs, as well as the familiar magic mirror. But more than anything, in *Stardust* and *Snow White and the Huntsman* the figure of the ancient crone for whom happiness, power and rejuvenation combine into an evil, potent mix offers the most powerful allusion to the 'wicked stepmother' of the Snow White fairytale.

This figure of the 'wicked stepmother' chimes with Jungian formulations of universal archetypes, such as the Mother, Father, the Child or the Trickster, that are inscribed within the collective unconscious, and which James Iaccino (1998: xi) suggests are 'forms without content' that find their 'expression in tribal lore, mythology, fairy tales, religious systems and primitive art'. Crucially, as argued by a cohort of scholars researching across literature and film, as diverse as Jack Zipes and Luke Hockley, archetypes should not be reduced to ahistorical or timeless formulations. Rather, a clear distinction needs to be drawn between archetype as a recurring form and archetype as meaningful figure. As Zipes suggests, 'social relations and psychological behaviour' are 'the very stuff which constitutes the subject matter of the tale' (1986, p. 1). To put this another way, post-Jungian theorists are crucially alert to the ways in which universal symbols are appropriated, re-visioned and accrue meaning within the symbolic order of particular times, places, social groups and practices. Thus crucially, myth and archetype are always culturally and historically specific as they play through both the conscious and unconscious of the symbolic order.

From this position, Zipes also forges a link between traditional myth and fairytale, and *Mythologies*, Roland Barthes' (1973 [1953]) account of modern myth. Barthes suggests that the denotations and connotations of any sign or image produce chains of signification that accrue a multiplicity of meanings in ways that effectively efface the arbitrary link between sign and meaning. In this way, meaning production is made to *seem* inevitable and made to *seem* natural, rather than being a process of cultural production. Once the cultural production of meaning is obscured, and thus rendered 'natural', it becomes depoliticized speech and takes on the function of ideology. Barthes' formulation of mythology is of particular importance here since it is largely concerned with the growth of the ideological function as facilitated by the rapid global circulation of mass produced images. And, to state the obvious, the circulation of myth and archetype is similarly bound up in this rapid process of mythologization. In other words, in the Barthesian sense, myths and fairytales can be seen to perform *mythological* functions. More especially, archetypes are pivotal to this mobilization of ideology by myth and fairytale. Thus, despite their seeming timelessness, archetypes should always be seen both as the product of a specific time and place and as the articulation of culturally and historically specific ideologies. The meanings of archetypes are never neutral – rather they are bound up in the circulation of dominant ideologies of any given moment. With this said, questions concerning the ideological function of the old crone archetype in its recent articulations are raised: what meanings are currently inscribed on the old crone archetype in *Stardust* and *Snow White and the Huntsman*; what mythologies are brought into play by these narratives?

Myth, technology and believability

Before these questions can be approached some discussion of the mechanisms through which both archetypes and mythologies are secured within contemporary cinematic discourse is warranted. Central to this discussion is the importance of 'realism' and 'believability'. There can be little doubt that the popular reach of both *Stardust* and *Snow White and the Huntsman* is bound up in the broader success of contemporary fantasy films, such as the *Harry Potter* series and the *Lord of the Rings* cycle. This success can be attributed (in part at least) to the CGI (Computer Generated Imagery) technology that is coming to dominate mainstream film and is wresting cinematic fairytales from their dominant Disneyesque animated form. As with the introduction of any new cinematic technology, such as happened with sound and colour, its arrival is in itself a source of curiosity and/or spectacle. Effectively, the changes wrought by technology to familiar stories, genres and forms become a major attraction for audiences and, of course, a source of profits for producers. At the very least, due to its cooption within the contemporary film industry, the crone archetype has a function within the capitalist economy. But this is not the whole picture because, paradoxically, the spectacle of CGI is predicated on its capability to disappear from the screen; to produce its special effects and yet leave no disruptive traces of technological intervention. In this way, the 'reality' effect of CGI plays a part in securing the ideological function of the crone because it enables filmmakers to realize the most fantastical imaginings of location and character with no disruption to believability. For example, in the course of *Stardust*, the crone Lamia undergoes several instantaneous and seamless age transitions as her rejuvenating magic is either depleted or restored.

In comparison, films made in previous decades that employed latex based prosthetic make-up to realize their aging effects struggled to secure the believability of similar aging transitions. For instance, the Hammer adaptation of Rider Haggard's

She (Dir., Robert Day, 1965) has its female protagonist, Ayesha (Ursula Andress), step for a second time into a sacred flame. This reverses the flame's rejuvenating effects and triggers an accelerated aging process that concludes with her disintegration into a pile of dust and rags. Shot as a series of cuts between a group of horrified onlookers and close ups of hands and face that signify a degenerative aging process, the mechanics of Ayesha's rapid aging are evident in a prosthetic facial overlay that does not quite reach her eyes, which thus retain a disturbing youthfulness, whilst Andress' face is fixed into an immobile and expressionless mask that draws attention to its artificiality. Crucially, unlike the effacement of CGI aging in *Stardust* and *Snow White and the Huntsman*, this kind of visible prosthetic aging ruptures the suspension of disbelief that stitches audiences into the 'realist' diegesis (on-screen world) of the film. With the rupture to the seam of 'realism' also comes a rupture to the mythological and ideological operation of archetype.

It is always worth restating the truism that realism is never an unmediated reflection of the real world, but rather it is itself an illusory special effect: a construction of an ostensible reality mediated through a variety of cinematic conventions in which time, space and character are woven together into a coherent diegetic world. The numerous versions of realism such as documentary realism, British social realism, Italian neo-realism, or Hollywood classic realism are a useful reminder that realism is never simply a given, but that its conventions are culturally and historically specific and that the exigencies of time, taste and cinematic technologies such as camera, sound, colour and editing techniques intersect to render realism a fluid and mutable formation that crosses genres and film forms in producing that suspension of disbelief that secures cinematic spectacle as a believable and knowable world.

Arguing that a film's *believability* is the crux of cinematic realism, rather than its capacity to reflect the extra-diegetic (off-screen) world, Steve Neale (1981) adopts a term from literary criticism, verisimilitude, to underline the fact that in fictional genres, 'reality' is always constructed. In literary criticism, verisimilitude means believability and/or faithfulness, which Neale suggests are organized in relation *both* to the conventions of specific genres and to recognizable societal norms. For Neale, the believability of cinematic fictional worlds stems from the combination of what he terms generic verisimilitude (faithfulness to genre) and cultural verisimilitude (faithfulness to everyday reality). This combination of cultural and generic verisimilitude renders plausible the most improbable and/or fantastical scenarios, such as invisibility, time travel, and special powers of all kinds. Christine Geraghty (1997) usefully sums up:

> Whereas generic verisimilitude allows for considerable play with fantasy *inside* the bounds of generic credibility (e.g. singing about your problems in the musical; the power of garlic in gothic horror movies), cultural verisimilitude refers us to the norms, mores, and common sense of the social world *outside* the fiction.
>
> (Geraghty, 1997, p. 360)

Following Neale and Geraghty, we can see that, while CGI technology plays a part in securing the fairytale realism and generic alignment of *Stardust* and *Snow White and the Huntsman*, the believability of their narratives cannot be reduced to such factors. Vitally, it is equally the case that their believability and realism are dependent on a recognizable cultural verisimilitude and the extent to which they reference the apparent everyday norms, mores, and common sense. Indeed, even with the 'magic' of CGI technologies, if cultural verisimilitude is ruptured or disturbed in some way, then the believability of the story and its characters breaks down. By the same token, if believability breaks down, the capacity of myth and archetype to articulate ideology, that is to be *mythological* in the Barthesian sense, is similarly unsettled. Thus, the stakes of cultural verisimilitude reach beyond the formulation of a believable diegesis, and extend to the circulation and recirculation of ideological mythologies as they flow between the diegetic and extra-diegetic world. It is this circuit of discourse (du Gay in Hall, 1997, p. 1) that flows between audiences and producers and enables archetypes to be continually refreshed. It allows archetypes to be rendered contemporaneous, relevant and believable and thus secured for the ideological work of mythology.

Embodied archetypes and myths of aging beauty

One of the key ways in which *Stardust* and *Snow White and the Huntsman* secure cultural verisimilitude, and hence historically specific ideological functions for their archetypes, is through the bodies of stars, and those supporting actors who never achieve the luminary status of stardom, whose flesh and blood populates and inhabits the spaces and action of CGI created worlds, and which, following Iaccino, gives embodied content to archetypal forms. Indeed, the bodies of stars also bear testimony to a lived connection between the diegesis of the film and the everyday practices of the extra-diegetic world – a connection that both prefigures and extends beyond the running time of the film. In his study of the emergence of film stardom in Hollywood's burgeoning studio system of the 1920s, Richard de Cordova (1999) makes the point that actors and actresses are transformed into stars in, and through, the publicity circuits of magazines and radio (we can now include TV and the world wide web in this process) that extend knowledge of stars beyond the diegesis of the film and take in their private as much as their public lives. As testified by the likes of Rudolph Valentino or Marilyn Monroe, the death of the actor or actress does not spell the death of the star image, and like archetypes, they become signifying systems available to subsequent generations. Whilst this does not necessarily render the star timeless in the manner of a Jungian archetype, it certainly enables a correlation of temporal longevity to be drawn between archetype and the body of the star: a longevity that extends beyond on-screen verisimilitude.

And this correlation between archetype and star is a site where we can begin to see the mapping of historically specific meanings onto universal archetypal forms, since the bodies of stars are never neutral and are always inscribed with multiple significations. Theorists of stardom such as Richard Dyer (1979, 1986) argue that stardom cannot be reduced to marketing strategies and film industry economics, and that stardom exceeds the particularity of a given actor or actress. Rather, stars are produced at the intersection of marketing and publicity discourses, on-screen performances and off-screen publicity and media events. Consequently, stars need to be understood as 'always extensive, multimedia, intertextual and as complex and polysemic signifying systems that are fully implicated in the circulation and reproduction of dominant discourses and ideologies' (Dyer, 1979, p. 3). Crucially, one of the ideological functions of stars is the embodiment of social values. As Dyer writes, stars function as:

> embodiments of the social categories in which people are placed and through which they make sense of their lives, and indeed through which we make our lives – categories of class, gender, ethnicity, religion, sexual orientation and so on.
>
> *(Dyer, 1986, p. 18)*

To rephrase Dyer, stars make discursively produced identities *seem* as if they are biological, and hence, essential properties of the body. Thus stars can be seen to operate as a type of Barthesian myth in that they serve to efface the cultural production of identity categories and operate to depoliticize the meanings of identity categories by rendering them as biologically determined. From here it is not an unreasonable leap to assume that the embodiment of the crone by Pfeiffer and Theron in *Stardust* and *Snow White and the Huntsman* can tell us something about contemporary discourses of old age femininity.

With their storylines about the crone's pursuit of everlasting youth and beauty, it is strikingly obvious how the cultural verisimilitude of both *Stardust* and *Snow White and the Huntsman* connects to the growth of those rejuvenation industries, both surgical and cosmetic, that in contemporary western cultures shape ideals of femininity and which also serve to pathologize the signs of aging as inscribed on the body. This follows the gerontological paradigm in which old age is produced as a period of decline and its subject as a dying entity. As Pamela H. Gravagne observes:

> No matter how healthy and alive, no matter how functional and creative, the aged body was seen at one and the same time as pathological, since changes attributed to age were read as due to disease, and normal, since these changes were to be expected.
>
> *(Gravagne, 2013, p. 18)*

The archetypal crones of *Stardust* and *Snow White and the Huntsman* exemplify this paradigm in that their search for happiness is conflated with their seeking a curative for a pathologized old age.

Whilst the circulation of the crone archetype has always articulated some of the cultural anxieties about aging, especially for women whose identities and sense of self-worth are problematically imbricated in discourses of idealized beauty, the problem is particularly evident in contemporary culture due to the attractions of 'successful aging' discourses. This discursive formation first emerged in the late 1980s (Rowe and Kahn, 1997), just as the aging population began to be constituted as a problem in want of a solution, rather than as a marker of the West's social progress. Byrnes and Dillway summarize the successful aging configuration as being a regulatory regime concerned with 'the avoidance of disease or disease susceptibility, a high cognitive capacity, and active engagement with life' (Byrnes and Dillaway, 2004, p. 67). This model of supposed successful aging is now hegemonically established as the common sense alternative to, and remedy for, a burdensome, vulnerable old age with its attendant economic and emotional costs to the state, to communities, to families, and to the individual old person.

It is largely self-evident that because of their ongoing careers, their continued presence on our screens, their high profile appearances on chat show sofas and within broader circuits of media culture, and through their seemingly perpetual desirability (as actors in the film industry workplace and/or as sex objects in the circuits of cinematic desire) aging stars function ideologically to embody and naturalize the active engagement with life discourse that is central to successful aging agendas. As I argue fully elsewhere (Dolan, 2013a), aging stars also embody the formation of successful aging as it is organized around gender-specific discourses of firm and hard, which for masculinity is all too frequently reduced to sexual function (and the profits of Viagra). For femininity, successful aging is predicated on its insertion into what Naomi Wolf (1990) has termed the 'beauty myth': that panoply of procedures, processes, products and panaceas that commodify women's bodies, even as they interpellate female consumers into the mythology's ideological purview through its promise of better looks, and hence, happiness. It is a central plank of Wolf's argument that the attention paid by stars to their appearance, and the extent to which they implicitly or explicitly endorse the equation of beauty and happiness ('We're worth it!') position them to embody, naturalize and disseminate an ideology of beauty. By extension then, older female stars can be seen to embody 'successful aging' as it intersects with 'the beauty myth', and thus, their bodies can be recognized as sites where a new 'aging beauty myth' is constituted and naturalized.

However, we also need to acknowledge that for female Hollywood stars, and other national cinemas that adopt Hollywood aesthetics and forms in the competitive frame of the global film economy, old age commences at a much younger chronological age than it does for the majority of women. As far back as 1973 Molly Haskell observed that the elision of beauty and youth that underpins Hollywood casting impacted upon the professional longevity of female stars, who at the first visible signs of aging were deemed too old or over-ripe for a part – except as a marginalized mother or older sister. Meanwhile, the careers of their similarly aged male counterparts were, and continue to be, shored up by hetero-normative, romantic couplings with much younger female stars, both on and off screen (Haskell, 1973, p. 14). This has implications for the embodiment of the Aging Beauty myth by Theron and Pfeiffer. At the time of filming Theron was 37, and therefore just too young to convincingly wear the mantle of the aging beauty without support from

CGI morphing. Meanwhile, at 45, in the everyday world outside the film's diegesis, Pfeiffer is also a young woman. Yet, within the Hollywood paradigm, she is already 'over the hill' and an ideal site for the embodiment of the Aging Beauty myth, as it resonates with her extra-diegetic existence and with the CGI manipulations age that are a conceit of *Stardust's* narrative.

With that said, the ideological imperative of the Aging Beauty myth can be readily recognized in the proliferation of post-menopausal female stars such as Meryl Streep, Helen Mirren, Judi Dench, Ellen Burstyn, Diane Keaton, Julie Christie and Glenn Close, who since circa 2000 have been nominated for their performances at Oscar and BAFTA ceremonies. Whilst we might be tempted to applaud this alleviation of the longstanding sexist/agist regime that for decades has impacted on Hollywood's casting practices, there is little to celebrate in the disturbing and striking normative 'whiteness' embedded in this new visibility of aging female stars. It is troublingly noteworthy that stars like Angela Bassett and Whoopi Goldberg, whose youthful successes have already thrown into relief the acute marginalization of non-white actresses in the Hollywood paradigm (cf. Tasker, 1988), are excluded from both this celebration of aging female stardom, and major roles in prestigious films. Whilst Bassett has been sidelined into less prestigious television roles, Goldberg is literally rendered invisible through recent performances in which she is heard rather than seen, as a documentary film narrator or as the voice of Stretch, an animated character in *Toy Story 3* (Dir., Unkirch, 2010). Alternatively, she is pushed to the margins in cameo roles as herself. Such exclusionary practices are highly problematic not only because they marginalize non-white older stars, but because they also reproduce the ubiquitous and pernicious white, racial privilege that is normalized and rendered ideologically hegemonic through the embodiments of Hollywood's star system (Dyer, 1979).

The Aging Beauty myth, archetype and the unconscious

One conclusion that can be reached from the above discussion is that through films like *Stardust* and *Snow White and the Huntsman*, Hollywood and its ilk are mapping the myth of Aging Beauty, and its attendant ideologies, onto the archetypal crone, which here is self-consciously consumerist and self-consciously white. Conversely, the repressed unconscious revealed by this version of the archetypal crone is knowledge and appreciation of those female forms which through body size or skin colour do not conform to the myth. As I will elaborate, this is not the only unconscious repression to rupture the ideological seam of aging beauty. Leaving aside rare exceptions such as Judi Dench who, as Christine Geraghty (2002) has argued, helps mark the difference between the dame of American glamour and the ladylike dame of British theatrical prestige, the new visibility of aging female stars is largely contingent on the ability of older stars to dispel the signs of aging on their bodies (Dolan, 2013b). In the Aging Beauty myth, the privileged white bodies of older female stars are characterized by smooth brows, slender legs, flat stomachs, and pert breasts and buttocks. These aging female bodies are seemingly unmarked by pregnancy, or injury, or surgery or overindulgence and thus play a pivotal role in securing the perfection implied by the myth. Typically, many of the procedures used to attain this perfection are obfuscated by accounts of gruelling hours in the gym and healthy eating regimes. Only rare exceptions such as Madonna and Cher make public the extent of time spent in clinics and treatment rooms; and of the skills of surgeons and beauticians that produce their bodies as ideals of feminine allure and as exemplifications of the Aging Beauty myth's achievement.

Of course, for the rest, as Vivian Sobchak (1999) reminds us, not all the glamour of rejuvenation can be attributed to the surgeon's knife, the rigours of the gym, or the potions and the lotions of the beauty clinic. Rather, the spectacle of smooth, firm, feminine bodies is equally reliant on post-production techniques such as air-brushing and computer graphic transformations, what Sobchak has termed the 'second operation of plastic surgery' (1999, p. 206). The artifice of these transformations has led to consumer protests and legal action on both sides of the Atlantic. In 2012, the UK's Advertising Standards Authority (ASA) ruled that the L'Oreal campaign faced up by Rachel Weisz was exaggerated and misleading and banned it, although the watchdog agency rejected complaints about a separate L'Oreal commercial for a moisturizer featuring a photograph of actress Jane Fonda (Reuters, 2012). It also banned some Photoshopped cosmetics advertisements featuring Julia Roberts and Christy Turlington. In the USA, after the National Advertising Division (NAD) of the Council of Better Business Bureaus ruled that a CoverGirl mascara advertisement was misleading, Procter and Gamble shut down the advertising. The NAD, which can issue rulings but cannot itself enforce them, said it was following the lead of its sister body in the UK. And, most importantly, as suggested by Sobchak, the artifice of the second operation of plastic surgery is not confined to advertising but is fully embedded in popular cinema where, because of the prevalence of the Aging Beauty myth in contemporary culture, it helps establish cultural verisimilitude.

The dependency of *Stardust* and *Snow White and the Huntsman* on the second operation of plastic surgery is a moot point. We can speculate that it is unlikely to have been used to rejuvenate the younger Theron, and that it was probably used to rejuvenate the older Pfeiffer. However, without access to specialist or archival knowledge, there can be no certainty here. What is certain is that in these films, CGI technologies of aging are used to establish a young–old binary that is itself mapped onto the bodies of the stars as archetype. And this embodied binary is organized around a conscious expression of white, normatively sized youthful beauty and an attendant repression into the unconscious of an inexpressible, delimited and unregulated old age femininity. Some mitigation is offered to this particularly vile articulation of the crone. For example, the mobilization of the crone archetype in these films is aligned with Lamia and Ravenna who, consistent with their fairytale origins, are constituted as unredeemably vain and evil. Because of this their ultimate demise seems to be a just and logical punishment for their murderous intent, and the underlying intent to defy the hands of time. It seems almost as if the films' closures that see Lamia and Ravenna punished for their evil intent serve to redeem the narratives themselves from their invidious mythologization.

However, whilst such a conclusion is fully supportable, it misses the polysemic complexity of these narrative resolutions by neglecting the continuing existence of Pfeiffer and Theron beyond the diegesis of the film, and thus misses the ideological contradictions inscribed on their bodies. Notably, the demise of Lamia and Ravenna is not the whole picture, because the bodies of Theron and Pfeiffer have a *visibly* continuing existence outside the diegesis of the film due to their appearances at high profile publicity events, premiere screenings and award ceremonies, where, in the manner of the ubiquitous make-over show, all traces of old age are seen to be eradicated, whilst their fully restored youthful glamour is revealed as a spectacle of ideal feminine beauty. This spectacle of glamorous, aging female stardom effectively reiterates popular cinema's longstanding endorsement of the beauty myth and its more recent cooption into aging femininity because of its continuing visibility beyond cinematic diegesis and its continuing inscription on the bodies of stars.

However, this endorsement is riddled with contradictions in that the extra-diegetic bodies of Pfeiffer and Theron shore up the Aging Beauty myth even as the diegetic bodies of Lamia and Ravenna are ostensibly punished. Moreover, those punishments are themselves troublingly complicated since they are symptomatic of popular cinema's ongoing and pernicious pathologization of older women's bodies. Crucially, whilst these punishments *culminate* in the deaths of Lamia and Ravenna, they *commence* when Yvaine and Snow White are rescued from the crones' all-consuming pursuit of the Aging Beauty myth. At this point, once the magic of rejuvenation begins to fail, Lamia and Ravenna's beauty is exposed as an artificial, prosthetic glamour that – akin to the slimy, rotting flesh of Frankensteinian monster horror – drips and peels from their decomposing bodies, revealing the underlying actuality of their old age, whilst also equating that 'truth' – that old age – with moral *and* physical degradation and corruption. In this, both films reiterate a familiar trope of pathologized and abject aging femininity that can be traced through the likes of *Sunset Boulevard* (Dir., Wilder, 1950), *Whatever Happened to Baby Jane?* (Dir., Aldrich, 1962), and *She* (Dir., Day, 1965), in which women are ridiculed, vilified and punished because they refuse the mantle of an aging femininity that is constituted through discourses of redundancy and abjection (Dolan, 2013a).

These films exemplify a pathologizing gaze frequently brought to bear on aging femininity within popular cinema. This formulation of the pathological gaze derives from Foucault who in *The Birth of the Clinic* (1963) suggests that the clinical encounter is structured through the clinician's gaze that seeks the signs of disease and abnormality on the patient's body through prior knowledge of normal, healthy bodies. It is in knowing the signs of the healthy body that the clinician can recognize the symptoms of the abnormal, and thus diagnose ill health. The clinical gaze is therefore split between knowledge of the normal and of the pathological. Building on Foucault's account of disciplinary knowledge, Stephen Katz traces how nineteenth-century gerontology emerged as a 'knowledge formation . . . linked to the disciplining of old age and the construction of specific subjects of power and knowledge' (Katz, 1996, p. 1). That is, chronological age was used to identify a distinctive and discrete group of subjects that were linked to a set of signs and symptoms that in turn were concretized as a 'problem' through pathologizing discourses and practices. Here then, mainstream films such as *Sunset Boulevard*, *Whatever Happened to Baby Jane?* and *She* can be recognized as performing the work of age categorization, whilst also mobilizing the split gaze that pathologizes the body of the older female star through its knowledge of a youthful norm that enables the signs of aging to be recognizable and readable; and for these signs of aging to be constituted as symptoms of abnormality. However, with *Stardust* and *Snow White and the Huntsman,* there is a *doubling* of pathology: a *doubling* that can be recognized in the punishment of Lamia and Ravenna because, effectively, they are pathologized for *both* the pursuit of the aging beauty myth *and* the signs of age exposed beneath its youthful veneer.

This doubling of pathology offers a neat fit with Sadie Wearing's account of the aging female body in contemporary media representations that cut across print and screen media through ubiquitous make-over shows and magazine features. Wearing suggests that many of these texts attempt to have it both ways insofar as they 'offer the fantasy of therapeutic rejuvenation while remaining firmly entrenched in a coercive and moralizing policing of aesthetic and gender norms that set the standards of both chronological decorum and time-defiance regulating' (Wearing, 2007, pp. 304–305). As Wearing explains, even as women are located in ideologies of rejuvenation, condemnatory and regulatory discourses such as 'acting your age' and 'mutton dressed as lamb' place strict limits on the terms of rejuvenation. In a similar vein, Diane Railton and Paul Watson (2012) trace such regulatory discourses in the contemporary vilification of Madonna that marks a radical shift in her image from the lauded 'material girl' of the 1980s when her film-and-music-derived popularity was at its peak, to her current incarnation as an aging pop diva. Always a controversial figure because of her performance of pornographic gestures and use of fetishistic costume in her music videos and films, she nonetheless mesmerized with her ability to switch between distinct sexed and gendered identities by her proud display of a well-toned body that served to highlight gender performativity by unsettling existing assumptions of muscularity and self-determination being biological properties of the male body. However, since she reached her fifties, Madonna has been increasingly vilified in the press for the exposition of her flesh – a 'tawdry embarrassment' as Jane Fryer (2012) puts it.

Clearly, Madonna has breached the injunctions of chronological decorum and the likes of Fryer can be seen to be policing the regulatory terms of rejuvenation. Notably, in this regulation, there is a sharp contrast between the discourses surrounding Madonna's exposed flesh and that of Helen Mirren following a globally circulated paparazzi shot that carried the headline 'The Bikini Queen Reigns Supreme'. Where Mirren is lauded for her 'enviable curves and flat stomach' (Anon. a, 2008) and is held up as an exemplary representative of the aging beauty myth, Madonna is scorned because of her sinewy arms, gnarled, bony knees and 'wrinkled and vein-ravaged hands that reveal she is battling to defy the signs of aging' (Anon. b, 2007). Unlike Mirren, Madonna's skin is represented as bearing the signs of aging – it sags, it wrinkles, it is visibly veined. Therefore it seems as if Madonna's transgression of chronological decorum is not produced through the exposure of flesh *per se*, but rather, the terms of transgression are defined through the *type* of flesh on show, and by extension, by the signs of aging thus made visible. In short, Madonna displays the wrong kind of flesh to be allowed the burden of exposure because she embodies an incipient old age that ultimately cannot be contained, controlled, managed or concealed by cosmeceutical interventions.

The point that really needs to be made here is that the cultural verisimilitude of *Stardust* and *Snow White and the Huntsman* is highly reliant on its reiteration of a specific myth of Aging Beauty, whilst simultaneously it draws on the regulatory discourses that reflect those illuminated in the pathologization of Madonna: discourses that define and police chronological decorum. By the same token, this play of cultural verisimilitude illuminates some of the cultural anxieties (both public and personal) that attend the feared collapse of the Aging Beauty myth. As with the CGI-enhanced performances of Pfeiffer and Theron as Lamia and Ravenna, Madonna's flesh disturbingly foregrounds the myth's provisionality; its propensity to rupture, to break down and to revert to an underlying decay and degeneration that portend the final stages of life.

Here, then, is the nub of the matter: this flesh is not pathologized simply because it bears the signs of aging, but also because those signs of aging are a potent reminder of our universal mortality. Thus, in effect, the depoliticized speech of the aging beauty myth serves to silence mortality discourse, whilst the policing of chronological decorum forges a powerful alignment with western silences and taboos about death and dying. This silencing of mortality discourse returns the argument to archetype, and, following Bettelheim (1991), its propensity to symbolize the repressions of the unconscious. As Luke Hockley reminds us, archetypes 'encapsulate the totality of a psychological situation, both the aspects that are conscious, and the elements that are unconscious' (Hockley, 2001, p. 3). So, taking silence as a symptom of repression, it can be recognized that the breaches of chronological decorum represented by the punishment of Lamia and Ravenna in *Stardust* and *Snow White and the Huntsman* respectively are also breaches in the repressions of mortality discourse.

One further point needs to be made about the spectacular transition from beauty to abjection, from youth to decrepitude, made by the crone archetype. Because these transitions conclude with Pfeiffer and Theron marked with the signs of old age, old age is fixed as an unavoidable stage of life; a stage that may be temporarily forestalled, but one which will inevitably take its course. Thus, old age is represented as a fixed and knowable property of the body, and as an embodied, and hence biologically determined stage of life. The extent to which we should see biological aging as a fixed and knowable given has been complicated by cultural gerontologists who argue that 'old age' is a naturalized, discursive identity formation akin to gender, race, class or sexuality. For instance, Pamela H. Gravagne (2013) draws parallels between Judith Butler's (2003) account of gender performativity and the cultural construction of old age. Butler argues that gender is brought into being by social agents who 'constitute social relations through language, gesture, and all manner of symbolic social signs' (Butler, 2003, p. 413). It is in the reiteration of speech, gestures and actions that gender difference is secured and gender roles are prescribed. As Gravagne concludes, 'If gender (age) is performative, rather than expressive, then it is not performed to express or disguise an interior self, but to produce a recognizable self in the interests of a "social policy of regulation and control" (Butler, p. 423)' (Gravagne, 2013, p. 15).

To conclude, this then suggests two points. First, the regulatory discourses embedded in the punishment of Pfeiffer and Theron as Lamia and Ravenna extend to include the ongoing construction, reiteration and embodiment of old age performativity. And, crucially, the labour of this cultural production is rendered mythological in the Barthesian sense, even as it is inserted into the frame of myth and fairytale by the appropriation of the Snow White story. Second, the 'aging beauty myth', and its alignment to the cultural verisimilitude of *Stardust* and *Snow White and the Huntsman*, is, *simultaneously*, a reiteration of embodied old age performativity (the speech, gestures and actions of old age) *and* an opportunity to recognize the cultural construction of age through Pfeiffer's and Theron's CGI-enhanced performances of rapid age transitions. And it is that opportunity that bears the brunt of repression heaped onto the archetypal figure appropriated by these films. The violence of this repression is powerfully symbolic of an urgent and pressing anxiety about threats to the ideological seam of old age performativity. It marks a similarly urgent and pressing need to repress into the cultural unconscious any conscious awareness of old age performativity. Finally, it also marks a no less pressing and urgent need to secure the mythological alignment between old age performativity and the illusion of conscious embodiment.

References

Anon. a (21 July 2008). 'Helen Mirren The Bikini Queen Reigns Supreme at 63'. www.mailonsunday.co.uk/tvshowbiz/article-1035510/Helen-Mirren-bikini-queen-reigns-supreme-63.html.

Anon. b (18 June 2007). 'She's So Vein: The Very Veiny Hand of Madonna'. *Mail Online*. www.dailymail.co.uk/tvshowbiz/article-462819/Shes-vein-veiny-hand-Madonna.html.

Barthes, R. (1973) [1953]. *Mythologies*, London: Paladin.

Bettelheim, B. (1991) [1976]. *The Uses of Enchantment: The Meaning and Importance of Fairy Tales*, London: Penguin Books.

Butler, J. (2003). 'Performative Acts and Gender Constitution', in *The Feminist Theory Reader*, eds C. McCann and S. Kim (pp. 462–476), New York: Routledge.

Byrnes, M. and Dillaway, H. (2004). 'Who is "Successful" at Aging? A Critique of the Literature and Call for More Inclusive Perspectives'. Paper presented at the American Sociological Association meetings, San Francisco. http://citation.allacademic.com//meta/p_mla_apa_research_citation/1/0/8/3/1/pages108312/p10831-1.php.

Campbell, J. (1993) [1949]. *The Hero with a Thousand Faces*, London: Fontana Press.

De Cordova, R. (1991). 'The Emergence of the Star System in America', in *Stardom: Industry of Desire*, ed. G. Geraghty (pp. 16–29), London: Routledge.

Dolan, J. (2013a). 'Firm and Hard: Gender, Old Age and Hollywood's Gaze', in *De-Centring Cultural Studies: Past, Present and Future of Popular Culture*, eds José Igor Prieto-Arranz, Patricia Bastida-Rodríguez, Caterina Calafat-Ripoll, Marta Fernández-Morales and Cristina Suárez-Gómez (pp. 217–246), Newcastle: Cambridge Scholars Press.

Dolan, J. (2013b). 'Smoothing the Wrinkles: Hollywood, "Successful Aging" and the New Vvisibility of Older Female Stars', in *The Routledge Companion to Media and Gender*, eds C. Carter, L. Steiner and L. McLaughlin (pp. 342–352), London and New York: Routledge.

Dyer, R. (1979). (New edn, 1998). *Stars*, London: British Film Institute.

Dyer, R. (1986). *Heavenly Bodies: Film Stars and Society*, Basingstoke: Macmillan Press.

Foucault, M. (1963). *The Birth of the Clinic: An Archaeology of Medical Perception*. Translated 1973. London: Tavistock Publications.

Fryer, J. (19 July 2012). 'Sorry Madge You're Now Just a Tawdry Embarrassment: She's a Fan. But after Sitting Through the 53-Year-Old's Lewd, Expletive-Ridden New Show, Jane Fryer Is Not Happy'. www.dailymail.co.uk/news/article-2175666/Madonna-Hyde-Park-review-Sorry-Madge-youre-just-tawdry-embarrassment.html#ixzz22Bs6f36e.

Furby, J. and Hines, C. (2012). *Fantasy*, London and New York: Routledge.

Geraghty, C. (1997). 'Genre and Gender: The Case of the Soap Opera', in *Representation: Cultural Representations and Signifying Practices*, ed. S. Hall (pp. 337–386), Milton Keynes: Open University Press.

Geraghty, C. (2002). 'Crossing Over: Performing as a Lady and a Dame', *Screen* 43(1): 41–56.

Gravagne, P. (2013). *The Becoming of Age: Cinematic Visions of Mind, Body and Identity in Later Life*, Jefferson NC and London: McFarland and Company.

Hall, S. (1997). *Representation: Cultural Representations and Signifying Practices*, Milton Keynes: Open University Press.

Haskell, M. (1973). *From Reverence to Rape: The Treatment of Women in the Movies*, New York: Holt, Rinehart and Wilson.

Hockley, L. (2001). *Cinematic Projections: The Analytical Psychology of C. G. Jung and Film Theory*, Luton: University of Luton Press.

Iaccino, J. (1998). *Jungian Reflections Within Cinema: A Psychological Analysis of Sci-Fi and Fantasy Archetypes*, Westport CT: Praeger.

Katz, S. (1996). *Disciplining Old Age: The Formation of Gerontological Knowledge*, Charlottesville: University Press of Virginia.

Neale, S. (1981). 'Questions of Genre', *Screen* 31(1): 45–66.

Railton, D. and Watson, P. (2012). '"She's So Vein": Madonna and the Drag of Aging', in *Aging Feminities: Troubling Representations*, eds J. Dolan and E. Tincknell (pp. 193–204), London: Cambridge Scholars Press.

Rowe, J. and Kahn, R. (1997). 'Successful Aging', *The Gerontologist* 37: 433–441.

Sobchack, V. (1999). 'Scary Women: Cinema, Surgery and Special Effects', in *Figuring Age: Women, Bodies, Generations*, ed. K. Woodward (pp. 200–211), Bloomington and Indianapolis: Indiana University Press.

Tasker, Y. (1998). *Working Girls: Gender, Sexuality and Popular Cinema*, London and New York: Routledge.

Tasker, Y. and Negra, D. (2007). *Interrogating Postfeminism: Gender and the Politics of Popular Culture*, London: Duke University Press.

Wearing, S. (2007). 'Subjects of Rejuvenation: Ageing in Postfeminist Culture', in *Interrogating Postfeminism: Gender and the Politics of Popular Culture*, eds Y. Tasker and D. Negra (pp. 277–310), London: Duke University Press.

Wolf, N. (1990). *The Beauty Myth*, London: Vintage.

Zipes, J. (1986). *Don't Bet on the Prince: Contemporary Feminist Fairy Tales in North America and England,* New York: Methuen.

Zipes, J. (1994). *Fairy Tale as Myth/Myth as Fairy Tale*, Lexington: University Press of Kentucky.

5

FINDING THE GOLDEN EGG

Illusions of happiness in an age of consumer capitalism

Catriona Miller

Introduction: money and civilisation

Money, wealth and possessions all appear to be the obsession of a contemporary capitalist culture. There is a corresponding tendency to think fondly of the past as a simpler and less materialistic time. However, concerns with ownership, wealth and trade can be traced back to the dawn of recorded human history. Sumerian is one of the earliest known forms of writing and it was partly developed to enable accounting. The clay tokens, or 'count stones', were used as a primitive accounting system as early as 8000 BCE (Coulmas, 2003, p. 4) and as writing developed further it is noted that the 'earliest inscriptions record land sales, focusing on named individuals and suggesting greater social emphasis on personalised wealth' (Crawford, 2013, p. 99). It is reasonable to consider that in part the spur to develop writing was the need to record transactions and to track ownership.

This chapter will take a look at the depiction of the desire for money, the acquisition of wealth and its consequences, which forms a significant part of the folk and fairy tales of Western culture, before considering how traces of these tales can be found within more contemporary media texts such as *Citizen Kane* (Dir., Welles, 1941) and *Pretty Woman* (Dir., Marshall, 1990). It will also consider how well these stories fit within the context of the consumer capitalist culture within which much of the world now exists, and the growth of advertising which helps to sustain it.

The tradition of folklore and fairy tale

In traditional folk and fairy tales, there are a wide variety of stories associated with wealth and fortune. As is often the case with folk tales, they do not all make the same point: some are exhortative, while others are admonitory. Of the first type, tales such as *Jack and the Beanstalk* (Lang, 1890/1966) for example, and *Aladdin* (Lang, 1889/1965), drawn from Burton's 1885 version of *One Thousand and One Nights*, both tell the story of the poor young hero stepping out into the world to find his fortune. This might appear to suggest that the winning of a fortune is a suitable goal for the hero, but not so, at least not directly. In fact, it is important to note that whilst setting out to search for the means to feed one's starving mother or family is acceptable, seeking a fortune for its own sake is not and action at the expense of others is also not tolerated.

For example, in *The Grateful Beasts* (Lang, 1894/1966) (collected originally from Hungary by Hermann Kletke), three brothers all set out to find their fortunes, but the two older brothers do so at the expense of the youngest, Ferko, whom they cripple and blind to get his bread and then leave him for dead. Through some luck, the youngest brother overhears ravens talking about how to restore his sight and mend his broken legs. The young man heals himself and then uses this knowledge to heal first a wolf, then a mouse and finally a queen bee of their own injuries. In turn, they help him against his older brothers, now at court, who whisper to the king that Ferko is a magician. After Ferko passes several trials, the wolf eventually eats the brothers and the king, leaving Ferko to marry the princess and take over the kingdom.

Thus we can see, as demonstrated by the fate of the two older brothers, that setting out to win gold or fortune for its own sake and *at any cost* is likely to end in disaster for the greedy quester. By way of contrast, virtuous and honest heroes are usually rewarded for helping the less fortunate by coming into a large fortune of some kind. On closer examination, it does strike an odd note that in many cases material good fortune is the reward for a brave and moral hero and that the good fortune takes the form of treasure, gold or money, or a more generalised kind of wealth associated with marrying a princess and inheriting a kingdom. The message of these tales is that while seeking fortune is wrong, wealth may still be the reward for virtue.

It also worth noting that there is a gender distinction in these kinds of stories. Heroines are rarely out in the world to seek their fortune. Instead they tend to be forced out of their homes (often by a stepmother jealous of the younger woman), thus are seeking a husband and a new home. This is demonstrated in stories such as *Little Snow White* or *The Six Swans*, both collected by the brothers Grimm (Grimm, 2007), or *Cinderella* by Perrault (Perrault, 2010). As Pratt (1981) has noted, the 'return' is particularly problematic for female heroes, and there is rarely a kingdom (queendom) for her to inherit. Instead, in traditional tales the reward for a heroine is usually couched in terms of finding the right (rich) husband. So the happy ending for the righteous hero is material good fortune, whilst the happy ending for the righteous heroine is marriage to a hero.

The second type of story associated with wealth is distinctly more cautionary. For a very brief example, one of Aesop's fables, *The Goose That Laid the Golden Egg*, proves a useful specimen. In it a man and wife possess a goose that gives them a golden egg each day. However, they are not content with this state of affairs and cut the goose open, thinking to find more gold inside. Instead, the goose is dead and they have lost their daily egg. The moral of the tale being, 'Much wants more and loses all' (Aesop et al., 1912/2003, p. 15). In another cautionary tale from the classical period, King Midas (Ovid, 2008) responds to the god Bacchus's benevolence by asking that everything he touched might turn to gold, little realising that he would never be able to eat or drink again. Eventually, the god relents and Midas is relieved of his gift, retiring to the mountains to live in poverty.

In seeking to understand such tales, one interpretative approach might tend towards the suggestion that the material wealth of the reward is a metaphor, and that the gold, money, gems, etc. act as proxies for treasures of another order: wisdom, compassion, courage and so on. Thus the greedy who pursue money for its own sake, or misers who jealously hold onto their money, are the villains of the piece who come to grief or are overthrown, leaving the heroes to live happily ever after. A Jungian perspective might further suggest that these stories outline a path of individuation, which can be briefly defined as 'a person's becoming himself, whole, indivisible and distinct from other people or collective psychology' (Samuels et al., 1986/1991, p. 76). Individuation, however, is perhaps best understood as a metaphor for a 'sifting of personal and collective material' (Hockley, 2007, p. 14) that an individual undertakes in order to differentiate who one is from the culture and society within which one lives.

Individuation can be said to fall into two main parts – the first being an 'initiation to outward reality' (Jacobi, 1942/1973, p. 108) often characterised by the narrative form of the hero's journey (Campbell, 1949/2008). The hero (the ego) overcomes shadow monsters and other temptations (from the unconscious), making ethical choices, leading to a more conscious personality.

Of course, many of these traditional fairy tales are still being directly retold, often for children by the Disney corporation for example. Animated films such as *Cinderella* (Dir., Geronimi, Jackson, and Luske, 1950) or *Aladdin* (Dir., Clements and Musker, 1992) are one style, but there are also non-Disney live action versions of fairy tales in circulation, such as *La Belle et la Bête* (Dir., Gans, 2014), as well as more camouflaged and reworked narratives offering stories of the poor but honest hero finding his way in the world. *Pursuit of Happyness* (Dir., Muccino, 2006) is one such example. In this film, single father Chris Gardner (Will Smith) determines to provide a better life for his family by becoming a stockbroker, even though that entails a six-month unpaid internship with no guarantee of a job at the end of it. The title refers to the American Declaration of Independence, which offers 'preservation of life, liberty and the pursuit of happiness' (Rakove, 2009, p. 77) as examples of the 'inalienable rights of man'. The misspelling of 'happiness' arises within the film from a sign painted by the Chinese owner of a day care centre that Gardner's son attends. After the child's mother leaves, Gardner becomes his son's sole carer, and then becomes homeless but doggedly perseveres through all hardships to become a successful stockbroker. It is interesting that one thread on the imdb.com ("Capitalist Indoctrination?" n.d.) webpage discussing the clear association of happiness with material riches extended to eight pages of, at times, heated debate. The pursuit of happiness is such a constituent part of the common sense mythos and cultural backdrop of America today that virtually any criticism is cast automatically as denigrating the mainstream where freedom is equated with the freedom to pursue wealth (Burnett, 2012). The capitalist context of this film makes some changes to the folk tale narrative. Chris Gardner is portrayed as a good father, being willing to do 'whatever it takes' to create a more affluent future for his son, whilst it could be argued that being a good father is more than being a good provider. We will return to the issue of capitalism later.

The more admonitory tales are repeated in celluloid too. *Citizen Kane* (Dir., Welles, 1941) is perhaps one of the best-known films of all time. It begins with Kane (Orson Welles) dying in his huge mansion with only employees to care for him, but the first real introduction the audience has to the character of Kane is in the form of a newsreel reporting his death, entitled 'Master of Xanadu'. Although purportedly about Kane, it begins by describing in some detail the house he built. In some ways, the house, named Xanadu (after the Coleridge poem, *Kubla Khan*, published in 1816), appears to be Kane's life's work. The newsreel describes the huge effort and wealth required to build the house and to collect its contents; in fact, 'So much it can never be catalogued or appraised. Enough for ten museums. The loot of the world . . . Xanadu is the costliest monument a man has built to himself!' So declares the newsreel. Kane, despite being a reluctant millionaire, having failed at all the relationships in his life, in the end has nothing but his fortune.

The Great Gatsby (Dir., Clayton, 1974) based on the 1925 novel by F. Scott Fitzgerald, is also of interest. In it money appears as a corrupting influence. Daisy (Mia Farrow) and her husband Tom (Bruce Dern), and perhaps too the narrator Nick (Sam Waterston), exist in an empty, hedonistic life style, that Jay Gatsby (Robert Redford) wishes to join, if only to be found worthy of Daisy's love. Gatsby, the penniless lieutenant, emerges from the war with a tremendous fortune, designed to give him entrée into Daisy's privileged world, but instead Gatsby is destroyed. In this case money is a means to an end, rather than the goal in itself, but none the less, the hero has come by the money in mysterious circumstances and is thus not able to reap the rewards he dreams of. *The Great Gatsby* was remade by Baz Luhrmann in 2013, but both film versions offer a frenetic, Dionysian vision of Gatsby's parties, as an image of the desperation of the roaring twenties, just prior to the stock market crash of 1929. There is little here to admire in the world of the very rich.

For the heroine too, there are plenty of film narratives that follow the fairy tale model, for example *Sabrina* (Dir., Wilder, 1954) in which the chauffeur's daughter Sabrina (Audrey Hepburn) falls in love with David (William Holden), the feckless younger brother of her father's rich employer, but in time comes to appreciate the steadier charms of older brother Linus (Humphrey Bogart). *Sabrina* was remade in 1995, directed by Sidney Pollack, with Harrison Ford as Linus and Julia Ormond as Sabrina. Perhaps more controversially, there is *Pretty Woman* (Dir., Marshall, 1990) where a prostitute from the wrong side of the tracks, Vivian (Julia Roberts), wins her 'prince', businessman Edward (Richard Gere) through her personal qualities and beauty.

Examining modern day films in terms of their underlying fairy tale narratives is not without merit and, as suggested with fairy tales, can often yield useful insights.

Closer consideration of the films from a more Jungian perspective would also undoubtedly reveal elements of individuation narratives. However, all these stories (folk tale or film) raise an interesting point because, whether one approaches them metaphorically or attempts to stick to what is on the page and screen, the fact is the rewards for good choices and 'happily ever after' are closely associated with material wealth. Even if the wealth is taken as a metaphor, the vehicle of meaning relies on the association of plentiful material goods with reward and happiness.

'Happily ever after' is a concept that requires further consideration because happiness is a term that is very often simply taken for granted in discussions and is likely to be regarded as self-evident and transparent, but as one writer in the introduction to his history of happiness lamented, happiness was 'so elusive, so intangible . . . this "thing" that is not a thing, this hope, this yearning, this dream' (McMahon, 2007, p. xi) that he wondered how to go about pinning it down. Another writer simply notes that happiness 'is a contested concept' (Greve, 2011, p. x).

It is certainly a complex business tracing the history and meaning of the term, or to come to a definition. It is outside the scope of a chapter such as this to do justice to such complexity, but it is important to note that the idea of what constitutes happiness has shifted and evolved, changed its meaning, and moved from something that relied entirely on chance, to something (or at least the pursuit of it, as noted above) tantamount to a universal right. For the classical Greeks, happiness was not a feeling, rather it was a characterisation of a whole life that could only be reckoned after death. In medieval Europe, happiness too was linked with a moral Christian life, but true happiness could only be guaranteed in the heavenly afterlife. It is only with the discussions of the eighteenth-century Enlightenment and onwards that happiness became something 'to which all human beings could aspire in this life' (McMahon, 2007, p. 13), a point of view that began to have wide-ranging ramifications for public policy, for along with Enlightenment ideas came the Industrial Revolution and the exponential growth of capitalism. Indeed, the dominant mode of Western society became a capitalist one. In more recent times a culture has grown up around the constant consumption of material goods, to the point where it is often dubbed consumer capitalism.

This consumer capitalist mode, which can be understood as 'an organisation of the political economy in which the institutionalised interests of consumers set the terms for government policy formation and for company-level product market strategies' (Trumbull, 2006, p. 3) (where populations are addressed more often as consumers than as citizens), has had an effect upon the understanding of happiness itself, even though economists on the whole 'do not even like the question: "what is happiness?". To them happiness is not a concept clearly distinct from pleasure, satisfaction or welfare' (Bruni and Porta, 2006, p. xvii). Instead, they prefer to measure 'income as a suitable though incomplete proxy for human welfare' (Frey, 2008, p. 3). Nonetheless, the connections between economics and happiness studies have grown.

Interest in 'happiness economics' could be said to date back to the 1970s with Richard Easterlin's contribution (Abramovitz et al., 1974) in which he articulated what has come to be known as the Easterlin paradox. He found that within a given country, people with higher incomes are more likely to report being happy, but only up to a point. Subsequent rises in income did not raise happiness levels to the same extent. Taking care of basic needs (food, water, housing) did improve happiness dramatically but the higher up Maslow's hierarchy of needs (Maslow, 1943) one goes, the less the positive effect of greater material wealth.

Attempts to explain this paradox led to a mushrooming of studies on income and happiness, to the extent that one might suggest that there has been something of a 'happiness turn' in economics with growing efforts to measure a society's 'gross domestic happiness', rather than simply its gross domestic product. This shift has been championed by Bhutan ("Gross National Happiness" n.d.), but in 2010 British prime minister David Cameron declared that it was 'time we admitted that there's more to life than money and it's time we focused not just on GDP but on GWB – general well-being', and announced plans to measure happiness as an indicator of national progress, instead of relying solely on GDP "WHO – the Hapiness Effect" n.d. The Office for National Statistics in the UK has subsequently been busy developing ways of measuring this ("Measuring National Well-being" n.d.).

It is worth repeating that defining 'happiness' has been, and continues to be, a hotly debated topic within such studies, with many researchers settling instead upon the term coined by Diener (1984), Subjective Well Being (SWB), as the best measurable proxy. SWB is usually deemed to be made up of several strands that receive differing degrees of emphasis depending on the type of research being carried out. In fact, it has proved useful to draw a distinction between two types of happiness (Deci and Ryan, 2008). On the one hand there is a *hedonic* idea of happiness (drawn from Epicurus) where pleasure is maximised and pain minimised. In subjective well being studies, hedonic 'happiness' is explored with questions around feelings of enjoyment, and positive as well as negative affect (such as depressive symptoms). On the other hand there is the *eudaimonic* (sometimes spelled *eudemonic*) idea of happiness (drawn from Aristotle) which places more of an emphasis on achieving well-being through the fulfilment of one's individual potential within society. Notwithstanding, as Aristotle made explicit in his *Rhetoric*:

> We may take happiness as prosperity combined with virtue; or as independence of life; or as the secure enjoyment of the maximum of pleasure; or as a good condition of property and body, together with the power of guarding one's property and body and making use of them. That happiness is one or more of these things, pretty well everybody agrees.
>
> (Aristotle, 2012, pp. 22–23)

Virtue *and* prosperity feature in this definition. Those attempting to measure subjective well-being in relation to this version of happiness ask questions to do with purpose in life, fulfilment, self-acceptance and control (Dolan and Metcalfe, 2012).

To return briefly to fairy and folk tales, at least to some extent both *hedonic* and *eudaimonic* versions of happiness require money. So it is perhaps unsurprising that taken on a fairly straightforward level, fairy tales bring these two elements together as they offer narratives where material good fortune is the reward of a life well lived. To borrow the terminology of SWB studies, a *eudaimonic* life results in *hedonic* happiness. This is the 'happily ever after' of the fairy tale.

The Easterlin paradox, however, encapsulates a problem for the modern consumer: 'happiness wears off when it is generated by material things. Satisfaction depends on change and disappears with continued consumption. This process of hedonic adaptation induces people to aspire ever more' (Frey, 2008, p. 40). Hedonic adaptation, as this phenomenon has been dubbed, takes into account two factors that may help to explain the Easterlin paradox. First, social comparisons appear to play their parts as people tend to compare themselves to others within their community. Second, as income increases, so too does aspiration. In fact, preference drift outbalances the welfare effect of income gains (Frey, 2008). This means that in the consumer culture of the contemporary era, 'happily ever after' is a perpetually receding dream. The need to acquire ever greater wealth to enable ever greater consumption can never come to an end because the law of diminishing returns (hedonic adaptation) means the more one has, the more one's neighbours have, the more one wants. Happiness becomes related to the constant growth and expansion of wealth, perhaps in the same way as economies tend to be assessed on their rate of growth rather than on more absolute measures.

However, the situation has grown even more complex, for in the twenty-first century consumption is no longer simply a matter of the physical consumption of material goods, for consumption today includes the consumption of symbols, and it may be useful at this point to consider exactly what has changed in today's capitalist economy.

Marx, in his extensive analysis of capitalism, introduced the ideas of 'use value' and 'exchange value' in which one type of good could be exchanged for another, with a perceived equivalence. It was a 'perceived' equivalence because exchange value could not be fixed, depending as it did upon a variety of factors, such as scarcity. Marx also noted that a 'commodity' was worth more than its simple use value because it was transformed through labour, suggesting that the 'form of wood, for instance, is altered if a table is made out of it' (Marx, 1867/1976, p. 163). Even within the nineteenth century, the economy had already moved away from the original use value of items towards understanding them in terms of exchange value, which increasingly meant money, or monetary value.

For Marx, the role of money as a medium of exchange in capitalist society obliterated the original use value of goods, and opened up space for a different kind of meaning beyond even exchange value. By the second half of the twentieth century this additional meaning grew ever more accentuated and was dubbed sign value (Baudrillard, 1981/1994) as commodities were perceived to denote intangible qualities like style, gravitas, or youth. It was a *sign* value, because, drawn from the semiotic understanding of the sign, there was a signifier and a signified, which had only an arbitrary relationship, but which, nonetheless, was socially understood. To be fair, Marx had discerned this possibility himself, describing value as something which:

> transforms every product of labour into a social hieroglyphic. Later on, men try to decipher the hieroglyphic, to get behind the secret of their own social product: for the characteristic which objects of utility have of being values is as much men's social product as is their language.
>
> *(Marx, 1867/1976, p. 167)*

However, as the twentieth century progressed, it began to be further understood that it was not just a question of Western culture becoming more materialistic, that is, just wanting to have *more* of everything (as a sign of accumulated capital), rather that material goods and their production, exchange and consumption began to be understood within a cultural matrix. Consumption in a postmodern context was no longer so much a consumption of a material utility but instead a consumption of signs – a cultural economy where symbols were exchanged as much as (or perhaps more than) material utility.

An example of this can be found within the online metaverse of Second Life, which was launched in 2003. Inspiration for the platform came from Neal Stephenson's 1992 cyberpunk novel *Snow Crash*, which described both the metaverse and its avatars. Second Life reached its peak of users around 2006, but although these have dropped it still had healthy numbers of regular users in 2014. Players can use code to create objects within the game. However, Second Life has an in-world currency called the Linden dollar, which has a real-world value. Using Linden dollars, avatars (the players' in-world representatives) can buy appearances and abilities (a better quality or rendering of hair or a more realistic animation of walking), as well as houses, cars and fashions. For example, Adidas created a store where avatars could purchase branded trainers (Bannister, 2006). The trainers gave the avatars extra ability to jump and bounce within the game. Of course, all the player is purchasing is permission to use a section of computer code, but 'first impressions matter in virtual worlds too' (Weibel et al., 2010). The better realised the avatar (the better quality the coding, the more customised), the higher the status of the player. In this scenario exchange value and sign value are completely dominant.

However, there is still a question around the mechanism for investing a commodity with this additional sign value. Custom and practice, alongside historical precedent, undoubtedly play their part but on their own these do not account for the speed and reach of ever-novel sign values associated with commodities in the contemporary era. To be sure, the churn of commodity consumption, which leads to hedonic adaptation, is facilitated and encouraged, at least in part, by *all* media representations of 'the perfect life'. The further discussion of traditional narrative formats such as feature film or television drama could yield useful insights here, but I would argue that searching for 'myths of money' within those traditional drama forms may be missing the point, because more common by far in the era of consumer capitalism are the ubiquitous micro-narratives of advertising.

The role of advertising

It is difficult to get hard data on exactly how much advertising any one person is confronted with on a daily basis. However it is much easier to get information on the health of the industry in terms of expenditure, growth and profit (Segment Specific Insights for the Entertainment and Media Outlook (PWC), n.d.), and the fact is that 'advertisements saturate our social lives' (Goldman, 1992, p. 1). To illustrate this point, it is instructive to consider how much time elapses each day between opening one's eyes in the morning, and hearing or seeing one's first advert (television, radio, newspaper, billboard, internet, mobile phone and so on).

Advertising narratives are in essence very straightforward. Although their flavour might have altered over the years and they tell a simpler story about wealth than the one that is voiced in folk and fairy tales, advertising tells a story of desire fulfilled. The viewer is presented with a vision of happiness where the acquisition of goods and services, or perhaps more specifically brands (which may embody a whole set of sign values), will allow the consumer to attain a similar level of delight to that depicted.

As early as 1930, the trade paper *Printer's Ink* noted that 'advertising helps to keep the masses dissatisfied with their mode of life, discontented with ugly things around them. Satisfied customers are not as profitable as discontented ones' (Ewen, 2008, p. 39). And at least initially, advertising tended towards the AIDA model (Attention, Interest, Desire, Action) of attempting to persuade the consumer to buy this or that particular brand or product. This style of advertising might best be typified by the Lifebuoy soap adverts ("Lifebuoy Soap" n.d.) of the 1960s. Lifebuoy did not invent the term BO (Body Odour) – that honour going to a woman's deodorant called 'Odo-Ro-No' in the early twentieth century – but Lifebuoy did much to popularise it and used it extensively in their advertising campaigns for toilet soap. It named a problem, then gave the answer: use Lifebuoy soap to guarantee 'personal freshness', and social and career success is sure to follow. This formula was used for both men – an airline pilot who had trouble getting the girls – and women – a fashion designer who had trouble getting her boss's attention, for example. In fact, this approach has not been entirely abandoned, as a visit to Unilever's website confirms. This model is still being used today in the Lifebuoy Lemon Fresh campaign, where a teenager will not raise his arms because of his body odour problem, but is saved through the intervention of a scientist who tells him that Lemon Fresh soap will cure his problem.

However, although this type of advertising persists, it is being supplanted by what might loosely be termed postmodern advertising, where commodities are given ever more arbitrary cultural meanings. 'Advertisers attach signifiers to disparate objects and just as rapidly detach them, in the mischievous pursuit of novelty and difference. In the hyperreal world of postmodern advertising, everything mutates into everything else, all is image, appearance and simulation' (Odih, 2007, p. 248). Advertisers no longer tell the viewer what the product can do for them (cleaner teeth, fresher smell, faster car); instead they seek to show the viewer how the product or, increasingly, the brand will make them *feel*. The brand is a key component of postmodern advertising, because it can be extended across multiple products.

> A brand is a promise of satisfaction . . . a tangible, symbolic system created by a producer to evoke an IN-tangible notion in a customer's mind. The system comprises a discrete identity – name, logo, colour, visual style, tone of voice, product design, package design, advertising, approach to a customer service, and environmental design – associated with an insight involving rational product benefits, emotional desires, and personal aspirations.
>
> *(Healey, 2008, p. 248)*

This is a complex phenomenon but one which postmodern consumers understand very well. A renowned example is the Cadbury's Gorilla advert ("Cadbury Gorilla Drummer" n.d.) which was a huge success, giving Cadbury a significant bump in sales across all its products (record revenue growth of 7 per cent, Cadbury's best for a decade, with global sales up 11 per cent ("We Are Fallon"), despite the fact it had nothing to do with chocolate in general or Cadbury's milk chocolate in particular, apart from the purple colour coding associated with the Cadbury logo. However, what the advert *did* was to create emotionally compelling images, sounds and micro-narrative (the gorilla waits with obvious anticipation for the famous drum break in the Phil Collins song 'In the Air Tonight') with a payoff that left the viewer feeling good and a tag line, 'A glass and a half of full of joy', that did not appear to be demanding anything (Heath, 2012). Hockley discusses the use of anthropomorphic animals in advertising, suggesting that such images may straddle the divide between conscious and unconscious and as such become recipients of unconscious projections (Hockley, 2007, p. 84), which raises some interesting possibilities in understanding the success of this advert. The gorilla is a very close genetic relative of the human, and perhaps in this context is permitted to enjoy the full potential of that famous drum break without embarrassment. The advert created feelings of amusement and congeniality which were then associated with the Cadbury's brand.

To give another example, the 2008 'I am Mercedes Benz' campaign ("Presence: I Am Mercedes Benz" n.d.) only tangentially featured the car that was ostensibly the subject of the ads. The advertising agency said:

> Our challenge was to get younger drivers to change their view of Mercedes-Benz by injecting dynamism into the brand. The campaign was created to bring to life the qualities that make Mercedes-Benz special, such as 'Presence', 'Attraction' and 'Ambition'. In all three ads, actors are used to personify the brand, showing us that Mercedes-Benz cars are far more than just metal, rubber, glass and plastic.
>
> *("Presence: I Am Mercedes Benz" n.d.)*

All of the adverts shared a similar mise en scène: chiaroscuro lighting, multiple focus pulls, dark urban streets, rain on windows, running dogs and, despite the occasional shots of the speeding car, a wistful melancholy air, imbued in part by the Nick Cave and Warren Ellis music (drawn from the film *The Proposition* (Dir., Hillcoat, 2005) which featured on two of the adverts). The actors associated with each advert delivered the low-key voice overs to invert the supposed title of the advert. The first ad, 'Presence', for example, featured Hollywood actor Josh Brolin, whose voice over purrs 'Presence is a curious thing. If you need to prove you've got it . . . probably never had it in the first place. It's not about ostentatious adolescent display. It should be something effortless.' The tag line on the screen was 'I am Mercedes Benz' alongside the Mercedes Benz logo. The adverts suggest a level of brooding, effortless chic tinged with urban angst and cynicism.

The advert tells the viewer nothing about the car's use value or, indeed, exchange value; rather it seems to suggest a direction of interpretation designed to add sign value to the car: that one could (should) embody these qualities, including perhaps the dynamism, the advertising agency hoped for. It is a car for serious people, as a quick comparison with Vauxhall Corsa's 'C'mon' ("Vauxhall Corsa C'mon Chase" n.d.) campaign featuring puppets would seem to indicate.

Postmodern advertisers no longer rely upon any demonstration of the product's use value. Instead they seek to imbue their products with a more dreamlike, less definable symbolism, attempting to construct images capable of invoking the unconscious projections of potential consumers (as Hockley suggests regarding the use of animals in advertising). Within a world of consumer choices there are many brands of chocolate and car to choose from, but individuals begin to make decisions based upon the apparently arbitrary associations between brand and product because 'rather than unreflexively adopting a lifestyle through tradition or habit, the new heroes of consumer culture make lifestyle a life project and display their individuality and sense of style in the particularity of the assemblage of goods, clothes, practices, experiments, appearance and bodily dispositions they design together into a lifestyle' (Featherstone, 1991/2007, p. 86). In particular, brand values are understood within any given cultural milieu to denote a variety of qualities that the consumer chooses to associate with him/herself. Everything from choice of toothpaste, shampoo and clothing to car, home, holiday via music, film and art preferences have become associated with brands and commodities, and even the choice *not* to choose brands is a consumer choice. In the early twenty-first century, the overwhelming attraction of commodities is understood to lie in their symbolic qualities where consumer capitalism promotes *appearance* as the prime arbiter of value and sees self-development above all in terms of display.

Commodity, persona and self

So the postmodern consumer capitalist individual's enunciation of identity is largely framed in terms of material goods and branding. In a consumer culture, a 'sense of self' is in part created by our consumption habits and acquisitions. It need not be conspicuous as such – an ostentatious display of wealth – rather we simply use the signs of our consumption as outward display of personality. As one writer notes:

> Western consumption is unique in that identity becomes vitally and self-consciously enmeshed in stories that are read by consumers into innumerable, relatively mundane, mass-produced objects that they buy, use or own . . . promising to act as the raw material out of which our individual identities may be fashioned.
>
> *(Gabriel and Lang, 2006, p. 86)*

The acquisition and display of goods becomes a proxy for the development of the individual self. However, there is a slippage between straightforward display – 'I am the kind of person who has these things' – and a more generative association between commodity and consumer – 'to be the kind of person I want to be, I must have these things' – which suggests a mutually reinforcing cycle of desire, aspiration and display, as the earlier mention of hedonic adaptation alluded to.

It has another consequence. As Giddens puts it:

> The project of the self becomes translated into one of the possession of desired goods and the pursuit of artificially framed styles of life . . . The consumption of . . . goods becomes in some part a substitute for the genuine development of self; appearance replaces essence as the visible signs of successful consumption come actually to outweigh the use-values of the goods and services in question themselves.
>
> *(Giddens, 1991, p. 198)*

Of course, Giddens does not use 'self' in the Jungian sense here, but it might be tentatively suggested that in the era of postmodern consumption, the process of individuation is being derailed into ever greater emphasis upon building the persona, a term which 'derives from the Latin word for the mask worn by actors in classical times. Hence, persona refers to the mask or face a person puts on to confront the world' (Samuels et al., 1986/1991, p. 107). Jung defines it thus:

> The persona is a functional complex which has come into existence for reasons of adaptation or necessary convenience, but by no means is it identical with the individuality. The function-complex of the persona is exclusively concerned with the relation to the object [that is, the outside world]. The persona . . . is a compromise between individual and society as to what a man should appear to be.
>
> *(Jung, 1971, para. 801)*

As noted above, the process of individuation refers to 'a person's becoming himself, whole, indivisible and distinct from other people or collective psychology' (Samuels et al., 1986/1991, p. 76). Jacobi indicates that it falls into two main parts.

The first is the 'initiation to outward reality' (Jacobi, 1942/1973, p. 108) of which development of an appropriate persona is part. 'It aims at the adaptation of the individual to the demands of his environment' (ibid.). The folk and fairy tales discussed above suggest that the process of becoming adapted to the outer world requires acts of honesty and courage in the overcoming of shadow monsters, in order to marry the princess and claim the kingdom, or, at least, to take one's place in society. In contemporary times, instead, the consumption and display of symbols via commodities play a strong role in construction of the persona. It is interesting that Jacobi adds: 'the persona involves not only psychic qualities but also forms of social behaviour and our habits of personal appearance, posture, gait, dress, facial expression, the quality of our smile and our frown, even our way of wearing our hair' (Jacobi, 1942/1973, p. 28).

A persona working well is like a supple skin regulating contact between the inner and the outer worlds, adjusting according to context, and any individual will have several personae to call upon, related to and affected by, for example, cultural context, gender identity, age, professional status and so on. In postmodern times, it appears that individuals have more personae than may have been the case in the past. For instance, a bank manager in the 1960s was expected to conduct his life with a certain probity and seriousness associated with a job requiring a high degree of trust. Such a man (usually a man) would be expected to drive an equally serious car. The modern Bentley still trades in such images, as the promotional film for the 2014 Flying Spur ("The New Bentley Flying Spur" n.d.) model indicates. Words featuring in the film and the brochure are power (mentioned several times), elegance, intent, and performance. However, a contemporary bank manager might very well wish to project these qualities within the context of the workplace, but may on weekends drive the Beatnik-associated Volkswagen Type 2 camper van (the modern equivalent still referencing the 'dream machine' and spirit of adventure associated with the original ("VW California Beach Camper Van") in order to go surfing.

Such a combination of personae would have been unthinkable in the 1960s. In comparing the current websites for the Bentley Flying Spur and the Volkswagen California Beach (the name of one of the new camper van models) it is clear that it is not just a question of cost – they are both expensive vehicles – but the two cars are associated with radically different lifestyles: the Bentley offering itself as a symbol of the powerful, serious businessman; the California Beach associating itself with freedom and family adventure. The obvious suggestion is that to own such a vehicle is to partake in these associations, but association may not be a sufficiently forceful way of putting it. These dreamlike 'happily ever after' adverts set out to draw the unconscious projection of potential consumers to place themselves within the story. As Hockley points out, the 'purpose of the advertisement is to create a mini-myth that offers the opportunity for personal transformation' (Hockley, 2007, p. 80).

Thus commodity symbols acquired and displayed can do two things. First, they help to perform the persona (concerned with collective adaptation), and the acquisition of the 'right' symbols helps us to perform our social roles. However, the symbolic qualities may also be a kind of two-way street, at the same time offering the individual a way to construct that persona in the first place. Persona performance and commodity acquisition appear to go hand in hand where the nature of consumer capitalist society is such that adaptation to the external world is constant, not a once in a lifetime deal. Individuals are encouraged to have a greater variety of personae than ever before (as suggested by the example of the surfing bank manager) and whilst a well adjusted individual will be able to swap personae suitably to each situation, it is worth remembering that consumer capitalism is very happy to sell the accoutrements of any number of personae at the right price.

To return to the metaphor of the individuation process: after the adaptation to the outer world, there is a second part to the process, a turning back within, relating to a widening and deepening of the Self. The Self in Jungian vocabulary refers to an 'archetypal image of man's fullest potential and the unity of the personality as a whole' (Samuels et al., 1986/1991, p. 135). However, it appears that this second stage too is being constructed in terms of consumption, although it may be a more experiential commodity being sold, such as retreat holidays (see "The Retreat Company" n.d.; and any number of self-development courses). The process of becoming oneself also seems to be 'packaged and distributed according to market criteria' (Giddens, 1991, p. 198).

Thus within the consumer capitalist milieu, both persona and individuation begin to be constrained by the commodities available to carry symbolic meaning. And there is a further limiting effect that must be conceded. These commodity symbols are not freely available and this second limitation brings us back to the central concern of this chapter – money. A postmodern consumer may well be able to assemble any number of suitable personae from the bricolage of commodity signs surrounding them, but even if the sign value is of prime importance there remains an exchange value associated with goods and services. They all cost something. The freedom to build an appropriate persona and to explore the Self requires a certain level of material wealth, at least in so far as capitalism tends to package and present these opportunities to consumers.

The illusion of happiness held out to us by the micro-narratives of advertising is one where the careful acquisition and display of commodities offer to make manifest the identity of an individual, but it might be an illusion for two reasons. First because the desire to *be* a certain type of person is likely to be manufactured by such advertising narratives in the first place and they may further constrain the possibilities of that initiation to inward reality that Jung spoke of, by offering neatly gift-wrapped moments of inner experience and self-development. Second, because no matter how postmodern the advertising, no matter how far the sign value is built of arbitrary associations, it fails to indicate how money is to be gained in the first place. The happiness offered by advertising is illusory not because of hedonic adaptation *per se*, rather it is illusory because it misses out the need to have wealth. Sign value might very well be of prime importance in the selection of which commodities are to be consumed, but the consumption itself is possible only through exchange: money for commodity.

Money for its own sake may still be considered undesirable, or problematic, at least within the traditional narrative forms of film and television, but much of our contemporary consumer capitalist culture is built upon acquiring enough money to make those commodity purchases that will constitute our identity, both outward (persona) and inward (self). Ability to consume goods/experiences is essential for the construction of persona and exploration of self; at least, that is the illusion presented to us in postmodern consumer capitalism, and we are not encouraged to dream outside of that ideological envelope.

So there is a dissonance about the myths around wealth in a consumer capitalist era. Western society has changed as 'economic, socio-cultural, and psychological transformations, which have accelerated since the 1950s have produced mass consumer societies characterised by mushrooming credit facilities, overwhelming consumer choice, and a central role for consumption in everyday life' (Dittmar, 2007, p. 2). Consumption has shifted from an occasional activity to one that is central, at least for the urbanised inhabitants of the world's megacities.

However, this shift has not been radically addressed in the traditional narrative formats of feature film and television. Audiences are still being told the old tales, but the setting of the stories contains an unspoken change. The display of commodities in feature films is in some ways unrelenting. The fairy tales are still there, *Cinderella*, *Beauty and the Beast*, and *Aladdin*, for example, but now contextualised within the framework of the Disney corporation, where they are increasingly positioned as vehicles for consumption of the commodities associated with the films, ranging from bed linen to clothing, to lunch boxes, books and holiday destinations. There are also those rags-to-riches narratives of less obviously folk tale origin such as *Pursuit of Happyness* and *Pretty Woman*, but here the acquisition of wealth simply leads to the ability to consume. Chris Gardner is set upon this journey to wealth through the sight of a happy man emerging from a red Ferrari. Vivian in *Pretty Woman* enjoys going back to the dress shop that refused to serve her to demonstrate how they have missed out on her new found wealth.

However, it seems likely that in terms of the myths that society tells itself about wealth, perhaps these traditional drama forms have been superseded by the micro narratives of advertising: thirty-second stories of happiness attained through commodity acquisition and display. The acquisition of material wealth is an underpinning constant in contemporary consumer capitalist society, which requires that consumption, it tells us, in order to both display and create identity.

However, with the global financial crisis of 2008 there may be countervailing forces at work. As Gabriel pointed out in 2006, 'changes in production, rapid technological innovation, population and environmental pressures, political uncertainties and trends toward globalisation of the media, all conspire to undermine the comfortable assumption of ever increasing consumption' (Gabriel and Lang, 2006, p. 188). For the first time since the Second World War it seems that the standard of living in the West is no longer rising. The complexities of the banking crisis have thrown into sharp relief the fact that money itself does not have a concrete reality. Rather it is a 'socially constructed (and continually re-negotiated) category, and is constituted by social relations between the monetary and other economic agencies in the society' (Smithin, 2000, p. 7). Money, the medium of exchange itself, is entirely symbolic. It is a human construct, a set of ideas, a symbol and yet it circulates as if it is a 'real' thing and as we move further into the twenty-first century, it may be that we find money itself is the biggest illusion of all.

References

Abramovitz, M., David, P. A. and Reder, M. W. (1974). *Nations and households in economic growth: Essays in honor of Moses Abramovitch.* New York: Academic Press.

Aesop, Ashliman, D. L. and Rackham, A. (2003). *Aesop's fables.* New York: Barnes and Noble Classics. (Original work published 1912.)

Aristotle. (2012). *The art of rhetoric.* London: HarperPress.

Bannister, L. (2006). In *Brand Republic News.* Retrieved from: www.brandrepublic.com/news/592537/.

Baudrillard, J. (1994). *Simulacra and simulation.* Ann Arbor: University of Michigan Press. (Original work published 1981.)

Bhutan_. (n.d.). Gross national happiness (bhutan_. [Web page]). Retrieved from: www.grossnationalhappiness.com/.

Bruni, L. and Porta, P. L. (2006). *Handbook on the economics of happiness.* Northampton MA and Cheltenham: Edward Elgar.

Burnett, S. (2012). *The happiness agenda: A modern obsession.* New York: Palgrave Macmillan.

Cadbury Gorilla Drummer. (n.d.). In Vimeo [Video File] Retrieved from: vimeo.com: http://vimeo.com/62839747.

Campbell, J. (2008). *The hero with a thousand faces.* Novato CA: New World Library. (Original work published 1949.)

Capitalist Indoctrination? (n.d.). In Internet Movie Data Base [Discussion Board] Retrieved from: www.imdb.com/title/tt0454921/board/nest/124044712?p=1.

Coulmas, F. (2003). *Writing systems: An introduction to their linguistic analysis.* Cambridge and New York: Cambridge University Press.

Crawford, H. (2013). *The Sumerian world.* London: Routledge.

Deci, E. L. and Ryan, R. M. (2008). Hedonia, eudaimonia, and well-being: An introduction. *Journal of Happiness Studies, 9*(1), 1–11.

Diener, E. (1984). Subjective well being. *Psychological Bulletin, 95*(3), 542–575.

Dittmar, H. (2007). *Consumer culture, identity and well-being.* Hove: Psychology Press.

Dolan, P. and Metcalfe, R. (2012). Measuring subjective wellbeing: Recommendations on measures for use by national governments. *Journal of Social Policy, 41*(02), 409–427.

Ewen, S. (2008). *Captains of consciousness: Advertising and the social roots of the consumer culture.* New York: Basic Books.

Featherstone, M. (2007). *Consumer culture and postmodernism.* London: Sage. (Original work published 1991.)

Frey, B. S. (2008). *Happiness: A revolution in economics.* Cambridge MA: MIT Press.

Gabriel, Y. and Lang, T. (2006). *The unmanageable consumer.* London: Sage.

Giddens, A. (1991). *Modernity and self-identity: Self and society in the late modern age.* Cambridge: Polity Press.

Goldman, R. (1992). *Reading ads socially.* Hove: Psychology Press.

Greve, B. (2011). *Happiness.* Abingdon: Routledge.

Grimm, J. and Grimm, W. (2007). *The complete fairy tales.* London: Vintage Classics.

Gross National Happiness (n.d.). In Gross national happiness. Retrieved from: www.grossnationalhappiness.com/.

Healey, M. (2008). *What is branding?* Hove: Rockport Publishers.

Heath, R. (2012). *Seducing the subconscious: The psychology of emotional influence in advertising.* Chichester: John Wiley and Sons.

Hockley, L. (2007). *Frames of mind: A post-Jungian look at cinema, television and technology.* Bristol: Intellect Books.

Jacobi, J. (1973). *The psychology of C. G. Jung; an introduction with illustrations.* New Haven CT: Yale University Press. (Original work published 1942.)

Jung, C. G. (1971). *Psychological types: The collected works* (vol. 6). London: Routledge and Kegan Paul.

Lang, A. (1965). *The blue fairy book.* New York: Dover Publications. (Original work published 1889.)

Lang, A. (1966). *The red fairy book.* Princeton NJ: Dover Books. (Original work published 1890.)

Lang, A. (1966). *The yellow fairy book* (2nd edn). New York: Dover Publications. (Original work published 1894.)

Lifebuoy Soap. (n.d.). In YouTube [Video File] Retrieved from: www.youtube.com/watch?v=Wure26PhGYo.

McMahon, D. M. (2007). *The pursuit of happiness: A history from the Greeks to the present.* London: Penguin.

Marx, K. (1976). *Capital: Volume 1.* Harmondsworth: Penguin. (Original work published 1867.)

Maslow, A. H. (1943). A theory of human motivation. *Psychological Review, 50*(4), 370.

Measuring National Well-being (n.d.) in (Office for National Statistics). Retrieved from: www.ons.gov.uk/ons/guide-method/user-guidance/well-being/index.html.

The New Bentley Flying Spur. (n.d.). Retrieved from: www.newflyingspur.bentleymotors.com/en.

Odih, P. (2007). *Advertising in modern and postmodern times.* London: Sage.

Office for National Statistics. (n.d.) Measuring national well-being. Retrieved from: www.ons.gov.uk: www.ons.gov.uk/ons/guide-method/user-guidance/well-being/index.html.

Ovid. (2008). *Metamorphoses.* Oxford: Oxford University Press.

Perrault, C. (2010). *The complete fairy tales.* Oxford: Oxford University Press.

Pratt, A. (1981). *Archetypal patterns in women's fiction.* Bloomington: Indiana University Press.

Presence: I Am Mercedes Benz (AMV). (n.d.). Presence: I am Mercedes Benz (AMV). [Web page]. Retrieved from: http://amvbbdo.com/work/campaign/mercedes-benz/iammercedesbenz/presence.

Rakove, J. N. (2009). *The annotated US constitution and declaration of independence.* Cambridge MA: Harvard University Press.

The Retreat Company. (n.d.). In The Retreat Company. Retrieved from: www.theretreatcompany.com/about/.

Samuels, A., Shorter, B. and Plaut, F. (1991). *A critical dictionary of Jungian analysis.* London: Routledge. (Original work published 1986.)

Segment Specific Insights for the Entertainment and Media Outlook. (n.d.). In Price Waterhouse Cooper. Retrieved from: www.pwc.com/gx/en/global-entertainment-media-outlook/segment-insights/index.jhtml.

Smithin, J. N. (2000). *What is money?* London and New York: Routledge.

Trumbull, G. (2006). *Consumer capitalism: Politics, product markets, and firm strategy in France and Germany.* Ithaca NY: Cornell University Press.

Vauxhall Corsa C'mon Chase. (n.d.). In YouTube [Video File] Retrieved from: www.youtube.com/watch?v=Tu2xcyifTAw.

VW California Beach Camper Van. (n.d.). In Volkswagan Vans. Retrieved from: https://www.volkswagen-vans.co.uk/range/camper-vans/california-beach/.

We Are Fallon. (n.d.). Retrieved from: www.fallon.co.uk/work/show/id/22.

Weibel, D., Stricker, D., Wissmath, B. and Mast, F. W. (2010). How socially relevant visual characteristics of avatars influence impression formation. *Journal of Media Psychology: Theories, Methods, and Applications*, 22(1), 37.

WHO-The Happiness Effect. (n.d.) In World Health Organization. Retrieved from: www.who.int/bulletin/volumes/89/4/11-020411/en/.

6

THE SELF-KNOWLEDGE INDUSTRY AND MYTHS OF HAPPINESS

Ryan Howes

Introduction

Wherever known reality stops, where we touch the unknown, there we project an archetypal image.

Marie-Louise Von Franz (1972)

Ladies and gentlemen, take my advice. Just pull down your pants and slide on the ice.
Dr. Sidney Freedman, M*A*S*H
(Metcalf, 1973, episode 53, season 3, 20th Century Fox)

The personal and confidential nature of psychotherapy renders it an ambiguous target inviting projection. Therapists cannot disclose the contents of their sessions due to professional and ethical constraints, and the stigma associated with therapy inhibits their clients from divulging their participation, let alone sharing the finer points of treatment. Add to this the overwhelming glut of diverse theories and techniques utilized in the profession, and a coherent, unified description of therapy becomes nearly impossible. People come to therapy seeking clarity, resolution, and ultimately happiness, but the process for achieving these goals remains a mystery. The popular representations are therefore reduced to stereotypes based on projection.

Nowhere are these distorted images more evident than in the television and film industry, with their long history of depicting therapy in a sensationalized form. The conscious goal of engaging entertainment produces the unconscious result of promoting therapist archetypes, each founded upon our collective fears and wishes. In this chapter I explore the myth of happiness as portrayed in the media's depiction of the self-knowledge industry.

The evolution of the self-knowledge industry

When Freud began to talk with hypnotized patients in the late nineteenth century as a method for symptom reduction and the recovery of traumatic memories, I doubt even his own grandiose fantasies could fathom the self-knowledge industry as it stands today. The language and culture of psychology permeate every facet of contemporary society.

Freud's surprisingly successful method of talking with patients about their hysterical paralyses morphed into the 'talking cure' treatment for a variety of psychological and physical maladies of the day, capturing the intrigue of the medical community and the ire of the general public. While his repressed-sexuality-focused theories lacked popular staying power, the novel approach of using conversation to reduce symptoms spawned an industry that supports hundreds of treatment modalities utilized by over a million therapists worldwide. Today, 3.2 million U.S. citizens, from the severely mentally ill to the 'worried well', seek treatment for a variety of emotional, relational, occupational, existential, or biological issues – the problems that get in the way of their happiness (Olfson and Marcus, 2010). It is because of Freud that a friend's dire complaints of psychological distress are likely to garner our flippant: 'You should talk to someone about that.'

The quest for happiness via psychotherapy takes on both implicit and explicit forms. For those suffering debilitating conditions like depression, anxiety, attention deficit disorders, phobias, or experiencing the effects of trauma or abuse, therapy is focused on reducing symptoms and thereby improving functioning through the resolution of their problems or learning to cope with and accept them. It is implied that one will be free to resume a happy life, or the pursuit of happiness, with these roadblocks managed. For others, the 'worried well' who have no significant trauma or affliction and are relatively functional in society, they may choose therapy as an explicit effort to find or achieve happiness. They want to make a good marriage great, seek to find their true occupational calling, or aspire to Olympic-level performance in their pursuit of choice. Abraham Maslow proposed that self-actualization, the fulfillment of one's personal potential, is the pinnacle of human development. Many people seek this top-of-the pyramid ideal, even if achieving this goal 'rarely happens . . . certainly in less than 1% of the adult population' (Maslow, 1962, p. 204).

Whether explicit or implicit, for many clients happiness is the carrot dangling from the end of the therapeutic stick. They spend countless hours and untold financial resources on this quest for happiness in the therapy office. Therapists would be misrepresenting their work if they were to guarantee happiness as a result of therapy, as this goal is rarely achieved. Still, you won't find a therapist's website, advertisement, or consent form that bluntly states happiness won't be obtained through therapy. Happiness via psychotherapy may be a byproduct of the treatment, so the myth perpetuates.

Does therapy help?

Citing years of research in his 2004 TED Talk, Positive Psychology founder Martin Seligman said: 'Psychology and psychiatry over the last sixty years can actually claim that we can make miserable people less miserable, and I think that's terrific' (Seligman, 2004). Indeed, numerous comprehensive studies have shown therapy to produce a moderate to large improvement in health as compared with a non-treated control group or patients who only took medication (Shedler, 2010). The specific technique makes some impact, but the current wisdom points to the functionality of the therapeutic relationship as the primary agent of change. The healing power of an authentic, compassionate relationship that challenges when necessary is the prototype of a helpful therapeutic relationship, which will vary from client to client, therapist to therapist (Cooper, 2008).

How, exactly, does therapy help people achieve happiness? Herein lies the central problem with the myth of happiness in the self-knowledge industry: the answer is complicated and ultimately unpredictable. Therapy occasionally helps people achieve happiness, and when it does, the experience is fleeting, as it is for everyone else. Furthermore, the paths used to reach this lofty goal are as diverse as humanity itself. Therapy can help some people feel happy some of the time through mysterious methods.

Through both anecdotal evidence and research data we know therapy helps, which is why the field continues to grow. Many of us have experienced our own healing and thriving through therapy, or we have seen the benefits it appears to have produced in loved ones. It does help, but it is difficult to pinpoint why. The very nature of therapy makes this discovery extremely difficult.

Therapy's negative stigma

In an over-sharing era where we tweet photos of every meal and report our intimate thoughts and physical symptoms on social media, therapy remains hidden under a shroud of secrecy. The antiquated ideas that mental problems were caused by evil spirits or a wandering uterus – the original theory behind hysteria – have fortunately left our common understanding, but the inane belief that 'you must be crazy if you're in therapy' is proving quite difficult to shake. Therapy clients still sneak away to an unspecified weekly 'appointment' due to fear of being discovered and branded 'crazy' or 'unstable'. Meanwhile, they will freely discuss with friends and coworkers the details of their medical, dental, or chiropractic checkup. And that is the attitude of the fortunate minority who actually come to therapy. We can only assume millions who would benefit from therapy are partially dissuaded due to the stigma against seeking professional psychological help, and in having an emotional, cognitive, or relational issue in the first place.

Research supports the idea that mental health stigma has a prohibitive effect that prevents people from seeking help. On average, people with mood disorders delay treatment six to eight years, a number that rises to nine to twenty-three years for anxiety disorders (Wang *et al.*, 2007). While there may be multiple factors at play, the idea that stigma could contribute to waiting this long for treatment is a serious cause for concern. When someone would rather suffer from severe anxiety for *twenty-three years* than face the stigma of psychological treatment, it is safe to say that the mental health industry has an image problem.

Furthermore, as long as 'You need therapy!' and related taunts are an acceptable retort to any annoying acquaintance, we will have a therapy stigma. The statement is a criticism, an insult, and portrays therapy as a remedial tool to correct irritating behavior; not the compassionate promotion of a valid treatment modality or a process that facilitates self-actualization.

The confidentiality dilemma

Unfortunately, the most simple and clear way to demystify psychotherapy is unethical. People come to therapy to discuss issues in their lives that are not public knowledge: their depression, their abuse history, their love affair, their sexual problems, their phobias, etc. In order for clients to feel safe enough to reveal these problems and ultimately find healing, they need to know their work in the therapy office, including their very participation in therapy, will remain confidential. For over a century, the bodies that govern psychotherapy have recognized the primary importance of privacy within the therapeutic relationship, therefore Rule #1 has been, and will continue to be, confidentiality. With a few rare legal exceptions involving the safety of the client and those around them, what happens in therapy stays in therapy. In essence, we therapists are professional secret keepers.

For example, when I return home from a day of work as a psychologist in private practice, my wife, like every significant other on the planet, will ask me about my day. Despite the love and trust my wife and I share, my response is censored. 'A good day,' I might say, 'some tough challenges and rewarding moments.' If the day brought forth some new insights about me and my work, I might add: 'I noticed it was hard to focus this morning, probably because I didn't sleep' thanks to our 2-year-old experiencing the tribulations of potty training. But I cannot mention the specifics of my sessions. I cannot talk about my depressed client who hides her suicidality. I cannot talk about the conflicted man who is sleeping with his secretary. I cannot gossip about the minor celebrity client with some TMZ-worthy drama brewing. I cannot share the awkwardness of the client who believes I'm the reincarnation of his deceased sister. And I certainly cannot talk about the deceitful client whose spouse works peripherally with my own wife. I cannot even share this information with you without telling you these clients are de-identified composites who may or may not be fictional. If therapists could share how we work with as much openness as a carpenter walking through a model home or a chef in an open kitchen, our work would be demystified. But in doing so we would lose a cornerstone of the profession, confidentiality, and most of our clientele along with it.

Projection turns against us

One of Freud's many contributions was the concept of projection – the idea that people may unconsciously ascribe their own feelings or characteristics to others. In everyday life, it is a cheating husband who suspects his wife is having an affair, or a grumpy boss accusing his secretary of having a bad day. Acknowledging these feelings are their own feels like too great a challenge for them in that moment, so they externalize and often criticize them in others.

Freud believed greater ambiguity pertained to projection, which led to the analytic stance of presenting as a neutral 'blank screen' to elicit the projections of patients. A competent analyst could elicit and save these misplaced feelings, then feed back the projection to the patient in an interpretation. For example: 'You seem to assume I'm going to reject you, much like you described your mother. I wonder where else you have this response in your life.' This is one method for making the unconscious drives and impulses conscious, which is the primary healing modality of psychoanalysis.

If therapists cannot give honest, accurate accounts of the work they do, and clients are so ashamed of seeking talk therapy that they are unable to discuss their therapeutic work with friends, the whole field is a blank screen, an industry primed for projection. Therapy and therapists become Rorschach inkblots for society to project their own fears and wishes upon, with nary an argument from the silent participants. Jung often addressed projection, concluding:

> The effect of projection is to isolate the subject from his environment, since instead of real relation to it there is now only an illusory one. Projection changes the world into the replica of one's own unknown face . . . The more projections are thrust in between the subject and the environment, the harder it is for the ego to see through its illusions.
>
> *(Jung, 1959/68, para. 17)*

Therapists on screen, therefore, may be more an amalgam of the screenwriters' and directors' own internal dynamics than a balanced representation of healing professionals. When pen meets paper, the character that emerges reflects their stereotypes and deeply held beliefs of emotional caregivers, from the strong to the seductive to the silly to the sadistic.

The epigraph above speaks to this. In the midst of the bloody chaos in a mobile surgical hospital during the Korean War, psychiatrist Sidney Freedman distills wisdom formed by years of training and experience into his most famous sound bite: pull down your pants and slide on the ice. The recommendation is either absurd or profound. Is he a fool? Does he have some transcendent knowledge? Are these loving words of levity spoken in a language his friends can understand? Is this reassurance from a loving father? This statement says more about the writer or society than the profession as a whole, as do most therapist depictions.

Therapists as archetypes on screen

Marie-Louise Von Franz's statement that 'wherever known reality stops, where we touch the unknown, there we project an archetypal image' (1972, p. 201) is most evident in the media's handling of the self-knowledge industry. The great mystery of what happens behind closed doors, beyond the white noise sound screen machines, is tantalizing fodder for screenwriters. Screenwriters devoted to motivation and character will salivate at the chance to look behind the façade into a therapy session, where true selves are unveiled and therapists react. As the storytellers attempt to unravel the mystery of therapy and therapists, a pure glimpse into the drive and motivation of human nature, known reality inevitably reaches its limit and they are left to project their own wishes and fears. These projections help form the archetypical therapists we see on screen today.

If the self-knowledge industry is to have a fair chance at reaching potential clients who could benefit from its services, we need to distinguish fact from fantasy in these archetypical portrayals. This chapter looks at several common therapist archetypes depicted in the media, distinguishing reality from artistic license. I have chosen to explore this phenomenon in light of six prominent archetypes: King/Queen, Warrior, Magician, Lover, Fool, and Shadow.

The King/Queen

Many of us hope to find a stable, older, wiser mentor who will show great interest in us and guide us through the treacherous pitfalls of life. We imagine an unflappable rock of a person who will tolerate our immaturities and love us in spite of them. We want to know someone is in charge, and that they have our best interests in mind. This is the good father or mother; one who will correct and guide as needed, accept our flaws and shortcomings, but love us all the while. It is to them we say: 'Please let me take the wheel but tell me where to go, I've never been here before.'

The King/Queen archetype, the embodiment of ultimate wisdom and harmonizer of chaos, is the most favorable and positive (perhaps idealized?) therapy archetype. Moore and Gillette (1990, p. 49) describe this type as 'seasoned and complex, wise, and in a sense . . . selfless'. They have a storehouse of knowledge and perspective and patiently guide others toward the goal. This patience is an important element, as their subjects often require many hours of repetition and test limits throughout their relationship. The King or Queen needs to stay strong despite the boundary-pushing tendencies of their subjects.

On screen, relatively few therapists embody the King/Queen archetype. Bob Newhart's comedic role as Dr. Robert Hartley in *The Bob Newhart Show* (1972–1978, Davis, CBS) was the straight man to the absurd comedic stylings of his patients and acquaintances. He gave sound psychological advice despite the bizarre, neurotic requests of his clientele. More recently, Mariah Carey's role as social worker Ms. Weiss in the movie *Precious* (Dir., Daniels, 2009, Lionsgate) stands up for the title character as she confronts her abusers. Lorraine Bracco's strong depiction of Dr. Melfi in *The Sopranos* (Chase, 1999–2007, HBO) may best represent the unflappable quality of the Queen as exemplified in this scene with her gangster client Tony Soprano:

Dr. Melfi: Do you want to tell me what you're thinking?

Tony: Believe me you don't want to know. You want to know what I'm thinkin'? Seriously. I'm thinking I'd like to take a brick and smash your fucking face into fucking hamburger.

Dr. Melfi: Do you think making hamburger out of me would make you feel better?
Tony: Mother of Christ. Is this a woman thing? You ask me how I'm feeling.
 I tell you how I'm feeling and now you're going to torture me with it.

To my point about strength and patience, not many therapists would stick around after a client threatened to smash their face into hamburger with a brick. Dr. Melfi does, through this and many other sessions, sometimes just as challenging.

But the King/Queen archetype is also compassionate, as seen in Judd Hirsch's Dr. Berger in *Ordinary People* (Dir., Redford, 1980, Paramount), as he treats a young man suffering from the loss of his brother and the resulting disintegration of his family:

Conrad Jarrett: I'm so scared! I'm scared.
Dr. Berger: Feelings are scary. And sometimes they're painful. And if you can't
 feel pain . . . you won't feel anything else either. You know what I'm
 saying?
Conrad: I think so.
Dr. Berger: You're here. You're alive. Don't say you don't feel that.
Conrad: It doesn't feel good.
Dr. Berger: It is good. Believe me.
Conrad: How do you know?
Dr. Berger: Because I'm your friend.

Dr. Berger becomes the stable object for Conrad to lean upon as his world falls apart, someone who assures him that his internal experience makes sense and that he will support his external world. He will be his friend, after all.

The King/Queen archetype accurately portrays many elements of the therapeutic relationship. Therapists are trained to make the client the focus of treatment, and to make their own needs and issues secondary during the therapy session. We work to maintain a stable, predictable environment in therapy, adhering to the 'frame' of therapy where we maintain the same physical environment, the same time and role boundaries, and most importantly the same approach to the client and their problems. We work to understand our own issues so that a client's accusations or feelings toward us are recognized as reflections on their experience and not a cause for us to become defensive. In essence, we all want to be strong and wise Kings and Queens, even though we often fail. This archetype is also inaccurate as it sets an impossibly high goal for most therapists. Invariably, therapists will have off days, blind spots, and unresolved issues that impede their work with their clients. Furthermore, the role of King/Queen implies a leadership position that many therapists do not believe in. It is not the therapist fixing the client, but a more egalitarian approach of therapist and client working together toward a common goal.

The Warrior

We do not typically think of therapists as warriors. Often described as the 'touchy-feely' storefront to the 'soft-science' of psychology, psychotherapy is rarely equated with battle cries and fisticuffs. It seems the oil of conflict does not mix with the water of the healing profession. But conflict is interesting, and simpatico does not make for engaging television. The popular media frequently employ the myth of the Warrior therapist to draw in viewers by promoting a mild paranoia: maybe even my caregiver is out to get me.

Moore and Gillette (1990, p. 80) describe the Warrior archetype as characterized by aggressiveness and awareness, someone who is both a strategist and a tactician. Winning the battle is their primary goal, one they reach through drive and cunning. While the Warrior's victory may ultimately benefit people, relationships are not their primary focus. Warriors tend to have a loyalty to something, an ideal, a pledge – in the case of a therapist, perhaps a theory, but this is often a transpersonal commitment, larger than individuals (Moore and Gillette, 1990, p. 84). How in the world might this relate to psychotherapy?

The language of hostility is a staple in mental health. Many clients describe how they 'battle' depression or 'fight' negative self-talk. They speak of internal 'conflicts' and the 'clash' between right and wrong raging inside. This language, typically reserved for warfare, is often employed to describe an individual's relationship with their malady.

By the way, we therapists recognize this lexicon and advertise our services to the 'struggling' masses, offering victory, peace, acceptance, and resolution. We promote our empathy, support, and safety within a non-judgmental atmosphere. Peruse any therapist directory and you'll find variations on this theme: 'You are at war with your issues; come to my sanctuary to find a peaceful resolution.' Ironically, we professional pacifists embrace the war metaphors.

Our theories support this collaborative, peacemaking stance. One of the primary tenets of Carl Rogers' Client Centered Therapy is unconditional positive regard, rooted in a belief that clients can find their own solutions if provided an environment of empathy and warmth. Irvin Yalom's Existentialist/Humanistic approach envisions therapists and clients as 'fellow travelers', engaging life together in a mutually supportive relationship. Even the neutrality inherent to the psychodynamic theories has the goal of eliciting projection and transference in order to bring insight to negative relational patterns – it is not therapist vs. client, but therapist and client working together to understand the debilitating unconscious projections that wreak havoc in their significant relationships. If there are battles waged in depth psychology, they are against resistance and distortion, not against the client's true self.

The Therapist-as-Warrior archetype blurs this distinction in popular media. Often based in a fragile narcissism that manifests as a perpetual need to be right and win, the Warrior's office is a battleground that pits the highly trained therapist against the wounded, often resistant client. Armed with professional jargon and honed debating skills, the therapist attacks not just the pathology, but the client as a whole. The Warrior eschews collaboration and empowerment in favor of pounding the client into submission: if you admit you are doing things wrong and choose my way instead, you might find a meaningful life.

In 2008, HBO launched *In Treatment*, a drama about psychologist Dr. Paul Weston (Gabriel Byrne), his sessions with his clients and his meetings with his own therapist/supervisor/couples counsellor (Dir., Levinson, 2008, HBO). While Weston developed into a multi-faceted character over the series' three seasons, as a therapist he most often embodied the Warrior archetype. This loyal, energetic, self-sacrificing therapist appeared to value passion and purpose over self-care. While this may be a temporary ideal for many clients, it also presents great risk for Paul where hasty efforts are employed and his depleted resources result in implosion.

Paul unveils his Warrior proclivity early, in his first session with Alex, a distressed Navy fighter pilot (Alex, Week one, 1.02):

Alex: So, are there any rules?
Paul: Rules?
Alex: Ground rules. Anything I should know before we start?
Paul: Oh . . . Not really. It's more or less . . . It's more or less up to you.
Alex: Oh, right, right. I'm a customer.
Paul: Yeah. Though in my profession we say that the customer is always wrong.
[Alex looks surprised at Paul]
Paul: That's a . . . It's a therapists' joke.

The customer is always wrong. While this is presented in a light-hearted manner at first, it typifies Paul's approach in the majority of his therapy sessions. His style is so aggressive; he and his clients frequently begin to argue before they have taken a seat. He argues his logic against their beliefs, trying to show them they are wrong to believe as they do.

There is an old saying often shared in couples therapy: 'You can be right *or* in relationship.' The desire to win feels natural, particularly among competitive, aggressive people. But in the context of relationship, the idea of winning must shift from individual victory or victory for the couple as a unit. The member of the dyad who wins the argument enjoys the self-satisfaction of conquering the foe, but the foe happens to be your significant other, who is now dejected, possibly hurt, and at best, the loser. While one member feels victory, the relationship is no stronger. What did you really win?

The therapeutic dyad is no different. If a therapist's goal is to 'win the session' by posing the stronger argument to obliterate the client's logic, they may win the debate, but the relationship loses. The client is left with the idea that they are an idiot causing all their own problems; hardly an empowering outcome. The myth of the Warrior therapist may indeed be the prototype for some clinicians, but I doubt there are many combative therapists who build a caseload and stay in practice for long. Clients in need of care and understanding, collaboration rather than conflict, empowerment instead of belittling, will not stay with a Paul-style therapist very long.

The Magician

The concept of the 'magic pill' has a rich legacy in psychotherapy. Clients often seek treatment in search of that one nugget, the one solution, the silver bullet that will instantly turn their life around and make everything all right. The self-help book industry has capitalized on this myth with titles like *5 Steps to a Healthy Marriage* and *Resolve Depression in 10 Minutes a Day*. Popular media boil this down even further, suggesting one key insight will help a client regain their lost marbles. But it is rarely one factor that causes a person to tumble into mental illness, so a single intervention is not going to produce a magic cure.

Let us take a typical episode of *Dr. Phil* (2002, McGraw, Harpo), for example. At the beginning of the hour, a suffering client weepily presents a dysfunctional relationship or self-limiting belief. Dr. Phil intervenes to explore the symptoms, invariably states, 'how's that working for you?' and proffers his homespun wisdom. With ten minutes to spare, one of Phil's platitudes strikes pay dirt; the *Aha!* moment has arrived, and the client is in a stunned, sobbing state of shock and awe. The magic pill arrived before the closing credits, and a life is forever changed. As far as the viewing audience knows, that is. If I had a nickel for every client who asked if I could just be more like Dr. Phil . . .

According to Moore and Gillette, it is to the magician

> that people go with their questions, problems, pains, and diseases of the body and of the mind . . . He is the one who can think through the issues that are not obvious to other people. He is a seer and a prophet in the sense not only of predicting the future but also of seeing deeply.
>
> *(Moore and Gillette, 1990, p. 99)*

It is not surprising that this archetype is well represented in popular media depictions of therapists. People come to us for the same reasons, and we often present non-obvious solutions. We 'predict' future behavior based on past behavioral patterns and employ all methods of questioning, listening, and theory in order to 'see deeply'. We serve the same purpose of the magician, but we achieve our goals through non-magical means. Often our means are subtle, gradual, mundane; they may even seem boring if viewed by an objective outsider.

The magician is the embodiment of wisdom and knowledge, the insightful sage who values creative solutions to intricate problems. Dr. Sean Maguire (Robin Williams) from *Good Will Hunting* (Dir., Van Sant, 1997, Miramax) personifies this 'I know what will fix you' archetype and presents a high expectation of success for therapists and clients alike. His interpretation is precise and deep, and with one Howitzer intervention he delivers insight, catharsis, and lasting behavior change. In Will's case, he needed Sean to spend time building rapport, disclose his own issues, and then to administer the magic pill regarding Will's childhood abuse:

Sean McGuire: It's not your fault.
Will Hunting: I know that.

Sean McGuire: Look at me, son. It's not your fault.
Will: I know.
Sean McGuire: It's not your fault.
Will: I know.
Sean McGuire: No. No you don't. It's not your fault.
Will: I know.
Sean McGuire: It's not your fault.
Will: Alright.
Sean McGuire: It's not your fault . . . It's not your fault.
Will: Don't mess with me.
Sean McGuire: It's not your fault.
Will Hunting: Don't mess with me, alright. Don't mess with me, Sean. Not you!
Sean McGuire: It's not your fault.
Will Hunting: [tearing]
Sean McGuire: It's not your fault.
Will Hunting: [openly crying] Oh God! I'm so sorry. . .

The pill is administered several times. With deep eye contact. And an embrace. After that breakthrough, Will was able to leave Boston, follow his girlfriend, and pursue a life of happiness on the West Coast. Magic.

I am not denying the existence of breakthrough moments or powerful insights; these are wonderful gifts we occasionally find in therapy. Will's damaging beliefs and fears of intimacy certainly needed correction, and Sean found an effective way to challenge them. But I call into question the finality of the cure. Was that single insight enough to correct a lifetime of negative behavior patterns? Does absolution from past beliefs result in once-and-for-all behavior change? If Will's limiting belief came from one person, does one alternate belief from his therapist result in lasting change? What happens when yet another viewpoint from another significant figure arises? The symptom appears to be cured. The status of the deeper problem remains to be determined. But Will is gone now.

The distinction between therapist and magician lies in two areas – precision and time. Magicians are typically able to quickly administer one intervention that presents a cure. The therapeutic cure tends to be multi-faceted, often incomplete, and takes a long time. Take, for example, a woman who is depressed because she hates her job and believes she married and had children with the wrong man. This is not an uncommon presentation in therapy, and has no easy, magical solution. Staying with the job has challenges, as does leaving the job. The same thing goes for marriage. Or maybe her job and marriage dissatisfaction are merely symptoms of an underlying organic depression. We could spend weeks determining which is the chicken and which is the egg. It may take months or years in therapy for her to make decisions she can accept, even if they are imperfect.

As long as Hollywood sells the idea of the quick fix, the once-and-for-all permanent shift in therapy, we are setting clients up for disappointment. Abrupt change is rare and often unstable, we find lasting change often results from small, gradual adjustments that occur over time. But that is not as exciting. Nor as magical.

The Lover

When people envision a loving relationship they typically talk about feeling understood, accepted, supported, and cared for. They talk about how interested they are in one another and how their talks go to unprecedented depths of emotion and vulnerability. A healthy therapeutic relationship achieves a level of intimacy that approaches and occasionally surpasses it. It is not surprising that a wish for romance and physical intimacy occasionally arises.

As often as this wish arises, and as understandable as it might be, romantic relations between therapist and client are on par with breached confidentiality as a cardinal sin in the field. The potential for unequal power dynamics, exploitation, coercion, and the risk of therapists working unsupervised behind closed doors have made our governing bodies hyper-aware of any such contact between therapists and clients.

The wish for a therapist who empathizes with and merges with the client is well represented in the media, and reflects the Lover archetype whose deep desire for connection supersedes the reality of boundaries. Dr. Susan Lowenstein (Barbra Streisand) from *Prince of Tides* (Dir., Streisand, Columbia Pictures, 1991) and Dr. Libbie Bowen (Lena Olin) from *Mr. Jones* (Dir., Figgis, Columbia Pictures, 1993) depict therapists who care so much the boundaries do not matter. Kathryn Railly (Madeleine Stowe) from *Twelve Monkeys* (Dir., Gilliam, 1995, Universal Pictures), Cheryl (Helen Hunt) from *The Sessions* (Dir., Lewin, Fox Searchlight, 2012), and Katherine (Anna Kendrick) from *50/50* (Dir., Levine, Summit Entertainment, 2011) play a similar caregiver-becomes-lover role. We see this explicitly represented in Dr. Molly Griswold's (Rene Russo) turn as golfer Roy McAvoy's therapist/love interest in *Tin Cup* (Dir., Shelton, Warner Brothers Pictures, 1996), as she coaches him on his dating skills:

Dr. Molly Griswold:	All you have to do is walk up to this, this woman, wherever she is, look her in the eye – look at me, Roy – just look her in the eyes, that's right, let down your guard, and don't try to be cool or smooth or whatever; just be honest and take a risk. And you know what, whatever happens, if you act from the heart, you can't make a mistake.
Roy 'Tin Cup' McAvoy:	Dr. Griswold . . .
Dr. Griswold:	Yes?
Roy:	I think I'm in love with you.
Dr. Griswold:	What?
Roy:	From the moment I first saw you, I knew I was through with bar girls and . . . strippers and motorcycle chicks, and . . . when we first started talking I was smitten with you, and I'm smitten with you more every day I think about you, and the fact that you know I'm full of crapola only makes you more attractive to me. Usually I can bullshit

> people, but I can't bullshit you, and in addition you got, you got great legs, and . . . most women I'm thinking about how to get in their pants from day one, but with you I'm just . . . I'm just thinking about how to get in your heart, and . . .

Of course, they go on to live happily ever after. While the majority of the quote is Roy's declaration of love, the film makes clear the mutual interest. Dr. Griswold is the loving, accepting sparring partner for the feisty Roy, and allows the boundary to be broken for the sake of true love.

I should note two things. First, the therapist as Lover archetype in film involves almost exclusively female therapists with male clients. Second, the ethical violations are typically skirted superfluously by the therapist not acting contractually in a therapeutic capacity or some other such legality. Regardless, these are therapists who perform in a therapist capacity for their (male) clients and the relationship becomes romantic. The idea that this is wish fulfillment on the part of the writer, director, and/or general public is strongly supported.

According to Moore and Gillette (1990, p. 121), the Lover is: 'the archetype of play and of display, of healthy embodiment, of being in the world of sensuous pleasure and in one's own body without shame'. Lovers are the source of spirituality, empathy, and the feelings of others. Love and romance are their highest ideal, an impulse that supersedes the boundaries of the professional relationship.

Again, therapists do resemble the Lover archetype in several ways, sharing many deep emotional experiences on a very intimate level. But the boundaries involving romantic relationships are iron clad and rooted in a fundamental belief: therapy is designed to help people achieve a goal, not to be the goal. If a client seeks to find romance, therapy should help him or her uncover the obstacles preventing romance, not provide the romance.

The Fool

Perhaps the most common depiction of therapists in the media is the Fool, an absurd but comical character known for poor decision making, absent boundaries, and low self-awareness. Most are oblivious to their shortcomings and make clumsy attempts to hide strong impulses and emotions, to which they seem beholden. Most are fairly harmless to others, as they lack the skills to adequately plan or scheme, but as therapists in a position of some power, they can lead clients astray with their bumbling communication and emotional interference. For some reason, this is the popular therapist archetype.

In the film *Analyze This* (Dir., Ramis, Village Roadshow, 1999), Billy Crystal is cast in the role of Dr. Sobel, a burned out therapist quickly losing touch with his therapeutic standards. In one scene he meets with a couple in counseling and blurts out this advice:

> Here's what I think you should do, Elaine. I would do whatever he says. If he
> wants you to talk, talk. I would get on all fours and bark like a dog. I would
> do whatever it takes. Smoke some joints! Drink some wine!

While in some dramatic traditions the figure of the Fool is a source of wisdom, as in Shakespeare's plays, the therapist on TV and in film is regularly not invested with such insight. Starting with *Dr. Dippy's Sanitarium* (1906), Hollywood has long held to the comedic staple of the therapist buffoon. These fools come in the form of out-of-touch eccentrics (like Frasier Crane in *Frasier*, 1993–2004, Angell, Paramount Television), mentally unstable clinicians who are crazier than their clients (Lisa Kudrow in the television series *Web Therapy*, 2013, Bucatinsky, Is or Isn't Entertainment), one-note simpletons (*Saturday Night Live's* Stewart Smalley by Al Franken, 1975–present, Michaels, NBC), or inept burnouts like Dr. Sobel. They typically portray a veneer of aristocratic or academic acumen that is fragile and soon displays the neurotic, narcissistic personality underneath. They provide an easy target for the dismissal of psychotherapy as a pointless quest led by clueless oafs.

One of the most prominent therapist fools is Dr. Leo Marvin (Richard Dreyfus), who loses his grasp on reality when a patient (Bill Murray) follows his family on vacation in *What About Bob?* (Dir., Oz, Touchstone, 1991):

Dr. Leo Marvin: You understand, don't you? There's no other solution. You won't go away.

Bob Wiley: I will.

Dr. Leo Marvin: No, you won't. You're just *saying* you will! But then, after I don't kill you, you'll show up again. And you'll do something else to make everyone in my life think you are wonderful and I'm a schmuck. But I'm not a schmuck, Bob, and I'm not going to let you breeze into town and take my family away from me, just because you're crazy enough to be fun.

The inaccuracy of this archetype lies in the ineptitude of the Fool. Therapists attend several years of education beyond college where they are evaluated not only on their coursework, but on their abilities as therapists. Their work is supervised, sometimes video or audiotaped, and evaluated by licensed clinicians periodically. If a student repeatedly proves inept as a therapist, they are asked to leave the program. Schools do not want to graduate poor therapists, as they will reflect poorly on the school. In the USA, beyond graduation, there are 1,000 or more hours of supervised work in conjunction with a comprehensive licensing exam that tests clinical knowledge as well as an understanding of legal and ethical issues. Again, if a clinician is inept they may not be able to pass these tests. After licensure, there is the capitalistic valuation based on performance. If the clinician is unable to connect with, and ultimately help, their clients because they are playing the fool, the clients simply will not return, which will come to the attention of their boss or will result in an empty private practice caseload. Truly inadequate therapists tend to flub their way out of a job. Leo Marvin would not be known as a successful therapist, even if his book was a bestseller.

Why does this stereotype continue to thrive? A common public belief is that therapists are drawn to the profession because they themselves are mentally unstable people who are trying to sort through their own issues by diving into psychology as a profession. I used to feel angry and defensive when I heard this, believing the homespun wisdom was completely wrong – therapists were healthy people trying to help others, nothing else. But after two decades in the field my view has become nuanced. I have come to understand that many people drawn to a career in therapy tend to have a personal reason for seeking this kind of work, whether an affliction of their own or of a loved one, and their own quest to find answers motivated them to deeper study and eventually pursuit of a career in the field. I do not think this means that all therapists are mentally unstable, but that many have experienced their own emotional hardship that gives them the motivation and empathy to treat others. I would now say yes, many therapists do bring some emotional baggage into this work, and it is this very experience that helps them to be caring, attentive therapists.

I point this out to say if there is accuracy in the Fool archetype, it lies in the fact that we are all human. Clients may wish for King or Queen therapists who have strength and understanding with no blind spots, but more often we find therapists to be human beings with quirks, inadequacies, and many of the annoying traits we find in friends and family. What sets therapists apart is not the perfection they have attained in their personality or personal life, but their strong desire to understand and help others.

The Shadow

The evil, sadistic therapist is another common type seen on screen. These healing professionals choose to use their considerable psychological knowledge to injure, control, and even kill their patients because it brings some personal satisfaction. These 'evil doctors' tend to be sly, brilliant, and even charming, luring their victims in with a seductive quality.

The Shadow embodies all that is negative, dark, and kept from the conscious self. According to Jung the Shadow is not a person but an aspect of everyone's personality that we try to keep hidden because of its unpleasant, selfish desires. Due to our lack of awareness, the Shadow is therefore highly prone to projection onto others.

On-screen examples include psychiatrist and pedophile Peter Teleborain (Anders Ahlbom) from *The Girl with the Dragon Tattoo* series (Dir., Fincher, Columbia Pictures, 2011), the Santa-condemning Dr. Rogers (William Forrest) from *Miracle on 34th Street* (Dir., Seaton, 20th Century Fox, 1947), and the iconic psychopath psychiatrist Hannibal Lecter (Anthony Hopkins) from the *Silence of the Lambs* movies (Dir., Demme, Orion Pictures, 1991). Each uses their position of power to betray the Hippocratic oath. Some, like *One Flew Over the Cuckoo's Nest's* (Dir., Forman, United Artists, 1975) Nurse Ratched, are not specifically therapists but play a therapeutic role, as in this scene where she discovers psychiatric patient Billy Bibbit has engaged in some forbidden behavior involving alcohol and women who snuck onto the unit:

Nurse Ratched: Aren't you ashamed?
Billy: [confidently stutter-free for the first time in the film] No, I'm not.
[Applause from friends]
Nurse Ratched: You know Billy, what worries me is how your mother is going to take this.
Billy: Um, um, well, y-y-y-you d-d-d-don't have to t-t-t-tell her, Miss Ratched.
Nurse Ratched: I don't have to tell her? Your mother and I are old friends. You know that.
Billy: P-p-p-please d-d-don't tell my m-m-m-mother.

Within minutes Billy has taken his own life and Nurse Ratched has regained control over her unit.

The accuracy of the therapist Shadow archetype lies in the fact that everyone has a shadow, including therapists. Regardless of how many degrees, training experiences, or years of their own therapy the clinicians have had, we still possess a shadow. We employ these training and competency safeguards to help clinicians become aware of their blind spots, but it is inevitable that an unconscious thought, feeling, or attitude will occasionally sneak through. The purpose of supervised training is not to eliminate the issues in the clinician's life, but to help them become aware of potential blind spots and seek assistance when they find them. Sometimes we catch them, sometimes we do not.

The inaccurate part is the implication that a significant number of therapists are driven by their Shadow. While I have never met any personally, I cannot refute the idea that sociopathic therapists have graduated and become licensed to practice psychotherapy for the purpose of control and the intent to cause harm. With 1,000,000 therapists in the United States, I must believe some bad eggs made it through the system. But in general I must point to my own experience of therapists in training. They are people who want to give, either because they feel fortunate to have an abundance of resources or because they have been through hardship and want to give back. They deeply desire to help people. They occasionally cause problems by crossing boundaries with good intentions or offer hope they cannot deliver, but they generally intend to behave ethically. I have noticed in my work as a supervisor how many more people I need to restrain from giving too much versus the withholding therapist who gives too little or does not care enough. Selfishness is not a problem I encounter very often. Reining back therapists who want to give too much, however, is a major part of my job.

Conclusion

It is often tragic to see how blatantly a man bungles his own life and the lives of others yet remains totally incapable of seeing how much the whole tragedy

> originates in himself, and how he continually feeds it and keeps it going. Not *consciously*, of course – for consciously he is engaged in bewailing and cursing a faithless world that recedes further and further into the distance. Rather, it is an unconscious factor which spins the illusions that veil his world. And what is being spun is a cocoon, which in the end will completely envelop him.
>
> *(Jung, 1959/68, para. 18)*

In the quotation above, Jung highlights the pitfalls that belie a lack of self-awareness. While humankind is capable of making the requisite changes, we continue to spin our cocoon in an oblivious rage. The common theme of this chapter is a call for clarity on three levels: First, therapy is a complex relationship that is difficult to represent through our current media conventions. The self-knowledge profession needs to make a stronger effort to clearly explain, in accessible language, the methods by which we practice. Second, the media reflects the extremes of therapy to entertain, which perpetuates ideas of therapy as represented through archetypal roles of the therapist and its impact on the client. Using clear information from the therapeutic community, the media can send a more accurate message about the specifics of psychotherapy, which is less sensationalized than the current use of archetypes but no less intriguing and transformational. Finally, therapy as a profession would be better served by increased education and demystification of the therapeutic process and efforts to de-stigmatize therapy so clients can give honest accounts of their experience in therapy to challenge harmful stereotypes. Only then can therapy make a decent attempt at promoting contentment, control, and ultimately give a realistic assessment of the potential for happiness. Both the media and the therapeutic profession can more clearly represent the reality of the myths and fairytales of happiness as a product of self-knowledge. The truth may set you free, but it will not always make you happy.

References

Cooper, M. (2008). *Essential research findings in counselling and psychotherapy*. London: Sage.

Jung, C. G. (1959). *Phenomenology of the spirit in fairy tales* (R. F. C. Hull, trans.). In H. Read, M. Fordham, and G. Adler (series eds), *The collected works of C. G. Jung* (vol. 9 pt. ii, paras 17–18). New York: Pantheon. (Original work published 1948.)

Jung, C. G. (1959/68). 'The Shadow' (R. F. C. Hull, trans.). In H. Read, M. Fordham, and G. Adler (series eds), *The collected works of C. G. Jung* (vol. 9 pt. ii. Aion). New York: Pantheon. (Original work published 1948.)

Maslow, A. H. (1962). *Towards a psychology of being*. New York: Van Nostrand.

Moore, R. and Gillette, D. (1990). *King, warrior, magician, lover*. New York: HarperOne.

Olfson, M. and Marcus, S. C. (2010). National trends in outpatient psychotherapy. *American Journal of Psychiatry* 167(12), December, 1456–63, doi: 10:1176/appi.ajp.2010.10040570. Epub 2010 Aug 4.

Seligman, M. (2004, February). Martin Seligman: The new era of positive psychology [Video file]. Retrieved from www.ted.com/talks/martin_seligman_on_the_state_of_psychology. html.

Shedler, J. (2010). The efficacy of psychodynamic psychotherapy. *American Psychologist* 65(2), February-March, 98–109. doi: 10.1037/a0018378.

Von Franz, M. L. (1972). *Patterns of creativity mirrored in creation myths (Seminar series)*. New York: Spring Publications. ISBN 978-0-88214-106-0. Found in M. Gray (1996), *Archetypal explorations: an integrative approach to human behavior*. New York: Routledge, p. 201.

Wang, P. S., Angermeyer, M., Borges, G., Bruffaerts, R., Chiu, W. T., de Girolamo, G., Fayyad, I., Gureje, O., Haro, J. M., Huang, Y., Kessler, R. C., Kovess, V., Levinson, D., Nakane, Y., Oakley Brown, M. A., Orinel, J. H., Posada-Villa, J., Aguilar-Gaxiola, S., Alonso, J., Lee, S., Heeringa, S., Pennell, B. E., Chatterji, S., and Ustun, T. B. (2007). Delay and failure in treatment seeking after first onset of mental health disorders in the World Health Organization's World Mental Health Survey Initiative. *World Psychiatry* 6, 177–185.

7

THE SHADOW OF REDEMPTION

The Grail and the self-knowledge industry

Joanna Dovalis

Introduction

The uncertainties and discontent in modern Western life have pressed each of us to turn to our psyche and ask, 'Who am I? Where do I belong? What is my journey, my passion?' The self-knowledge industry, in its diverse and varied forms, has been a cultural response to this psychological need. The industry aims to help individuals improve their lives by focusing on all parts of the human experience, including the emotional, physical, spiritual, and intellectual domains. Psychotherapy plays a significant role in modern society and it too is part of the self-knowledge industry. To understand the quest of the knowledge seeker, we will enter the therapy room.

A person must create life experiences that initiate the process of individuation, and those experiences translate to psychic events that lead to consciousness. In this chapter, the quest for healing and self-awareness is illustrated by examining the therapy sessions of the client Walter in Season 2 of the HBO television series *In Treatment* (Dir., Garcia, 2008). His journey will be compared to the mythical story of Perceval and his relationship to the Fisher King on his vision quest for the Holy Grail. Perceval and Walter are symbolic of the modern man who has overly identified with the intellect at the peril of the feeling life. And like Perceval, Walter's healing embodies the midlife journey that requires a confrontation with the unconscious and the breakdown of the persona, leading to the discovery of the Self – the core of one's being.

The quest of the knowledge seeker is a developmental journey that may heal the split from our own authentic natures, where all psychological and emotional problems originate. In order for self-knowledge to lead to happiness, it must be used as a means for understanding and insight. In other words, the quest to truly learn about oneself is a place of psychic integration and redemption. Development of a conscious ego does not solely depend on knowledge or intelligence, but develops through the healing of the feeling function in the light of self-knowledge *and* reflection. From this it follows that insight and therapy would be greatly enhanced by examining the correlation between myth and psychological symptoms. Guided by the Hermit and the Analyst, our travelers Perceval and Walter will navigate through the travails of the unconscious.

A summary of Perceval and the Fisher King

The quest for the Holy Grail exists in many forms. An early version is *Perceval, ou Le Conte du Graal* by Chrétien de Troyes (c. 1180), a living myth that transmits through outer and inner realizations.[1] It entails an end-of-days aura that connotes a complete life as one that is lived to its end; the Holy Grail is attained only by those who have truly lived their own lives. Laden with poetic fantasy and symbolism, the object of the quest lends itself to myriad experiences and psychological interpretations. This makes its metaphorical power the *sine qua non* for private revelations and transformations.

A summary of Perceval and the Fisher King will serve our understanding of the character Walter from *In Treatment*. The story of the Grail coalesces around Perceval, an innocent fool who becomes the embodiment of healing compassion. His story is a chronicle of the feeling part of man that has been wounded, likened to the current dilemmas of our intellectually driven modern life. His vision quest for the Grail is closely bound by his relationship to the Fisher King and, as a consequence, the growth of consciousness.

Perceval grows up in the care of his mother, who raises him in loneliness and deliberately keeps him sheltered from the intrigues of courtly life. Appearing at three significant points in the narrative, she brings the feminine dimension of healing and wisdom to her son. As a fatherless son, rather than being compelled toward regression, Perceval carries a strong desire for a life full of experience and action. His independent nature draws him away from his mother and toward essential separation, which eventually leads him to the holy vessel.

During his travels, Perceval meets the Fisher King, the prince Amfortas who bears an injury to his groin that was caused by his own greedy appetites. The King can only be restored to health by an exceptional knight who asks a certain question. Perceval is banished from the Grail Castle for not asking the correct question regarding the Grail; he must leave to create life experiences that will prepare him for his ultimate return. But he must first conquer guilt. He initially refuses to discard his mother's handmade garments, despite the fatherly advice from his teacher Gornemant de Goort. But as Jung (1956) explains in *Symbols of Transformation*, the longing for the mother can also be understood as an unconscious urge for rebirth and transformation of the personality. It is not until later in his midlife that Perceval grows weary of living the hero's journey and succumbs to removing the garments by his own volition. The shedding of the garments represents Perceval's psychological navigation through the midlife transition and his conquering of guilt, which he was previously unable to accomplish. As Emma Jung and Louise von Franz (1998) describe, 'Perceval's guilt was twofold: he did not attend to his mother nor did he ask about the Grail – and the latter offence is actually described as a consequence of the former' (p. 181). The growth of consciousness moves forward with an awareness of this powerful emotion, reflecting a healing of the feminine principle and wounded feeling function. That is, guilt, which carries both spiritual and psychological dimensions, is necessary to contend with the shadow and prepare the personality for contact with the Self.

Perceval's healing of the Fisher King

The Fisher King is too ill to live but is unable to die, a state that Stein (1983) calls psychological liminality – a transitional place in which there is an amputated past and a vague future. Liminality is the psychological territory of shadow consciousness, where the presence and the role of the archetypal unconscious is represented by Hermes, the god of travelers and passages. The King's ailment is descriptive of anxiety and depression, the anguish that is experienced in the transition of midlife during which there is an absence of and alienation from oneself and, consequently, from others. His suffering can only be assuaged by fishing, which stands as a metaphor for the way a wounded person's life is only bearable when he or she is engaged with the inner life and the dark waters of the unconscious. As described by Stein (1983), 'It is a long dark night of the soul, a descent into regions of feeling and of experiencing that comes quite unexpected and certainly unsolicited' (p. 23). While unconscious depression does not heal, conscious depression or suffering can lead us to the source of transformation and renewal. It is during a time of incubation and stillness, rather than stagnation, that something new can become known. At these crucial moments of transition and disillusionment, it is possible to transcend suffering and experience healing. Thus, the Fisher King also represents the requisite of a psychological wound in order for a new consciousness to emerge.

Perceval must leave the Grail Castle and search the lower world of Klingsor and Kundry, meaning he must visit the unconscious shadow within as a means to overcome the appetites of the flesh. For twenty years, he slays dragons and rescues maidens, surviving attempts on his life and on his virtue. While traveling, he is confronted by pilgrims who tell him to visit the local hermit. They give him the same directions he had received as a youth when he had first stumbled upon the Fisher King. He is told to go down the road, turn left, and cross the drawbridge to find the Grail Castle. Building this psychological bridge between ego-consciousness and the unconscious is both the central task of midlife and also serves as the transcendent function in the journey of individuation.

Perceval confesses to the Hermit the worst mistake of his life; he had failed to ask the question of the Grail, which would have relieved the King's suffering. A moment of *kairos* (a supremely opportune time) immediately creates understanding for Perceval. He realizes that his principal duty in life is to heal the Fisher King and thereby, psychologically, to heal his own wounds and put down the armored defenses of the ego and surrender to the Self. This fortunate moment reveals the presence of Hermes converging in a moment of synchronicity. Here, two vectors meet, the intentionality of the ego and the archetypal realm. When at last he returns on Good Friday to the Grail Castle, he bears the spear of Longinus and with it touches Amfortas's wound, which is at once remarkably healed. This resonates with Gawain's declaration to King Arthur at the Round Table, 'We have won everything by the lance and lost everything by the sword'. The lance represents the high value placed on the feeling life, achieved by discrimination, sacrifice, and the work of consciousness, whereas the sword is symbolic of the force and power of the armored ego. The breach of the feminine that contains the vessel has at last been sealed, and the eponymous hero returns from his quest to assume his place among the knights of the Grail, his compassion enlightened.

Finding his way back to the Grail Castle in midlife, Perceval has asked, "To Whom Does the Grail Serve?" and has, therefore, made a commitment to take the conscious path. The wounded Fisher King is healed and dies exactly *three* days later, a spiritual ascension signifying that the wounded part of the self has been released as the shadow has served its purpose. The ego defenses have been defeated, allowing the spiritual self to attain its divine heights by moving into alignment with one's authentic nature. Perceval has successfully shifted the center of his personality from a persona orientation to that of the Self.

In Treatment: Walter's burden

In Treatment (Dir., Garcia, 2008) is set within the psychotherapy sessions of four patients and their therapist Dr. Paul Weston (Gabriel Byrne). Paul's supervision sessions with his psychotherapist Gina (Diane Wiest) reveal his own internal conflicts in his personal and professional life, which helps him find his way through the healing process. One patient in particular struggles to find himself amidst a lifetime of guilt and searching for acknowledgment of his deeds: Walter (John Mahoney) is a high-powered executive who initially sought therapy at the urging of his wife but eventually continues to attend sessions of his own volition. Throughout the seven-week season, Walter battles with himself as he confronts the emotional turmoil he has carried since childhood. Walter's seven therapy sessions are described here from a depth perspective that relates Walter's life experiences to those of Perceval, and, ultimately, to Paul.

Session 1: Walter, CEO

Walter's first therapy session sets the stage for the unraveling of his childhood sorrow. He enters the therapy room and shakes the doctor's hand. He is noticeably anxious and rather pompous, expressing his worry about having 'nice things', such as his cashmere coat. He says, 'The trouble with having nice things is you have to worry about them.' He looks at his watch frequently, wanting to move along quickly, the gesture being an obvious sign that he is under a great deal of psychic pressure. He attempts to take immediate control of the session, instructing Paul to start the process by telling him everything he knows about him. When Paul replies that he knows nothing about him, Walter is completely shocked, comparing Paul to college students who ignore the most relevant part of the newspaper – the business section. Walter's name is apparently strewn across the business section, as he is the CEO of a company that has caused many deaths as a result of its contaminated infant formula. Paul reacts nonchalantly to Walter's belittling comments.

The uneasiness of the first session lingers as Walter continues to engage Paul in a power struggle for control over the session. Walter knows no other way to handle himself but as the executive who controls and manages others. He expresses that his greatest concern is his inability to sleep, which is symbolic of his inability to surrender and let go. Lack of sleep affects his ability to function in his high-power position. He must sleep in order to be at the top of his game.

The topic shifts to Walter's family. He is the father of two boys who have 'launched', but he speaks mostly of his daughter Natalie. He is noticeably happier when speaking about her, softening his tense demeanor, until he reveals that she is now working in a clinic in Rwanda. He reads aloud a letter from his daughter in which she tells him she has never felt so alive and has come to realize that life is about helping people. Unable to understand her perspective, Walter is terribly worried and angry about her being so far away, vulnerable while living in a Third World country. Paul confronts Walter's fantasy of flying to Rwanda to bring her home and explains the difference between stability and security. Walter becomes angry at Paul, telling him he does not need his 'god damn permission' to decide how to respond to his daughter. Much like Perceval's refusal to take guidance from Gornemont to separate from his mother's apron springs, Walter rejects his therapist's help.

When Paul asks Walter who he can talk to about his feelings and experiences, Walter replies that there is nobody. His boys wouldn't understand, and he doesn't want to worry his wife Connie. He reports that his wife used to call him 'Superman' and that he served in the Vietnam War. He is clearly discomforted by his inability to handle anxiety and insomnia at the cost of losing the respect and clout he has earned throughout his life.

Paul explains to Walter that therapy is a process that takes time, but Walter insists he does not have 'the luxury of time'. He then collapses to the floor, gasping for air, apparently unable to breathe. Paul attempts to help Walter recover from the attack. When Walter gets up, he says 'They always go away', and leaves the room.

Like myths and dreams, Walter's first therapy session reveals a self-portrait of the troubled regions of his psyche. His desire to bring Natalie home speaks of separation anxiety, as her growing independence brings a painful change that he equates to the loss of love. His anxiety attack is a somatic manifestation of a memory deeply buried in the recesses of his unconscious. Like Perceval, losses of this magnitude imply a loss of the heroic defense and have crossed the psychic boundary into his body.

Thus, the core theme of Walter's first session is separation, the first major task in the long process of psychological change that occurs in midlife. According to Stein (1983), one must separate from an earlier identity with the persona, equivalent to Erik Erikson's (1968) psychosocial stage of *identity vs. role-confusion*. The persona is the public face or mask a person wears to fulfill his or her social, gender, or developmental roles. During the breakdown of the persona, two repressed and unconscious elements of the personality are released: (1) the rejected and inferior person that one has fought against becoming (the shadow), and (2) the contrasexual 'other' whose power one has always, for good reason, denied and evaded – the animus, the concealed masculine in women, or the anima, the feminine aspects of men (Stein, 1983).

Session 2: Walter's guilt

At the start of the next session, Walter apologizes to Paul for scaring him with the panic attack. Walter insists that Paul must have read about him in the newspaper this week; he believes someone at the *New York Times* is trying to bring him down by reporting damaging facts. Paul asks Walter if the criticisms might be coming from within the company. Walter acknowledges the possibility, but explains that his biggest concern is that his negative publicity may be jeopardizing his daughter's safety in Rwanda. It appears the therapist is attempting to discern how much of Walter's anxiety stems from his internal life rather than external circumstances.

Throughout his therapy sessions, Walter has kept his two cell phones on, constantly checking them and rejecting calls. Like Perceval, this behavior reflects his heroic need to be responsive to others, but might also be an unconscious strategy to interrupt any connection from forming between himself and the therapist – as well as his own feeling life. Paul gently responds to the shame driving Walter's defenses by inviting him to share what is on his mind. Walter talks about James, the son of the founder of his company, Mr. Donaldson. Walter and James had been in the war together, and Walter was asked by Mr. Donaldson to 'watch out' for his son. When the young man died in a car accident after the war, Walter felt responsible for his death. He carries this burden, believing that he could have prevented the death by taking better care of him as he had in Vietnam. Walter suffers from deep-seated guilt, the same emotional problem Perceval had to overcome. There are legitimate signs of a puer identification in both men, with the accompanying feelings of invulnerability and illusions of omnipotence. This prolonged psychological identification is organized around the defense of denial and embodies a lost part of an earlier self that belongs to the past.

Paul asks Walter about the anxiety attack he had experienced during the previous session. Walter admits he had had another attack in the elevator at work that morning, though he does not understand why he had the attack. Paul reveals a connection between the attack and a change in Walter's morning routine. Every morning for the last 30 years, Walter had spoken to Bob, the security guard of his building. That morning, Walter saw that Bob was not at work. The new security guard told him that Bob had dropped dead of a heart attack. Paul asks Walter if he missed seeing and talking to Bob, to which Walter replies, 'Not at all', that Bob meant nothing to him. At this point, it is apparent that it is not in Walter's nature to be so cold, a shadow reaction revealing his capacity to split off and defend against an unwanted memory. In present time, his response is a reflection of midlife death anxiety which may have more to do with his own unlived life rather than the fear of death. Paul offers his interpretation of the event, but once again, Walter becomes angry and shoots it down.

Walter then asks Paul which school he went to, undermining Paul's credibility as a tactic to regain his executive position during the session. Paul confronts the offensive question and asks Walter if he is concerned that Paul is not qualified to treat him. Paul's approach is effectual in eliciting additional self-revealing from Walter. Walter appears to have been unconsciously testing the waters with Paul to determine whether Paul is strong enough to take care of him. Walter explains that he has had the panic attacks since he was 6 years old. He tells the story of his 16-year-old brother Tommy who drowned. Tommy was the golden boy of the family, valedictorian of his class – he walked on water. After the death, Walter's father told him that Tommy's bedroom was now Walter's. Walter now knew why his parents had him; Walter was the spare, Tommy's replacement. And thus, Walter's attacks began as he slept with death in his brother's bed. He never told his parents about the attacks, a reflection of how his parents were no longer present to him.

The therapist asks Walter how his parents had grieved over their lost son. Walter recalls that his mother's beautiful hair had turned gray overnight. It was as if his real mother was trapped someplace far away. He remembers feeling sorry for his father. Paul explains to Walter that his parents had placed a heavy burden on him. He tied Walter's use of the word 'disappear' when speaking of Natalie and the security guard to his childhood trauma. Once again, Walter is unable to see any connection. Paul then asks him if he felt his parents wanted him to fulfill his brother's potential. Walter responds that no one could do that.

Paul tells Walter he has a disproportionately stressful response to present time events that precedes Bob and Natalie and that he doesn't trust people to ever come back if they leave him. Walter ponders whether his sleeplessness started when his daughter left for Rwanda. He asks Paul for medication, his first attempt to ask for help and to make a connection between his symptoms and his inner life. Paul agrees to call Walter's doctor about a prescription, but insists that it is important for them to continue to work in therapy. Walter stands up and begins to pay Paul. Paul tells him it isn't necessary to pay weekly, but Walter insists, quoting his father, 'Pay as you go.' Perhaps, because paying weekly allows Walter the psychological freedom to end therapy at any time, he believes it will prevent him from entering the dangerous waters of vulnerability. As such, it is a misguided attempt to keep himself safe from his fear of drowning in a bottomless sea of emotions.

Session 3: A trip to Rwanda

Walter begins the third session just as before, with a determined, down-to-business demeanor. He is once again completely in charge as he manages urgent calls about his business, despite his request that his secretary not call him for the next 40 minutes. Walter uses the metaphor, 'It is no time to tread water', in reference to the business crisis – an interesting use of language that casts light on the presence of his brother's drowning inhabiting his psyche. Paul suggests they reschedule their appointment. Walter pulls cash out of his pocket as he tells Paul that he values his time and wants to compensate Paul for rescheduling a previous session. Paul refuses to accept the payment, which far exceeds the normal fee for his appointment. Walter uses money as a means to free himself from the guilt he feels inside and to ensure that his connection to Paul has not been harmed. Walter finally succumbs to shutting off his phone.

Paul confronts the pressure Walter is feeling, encouraging him to slow down in response to the breaking crisis. Walter then admits he has spent the last 42 out of 72 hours on a plane; he had flown to Rwanda, 'to bring Natalie home'. He and Natalie had talked or e-mailed every day of her life, but lately he had not heard from her at all. Instead, Natalie had e-mailed her mother a worrisome letter about her father. Walter concluded that she must have been in trouble and that she needed him. Similar to the years Perceval spent saving maidens in distress, Walter has projected his own wounded anima onto his daughter and is impelled to rescue her from harm.

Paul asks Walter if Natalie had asked him to come, and wonders why he would choose to fly to Rwanda while his company was in the middle of a crisis. Although Walter clearly operates from a dominant-thinking function, his choice reveals compulsive psychic pressure coming from his unconscious feeling life. Perceval's and Walter's destinies depend on the conscious recognition that they are living out the fate of their childhood losses; they are trapped in the hero's role and identity inherited from their pasts and, so, they must journey.

Walter describes Natalie's appearance as he confronted her in the small village. His little girl had transformed into a stranger. She stood in front of him, shoeless, holding a baby in her arms. She was so thin, and had cut off her hair, the image linking the early trauma of how his mother's hair had dramatically faded to gray overnight after his brother's death. Walter was unable to recognize Natalie. He knew she must have been hiding something from him, just as he had felt his mother had been trapped someplace far away. With his early trauma fully activated, he had insisted that Natalie go home with him. Natalie had said she was busy and told her father to go to the hut and rest. Disgusted by the impoverished conditions, a projection of his Fisher King wound, Walter began to pack up all of her belongings. When she discovered what he had done, Natalie screamed at her father and told him, 'Go fuck yourself.' Natalie's adolescent rage reflects her desperate need to continue the separation process from her father. Needless to say, Walter's heart was broken. Paul confronts Walter's inability to tolerate his daughter's separation by describing Walter's domineering and obsessive behavior, sabotaging her chance to grow up. Paul strongly encourages Walter to think about the way he had responded to his daughter and encourages him to let Natalie be, to let her go.

Obviously shaken, Walter stands and rummages through his coat pocket, looking for a Xanax tablet. He then recalls a recent bad dream in which he was back at his parents' house in Tommy's room, feeling suffocated. Walter continues to call his own bedroom 'Tommy's room', a metaphor for living his dead brother's unlived life, with no space for his own dreams. Paul asks if Tommy has been on Walter's mind since Natalie left. Paul continues to explain Natalie's need to separate, emphasizing that it is something Walter has never been able to do. Paul acknowledges that separation must feel like abandonment to Walter, similar to when Tommy had left him. He reminds Walter that Natalie had attempted to talk to him, but he had refused to hear what she had to say. Paul points out that this may be the first time that Natalie's wants are not the same as her father's.

While growing up, Natalie's strong mind had been validated by her father, and as a *father's daughter* in the Jungian perspective (Murdock, 1994), she has proven to be very successful. It is the security of their relationship that has allowed her to confront him. However, as Natalie attempts to define herself, Walter's feelings of connection are threatened. He admits that she doesn't need him anymore, so she must be done with him. Again, Walter's use of language links to his inner life, as the 6-year-old boy who felt his parents were 'done with him' when Tommy died. Walter's need to be useful had always been the adhesive that ensured a connection to others. He gathers his belongings while stating that the company cannot get rid of him, because he is the glue – Mr. Donaldson cannot survive without him.

Session 4: Walter's resignation

Walter enters the therapy room wearing casual clothes, not his typical business attire. He explains that his Blackberry was taken away from him along with his job and reputation. Like the Fisher King, Walter has entered the second stage of the midlife transition, liminality, a time when the ego is unable to fully identify with a former self-image. Walter must find the 'corpse' and identify the original source of pain, and then put the past to rest by grieving, mourning, and burying it (Stein, 1983). Hermes, the father of alchemy, is the guide into and out of this darkness. And Paul's help can only offer a Hermetic pathway through the travails of Walter's unconscious pain as he leads Walter's perplexed ego on the path to even deeper liminality.

Paul had read the newspaper headline earlier that morning: 'CEO forced to resign'. Walter insists that he had done everything right and played by the rule book, precisely how a company should respond to a lethal crisis. However, once he had taken responsibility, he was pushed out. He states that the world is more predatory than it used to be and regrets letting his guard down, which reflects the wounded feeling function as a casualty of modern life. Paul interjects and asks Walter if he has been eating and sleeping, looking noticeably concerned when Walter tells him he has needed to take pills to sleep. Paul gently approaches any thoughts of suicidal ideation. Walter's heroic mode of functioning is completely compromised with this clear-cut defeat. A crack has opened between Walter's ego and persona, creating a place for the shadow personality to emerge. Like Perceval, he has been thrown out of the Grail Castle and, in solitude, must visit the unconscious shadow in order to find his way back.

Walter expresses how ironic it is that now that he has the time to talk, it is too late to help. He feels like an old man who has stayed in the game too long. Although he has had a great deal of support from family and friends, it gives him no comfort. It is apparent that Walter feels completely alone as he struggles with a deep sense of shame. Reflecting on his friend Dean, Walter says he cannot stand people who fool themselves; Dean was fired and had 'lived out his usefulness'. Paul mirrors back Walter's own confession that his life is over, just like Dean's. Walter asks Paul what he thinks of him, but does not give him time to respond. He quickly moves into a negative projection, stating that he knows what Paul thought of him the first time he came to therapy: he was a greedy man who let babies die. Paul confronts Walter's distortion and, says, 'The truth is, I'm angry at the deep sense of betrayal you have experienced, and the way they have treated you,' emphasizing that he believes Walter is a man of integrity. Walter's deep sense of loyalty and integrity is analogous to that of Perceval – the exceptional knight.

Walter talks of a belief that he has instilled in his young business students: once a company loses its name, it loses everything. This creates a space for Paul to ask Walter about his relationship with Mr. Donaldson and to question Walter's profound loyalty to him. Walter insists that Mr. Donaldson had not asked for his resignation, that he had simply yielded to the social pressure of the situation. But then Walter explains the matter-of-fact manner in which Mr. Donaldson had let him go; he had told Walter the situation was 'too bad' and wished him luck. After 35 years of devotion to Mr. Donaldson's company, Walter was bid farewell without so much as a pat on the back. Mr. Donaldson's decision reveals the temperament of the archetypical senex, who might be not only cold, but also distant.

After this situation, Walter is left feeling that he has trusted the wrong people in his life. He turns to the memory of his friend James, Mr. Donaldson's son. Walter reveals that James was actually a reckless young man who had eventually driven his car into a tree. Walter had resolved his guilt by becoming James's replacement, Mr. Donaldson's lost son. With candid fervor, Paul expresses his authentic feelings of disgust; after making Mr. Donaldson one of the richest men in the country, how could he have released Walter from his duty in such a cool, impersonal way? Interestingly, Johnson (1995) describes coolness as one of the characteristics of a Fisher King, a wounded man.

At this point, Paul links the two crises in Walter's life: Natalie's departure to Rwanda and the corporation's contaminated baby formula. He explains to Walter that his choice to fly to Rwanda was his attempt to bring things to a head, an action intended to relieve the intense psychic pressure he was experiencing. Paul continues to confront Walter's deep-seated feelings of guilt and his feeling of responsibility for the infants' deaths, despite having done everything possible to respond to the situation. Paul confronts Walter's punitive superego and explains that he is punishing himself by continuing to question why he had not done more. Walter concedes by saying that he had no choice, that it was his fault.

Paul then deals with Walter's father complex and explains that he speaks about Mr. Donaldson in the same way one would speak of a father, which prevents him from acknowledging Mr. Donaldson's role in the crisis. This prompts Walter to supply a deeper revelation of what had happened on the day of his brother's death.

Tommy had come into Walter's room that night and told him that he was going to jump into the quarry. Little Walter, being only 6 years old, had cheered on his brother, telling Tommy that he knew he could do it. So Tommy jumped.

Thus, at the age of 6, Walter had taken full responsibility for his brother's death. He owed his parents his own life in return. Walter's idealization of his older brother had partnered with his feelings of omnipotence. Together, these two normal childhood stages had created the perfect storm to fuel his extraordinary guilt. He was culpable in his brother's death and had transferred the overwhelming responsibility to present time – only this time, he is a baby killer.

Session 5: Descent to Hades

Walter's fifth therapy session takes place in a hospital room where Paul has come to visit him after he has supposedly had a bout of food poisoning. Walter sits in bed, explaining to Paul that he had felt a chill and assumed he was ill from something he had eaten. Walter reveals that Natalie is visiting from Rwanda. He suspects she only came to visit out of guilt after her mother had told her of his lay off. Walter's sons had also visited, but their presence had been awkward, making conversation with their father difficult under the recent circumstances. Walter reports that his mood had improved upon Natalie's arrival. She had attempted to talk to him about the incident in Rwanda. His isolation was upsetting to her, so she was constantly urging him to leave his bedroom, to get dressed, to have a life again.

Paul confronts Walter about the alleged food poisoning, admitting that he knows Walter's stomach was pumped upon arrival at the hospital. Walter quickly takes control of the conversation, telling Paul to not worry, that unlike his recently deceased client, Walter's family would not sue him. Walter admits that he had had Paul vetted at the start of their therapy sessions, though he had found out about the lawsuit too late. Walter's aggressive stance reveals his repressed guilt and anger as he moves into a splitting defense, identifying with what he perceives as Paul's negligence by stating, 'We both have blood on our hands.'

Walter romanticizes his suicide attempt as 'a millionaire's death' – hoping to just go to bed one night and not wake up. He admits to taking the pills, wanting to end the nightmare. Having lost all personal value, Walter believes he deserves the recent chain of events and that everyone would be better off without him. He blames himself for the death of his brother, his friend James, and now, the babies. In the ultimate act of aggression, he had imposed the death sentence on his own life, his punishment for the unforgivable. Paul points out that Natalie would have never been able to forgive herself; her life story would have become a repetition of Walter's own. Walter pleads with Paul to minimize his medical condition, to tell Natalie and the doctors that he is fine, but Paul explains that he should be kept under observation. Defending himself against his sense of powerlessness, Walter threatens to call his lawyer, to which Paul challenges him to 'Get in line'.

Common to all transitional periods, the psychological task is to confront repressed elements within the personality as they return to consciousness. This stage in the midlife journey can be displayed in regressive, even pathological, acts. Again, much like Perceval's need to wear his mother's handmade garments, Walter has tried to return to the realm of the mother. His suicide attempt expresses a yearning for symbiotic union with the mother he had lost, reflecting his heightened need for nurturing and connection. He has traveled to Hades to find his mother who has been trapped far away since his brother's death. 'Until the pit of death is entered, the process of internal transformation cannot move to its conclusion, for at midlife, too, a new person is born' (Stein, 1983, p. 108). In this stage of therapy, Walter must re-establish a connection between his ego-consciousness and its source – the maternal unconscious and wounded feeling function. Walter's relationship with his daughter must move from an external projection of his own anima. He needs to discover what Natalie found in Rwanda: a sense of vitality and purpose in life.

Paul and Natalie talk with each other in the hall after Walter forces Paul out of his room. Natalie confides that her mother does not handle stress well; Connie has been in rehab several times for addictions to booze and pills. Paul is surprised at this disclosure, given Walter's consistent idealization of his wife. It is now clear that Connie's addiction is a replication of Walter's own absent mother. It was his duty to care for them both.

The psychological merger of his mother and his wife reveals an interrupted developmental stage, due to his early childhood trauma, that is responsible for his illusions and, thus, many of the critical life choices Walter has made and now regrets. When one is unable to integrate painful feelings, the defense of splitting is employed; people or events are viewed as *all good* or *all bad*. Walter has used the defense mechanism of idealization, attributing exaggeratedly positive qualities to not only his wife and daughter, but also to Mr. Donaldson and his brother. At other times, Walter has employed its binary opposite – devaluation – in regard to Paul and, even more dangerously, to himself.

Session 6: Vulnerability

Natalie escorts Walter to Paul's office for therapy. Since his suicide attempt, Walter is under constant supervision by the hospital staff and his wife and daughter, which deeply humiliates the former executive. This tight supervision is analogous to the necessity of guidance by the feminine and the psychological vigilance required during the midlife transition. Walter cajoles Paul, confiding that the hospital staff are not bright, unlike Paul, who Walter considers his equal. Paul confronts Walter's proclamations, having felt devalued by Walter in the past. He continues to approach Walter in a very direct manner to determine Walter's motive for flattery. Walter admits that he cannot relate to other patients and insists that he does not belong in the program.

Paul creates a therapeutic opening for Walter to express his feelings by recognizing that Walter might be angry that Paul had not saved him from his depressive episode. Walter admits that one of the psychiatrists described Paul as reckless for opening Pandora's box at the wrong time. This accusation is counter to many psychoanalytic thinkers who believe every patient owes it to himself to have at least one breakdown (Panajian, 2012). Having navigated through the dark night of the soul himself, Paul is not afraid to go on the journey with his client. In the words of Jung:

> So long as you feel the human contact, the atmosphere of mutual confidence, there is no danger; and even if you have to face the terrors of insanity, or the shadowy menace of suicide, there is still that area of human faith, that certainty of understanding and of being understood, no matter how black the night.
>
> *(Jung, 1926/46, para. 181)*

Pleading for Paul to release him from the hospital, Walter abandons his young manipulative tactic and speaks more directly. Paul insists that the therapy continue and that Walter must become honest. Walter concedes and begins to talk about his shameful experience. He reveals that he had not wanted Natalie to know about his attempted suicide; that the hospital has been hell for him, leaving him with nothing to do; that he used to be such a busy man, but now felt uncomfortable with 'wasting time'. Walter's busyness had been a useful defensive strategy to keep unwanted feelings and memories at bay. Paul responds by suggesting he use the time to reflect on his inner life, which Walter validates by admitting that Natalie tells him he should listen to his inner voice. He walks to the window and comments that Paul lives on a pretty street – perhaps a first indication that not only is the depression beginning to lift, but also that he is ready to surrender to the geography of the inner life.

Walter sits down and asks Paul what he would have done in his situation. Paul mirrors Walter's inner life by telling him that he understands how hopeless he must have felt and how he had wanted a way out. Paul then declares that the worst night of his life has passed. Walter says he has tried to come up with ways to stop feeling and that he had always been able to carry on working, but not this time. He was not aware of this Other Walter who crumbled under pressure. Paul suggests that the Other Walter may have space to emerge, now that Walter's time is not occupied by the relentless demands of his work life.

Paul then refers to Connie's history in rehab, surprising Walter to the point of anger. Paul engages in the learning moment by explaining that 'This is what people share in therapy', expressing his desire for Walter to be up front and honest. Walter regresses to his core belief, claiming responsibility for his wife's inability to cope. He believes his frequent absences had caused her to slip. He feels bad that he is no longer the rock he used to be, that he is no longer her 'Superman'. Walter has had to face the complete failure of his omnipotent self and, like Perceval, his identification with the defensive structures of the heroic ideal has cracked. Paul expresses empathy with the toll it has cost Walter to have always been the hero, on the front line since Tommy's death. Paul makes Walter understand that he does not know how to not be in charge or how to play. It is time to release Little Walter from the darkness and to reconnect with the part of himself that was left behind when his brother died; Little

Walter is the part of him that wants to live. In a cathartic moment, Walter begins to sob. Paul, the healing father, walks over to him and Walter holds onto Paul's leg for dear life while he cries. Although he remains standing, Paul stays close, knowing that Little Walter needs to finally feel his proper size, to feel the presence and care he has never known.

Session 7: The conscious path

Walter's final session illustrates his ensuing closeness to his therapist. Paul responds with warm understanding to Walter's disruption of another couple's therapy when he eagerly enters the therapy room before his appointment time. Therapy begins at the moment of contact, the interruption showing positive signs of childlike spontaneity and safety in the relationship Walter now has with his therapist. Paul is becoming an internal object, available to Walter in a way that his parents were unable to be.

Walter expresses his gratitude to Paul for facilitating his discharge from the hospital. He tells Paul he has been working in the yard, pruning and cutting down the brush, which Paul points out as analogous to the pruning he is doing in therapy. Paul then addresses Walter's emotional breakthrough in the last session, though Walter acts as if he does not remember, reflecting the subtle interplay between resistance and submission during therapy. Paul reminds him that he was quite moved about the possibility of finding the lost Walter. Paul's intervention stimulates a dream memory for Walter. Mr. Donaldson had called him in for a meeting in an old garage. They had shaken hands, then Mr. Donaldson had explained that they had traced the source of the contamination – some nut had tampered with the product. Walter had felt vindicated. The 'old man' had apologized and admitted that letting go of Walter had been the biggest mistake he had ever made. Walter had tried to answer him, but he was unable to speak.

The dream indicates that Walter's superego is loosening its tyrannical grip on his psyche, and he has made contact with the original source of his pain, relieving his guilt. Just as Perceval had felt deep regret for not asking the question of the Grail to end the Fisher King's suffering, Walter had not thought to ask the question about his own divine child: Little Walter. His silence in the dream not only signifies the releasing of the wants of the ego, that he no longer desires his executive position in the company, but also symbolizes a connection to the divine part of himself that has no language.

Walter then associates the feelings of the dream with his father. After Tommy's accident, Walter's father could not sleep and worked the graveyard shift, a memory that conveys an image of his father as 'the walking dead'. He would peek at his father while he worked in the garage, stealing moments of connection. Walter recalls the way his own sons would spy on him, but says his sons are no longer interested in him. Paul emphasizes that Walter now has time to work on repairing his relationship with his sons. Walter also recalls making his mother two drinks in the evening. She would retreat to her bedroom to smoke, causing catastrophic worry in the young boy as he imagined a fire would ensue. Paul validates Walter's perceptions of his parents, acknowledging how grief-stricken they were, but like Perceval, Walter was a lonely little boy who had needed them. Johnson (1995) emphasizes that 'the problem of loneliness is an expression of the wounded feeling function' (p. 26).

Walter recounts his father's idea to move to a new home, though his mother had not wanted to move. Walter would ride his bike to his old house and sit for hours, waiting for Tommy to come home. With only feelings of duty and loneliness to occupy the new house, Paul suggests that rather than looking for Tommy, perhaps Walter was looking for someone else – his lost self. Paul asks Walter if he remembers crying when his brother died. In a struggle to recall the memory, Walter admits that yes, he had cried, but that his father had picked him up firmly by the arms and told him never to cry in front of his mother. A young boy could only interpret this action as a demand to hide his feelings in order to avoid causing harm. Little Walter and his feeling life were banished.

Walter takes a drink of water and says, 'Walter the CEO is gone now.' Paul says the crash was inevitable. Walter asks Paul if this is what he had wanted, to break him down in therapy. Walter is still confused about the ego-driven life, full of its own agenda and strategies. He says he missed his life; at 68 years of age, he had not taken a moment of life for himself. Paul insists that now is the time to stop taking care of everyone else. Walter must choose to do one of two things: Paul could help wrap him back up, or they could take a deeper route and continue their therapeutic work to achieve a new way of being. Paul admits the therapeutic path would require Walter to come to therapy more often. As an innocent child, Walter asks if Paul would really want to spend more time with him. When Paul replies that he would, Walter stands up and asks with enthusiasm, 'When do we start?'

Redemption

Paul, our Hermetic Analyst, has guided his client through his midlife journey and the dark night of the soul. Following Perceval's course of action, Walter agrees to take the conscious path, ready for the third phase of the midlife transition, that which Stein (1983) calls the phase of reintegration. The main undertaking of therapy at this stage is to help the client endure the tension of the opposites, as he or she continues to heal the splits between the conscious and unconscious fields of awareness. By tapping into the inner realms of the psyche, distorted projections continue to be examined, allowing change and growth to occur in the transformation of the personality.

The goal of therapy is not to reach some illusory state of happiness, but to release oneself from the grips of internal angst and the turmoil that lives in the unconscious. Just as Walter must contend with his own emotional life, Paul, the wounded healer, is also on the Perceval journey searching for the Grail. Thus, therapy provides a place for both client *and* therapist to become fully human, to share in the peace of mind and self-love that come along with connection.

Therapy offers a road back to the Grail Castle, a miraculous place of healing and deeply felt compassion. But, just like our nightly dreams, the Grail Castle disappears, waiting to be discovered by the dreamer who asks the right question. In the confines of the inner life we call to memory what has been forgotten and retreat into the darkness for illumination. For those who are courageous enough to take on the dangerous journey of individuation, the Grail is within reach.

Like the Grail, therapy does not offer a blissful state of happiness; rather, it contains suffering and redemption manifested in self-awareness. The Shadow leads the psychologically curious to understanding; the Shadow terrifies because it forces one to experience the searing union of the healing and regimented parts of the psyche. And it is in this worthy event that the seeds of its own disillusionment are contained, and when integrated, create a space for the Self to find its individual expression. When asked whether modern man would make it, Carl Jung replied, 'If enough individuals will do their inner work.' Modern troubled knights must choose to take the conscious path on their search for the Grail. And the self-knowledge industry serves to guide them along the journey.

Note

1 Special thanks to Ken Friedenreich for his contribution to the review and historical context of the Grail story.

References

de Troyes, C. (c. 1180). *Perceval, ou le conte du graal.*

Erikson, E. H. (1968). *Identity: Youth and crisis.* New York: Norton.

Johnson, R. (1995). *Fisher King and the Handless Maiden: Understanding the wounded feeling function in masculine and feminine psychology.* New York: HarperCollins.

Jung, C. G. (1926/46). 'Analytical Psychology and Education'. In *Collected Works of C. G. Jung, Vol. 17.* Princeton, NJ: Princeton University Press.

Jung, C. G. (1956). *Collected Works of C. G. Jung, Vol. 5: Symbols of transformation.* Princeton, NJ: Princeton University Press.

Jung, E. and von Franz, M.-L. (1998). *The Grail Legend.* Princeton, NJ: Princeton University Press.

Murdock, M. (1994). *Fathers' Daughters.* New York: Fawcett Columbine.

Panajian, A. (2012, May). 'The Relationship of Freud's Splitting of the Ego, Dissociation, and Borderline Disorders'. Paper presented at the Clinical Dialogues, C. G. Jung Institute of Los Angeles, Los Angeles.

Stein, M. (1983). *In Midlife: A Jungian perspective.* Woodstock, CT: Spring Publications.

SECTION III

May all your Wishes come True

Luke Hockley and Nadi Fadina

May all your wishes come true – it sounds like a dream, and the hope for a happier life is something we can all identify with. That is why there is a moment of recognition when we hear Walt Disney's Cinderella sing, 'A dream is a wish your heart makes, when you're fast asleep.' However, some years before the animation of Cinderella, Sigmund Freud sounded a more cautionary note, observing that dreams are not as innocent as they first appear, any more than fairytales are simply children's stories. In his researches into the structure of the psyche, Freud identified the psychological mechanism by which dreams come to contain an element of fantasy. He termed the process 'wish fulfilment'. Distancing himself from Disney's Cinderella, the wish he described turns out to be a dark one – namely, the Oedipal desire to symbolically murder our parents. Such family dynamics are present in every aspect of life, and we can see them enacted in reality television programmes, such as *The Apprentice*, where the central dynamics are power and control. Lord Sugar's catch phrase 'You're fired' is a symbolic act of filicide that is designed to crush the Oedipal pretensions of his employees.

Freud thought that while it would not make us happy it was nonetheless essential that we acknowledge the dark side of life. He suggested that becoming aware of the ways in which we are driven by unconscious thoughts has the effect of lessening their grip on us, and we feel more in control of our lives. Of course, the impossibility of this Oedipal drama means that these murderous desires have to be hidden, and consequently they present themselves in other ways, for example in dreams. One of Freud's enduring observations has been the insight that dreams are primarily sexual in their meaning, and that their images are populated with disguised latent Oedipal meanings that lie beneath their seemingly innocent surface. Freud depicts us trapped in a drama whose narrative cannot be fully concluded. It is certainly the case that for many of us it often appears that there is no way out of life's difficulties, Oedipal or otherwise, and this can be a profoundly depressing realization.

When it came to the role that dreams play in our lives, Jung adopted a rather different view. He thought dreams depicted the actual situation in our unconscious and not a hidden and disguised sexual one. For Jung, the dream mechanisms that Freud outlined were unnecessary, as dreams simply represent the psychological reality of what is happening in our lives. However, a complication comes about because Jung came to see that dreams use a symbolic language. Today, few of us are well versed in how to interpret such messages and the psychological meaning of symbols both in dreams and in popular culture is something that has largely been lost. Consequently to understand our dreams, and how they relate to our cultural lives, it is necessary to understand their symbolic imagery. This is significant, as without this distinction we treat psychological symbols and mythological images as though they were real – something which modern advertising plays on.

In 'The Emperor's New Clothes', Hans Christian Anderson illustrates how it is possible to be duped into thinking that what we wear hides who we are, when actually the naked truth about ourselves is exposed to the world. The story reveals what happens when we come to believe that an illusion is real, or when we confuse the symbolic and the material – when we mistake the fabric of reality for the substance of our being. Regardless of whether we are draped in actual clothes or social rituals, we wear them in a symbolic manner. The same is true of the other goods with which we adorn our homes and ourselves. What the Emperor eventually realizes is that he needs to decide for himself how he wants to be-in-the-world. His decision is to wear real clothes and not imaginary ones and in doing so, he chose not to live his life clothed in a transparent illusion – he no longer wanted the consumerist fantasy that had been woven by the sycophantic flattery of his tailors. In a similar vein, each one of us needs to decide how to 'be' in the world. The story speaks to our need for psychological truth in the ways we live our lives, and it also shows how important it is for us to be authentic and true to our self.

Being-in-the-world in such an honest way is not an easy task. To take a compelling example, we all know that we are going to die. However, that is not the same as facing and accepting the reality of death as part of our daily life. Mostly we choose not to think about our own mortality, or that those we love will also die. Instead we seek happiness through transforming ourselves. We think that the deep undercurrents of existential anxiety, that we all experience, can be transformed, or at least displaced, through buying new things, by 'making over' our homes or our appearance, or by getting a new job. However, as 'The Emperor's New Clothes' reminds us, clothing ourselves in happiness is not the answer because it turns out to be nothing more than an illusion. Instead we need to accept life for what it is, and to recognize when we are being deceived. In so doing we learn how best to cope with life's difficulties.

This suggests a certain stoic approach to life, in which what matters most is the outlook on life that we adopt. The Stoic philosophers of early Greece and Rome included Epictetus, Seneca and Cicero. At the core of their philosophy is the idea of an 'excellence of character' in which a rational outlook on life is cultivated. The reason for such cultivation is that it leads to mental satisfaction – knowing that we are living life in as thoughtful and reasonable a way as possible is satisfying to us. The very things we pursue in our search for happiness such as money, a better job and material possessions will always fail to live up to our expectations. They fail to make us happy. What matters more is the mental stance we take towards relationships, emotions, our health and the way we age. None of these parts of life are in themselves good or bad (though it is better to be healthy than ill, for example). What is more important is that we adopt a rational and thoughtful approach towards life. Or so the Stoics thought.

Coping with life's difficulties, including the reality of death, is something that the characters of Nordic noir know about. Recently the genre has gained an unexpected popularity, perhaps as a result of its existential Scandinavian approach to life's anxieties. We might say there is something both philosophical and psychological in its worldview. In particular, the detectives in these television programmes live in what is both a rational and a thoughtful manner, but they are also driven. They appear to be at the mercy of their inner demons and there is a certain gothic romanticism that permeates their lives. Henry Fuseli's painting titled *The Nightmare* (1782) depicts an imp sitting on the chest of the dreamer and, in a semi-autobiographical manner, it could easily hang on the walls of detectives Lisbeth Salander or Sarah Lund. In the painting the brooding imp looks out of the canvas directly into the eyes of the viewer. In a similar manner, and in the intimacy of our living rooms, the murders which Salander and Lund deal with stare us directly in the face. What *The Nightmare* and Nordic noir share is an acceptance of life's demons, as they sit right on top of us.

As the narrative arc of these long-running television series unfolds, they uncover how each of the characters turns out to harbour some unexpectedly dark secret. The investigations reveal that underneath the respectable personae of teachers, politicians and the police themselves there is something either menacing or shameful. In this case it is not an Oedipal fantasy that waits to be revealed. Instead it is the realization that regardless of appearances each one of us has a shadow side. Transforming the appearance of a character is a familiar fairytale trope. Its purpose is normally to disguise an evil intent, and part of the appeal of Nordic noir is its existential insistence that the dark side of life is an intrinsic part of being human.

As the demands of an existential life are too much we choose instead to live as though we are in a sort of fairytale, where our lives can be magically transformed. Challenging this misperception, what Freud, Jung and the existential view of the world all show is that it is possible to live in a way where we are ourselves, even if that means we are out of step with everyday society. This does not require magic; it is in fact quite rational. That said, in our contemporary culture it is a brave person who adopts a stoic attitude. Instead we look for quick solutions that we can purchase – solutions that are about turning ourselves into something we are not. It is rare indeed to find anyone suggesting that happiness stems from being yourself – unless of course they are promoting a book, download or DVD on the topic.

One way we believe we will become ourselves is by marrying someone else. It is as though psychologically we feel incomplete and that we hope for a greater sense of wholeness. We imagine this will come from living our lives with someone else, and wedding rings, with their unbroken band of precious metal, symbolize the seamless unity of the relationship. Of course many fairytales end in marriage, even if the sad reality is that many marriages are far from being fairytale romances. The myth of personal transformation, be it through marriage or any other means, is just that, a myth — it is a symbolic way of understanding how we cope with the daily difficulties of life. When it comes to fairytales we make the distinction between myth and reality — no one actually believes that Cinderella is about wearing the right shoes for the evening out, or that the Three Little Pigs are promoting home improvements. Even so advertisers, and the seemingly endless stream of reality television makeover programmes, would have us believe that happiness lies in having a home in the countryside (preferably a brick one) or in knowing who to 'Snog, Marry or Avoid'.

Television programmes, which offer to transform our lives by changing the material conditions of our existence, turn what should be a symbolic and metaphorical insight into a commercial product. In doing so the psychological relevance of the message is lost, as its commercial value is leveraged. To borrow a different image, this time from Norse mythology, the rainbow bridge Bifröst illustrates the symbolic connection that exists between the world of the gods (Asgard) and the human world (Midgard). The rainbow symbolizes the bridge between two worlds — between the inner world of the imagination and the physicality of the material world. Popular folklore has it that at the foot of the rainbow there is a pot of gold. However, happiness does not come from the search for something precious and, like the imaginary pot of fairy gold, it turns out that it is unobtainable. Instead, happiness comes from understanding that the best way to be rich in life is to accept the state of our human condition and for us just to be the people we are.

8

ENGAGING MARRIAGE

Rom coms and fairy tale endings

Heather Brook

Hollywood romantic comedies draw on myths of happiness in direct and often obvious ways. Cinderella stories are a staple narrative of mainstream romance, as are a number of other fairy tales. This chapter considers the ground shared by mainstream, wedding-themed movies and fairy tales. It takes, as its starting point, Alexia Panayiotou's (2010) assertion that 'films are . . . the equivalent of modern-day myths' (p. 660), and works with Celestino Deleyto's (1998) rejection of the idea that films *either* reinforce *or* challenge the status quo (p. 40). Hilary Radner's (2011) similarly appealing approach is that films do not merely reproduce domination, but rather 'reproduce, modify and critique' discursive formations, and as such can reveal 'the tensions and controversies of an era' (p. 2). In a climate of high divorce rates and flexible family formations, wedding movies offer a particularly intriguing source of social pleasure. Indeed, the enduring popularity of wedding-themed movies (especially as romantic comedies, but in fact spanning a range of genres) speaks to the wedding as a site of continuing interest and anxiety. In this chapter, I begin by outlining some of the features common to fairy tales and popular wedding movies like *The Wedding Planner* (Dir., Shankman, 2001), *27 Dresses* (Dir., Fletcher, 2008), and *Bride Wars* (Dir., Winick, 2009). Having mapped this common ground, noting its historical highpoints and attending to how current anxieties might be reflected on screen, I will outline how the fairy tale elements of wedding movies can be analysed using two particular feminist lenses: first, the feminist critique of marriage and its cultural mystification; and, second, feminist accounts of the gendered power relations inherent in viewing. My approach is interdisciplinary and feminist, drawing on the political and sociological frameworks that shape contemporary social and cultural studies, particularly those that take popular movies to be 'important and complex social documents in their own right' (Radner and Stringer, 2011, p. 3). The chapter ends with a warning not to dismiss or devalue those cultural products enjoyed by women, and certainly not to deride women who enjoy them. Instead it suggests that it is more useful to enquire about the social conditions that endow gendered cultural forms with meaning and pleasure in our lives.

Contemporary, mainstream wedding movies typically share a number of features with classic fairy tales (Tasker, 2011, p. 67; Greenhill and Matrix, 2010b, p. 4). Similar narratives, characters and settings endure even as they are modified and updated. While many of the classic texts on film and myth take the action or adventure story as a formulaic template for screenwriting (Bordwell, 2006, pp. 33–34; Kapsis, 2009, p. 3), the connections between romantic comedy and fairy tales are just as clear (Bacchilega, 1997; Garrett, 2012), albeit more rarely acknowledged (Zipes, 2010, p. ix). Robert Murphy (2001), for example, describes British romantic comedies as 'urban fairy tales' (p. 297) rehearsing age-old stories of courtship as rescue. Hilary Radner (1993) likewise explores the consonances between mainstream Hollywood romances (in this case, focusing on *Pretty Woman* (Dir., Marshall, 1990)) and Cinderella stories. The re-tellings are never uniform, complete, or exact, of course, and in some ways the fairy tale elements rehearsed in contemporary movies offer just a sliver of the breadth and richness available in the fairy tale tradition, which is itself neither ahistorical nor universal. Nevertheless, certain elements recur so frequently as to suggest a meaningful and lasting connection. What follows illustrates how such connections are evident in plot, devices, character types, and settings.

Part of the pleasure in watching contemporary romantic comedies is their whole or partial familiarity. This familiarity begins at the level of plot. Popular Hollywood (and especially Disney) interpretations of fairy tales have revitalised and nourished the appeal of fairy tales themselves (Greenhill and Matrix, 2010a). On the page and on screen, romance inflected by the magic of fairy tales continues to draw mass appeal, particularly for women and girls. Similar stories are subject to endless variations, adapted in different settings in order to be refreshed over and over again, even as the circumstances and meaning of their telling change. This is the nature of 'genre' movies. Film genres are:

> categories identified by story, style, iconography, recurring stars, and formulas that get repeated – and remain box office draws – because they speak to cultural desires, anxieties, and fantasies. The romantic comedy film is one of our favourite stories about courtship, coupling, and falling in love.
>
> *(Mizejewski, 2010, p. 17)*

Weddings lend themselves to cinematic representation as points of narrative closure in which the 'natural' endpoint of a courtship plot is fulfilled, and as a visual spectacle in which every woman (and increasingly, every man too) is supposed to have a stake. The Cinderella story most familiar to me, for example, has more in common with romantic comedy genre movies than with Charles Perrault's or other 'classic' versions.[1] I would not suggest that fairy tales like 'Sleeping Beauty', 'The Ugly Duckling', and 'Cinderella' are precise templates for romantic comedy, but rather that there is movement and influence in both directions (Greenhill and Matrix, 2010b, pp. 1–3).

In romantic comedy movies, as in fairy tales, we witness an almost inevitably heterosexual love story (Kirkland, 2007; Moddelmog, 2009; Kaklamanidou, 2013, p. 8). Boy meets girl, misunderstandings, complications or obstructions prevent the couple coming together. Eventually those difficulties are resolved and the two are united with the explicit or inferred promise that they will live happily ever after. The classic Hollywood romantic comedy convention is for the wedding as happy ending (Deleyto, 2003, p. 170) – a convention that is reiterated in small-screen reality shows like *The Bachelor* (2002–present, ABC) and similar match-making entertainment.[2] Almost all rom com narratives include (among other conventions) two key elements: an awakening (literal or metaphorical, but usually both), at which point the true nature of one or both of the protagonists' feelings for each other are realised or revealed. There is also, often, an episode of magical (or somewhat magical) transformation. These are, of course, key features of a number of popular fairy tales (Zipes, 2006, pp. 99–100): they are stories which constitute cultural myths upon which both movies and social understandings more generally draw. Typically, in the course of the story's unfolding, we see at least one and sometimes several fairy tale episodes or elements.

From 'Sleeping Beauty', the motif of the heroine awakening to her rescuer is repeated in highly literal ways. In *27 Dresses* (2008), Jane (Katherine Heigl) takes a knock to the head in a scrum to catch a bride's bouquet, and passes out. When she wakes up, the camera adopts her point of view (in itself a singularly unusual moment) to introduce the male protagonist, Kevin. In *Bridesmaids* (Dir., Feig, 2011), Kristen Wiig's character Annie is first shown freshening up, applying make-up and fixing her hair. She slips back into bed with her (unsuitable) boyfriend, then feigns waking up shortly after he does. This is contrasted with a later scene in which Annie falls deeply asleep (without meaning to) in police officer Nathan Rhodes' (Chris O'Dowd) bed. This time, with Mr Right watching her sleep, she (really) wakes up. In *The Wedding Planner* (2001), Mary (Jennifer Lopez) draws on three different fairy tales in a matter of moments: losing a shiny shoe which her prince-to-be picks up ('Cinderella'), passing out and awakening ('Sleeping Beauty') surrounded by a number of small, playful people ('Snow White') in a child's bed ('Goldilocks').

The romantic comedy heroines in *The Wedding Planner* (2001), *27 Dresses* (2008), *Bride Wars* (2009), *The Proposal* (Dir., Fletcher, 2009), and even the brides in *Bridesmaids* (2011) and *I Love You, Man* (Dir., Hamburg, 2009) are all either daughters of a widower or entirely orphaned: like Cinderella, Sleeping Beauty and Snow White, they are motherless. Motherless heroines have been a staple of romantic comedy from its beginning: Steve Neale and Frank Krutnik's (1990) analysis of 1930s and 1940s romantic comedies argues that the absence of the mother means that male points of view (especially that of the heroine's love interests) dominate: 'the choices offered to [the heroine] tend almost exclusively to be in relation to men and what they desire of her' (p. 159; see also Henneberg, 2010). In *27 Dresses* (2008), Jane's younger sister, Tess, wins the attention of George – the man with whom Jane has long been in unrequited love – constituting another echo of Cinderella. (Plain) Jane is positioned as the dutiful, hard-working sister, while Tess is manipulative and spoilt. The female protagonists in these and many other wedding movies can be understood as what folklorist Steven Swann Jones calls the 'Innocent Persecuted Heroine' (Jones, 1993; Bacchilega, 1993). The archetype here is the underappreciated Cinderella figure made to undertake dirty, difficult, labour for others. The heroine in *27 Dresses* (2008) is again an instructive example here. Not only does Jane work long hours for a boss who fails truly to appreciate, reciprocate or reward her dedication, she also performs unpaid and exhausting event management work for her many marrying friends. The under-recognised Cinderella-heroine reappears in a range of similar incarnations: in *Bridesmaids* (2011), Kristen Wiig's Annie works at a job she hates and lives with appalling flat-mates (the inimitable Rebel Wilson and Matt Lucas as incarnations of the 'ugly stepsisters'); Sandra Bullock's Margaret in *The Proposal* (2009) is referred to as 'it' and 'the witch' by her colleagues; in *Bride Wars* (2009) Anne Hathaway's character Emma is relentlessly exploited by her teacher colleague, Deb (Kristin Johnston). Each character in her own way is constructed as a kind of 'innocent persecuted heroine'.

In wedding movies as in fairy tales, fairy godmothers figure as agents of magical makeovers. In *Bride Wars* (2009), Vera Wang is an invisible but pivotal fairy godmother. Recalling how frequently the heroines in romantic comedy are motherless, we should not be surprised to learn that fairy godmothers are thought by Vogler (1992) to convey the spirit of a dead mother (as cited in Garrett, 2012). In *The Proposal* (2009), Grandma Annie (Betty White) performs as an eccentric fairy godmother to Margaret (Sandra Bullock), as do the hotel manager (Hector Elizondo) in *Pretty Woman* (1990), and Michael Caine's character in *Miss Congeniality* (Dir., Petrie, 2000). In romantic comedy, the fairy godmother's job is, often enough, to match the heroine's outward appearance to some 'truth' about herself, prompting a realisation or awakening on her part. In *Bridesmaids* (2011) we see a more interesting take on this, with the transformation involving attitudes more than appearances. Here, the fairy godmother role is performed by Megan (Melissa McCarthy), who literally pummels some sense into the self-pitying Annie.

Moments of realisation and transformation in wedding movies often have direct fairy tale parallels in the material objects they feature as well as in the character-types wielding them. As Paula Cohen (2010) asserts, 'romantic comedies engage with material things in a particular way: they glory in them and glorify them' (p. 79). The *Sex and the City* movie (Dir., King, 2008) fetishises fashion in general, and shoes and handbags in particular (Doherty, 2010, p. 26). Wedding movies often involve a beautiful – even magically beautiful – dress, worn at some contemporary equivalent of the ball. In *What Happens in Vegas* (Dir., Vaughan, 2008), this is a formal, corporate event – at Joy's (Cameron Diaz) stockbroking firm's retreat, the protagonists slow-dance, and begin to recognise their mutual warming to each other. For Jane in *27 Dresses* (2008), the 'ball' is a small-town bar at which she and Kevin sing 'Benny and the Jets' while dancing drunk on the tables. The somewhat heavy-handed 'irony' here is that this moment occurs precisely when the heroine appears in her own casual clothes as opposed to someone else's idea of a beautiful (bridesmaid's) dress. These are just some of the many resonances linking fairy tales and romantic comedy. Some of the parallels are sweeping and obvious (as in retellings of 'Cinderella' like *Elle: A Modern Cinderella Tale* (Dir., Dunson and Dunson, 2010), *Ever After: A Cinderella Story* (Dir., Tennant, 1998) (Williams, 2010), and *A Cinderella Story* (Dir., Rosman, 2004); some are clear but not quite as direct: *Pretty Woman* (1990), *The Princess Diaries* (Dir., Marshall, 2001), *Never Been Kissed* (Dir., Gosnell, 1999); and others still are removed by degrees, with relatively minor or more subtle fairy tale references: *Hitch* (Dir., Tennant, 2005), *Bridesmaids* (2011).

Because of their similarities, fairy tales and romance genres have been subject to similar kinds of feminist critique.[3] In the first place, both genres have been dismissed as culturally lightweight (Rowe, 1979, p. 238; Kaklamanidou, 2013, p. 1). Though they are rarely labelled as such, 'dick flicks' – movies made about and for men – are generally deemed worthier and more important than those produced by or for women. So-called 'chick flicks' (movies aimed squarely at a female audience, usually with popular drawcards as their stars), including precisely the kind of romantic comedies and wedding movies discussed here, continue to draw critical and social scorn.[4] Betty Kaklamanidou opens her marvellous book with a quotation from journalist Mindy Kaling, who declares, 'saying you like romantic comedies is essentially an admission of mild stupidity' (Kaling, as cited in Kaklamanidou, 2013, p. 1), underlining the general derogation of 'chick flicks' and, of course, the women who enjoy them. Appraisal against a gendered double standard is apparent in reviews, too. If a romantic comedy is critically acclaimed, it will be described as offering something *more than,* different from and superior to chick flicks more generally; if a romantic comedy is panned, it will almost inevitably be derided as typical chick-flick dross. *Bridesmaids* (2011), for example, was praised for 'go[ing] where no typical chick flick does' (Dargis, 2011), and for offering 'a male, or male-seeming dimension that is not featured in all the other sugary girly rom-commy treatments' (Bradshaw, 2011). In contrast, *Bride Wars* (2009) was derided as 'chick flick hell' (Travers, 2009), 'an endurance test for straight men' (Robey, 2009), and 'everything reasonable people hate about so-called "chick flicks"' (Canavese, 2009). Some reviewers (with or without irony) condemned *Bride Wars'* sexism (Canavese, 2009; Murphy, 2009; Cockrell, 2009). The first step in any feminist treatment of fairy tales or romantic comedies, then, is to take them seriously.

To take comedy seriously is to invite consideration of paradox and ambiguity. Contemporary feminist understandings of romantic comedy, chick flicks, and the fairy tales they engage with or extend, are replete with complications (Greenhill and Matrix, 2010b, p. 20). In the early days of second-wave feminism, fairy tales and romance alike were more or less routinely denounced.[5] As the products of a relentlessly patriarchal society, they were said to teach women to be helpless, dependent, selfless, and to want above all to serve men – or one particular man, at least (Rowe, 1979, p. 237). Patriarchy's envoy is Prince Charming, and Cinderella and her sisters are his duped and servile subordinates. If admitting to enjoying romantic comedy is akin to broadcasting one's stupidity, to enjoy wedding rom coms, even secretly, may be to embrace one's inner moron. While the popular misconception of feminism as dour, humourless and ugly persists, the reality is that for feminist scholars and critics, taking romantic comedy seriously has not amounted to forgoing its pleasures and scolding its audience. Rather, a much more precarious line between criticising the socially subordinate place offered to women both on and off-screen, and affirming comfort and pleasure for women wherever it may be found, can be negotiated. In other words, contemporary feminist scholarship often endorses the pleasure women might take in their representation as romantic comedy heroines, even as the limitations of those representations and their effects are criticised. Women are not stupid for enjoying romantic comedies any more than men (or indeed women) are foolish for enjoying action movies or thrillers. With this caveat in mind, then, let us consider how contemporary wedding movies can illustrate some of the more trenchant elements of feminist critiques of romance.

One of the earliest and most enduring feminist critiques of romantic culture is its tendency, conspicuous in both fairy tales and romantic comedy movies, to figure weddings as moments of absolute and ultimate resolution. There is a strong Hollywood tradition in which weddings symbolise 'happily ever after'; they are the kissing culmination of 'the marriage plot'. In movies like *27 Dresses* (2008) and *The Wedding Planner* (2001) (and a multitude more) as in 'Cinderella', the heroine's anxieties and difficulties are eventually settled in her implied or explicit wedding and its promise of happiness ever after. It may be that weddings no longer constitute quite the clichéd happy ending they once did. I agree with Deleyto (1998) that this is at least partly because we no longer see marriage as the necessary gateway to sex (p. 41). In *Bride Wars* (2009), for example, both Emma and Liv already live with their fiancés. The wedding's function as a ritualistic induction to sex is outdated, and today weddings are as likely to be the *context* for action as its endpoint – this is evident in films as different as *Sex and the City* (2008), *The Hangover* (Dir., Phillips, 2009) and *Rachel Getting Married* (Dir., Demme, 2008). Weddings remain nonetheless strongly or even axiomatically associated with romantic closure. As Rosalind Gill and Elena Herdieckerhoff (2006) assert, 'monogamy represents narrative closure' (p. 492), and this is as true in movies as it is in the romantic fiction of their analysis.

Drawing on their trenchant and enduring critiques of marriage, feminists have pointed out that even though weddings are typically presented as emblems of conclusion, they in fact signal the beginning of married life. When the book is closed, or the credits roll, the carriage might turn back into a pumpkin, the prince back to a frog, and the real work of maintaining a long-term intimate partnership begins (Doherty, 2010, p. 26). For women, becoming a wife has often meant entering into a relation of structural subordination characterised by disadvantage, poverty, exploitation, and even violence (Brook, 2007, 2014). Gayle Rubin (1975), for example, famously argued that in the patriarchal economy, wives are objects of trade, and the terms of the bargain are decided almost entirely by men. (If this sounds anachronistic, consider the standard value of an engagement ring, the appropriate cost of which is often calculated as a proportion of the fiancé's wage.) In a similar vein, Christine Delphy and Diana Leonard (1992) assert that when women marry, their labour, in its many forms, is appropriated by men as husbands and patriarchs. Delphy and Leonard's Marxist framework may lack contemporary appeal, but their analysis of women's labour – including emotional and sexual work as well as domestic labour, housework, and household production – remains compelling. Women continue to shoulder a much larger share of housework than men, despite couples' protestations of egalitarianism in their domestic arrangements (Bittman and Pixley, 1997; Maushart, 2001). Far from designating a happy end-point, weddings may mark the festooned gates to endlessly mundane and subordinated wifehood.

This critique, echoed in a variety of ways by feminists analysing marriage across a wide range of times and places, sounds a generalised warning against romance and marriage. As Linda Mizejewski (2010) argues, romantic comedies make a spectacle of 'the extraordinary excitement of romance and gloss over the ordinary habits, duties, aches, and routines of long-term commitment' (p. 39). The critique invites the cynical suspicion that marriage must be dressed up and perfumed to be presented as the perfect romantic denouement in order to disguise its true ugliness and stink. The charges may seem heavy-handed, but the idea that in popular culture as in life, weddings serve as the pretty lure designed to trap us in unhappy matrimony is not without historical weight. As Mizejewski (2010) notes, '[m]any film scholars agree that romantic comedies emerged in the 1930s as a response to the decline of marriage and spiking of divorce rates in the previous 10 years' (p. 34), suggesting that whenever marriage is perceived to be under some kind of social threat, romantic comedy undergoes a revival. Similarly, the raft of divorce law reforms that occurred in the United States (and elsewhere) in the 1970s and 1980s prompted a resurgence of mainstream wedding-themed movies (Deleyto, 2003, p. 167; Mortimer, 2010, p. 17). Thus, while Gill and Herdieckerhoff (2006) marvel at 'the extraordinary tenacity of notions of heterosexual romance against the backdrop of significant cultural and demographic changes, including divorce on a hitherto unprecedented scale, an increase in the number of single person households, and a diversification of family forms' (pp. 489–490), that backdrop of change and anxiety might in fact fuel social or cultural desires to resolve those tensions.

The anxiety romantic comedies address, according to Mizejewski (2010), is the fear 'that men and women can't trust each other, that love may not be enough to fill the horrifying gap between the sexes' (p. 18). It might be argued, of course, that in its typical incarnation, romantic comedy creates as much as reflects gender difference (Lapsley and Westlake, 1992, p. 28), offering opportunities for pleasure as anxieties are produced and then neatly assuaged. In romantic comedies, as a rule, men and women are 'properly' different: opposites attract and even antagonise each other (Tasker, 2011, p. 67; Neale and Krutnik, 1990, p. 142; Doherty, 2010, p. 26), and love bridges all manner of differences (Kendall, 1990) – including class: *Wedding Crashers* (Dir., Dobkin, 2005), *Pretty Woman* (1990); ethnicity: *My Big Fat Greek Wedding* (Dir., Zwick, 2002), *Green Card* (Dir., Weir, 1990), *Hitch* (2005), *Something New* (Dir., Hamri, 2006); and even (though hardly typically or straightforwardly) disability: *Benny & Joon* (Dir., Chechik, 1993), *50 First Dates* (Dir., Segal, 2004). What has to happen in order to facilitate resolution is, more often than not, some kind of awakening on the part of the female protagonist. She must realise that she is a 'people-pleaser' like Emma in *Bride Wars* (2009), too controlling like Mary in *The*

Wedding Planner (2001), or too focused on her career like Margaret in *The Proposal* (2009). Like Goldilocks' porridge, she is in the first instance always and inevitably either lacking or excessive. The heroine who (eventually) recognises and corrects her faults (or has her faults identified and corrected by another) is the heroine who finds true love or, rather, love 'finds' *her*. Being corrected, transformed, and discovered by others, women are typically the done-to objects rather than the doing subjects of romantic comedy. The wedding as resolution, then, is a kind of bridle; weddings are women-wrangling solutions to the problem of 'unruly' women (after Rowe, 1995). It should be noted that the wedding is by no means the only solution, but walks hand in hand with consumerist alternatives, especially where women's unruliness is ostensibly evident in their appearance. The 'solution' may occur at the level of fantasy, on screen, in novels, or at the perfume counter, but it is not so much extraordinary as predictable. Thus, it is conceivable that while feminist critiques of marriage work to separate romantic love and marriage, fairy tale romantic comedies work – like all the king's horses and all the king's men – to put them back together again.

I have already suggested that romantic comedies seem to proliferate in response to social anxieties about marriage. That does not mean, however, that they do not change: as Peter Evans and Celestino Deleyto (1998) demonstrate, 'cultural variations [in romantic comedy] have been incorporated into the genre in several areas that attest not only to the genre's resilience but also to its flexibility to adapt to historical change' (p. 3). Given the reforms that are currently under way in many parts of Hollywood's global audience reach, we should expect cinematic responses to anxiety about same-sex marriage to be emerging and increasing. I would argue that this is precisely what is beginning to occur, not just in narratives focused around pivotal gay and lesbian characters, like *The Kids Are All Right* (Dir., Cholodenko, 2010), *Kiss the Bride* (Dir., Cox, 2008) or *In and Out* (Dir., Oz, 1997), but in movies whose action occurs at the boundaries of friendship and romance; the homosocial and the homoerotic; or, if I may, between bromance and homance. While I agree, for the most part, with Debra A. Moddelmog's (2009) view that Hollywood romantic comedies generally serve conservative and straight purposes, I am more hopeful than she that there is some room for more progressive political manoeuvre, even if those spaces are sometimes tight and awkward.[6]

I Love You, Man (2009), *Bridesmaids* (2011), *Bride Wars* (2009), and *Wedding Crashers* (2005) all include elements of the typical hetero-romantic comedy, but the centrality of the romantic relationship as opposed to a same-sex friendship is inverted. In standard hetero-rom-com fare, usually the same-sex friend is a source of advice (misguided or true) intended to complicate or progress the hetero-protagonists' love relationship. In these contemporary movies, however, love relationships are secondary to a central friendship. It is Liv and Emma's friendship in *Bride Wars* (2009) that is introduced, ruptured, then re-established (Winch, 2011); it is the central relationship of Lillian and Annie (and not Annie's emergent romance with Nathan) driving the narrative in *Bridesmaids* (2011); the duplicitous John and Jeremy's double-dating friendship is the key relationship in *Wedding Crashers* (2005); and it is Peter and Sydney's nascent friendship, not Peter's impending wedding, demanding resolution in *I Love You, Man* (2009). While falling clearly, woefully short of anything resembling Alex Evans' (2009) vision of even tentatively 'gay Hollywood' (p. 41), all of these movies, to different degrees, can be interpreted as having homoerotic as well as homosocial nuances. Perhaps that overstates things; perhaps what (partially) redeems these movies is not that they are especially amenable to homoerotic readings,[7] but rather that they are not merely or relentlessly homophobic. They may not constitute a rainbow panorama of inclusive sexualities, but perhaps they do show us glimpses, to borrow Deleyto's (1998) words, of how 'the contemporary tensions between heterosexuality, . . . homosexuality and homosociality find their way into the narrative structures of romantic comedy' (p. 53) even if they remain broadly heteronormative. Another way to consider this is to think about how these films demonstrate that heteronormativity is itself – like gender (Butler, 1990) – not immutable (Beasley et al., 2012).

In effect, feminist critiques contrasting the social conditions of marriage to its cultural packaging as the culmination of fairy tale romance amount to a critique of the mystification of marriage. The harsher aspects of the marriage-as-trap critique belie its complexity. The gendered work romance performs is lifelong, insistent, and deeply personal. We all know, for instance, that despite myriad references and consonances between cinematic and mundane life, what we see on screen are representations: we do not expect movies to mirror ordinary life in any precise way. Rather, even while we may be utterly absorbed and engaged with them, we know that movies are crafted, that they conform to any number of generic formulae, that they are cultural artefacts whose structure, situations, characters and rhythms differ markedly from ordinary life. The processes involved in watching and making sense of movies (and other representations) form the focus of a second, equally compelling vein of feminist critique.

While critiques of romance as mystification are sweeping and diverse, critiques of the gendered economy of looking are particular and profound, drawing on intellectually challenging psychoanalytic and philosophical frameworks. Laura Mulvey's work – beginning with her highly influential essay, 'Visual Pleasure and Narrative Cinema' (1975) – is the best known of these. Mulvey argues that the visual economy of cinema is gendered such that men are routinely figured as looking, while women are positioned as looked at. Complex relations of power and identification, repeated over and over again, mean that the 'male gaze', or the power not just to see but to organise visual meaning, becomes a mechanism of gender domination. The lesson is ubiquitous and strongly evident across a range of genres and styles (Martin and Kazyak 2009, pp. 328–332; Coca, 2011, p. 17). The tyranny of the male gaze does not mean that women cannot perform active roles, or that only men have the ability and means to envision films. Rather, it suggests a plausible rationale for women's objectification and its effects – including some aspects of viewing pleasure (Brook, 2008; Williams, 1984). The psychoanalytic contours of Mulvey and her contemporaries' accounts (Doane et al., 1984, for example) may be difficult to grasp in their entirety, but some of their insights can be illustrated in easy and immediate ways.[8]

To succeed in Hollywood, for example, women must be much more than merely excellent actors. To compete for most roles, they must also be young, slim, able-bodied, white, and, above all, beautiful (Radner and Stringer, 2011, p. 4). The New York Film Academy surveyed the 500 top-grossing movies released between 2007 and 2012. In these very popular films, nearly 30 per cent of women who appeared on-screen wore sexually revealing clothes, as opposed to only 7 per cent of men (New York Film Academy, 2013). When the camera pans a woman's body from toes to top, or zooms in on her breasts, or legs, or mouth, it adopts an objectifying male gaze. This objectification – or the process of turning a person into a thing – is, as Jean Kilbourne (1999) suggests, the first step in making violence against that person more acceptable.

It is not just that women are 'for' looking at; often, the camera follows a male character's point of view in watching a woman who does not, or cannot, look back. Women are symbolically or temporarily blinded, but remain visible. Consider, for example, the romantic cliché that when a woman removes her glasses she becomes instantly more beautiful, as if reducing her ability to see enhances her attractiveness as a vision. Women's vision is limited to a kind of internalised male gaze, or a kind of speculation as to how others might interpret the 'look' a woman exhibits. Women survey themselves (Berger 1972); we see female protagonists assessing and remedying their looks in familiarly feminine ways. In *Bride Wars* (2009), Liv and Emma go dress shopping, Liv goes to the hairdresser, Emma goes to a spray-tanning salon.[9] In *27 Dresses*, Jane models the eponymous bridesmaids' dresses for Kevin. In *Bridesmaids* (2011), the very first time we meet the heroine, Annie, she is sneaking out of bed to apply makeup and brush her teeth in order to 'wake up' looking pretty and fresh. Female characters often use mirrors, and as movie viewers, we watch women watching themselves. The cinema screen becomes, in effect, itself a kind of magic mirror. One interpretation of the frequency with which women are shown as self-surveilling mirror-users is that the dominance of the male gaze encourages women to participate in competing against each other for (objectified) attention. In this way, we internalise the male gaze and comply with its terms, even if individual women reject or contest its disciplinary tactics.[10]

The positioning of women as objects of sight is evident not just in movies, or even just in visual culture more generally (although it is certainly evident there): it is also part of fairy tale traditions. Snow White sleeps (eyes closed) in a glass coffin (remaining visible); Sleeping Beauty appears as an object of beauty, loved and courted by princes even though she neither sees nor speaks. Indeed, in Hollywood (as in governments, boardrooms, and classrooms) women have fewer speaking parts than men.[11] The romantic cliché sees the leading man silence his voluble and often complaining counterpart with – of course – a kiss. In a thoughtful and incisive analysis, Eleanor Hersey (2007) identifies what she describes as a new trend in romantic comedy. Hersey posits public speech-making by the romantic comedy heroine as kind of empowered alternative to a kissing or wedding resolution. Hersey's analysis is compelling, demonstrating how the female protagonists in *Miss Congenialty* (2000), *The Princess Diaries* (2001), and other popular movies are positioned as much more than docile objects of the (male) gaze. Certainly these instances signify something other than simple or total feminine submission. As such, perhaps Hersey can be read as warning against understanding 'the male gaze' as totalising and inevitable, instead confirming the versatility and variation apparent in romantic comedy.

The bigger picture, however, demonstrates that women do not share anything like equal screen time or equal spoils with men. Using Forbes' listing of the top ten male and female actors' earnings, the New York Film Academy (2013) revealed that '[i]n 2013 the highest paid female actor, Angelina Jolie, made $33 million, roughly the same amount as the two lowest-ranked men'. Further, 'of the sixteen biggest paychecks earned by actors per film, not a single one was earned by a female actor'. The Academy reported that women are underrepresented behind the scenes as writers, producers, cinematographers and directors, as well as commanding less screen time and competing for fewer acting roles than men (NYFA, 2013; Greenhill and Matrix 2010b, p. 16). Given these continuing gender inequalities, I am not as sure as Hersey (2007) that films in which the heroine leads, speaks, or rejects subordination 'represent the increasing presence of women filmmakers in Hollywood' (p. 151), nor that they comprise as strong a counterpoint to existing stereotypes as Hersey suggests.[12] Hersey recounts that in *The Princess Diaries* (2001), Mia (Anne Hathaway) eventually kisses Michael, who asks 'Why me?' Mia responds 'Because you saw me when I was invisible' (p. 155). I wonder, then, whether the movies Hersey highlights continue to figure a seeing and knowing male character, albeit one who recognises a more completely human female.

If it is not already clear that relations of looking are implicated in gendered power relations, consider how knowledge and looking are routinely likened in speech: when we understand, we say 'I see'; we 'take a closer look' or 'look into' matters requiring our attention; we 'speculate' on solutions to problems, offer 'insights', and so on. (Even the word 'theory' is etymologically linked to sight.) These kinds of utterances are consistent with a broader social discourse that analogises and equates knowledge and sight. Little wonder, then, that so many male protagonists in wedding movies know the heroine's desires or destiny better than she does herself. In *Bridesmaids* (2011), for example, Officer Rhodes (as Mr Right to Kristen Wiig's Annie) affirms Annie's vocation (she is a cake baker) at precisely the moment when she has given up on her cake shop. Indeed, in movies as in fairy tales, men (often literally) awaken women to their 'true' value; and that value becomes inextricably linked to their ability to be loved. The subject–object dichotomy is once again evident here: romantic comedy heroines are often the victims – or apparent victims – of unrequited or otherwise misdirected love. In the opening scenes of *What Happens in Vegas* (2008), for example, Cameron Diaz's character is dumped in humiliating fashion by her fiancé. We know a long time before they do that she and Ashton Kutcher's character are the 'right' match. This is another pleasurable manifestation of 'the male gaze' in that our position, as knowing viewers, is 'with' the male protagonist; as audiences we almost always identify 'perfect' love matches well before the couple involved does, and this knowledge usually comes to the female protagonist last of all. Key moments of transformation, then, usually occur not to the male protagonist but to the heroine, whose transformation tends to conform to the (knowing) male lead's vision of her.

Both of the feminist critiques outlined here – that wedding culture mystifies marriage, and that viewing experiences are thoroughly coloured by gendered power relations – have enduring analytical traction. Marriage continues to be presented, at least some of the time, as a destination for women, even if it is not necessarily the end of the line famously lamented by Betty Friedan (1963). Wedding magic is seductive, but the marriage trap is arguably and, for some women at least, not the shackle it once was (Spender, 1994). While divorce is certainly much more acceptable than it was thirty or forty years ago, and spinsters are no longer quite as obviously pitiful as they once were, marriage remains a social and mostly heteronormative expectation; weddings are still a source of heavily gendered pleasure. This does not mean, of course, that the desire to be married or to enjoy a beautiful wedding is foolish – far from it. Many people continue to take great comfort, nourishment, support and satisfaction in their marriage relationships in life as in movies. The pleasures of romance may be manufactured, and arguably fleeting, but that does not make them any less real.[13] Indeed, it is precisely because the coupled-up happiness depicted in wedding movies is not entirely illusory that our interest in it, and our hopes for it, are sustained.

Similarly, even though romantic comedy is routinely feminised and thus often subject to derision, feminist work from Janice Radway's (1984) ground-breaking work on women who read 'trashy' romance novels, to Hilary Radner's (2011) recent work on 'chick flicks', affirms that there is (or should be) no shame in enjoying activities that conform to gender norms, whether or not one is aware of those norms. Indeed, it seems likely that cultural forms or genres preferred by women are widely derogated simply *because* they are preferred by women. In other words, whatever women enjoy, value and create is deemed less worthy than what men do. (Imagine, for example, if knitting had the same social weight as, say, football. Champion knitters would be household names, there would be hours of expert stitch and pattern analysis on television, and there would be something disgraceful about wearing a machine-knitted scarf.) Enjoying 'princess' culture and wedding movies is in no way inherently or necessarily culturally inferior to more 'masculine' pursuits, even if their social value is heavily gendered and fiercely policed.

In the same way, (some) women's enjoyment of gendered beautification processes does not mean that women are vapid or vain. Women ought not to be criticised for equating beauty and happiness, or thinness and success. The processes of identification and representation discussed here are complex, and are so thoroughly social and yet immediately personal that it is all but impossible to step outside them. The cinematic Ugly Duckling's makeover implies, as do countless magazine articles and advertisements, that with the right magic, anyone can be made beautiful (Heyes, 2007; Jones, 2008). Such stories are not just about being chosen by a prince, but may also offer consolation to the spurned and the romantically 'invisible'. Being subject to an objectifying male gaze and negotiating its effects as competently as one can does not necessarily imply a docile acceptance of such conditions. Moreover, in the age of selfies, photoshopping, Instagram and other highly visual modes of self-presentation, it is not inconceivable that women's skills in self-surveillance might develop into something of a gendered asset, albeit in a relatively small and very partial sense. It is true, too, that men are being increasingly addressed as consumers of toiletries and cosmetics – even if they are addressed in markedly different ways from women. In relation to exercise programs, for example, the usual imperative is for women to become smaller/lighter but for men to become bigger/heavier. Similarly, ads for men's cosmetics associate the products with activity and energy, rather than simply 'correcting' defects or attracting admiring glances, as is more typical in advertising directed to women. In any case, bringing men into the fold of cosmetics consumption by elevating their anxiety about their looks is certainly nothing to celebrate (unless you hold shares in Unilever or L'Oreal). Perhaps the escalation of attention to personal appearance is just another grim symptom of consumer-culture decadence, where appearances matter more than substance, and where violence is ever more normalised.

It is not my intention, then, to conclude that women must 'rise above' our silly interest in romantic fairy tales if we are to embrace a feminist future. On the contrary, my interest lies in better understanding the conditions and mechanisms that underpin the gendered appeal of romantic comedies, wedding movies, and their fairy tale elements. Once these are clearer, one can see that enjoying wedding movies might be in some ways very much like participating in the lottery. We know that the odds of winning millions are remote, just as we know we are unlikely ever to experience the happily ever after fairy tale ending. Some of us buy lottery tickets even when we know that we are more likely to be struck by lightning twice than to win; some of us enjoy romantic comedy even though we recognise it as an idealised, manufactured, highly heteronormative and strongly gendered representation. Perhaps we pay, in both cases, not because we expect to win, but for the opportunity to fantasise that we might.

Having a critical attitude towards consumer capitalism's culture of affluence, waste, and poverty does not mean that there is no pleasure in imagining being rich, just as criticising heteronormative culture's stupid and damaging constructions of gender and sexuality does not make fantasies about being the object/subject of beauty and adoration redundant. Personally, I am not a romantic. But anyone can dream, and even feminists fall in love.[14]

Notes

1 See Zipes (2010) on the traffic between fairy tale traditions and Disney movies.
2 On 'makeover' movies more generally, including their relationship to weddings/marriage, see Ferriss (2008).
3 For interesting examples, see Joosen (2004); Lieberman (1989); Rowe (1979); Walker (1987); Pershing and Gablehouse (2010).
4 For discussion of 'chick flicks' and their features, see Radner (2011, pp. 36–39); Hollinger (2008); Ferriss and Young (2008). On moving beyond derisive attitudes to romantic comedy as a genre, see Deleyto (2009) and Garrett (2012).
5 For example, see Haskell (1974); for elaboration, Gill and Herdieckerhoff (2006); Garrett (2012).

6 Of course, they are not inevitably awkward – especially when treated by independent or non-Hollywood filmmakers. Consider, for example, the recently released *Blue is the Warmest Colour* (Dir., Kechiche, 2013), or *Better than Chocolate* (Dir., Wheeler, 1999).

7 See Doherty's (2010) scathing rejection of the possibility of *Bride Wars* being interpreted as 'a coded lesbian romance'.

8 Mulvey's work has been subject to critique and even auto-critique, and is clearly historically specific, addressing particular movie texts and not others. Aspects of her work are unappealing to me: for example, as a way to 'solve' or ameliorate the male gaze, Mulvey recommended non-narrative cinematic strategies. That such forms may be less popular than more familiar, mainstream movies speaks to her point, perhaps, but also indicates some limitations in her approach. For more, see Mulvey (2010) and Kaplan (2010).

9 For more on the intersection of beautification, consumption and gender in romantic comedy, see Winch (2011); for more on the gendered economy of looking and consumption, see Brook (2008).

10 The gaze is not just gendered, it also intersects with a range of other subordinating tactics, including, of course, racism. Moddelmog (2009) notes, for example, that 'a list of fifty love scenes in the top-grossing movies contains no scenes featuring people of color' (p. 164). For more on mirrors and their metaphorical and analytical uses, see Berger (1972), Bacchilega (1997, pp. 28–29), Grant (2011, pp. 293–294).

11 Only 30.8 per cent of speaking characters are women (NYFA, 2013).

12 For contrasting (feminist) interpretations of *Miss Congeniality* (2000), see Hersey (2007) and Sherman (2011).

13 See for example Hefner and Wilson's (2013) analysis.

14 Thanks to Sandie Price (personal communication, 2012) for this phrase, borrowed, in turn, from Stevi Jackson's (1993) article.

References

Bacchilega, C. (1993). An introduction to the 'Innocent Persecuted Heroine' fairy tale. *Western Folklore* 52 (1), 1–12 (Special issue: 'Perspectives on the Innocent Persecuted Heroine in fairy tales').

Bacchilega, C. (1997). *Postmodern fairy tales: gender and narrative strategies.* Philadelphia: University of Pennsylvania Press.

Beasley, C., Brook, H. and Holmes, M. (2012). *Heterosexuality in theory and practice.* New York: Routledge.

Berger, J. (1972). *Ways of seeing.* London: BBC/Penguin.

Bittman, M. and Pixley, J. (1997). *The double life of the family.* St Leonards, NSW: Allen and Unwin.

Bordwell, D. (2006). *The way Hollywood tells it: story and style in modern movies.* Berkeley: University of California Press.

Bradshaw, P. (2011, 24 June). Review of the movie *Bridesmaids. Guardian.* www.theguardian.com/film/2011/jun/23/bridesmaids-review

Brook, H. (2007). *Conjugal rites.* New York: Palgrave Macmillan.

Brook, H. (2008). Feed your face. *Continuum: Journal of Media and Cultural Studies* 22 (1), 141–157.

Brook, H. (2014). *Conjugality: governing marriage and marriage-like relationships.* New York: Palgrave Macmillan.

Butler, J. (1990). *Gender trouble: feminism and the subversion of identity.* New York: Routledge.

Canavese, P. (2009). Review of the movie *Bride Wars. Groucho Reviews* (online), Retrieved from http://grouchoreviews.com/reviews/3406

Coca, A. (2011). A reflection on the development of gender construction in 'classic' Disney films. *Amsterdam Social Science* 3 (1), 7–20.

Cockrell, E. (2009, 15 January). Review of the movie *Bride Wars*. *Sydney Morning Herald*.

Cohen, P. M. (2010). What have clothes got to do with it? Romantic comedy and the female gaze. *Southwest Review* 95 (1/2), 78–88.

Dargis, M. (2011). Deflating that big, puffy white gown (Review of the movie *Bridesmaids*). *New York Times*, 12 May 2011.

Deleyto, A. C. (1998). They lived happily ever after: ending contemporary romantic comedy. *Miscelánea: A journal of English and American Studies* 19, 39–55.

Deleyto, C. (2003). Between friends: love and friendship in contemporary Hollywood romantic comedy. *Screen* 44 (2), 167–182.

Deleyto, C. (2009). *The secret life of romantic comedy*. Manchester: Manchester University Press.

Delphy, C. and Leonard, D. (1992). *Familiar exploitation: a new analysis of marriage in contemporary western societies*. Cambridge: Polity.

Doane, M. A., Mellencamp, P. and Williams, L. (eds) (1984). *Re-vision: essays in feminist film criticism*. Los Angeles, CA/Frederick, MD: The American Film Institute/University Publications of America.

Doherty, T. (2010). The rom-com genre and the shopping gene. *OAH (Organization of American Historians) Magazine of History*, April: 25–28.

Evans, A. (2009). How homo can Hollywood be? Remaking queer authenticity from *To Wong Foo* to *Brokeback Mountain*. *Journal of Film and Video* 61 (4), 41–54.

Evans, P. W. and Deleyto, C. (1998). *Terms of endearment: Hollywood romantic comedy of the 1980s and 1990s*. Edinburgh: Edinburgh University Press.

Ferriss, S. (2008). Fashioning femininity in the makeover flick. In S. Ferris and M. Young (eds) *Chick flicks: contemporary women at the movies* (pp. 41–57). New York: Routledge.

Ferriss, S. and Young, M. (eds) (2008). Introduction: chick flicks and chick culture. In *Chick flicks: contemporary women at the movies* (pp. 1–25). New York: Routledge.

Friedan, B. (1963). *The feminine mystique*. London: Victor Gollancz.

Garrett, R. (2012). Female fantasy and post-feminist politics in Nora Ephron's screenplays. *Journal of Screenwriting* 3 (2), 177–196.

Gill, R. and Herdieckerhoff, E. (2006). Rewriting the romance. *Feminist Media Studies* 6 (4), 487–504.

Grant, B. K. (2011). 'When the woman looks': *Haute Tension* (2003) and the horrors of heteronormativity. In H. Radner and R. Stringer (eds), *Feminism at the movies: understanding gender in contemporary popular cinema* (pp. 283–295). New York: Routledge.

Greenhill, P. and Matrix, S. E. (eds) (2010a). *Fairy tale films: visions of ambiguity*. Logan: Utah State University Press.

Greenhill, P. and Matrix, S. E. (eds) (2010b). Introduction: envisioning ambiguity: fairy tale films. In *Fairy tale films: visions of ambiguity* (pp. 1–22). Logan: Utah State University Press.

Haskell, M. (1974). *From reverence to rape: the treatment of women in the movies*. New York: Penguin.

Hefner, V. and Wilson, B. J. (2013). From love at first sight to soul mate: the influence of romantic ideals in popular films on young people's beliefs about relationships. *Communication Monographs* 80 (2), 150–175.

Henneberg, S. (2010). Moms do badly, but grandmas do worse: the nexus of sexism and ageism in children's classics. *Journal of Aging Studies* 24, 125–134.

Hersey, E. (2007). Love and microphones: romantic comedy heroines as public speakers. *Journal of Popular Film and Television* 34 (4), 146–159.

Heyes, C. J. (2007). Cosmetic surgery and the televisual makeover. *Feminist Media Studies* 7 (1), 17–32.

Hollinger, K. (2008). Afterword: once I got beyond the name *chick flick*. In S. Ferriss and M. Young (eds), *Chick flicks: contemporary women at the movies* (pp. 221–232). New York: Routledge.

Jackson, S. (1993). Even sociologists fall in love: an exploration in the sociology of emotions. *Sociology* 27 (2), 201–220.

Jones, M. (2008). Media-bodies and screen-births: cosmetic surgery reality television. *Continuum: Journal of Media and Cultural Studies* 22 (4), 515–524.

Jones, S. S. (1993). The innocent persecuted heroine genre: an analysis of its structure and themes. *Western Folklore* 52 (1), 13–41 (Special issue: 'Perspectives on the Innocent Persecuted Heroine in fairy tales').

Joosen, V. (2004). Feminist criticism and the fairy tale. *New Review of Children's Literature and Librarianship* 10 (1), 5–14.

Kaklamanidou, B. (2013). *Genre, gender and the effects of neoliberalism: the new millennium Hollywood rom com.* London and New York: Routledge.

Kaplan, E. Ann. (2010). Is the gaze male? In M. Furstenau (ed.), *The film theory reader: debates and arguments* (pp. 209–221). New York: Routledge.

Kapsis, R. E. (2009, originally published 1991). Hollywood genres and the production of culture perspective. In T. Miller (ed.), *The contemporary Hollywood reader* (pp. 3–16). London and New York: Routledge.

Kendall, E. (1990). *The runaway bride: Hollywood romantic comedy of the 1930s.* New York: Knopf.

Kilbourne, J. (1999). *Deadly persuasion: why women and girls must fight the addictive power of advertising.* New York: Free Press.

Kirkland, E. (2007). Romantic comedy and the construction of heterosexuality. *Scope: An Online Journal of Film and TV Studies*, issue 9. Retrieved from www.scope.nottingham. ac.uk/article.php?issue=9&id=957

Lapsley, R. and Westlake, M. (1992). From *Casablanca* to *Pretty Woman*: the politics of romance. *Screen* 33 (1), 27–49.

Lieberman, M. K. (1989). 'Some day my prince will come': female acculturation through the fairy tale. In J. Zipes (ed.), *Don't bet on the prince: contemporary feminist fairy tales in North America and England* (pp. 185–200). New York: Routledge.

Martin, K. A. and Kazyak, E. (2009). Hetero-romantic love and heterosexiness in children's G-rated films. *Gender and Society* 23, 315–336.

Maushart, S. (2001). Wifework: what marriage really means for women. New York: Bloomsbury.

Mizejewski, L. (2010). Rules and unruliness: romantic comedy. In *It happened one night* (ch. 1). Oxford: Wiley-Blackwell.

Moddelmog, D. A. (2009). Can romantic comedy be gay? Hollywood romance, citizenship, and same-sex marriage panic. *Journal of Popular Film and Television* 36 (4), 162–173.

Mortimer, C. (2010). *Romantic comedy.* Routledge film guidebooks. London and New York: Routledge.

Mulvey, L. (1975). Visual pleasure and narrative cinema. *Screen* 16 (3), 6–18.

Mulvey, L. (2010). Afterthoughts on 'Visual pleasure and narrative cinema'. In M. Furstenau (ed.), *The film theory reader: debates and arguments.* New York: Routledge.

Murphy, K. (2009, 17 January). Review of the movie *Bride Wars*. *The Australian*.

Murphy, R. (2001). *The British cinema book* (2nd edn). London: British Film Institute.

Neale, S. and Krutnik, F. (1990). *Popular film and television comedy.* London: Routledge.

New York Film Academy (NYFA). (2013). Gender inequality in film. Published 25 November 2013; www.nyfa.edu/film-school-blog/gender-inequality-in-film/

Panayiotou, A. (2010). 'Macho' managers and organizational heroes: competing masculinities in popular films. *Organization* 17 (6), 659–683.

Pershing, L. and Gablehouse, L. (2010). Disney's *Enchanted:* patriarchal backlash and nostalgia in a fairy tale film. In P. Greenhill and S. E. Matrix (eds), *Fairy tale films: visions of ambiguity* (pp. 137–156). Logan: Utah State University Press.

Price, Sandie. (2013). Personal communication. 12 September 2013.

Radner, H. (1993). 'Pretty is as pretty does': free enterprise and the marriage plot. In J. Collins, H. Radner and A. P. Collins (eds), *Film theory goes to the movies* (pp. 56–76). London: Routledge.

Radner, H. (2011). *Neo-feminist cinema: girly films, chick flicks and consumer culture.* New York: Routledge.

Radner, H. and Stringer, R. (eds) (2011). Introduction: 're-vision'?: feminist film criticism in the twenty-first century. In *Feminism at the movies: understanding gender in contemporary popular cinema* (pp. 1–9). New York: Routledge.

Radway, J. (1984). *Reading the romance: women, patriarchy and popular literature.* Chapel Hill: University of North Carolina Press.

Robey, T. (2009, 9 January). Review of the movie *Bride Wars. The Telegraph* (UK).

Rowe, K. E. (1979). Feminism and fairy tales. *Women's Studies: An Inter-disciplinary Journal* 6 (3), 237–257.

Rowe, K. (1995). *The unruly woman: gender and the genres of laughter.* Austin: University of Texas Press.

Rubin, G. (1975). The traffic in women: notes on the 'political economy' of sex. In R. R. Reiter (ed.), *Toward an anthropology of women* (pp. 157–210). New York: Monthly Review Press.

Sherman, Y. D. (2011). Neoliberal femininity in *Miss Congeniality* (2000). In H. Radner and R. Stringer (eds), *Feminism at the movies: understanding gender in contemporary popular cinema* (pp. 80–92). New York: Routledge.

Spender, D. (ed.) (1994). *Weddings and wives.* Ringwood, VIC: Penguin.

Tasker, Y. (2011). *Enchanted* (2007) by postfeminism: gender, irony, and the new romantic comedy. In H. Radner and R. Stringer (eds), *Feminism at the movies: understanding gender in contemporary popular cinema* (pp. 67–79). New York: Routledge.

Travers, P. (2009, 8 January). Review of the movie *Bride Wars. Rolling Stone.*

Vogler, C. (1992). *The writer's journey: mythic structure for storytellers and screenwriters.* Studio City, CA: M. Wiese Productions.

Walker, M. E. (1987). Book review of Jack Zipes (ed.), *Don't bet on the prince. American Anthropologist* 89 (2), 511.

Williams, C. (2010). The shoe still fits: *Ever After* and the pursuit of a feminist Cinderella. In P. Greenhill and S. E. Matrix (eds), *Fairy tale films: visions of ambiguity* (pp. 99–115). Logan: Utah State University Press.

Williams, L. (1984). When the woman looks. In M. A. Doane, P. Mellencamp and L. Williams (eds), *Re-vision: essays in feminist film criticism* (pp. 83–99). Los Angeles, CA/Frederick, MD: The American Film Institute/University Publications of America.

Winch, A. (2011). We can have it all. *Feminist Media Studies* 12 (1), 69–82.

Zipes, J. (2006). *Why fairy tales stick: the evolution and relevance of a genre.* New York: Routledge.

Zipes, J. (2010). Foreword: grounding the spell: the fairy tale film and transformation. In P. Greenhill and S. E. Matrix (eds), *Fairy tale films: visions of ambiguity* (pp. ix–xiii). Logan: Utah State University Press.

9

THE MYTH OF AUTHENTIC SELF-ACTUALISATION

Happiness, transformation and reality TV

Greg Singh

> *The cult of the personality is a product of the myth of the individual. According to this myth, history is made by extraordinary men (and a few women), irrespective of social movements. The myth has two inflections. One stresses individual achievement through personal effort and competition, and particularly serves the interests of capital. The other is the folk myth (the Cinderella story or the Log-Cabin-to-White-House story) in which the individual succeeds through nature or fate, rather than effort, position or circumstance. The first inflection foregrounds labour, the second denies it and offers genius in its place. The myth of individualism, like all myths, is contradictory.*
>
> (Lusted, 1986, p. 73)

> *Cinderella is a symbolic narrative about how appearances can deceive, and how money to buy into a beautiful lifestyle isn't everything. Cinderella, recall, changes her outward trappings, not her face. [. . .] Evidently the ugly stepsisters should have got the Extreme Team to surgically trim down their feet (rather than struggling bloodily to force them into the glass slipper), because then they would become prince-marrying material.*
>
> (Heyes, 2007, p. 28)

The psychological effects of a twenty-first-century culture are already moving into an advanced stage of development; tentatively, and somewhat provocatively speaking, we might identify this stage as 'postmodern' or even 'post, postmodern'. My preferred term, following Marc Augé's *Non-Places* (1995), is 'supermodern' in acknowledgement of a peculiar phenomenon where the postmodern was in a sense always co-present with (or at the very least, germinant within) modernity. It is a transitory state of non-place, which is both alienating and disaffecting, and for which the genre of reality TV plays a key role in both reproducing and deflecting. Clearly there are a number of ways in which this idea is being addressed through both cultural and psychological theory and depending on whom one is reading this might be considered a nightmarish malady, or otherwise an opportunity for exploration and expression unbounded by the reactionary constraints of the past.

In her book *Jung, Irigaray, Individuation* Frances Gray (2008, p. 63) writes that:

> Myths, as bearers of symbol and meaning, tell stories that attempt to prescribe, explain and proscribe the dimensions of human being. The success or failure of each story is related to the constitution of the greater collective of which the discourse forms a part.

In tune with the very title of this book, relating to the myth of happiness, Gray's argument implies that in order to gain the happiness that so many of us seem to crave we would need to be 'successful' in navigating a path through the blind corners, dead-ends and red herrings of signs and symbols arising through myths in order to profit meaningfully from them. In other words it is necessary to listen to these myths and what they are really telling us through their use of symbols; what path are we on and how can we tell whether it is a 'right' path?

However, as implied in Gray's overview, given the context in which she addresses feminist philosophy in relation to Jungian psychology (to which I return later in this chapter), the paths that lie before us, whether trailed by us or laid for us, are characterised by proscriptions that we as social beings are subject to. In supermodern societies such as the one we find ourselves in today, the hyper-consumerist urge to follow an individual path, to 'find' oneself, or to reveal one's 'true', authentic self through making 'tough' choices, we find myths of self-actualisation and transformation to that end all around us. One of the richest examples of this (as well as, with all symbolic regimes) is reality TV though it is the most impoverished. This chapter seeks to explore some of the cultural effects of our times as reflected through the watchful lens of reality TV – that curiously always-already-hybrid TV genre that, whilst promoting lifestyles and aspirational narratives that promise happiness of one sort or another, seems to take in the aesthetics and concerns of a whole host of cultural phenomena from fashion and celebrity, to self- and home-improvement and all in between.

Reality/myth television

Reality TV programming shows and tells through the presentation of narratives of sometimes deeply moving 'personal journeys'; albeit narratives that are shared potentially by millions in a synoptic vision of 'one watched by many'. Through these personal journeys of others, viewers are invited to share in the emotion of the protagonists too – in a level of vicariousness unprecedented outside of religious rites and rituals. Indeed, as implied in the epigraph to this chapter, Lusted notes that a 'cult of personality' exists whereby television elevates ordinary people into the realm of the extraordinary, investing a select few with special properties (usually by virtue of success in some sort of performance – a task, or a contest – or even by virtue of being likeable – a judge panel or public vote).

This elevation in the popular imagination requires emotional investment and effort, encouraged through peripheral media coverage of the participants in commentary and news reports – what I would describe, following Stephen Heath (1981), as 'narrative image'. Heath describes narrative image as 'A film's presence, how it can be talked about, what it can be sold and bought on' (1981, p. 121). I have discussed this concept elsewhere (Singh, 2014) in relation to cinema's secondary and tertiary production practices, and it is useful when applied to moving image and media culture more generally. As Lawrence Kramer (2009) suggests, the concept translates especially well to series television: 'The episodes are concretizations of a general series plot that cannot be represented directly' (ibid., p. 202). This can be taken in two ways with regard to reality TV. First, in the sense that reality TV shows tend to be driven through character and personality, and the narrative drive towards achieving a state of self-actualisation – a narrative trajectory common to both factual and drama programming. Second, following John Ellis's 1982 discussion of narrative image, instances of a TV programme's narrative image, for example audition 'tapes' of contestants posted on the website accompanying a reality TV series, are enigmas: such materials are essentially offers or teasers, in which what is offered in the series (participants winning, losing, finding themselves and so on during the course of a programme episode) is a resolution to the promises of ephemeral marketing and promotional material.

As Lusted suggests, 'The myth of individualism', in my view the driving narrative underpinning success in reality TV, where people win or lose by the effectiveness of their labour or their genius, 'like all myths, is contradictory' (1986, p. 73). Analytical and depth psychology offer tools and methods through which we might explore such phenomena that link deep-seated meaningful acts allowing public 'buy-in' and emotional investiture with altogether more superficial trending behaviour, and this chapter will discuss these links to the psychological and political realities of myths of transformation towards a supposedly 'authentic' self-actualisation.

It ought to be noted that the fact that reality TV is viewed with such suspicion and even scorn in most academic scholarship (even some work in cultural studies that tends to be quite sympathetic to the consumption of such media) is partly due to an elitist attitude towards it as a trivial cultural form, and partly due to its hybrid nature, inasmuch as it tends to be neither entirely factual nor entirely fiction. As Annette Hill has noted, 'Reality TV is a catch-all category that includes a wide range of entertainment programmes about real people. Sometimes called popular factual television, reality TV is located in border territories, between information and entertainment, documentary and drama' (2005, p. 2). Therefore, whether or not such elitism and distrust that I have identified as associated with the 'genre' are misplaced, there seems little point in denying that a troublesome undercurrent in attempting to place reality TV within a generic taxonomy gives rise to some implications for both viewers and participants (how they are seen, and how they see themselves) featured in these programmes. This is worth a brief overview here, particularly from the media studies and television studies traditions of analysis, to which I shall give further treatment later in the chapter. The first question ought to be: well, what *is* reality TV?

Reality TV, like all television genres (if indeed it may be said to be a 'genre'), may be described as something of a hybrid that takes in a whole host of stylistic, formal and subject specifics. When taken as a whole, these specifics address many of the concerns of contemporary popular culture. There are programmes associated with hygiene (*How Clean Is Your House?*; *Embarrassing Bodies*); with finding a sexual partner or soul mate (*Snog, Marry, Avoid*); with revealing personal problems and talking about them in order to find a solution (*The Jeremy Kyle Show*); with talent competitions that have biographical components and occasionally a celebrity component (*Strictly Come Dancing*; *X-Factor*; *Britain's Got Talent*); with property (*Relocation, Relocation, Relocation*; *Grand Designs*; *Property Ladder*); programmes which frequently include a component of 'reinventing' oneself or one's lifestyle through property consumption; and, of course, with fashion, design, and personal appearance (*10 Years Younger*; Gok Wan's *How to Look Good Naked*).

In sum, this admittedly selective list indicates a number of things, but there are two commonalities in particular that seem to me to be of crucial significance. First, many or all of these subgeneric themes have a substantial crossover in terms of reality TV programming. Most tell (sometimes extraordinary) stories about ordinary people, 'real' people, sometimes revealing celebrities as being as 'normal' as their viewership, at others placing the mundane or everyday in wider social contexts (the medical profession, for example in the case of chemical peeling procedures featured in *10 Years Younger*, or the condition of the national economy, as is the case with property programming) in the name of consumer interests. Second, they are all kinds of programmes that tell their stories through some sort of transformation narrative, often framed in the convention of a 'personal journey' that the presenter or the protagonist or subject of the show undergoes (or is compelled to take on) in order to facilitate that transformation. These 'journeys' in reality television are for the most part metaphorical, although many examples exist where the participant undertakes a geographical journey through a place (*Long Way Down*), or a narrative one through history (*Vikings*); sometimes both, as in the case of Brian Cox and his *Wonders of the Solar System* series – a series hardly identifiable as reality programming by itself, but which undergoes its own personal transformation in the guise of fan videos as well as the transformation of Cox himself into a celebrity academic beyond television.

For Hill, 'Most television scholars who discuss reality TV tend to include a variety of television genres in their definitions of the "reality genre" precisely because reality TV borrows from so many different existing genres' (2005, p. 49). Bignell and Orlebar, for example, define reality TV as: 'A vague term for programmes where the unscripted behaviour of "ordinary people" is the focus of interest, where documentary observation is often combined with elements of the game show, make over or talent contest' (2005, p. 318). Obviously, this opens up the definition to a large selection of programming. For Casey et al. (2002, p. 196):

The label 'reality TV' encompasses a wide range of texts which take as their subject matter real lives, real-life situations and events, and first-person accounts of ordinary people (non-media professionals). Within this context, the personal, emotional and often intimate revelations of the first-person accounts are the driving force behind the narrative structure of these programmes, supported with actual footage (or dramatic reconstructions) of the events concerned.

In addition, following Jonathan Dovey's *Freakshow: First Person Media and Factual Television* (2000), Casey *et al.* state that 'reality TV is the perfect form for the times in which we live, in that it provides a cultural space where contemporary anxieties are played out within a dramatic structure and in an entertaining format' (Casey et al., 2002, p. 197). In other words, in addition to indifferent or distracted casual viewing habits associated with the way audiences have been found to watch television, the 'realities' played out in the narratives of such programmes have the potential to draw strong sympathy or antipathy precisely because audiences can relate to the people and the situations. Viewers sometimes recognise themselves in the participants of such shows, or understand the experiences as familiar, even though the truth claims of reality TV may not be taken very seriously and 'by its very nature popular factual entertainment sits in the spaces between fact and fiction' (Hill, 2005, p. 49).

It could be argued that this recognition of the familiar arises from the narrative work of an individualist myth, where participants in the programmes win against the odds. Again, Lusted sees these issues in television more generally as contradictory but powerful in terms of attracting the sympathy of viewers, precisely because viewers recognise a kindred spirit in the underdog: 'Within those contradictions the social groups who make up factions of television's audiences may also find alternative recognitions, affirmations and identifications that are even oppositional to the dominant tendencies of television's personality system' (1986, p. 74). I would argue that these contradictions have, if anything, intensified in the era of reality TV as television's 'personality system' offers up figures of derision and vilification – the notion of the celebrity 'Z-list': those personalities who, frequently emerging from reality TV coverage, rise to fame seemingly for no reason other than the coverage itself.

Yet, in a legacy from its humble docusoap and drama-documentary beginnings, reality TV programming invites audiences to experience the lives of other people (as ordinary people transformed into some kind of celebrity, or cases where celebrities are revealed to be ordinary) – a raison d'être which, for Bignell and Orlebar, 'carries an assumption of both realism and social responsibility' (2005, p. 106). Whether factual programming takes these assumptions seriously is up for question: the legacy of television documentary as a mirror on society – to presumably show the diversity of a society, and the issues that affect all within a society – seems to be wearing thin. For, as Bignell and Orlebar (2005, p. 115) continue:

Reality TV has emerged as a term that describes programmes characterised by a controlled environment, free of documentary's heritage of social issues. [. . .] The result is not the authenticity and explanation of documentary, but rather the spectacle of the everyday and an emphasis on the performance of identity.

This seems especially so in relation to makeover programming (of the body, the home, the car, pet or child behaviour) where the goal is to transform the subject undergoing the personal journey into something unrecognisable from what was there before; to transform the subject into its true essence, its authentic self. Dana Heller (2007, p. 3) takes this transformation narrative to its inexorable limit:

> contemporary makeover programming provides the paradigmatic example of reality television's prominence and far-reaching mass appeal. Specifically, that appeal lies in [. . .] a televisual performance that does not merely attempt to capture reality but transform it, with the ultimate aim of remodelling reality.

It is interesting that, if it is to be accepted that transforming reality is a goal of this form of programming, that transformation can occur unproblematically and without the need to address the social issues underlying the necessary 'problem' to which these 'solutions' are offered. Indeed, it may even be said that these programmes, with their melodramatic, personality-driven format, hardly need to do this; that they 'solve' problems that do not exist in the first place. In other words, the myth of happiness (i.e. 'if only this problem could be solved – only then, would I be happy') may itself be a social by-product of a process of being shown what dissatisfaction looks like, in turn engendering a sense of unease and unhappiness, which itself in turn prompts many of us to seek the easy distractions of reality TV programming, and so on. This is, obviously, a more disturbing trend, and one to which I return later in the chapter, with regard to gendered aspects. What seems obvious is that such programming functions semiotically as narratives of transformation, without the epilogue of social responsibility as a concern. Caroline Dover and Annette Hill (2007, p. 24) note of makeover show audiences that:

> Those who enjoy makeover shows do so because of the programmes' emotional and entertaining content; they do not tend to have high expectations of watching informative or true-to-life content. Our research shows that life-style programme viewers are not isolated viewers of this particular genre, but savvy viewers who are aware of general trends within non-fictional television.

However, as Roscoe and Hight have noted (2001, p. 8), in the first place:

> Documentary does not provide an unmediated view of the world, nor can it live up to its claims to be a mirror on society. Rather, like any fictional text, it is constructed with a view to producing certain versions of the social world.

So even though, as Bignell and Orelbar admit, documentaries claim to make an argument and centre upon evidence through a regime of realist representation, 'this usually includes some reliance on narration and interpretation. In other words, documentary always has a point of view, even if it claims to be a neutral one' (2005, p. 106). More often than not, this point of view places emphasis on the personal over and above any robust social commentary. The idea of television approximating what participants of factual programming repeatedly refer to as their 'personal journey' suggests that the myth of individualism has a fast hold on the schedules and, following Dover and Hill, audiences not only do not mind this but have an active preference for it.

This might be why aspects of melodrama have come to characterise most reality TV programming today. I return to the notion of melodrama towards the end of this chapter, as it seems to tie together the various strands of vicariousness and discourses of personal transformation that inhabit such shows. Following Annette Hill, one might say that melodrama and facts meld seamlessly, largely due to the contradictory nature of how audiences tend to assess participants of reality TV. For Hill (2005, p. 65), this is based upon a perceived:

> authenticity of real people's stories and situations within the performative environment of popular factual television. This mode of engagement involves criticism of the truth claims of reality programming, but also some degree of trust in the old adage 'the truth will out'.

Indeed, for analytical psychology, these overdetermined combinations of contradiction might reveal aspects of the symbolic in the genre. However, treated as they are in a literal and materialistic manner, such symbols are merely performative affectation.[1] Particularly striking examples of this 'real performance' of transformation may be found in a scan of lifestyle programming in particular, with its emphasis on conspicuous consumption, fashion and trends. I return to the makeover show as a particular instance of this in a moment. Before that I would like to discuss a very specific case in which a rather different kind of reality TV contest is caught in this journey of the 'makeover'.

'Disarm with charm' – gendered dynamics of reality TV

The latest series of *The Apprentice* (Series 9, BBC1, 2013) was a notable example of the kind of entrenched transformation narrative I have been describing so far. It featured a prize where the winner would get to set up their own enterprise, with a 50 per cent stake in the business owned by arch-entrepreneur and government business 'Tsar', Lord Sugar – presiding over and judging the budding entrepreneurs competing in the programme. The series saw the usual reality TV drama as the contestants fought it out for Lord Sugar's affections, at the same time undermining each other's efforts through subterfuge, self-declared psychological games, battles of wits and lots of shouting. Indeed, this scenario seems to visualise a much more pantomime-driven inflection of this Prince Charming character of fairytale – there seems to be precious little charm in Lord Sugar's arsenal of psychological weaponry. The contestants live in a shared house, and much like students in shared accommodation sometimes develop familial relationships that provide a support network and some much needed respite from the homesickness often felt under such circumstances. So the contestants developed sibling-like relationships which often spilled into the contest. Quite the Oedipal drama, then, this series of *The Apprentice* in common with previous seasons sought to represent the 'journey' of the contestants as they showed us that the world of business is a tough, dog-eat-dog world in which winners are celebrated (through meritocratic achievement and, importantly, 'self-made' individualist ascendance) and losers are cast aside as unsuitable 'entrepreneurial consorts' for Lord Sugar's attention. In the latest run of this programme the final rounds were (as notably and repeatedly reported in the tabloids) exclusively contested by female participants.

The series winner, Leah Totton, won with her idea to start up a chain of walk-in clinics where customers would be able to have consultations for cosmetic procedures and, provided they have the money, would be able to purchase treatments such as chemical peels, botox injections and skin-plumping, under the kinds of medical conditions that Totton (a medical graduate and A&E doctor) assured Lord Sugar would be implemented. It perhaps ought not to matter that former WAG Totton, 24 and now single, is a conventionally attractive young woman with an astounding collection of designer business clothes and a luxurious mane of blonde hair. The fact is, however, that the very same misogynist language I have just performatively used to describe her (note the careful inclusion of her marital status and age – an invariable inclusion in news reports about her, less invariable in the reports on her fellow male contestants) is the one constant that seems to characterise her public narrative image. Over a soundtrack of playful plucked strings at the start of her audition 'tape' for the series, posted on the programme's website,[2] Totton pronounces, 'I am vibrant, I'm ambitious and I'm pretty intelligent.' This opens up for the viewer a clear juxtaposition of beauty and intelligence, the cultural archetypical dyad that seems to signify that, somehow, these two attributes shouldn't be together. This is, of course, a nonsense as well as a mythology reinforced through the powerful narrative trope of surprise at the fact that someone *could* be both intelligent and beautiful. Indeed, more recently, such flimsy mythology in the name of 'surprise' turns of events has fallen apart in the face of mixed publicity in the events following the opening of the first Dr Leah clinic.

The very idea that personality can only ever be one thing or another thing might be overly simplistic. Indeed, it is something that we would probably find impossible to accept. Yet, it is a trope precisely because we see its like, repeated time and again in reality TV – particularly in formats where women compete, and where looks are foundational to a winning formula. One such example can be found in the reaction from the judges (Simon Cowell, Amanda Holden and Piers Morgan) to the first performance of 'I Dreamed a Dream' during the 2009 season of *Britain's Got Talent* (ITV, 2007–present).

Without trying to take anything away from Boyle, who is after all clearly a talented singer even if one may not consider her a particularly great one, there was an overwhelmingly positive response from the audience who, upon their initial encounter with Boyle, had been less than welcoming (Morgan: 'everyone was laughing at you. No-one is laughing now.') and now allowed themselves to be transformed by the fact that Boyle was anything more than what they had clearly assumed her to be. In Holden's words;

> I'm so thrilled because I know that everybody was against you. I honestly think that we were all being very cynical and I think that's the biggest wake-up call ever and I just want to say that it was a complete privilege listening to that.

The audience, whose noisy reaction was clearly an outpouring of collective trickster energy – an example of the trickster's general penchant for 'making, shaking and remaking of the social order', in Bassil-Morozow's words (2012, p. 7) – were now wholly on-side, overcompensating for their initial rejection of Boyle, whose looks have since been the subject of ridicule and hateful rhetoric from some quarters in the press. The point here is that the 'trick' being played (up for question as much as by and upon whom) seems principally to centre on the ambivalent notion that Boyle could deviate so sharply from the formula of expectations of the genre. For, as Morgan goes on to say, 'Amazing. I'm reeling from shock – I don't know about you two [looks to Holden and Cowell] but I can't believe it.' Indeed, neither, it seems, can Boyle quite believe it. Further reality programming featuring Boyle's career shows us the true face of the trickster collective, detailing the failure of Boyle to contain (for us, the audience) such a critical mass of contradictions. Her rather public break-down, and revelations in the tabloids of a 'tormented' soul suffering from Asperger's syndrome, indicate another example of how we are shown tortured genius as a mythology of the power of the journey towards happiness. In this respect, Boyle is repeatedly used as a recipient for trickster projections, and rather generally performs the role without necessarily being given the opportunity to deal with it.

Thus, in her audition video, Totton decides to play on this kind of ambivalence, this incredulity, as a fully conscious nod towards the mythos of the intelligent beauty. Even as she notes that 'I feel like I'm an excellent contender, I'm a very academic person . . . I'm a blue-sky thinker . . . ', rapid edits interject a sentiment which give the viewer the distinct impression that *she* feels that it needs to be said: 'I think I'm quite glamorous . . . I'm also a fantastic business mind . . . I've sort of got everything really'. The caption for the video anchors this persona as a way of communicating just *who* Totton is supposed to be: 'There's no need for bitchiness in business, says laid-back Leah. She prefers to "disarm with charm". And being a doctor, she's happy to get her hands dirty.' This is telling, and for a number of reasons. First, in terms of there being 'no need for bitchiness in business', this seems to make little sense in relation to a reality show where the raison d'être is to transform an ambitious but talented unknown into a business mogul, and apprentice to Lord Sugar. For, if it is indeed the case that there is 'no need for bitchiness in business', then why do repeated cultural images of Malthusian self-preservation saturate reality programming (and in *The Apprentice* particularly are not only unquestioned, but positively encouraged), and why are notions of so-called 'social Darwinism' so embedded in conventional world-views more generally? If anything, *The Apprentice* acts as an advertisement for survival-of-the-fittest attitudes. In terms of Totton's intention to 'disarm with charm' (in other words, the apprentice casts an irresistible spell upon the master; sets a glamour upon him), one needs only to refer to the book of clichés on the gendered ability to seduce the opposite sex as a somehow essential quality, charged particularly negatively in the case of women who are prepared to use these essential 'feminine wiles': the 'playing field' can never be level when one begins to analyse such social dynamics. For a start, why would women need to use 'feminine wiles' if everyone was treated equally, and everyone had an equal chance for success as the meritocratic mythology of modern Western democracies persists? A modern fairy tale, if there ever was. In addition, why then are women repeatedly exposed, humiliated and demonised in the media when they choose to use their looks to their advantage? This gendered division of labour, reflective of and reflected in a highly gendered media culture, has been subject to analysis and criticism and yet the mythology of equality persists: that those battles have been long won.

As Kate Millet pointed out (2000, p. 25) in 1969:

> While patriarchy as an institution is a social constant so deeply entrenched as to run through all other political, social, or economic forms, whether of caste or class, feudality or bureaucracy, just as it pervades all major religions, it also exhibits great variety in history and locale.

A radical feminist borne by the wings of the counterculture and the burgeoning civil rights and women's liberation movements of the late 1960s, Millet's views are quite clearly of their time. The arguments, as common in tabloid newspaper editorials as much as in lifestyle television and indeed in the classroom discussions of cultural studies students all over the UK, run that we are all equal now and indeed these battles have been won. It is with this in mind that we ought to pay close attention to Millet's argument: that although 'the principles of patriarchy appear to be two fold: male shall dominate female, elder male shall dominate younger', 'contradictions and exceptions do exist within the system' (2000, p. 25). In the cases of the sort under discussion in this chapter, I am concerned with moving from a systemic patriarchy in the purely socio-political sense, to a notion of the patriarchal image as a structuring principle, in a psychological sense, and back again. Millet's 'social constant' is, for me, a psychological reality also perhaps primarily so, following Samuels' (2009) politically charged analytical view of the structuring presence of collective psychology in the socio political sphere. The 'variety' of patriarchy that we are dealing with here is specifically transformed into its current image through the mythology of entrepreneurship – the third element of the caption anchoring Totton's audition into a specific meaning. In short, by declaring that Totton is 'happy to get her hands dirty', the idea of being a self-made free agent is promoted; a myth of individualism as a trajectory along which we all travel; the ultimate journey of the self, in media culture's own terminology, here coloured through the tint of manual labour, is transformed into skilled craftsmanship. In this case, Totton's profession-alised craftsmanship, in the medical and surgical precision of cosmetic procedures, is mirrored through her almost alchemical transformation from medical graduate to business partner of Alan Sugar, and her more general narrative image as an ambiguous brains/beauty personality.

Individualisation and individuation as distinct (mythical) processes

The philosopher Cressida Heyes has researched makeover and lifestyle programming in the UK, the US and Canada extensively, and it is useful here to turn to her Foucauldian-inflected analysis of makeover programmes to expand upon the kinds of ambiguities I have been discussing. Heyes (2007, p. 17) states that:

> The televisual makeover can be usefully interpreted, I argue, using the concept of normalization – that double and contradictory historical process Foucault describes by which developmental standards for populations are deployed to measure and enforce conformity at the same time as they generate modes of individuality. Normalization, on this view, both constrains (by compelling compliance with the norm) at the same time as it enables (by making certain forms of subjectivity possible), and, indeed, these two functions cannot be clearly separated.

In her essay '*Twilight*: Discourse Theory and Jung' Catriona Miller has shown that, although on the face of it, the Jungian depth approach and the Foucauldian discourse approach seem incompatible, she concludes that more work is needed in rethinking these two approaches as complementary, as they 'both arrive at the fuzzy boundaries of self and society' (2011, pp. 185–6). She writes (2011, p. 191):

> In some ways, perhaps, this is the biggest obstacle in bringing together a Jungian description with one based on discourse analysis. The ways in which 'identity' is thought to be constituted are in conflict. Discourse analysts tend towards the position that identity is produced by discourse. Jungians tend towards the idea that identity is a universal core arising from archetypes. [. . .] There is a sense in both perspectives, however, that there must be a link between the 'inner' subject and the 'outer' discourse, but how that link might work is unclear.

It is my contention that Heyes has identified a suitable discursive model to describe the psychosocial dynamics through which systemic patriarchy and the psychological image of the patriarch are two sides of the same narrative running through the myth of authentic self-actualisation in reality TV programming. I would suggest that, taken in this context, we can see that Miller's views can be adapted to think through the link between these two quite different but complementary processes at work in a larger psychosocial system. The more archetypical individualisation process, which takes its cues from a mythical narrative of progression towards an authentic self-actualisation in the trajectory of reality TV participants, ought to be accommodated as a discursive value within the altogether more depth-inflected process of individuation, to which Jung made such important contributions. The key to the difference in discourse and depth approaches is, to my mind, that they together form a cluster of processes. Indeed, some cultural theorists have been keen to view discursive formations of identity through the lens of psychology, in order to foreground interiorised psychological processes underpinning one's sense of self. Miller points to Stuart Hall's appropriation of Lacan in the service of this project, for example. She goes on (2011, p. 193, emphasis in original) to write that:

> It has been suggested in fact that any attempt to modify one's subject position within discourse (necessary if any possibility of resistance or the 'choice to act' is to be conserved) requires an 'emotional shift in being' (Hall, 1996). Emotion, although defined in a performative sense (one *does* emotion rather than *having* it), is seen as a marker of change.

What provides the motivation for such emotional shifts is an altogether bigger question. In the context of reality TV shows, one might speculate that the processes whereby the kinds of aforementioned 'alternative recognitions, affirmations and identifications' in personality-driven factual melodrama are psychological grounds within which such shifts in emotional investment and emphasis take place. The fact that reality TV tends to focus on the emotional aspects of personal journeys of transformation and the experiences that such transformations can offer is doubly significant here, as it seems to parody what is generally considered the altogether more serious and thorough-going psychic process of individuation.

That the deep processes are characterised by personal transformations (that often include profound and significant psychic insights and accommodations) ought to come as little surprise to Jungian scholars. Educational psychologists Robert D. Boyd and Jean Saul Rannells view these transformations in a thematic way (1990, p. 164). In contrast to Boyd and Rannells's view of personal transformation, the kinds of personal transformations taking place in reality TV more usually involve what I would describe as *archetypical* themes: themes revolving around pathways to individualisation rather than individuation. I deliberately use the term archetypical to describe this individualisation pathway, rather than the more conventional Jungian themes of archetypes as structuring principles, following on from my previous work in relation to this kind of abundant, excessive trope (Singh, 2011). This is a useful distinction mainly because the 'personal journeys' so often relayed to us in confessional forms in reality TV programmes, most often in testimonials by the participants themselves, are primarily constructs which engage myths of transformation at their most academicised, recognisable and repeatable.

'The transformative point-of-view', write Boyd and Rannells, 'is an overarching conceptualization of individuation symbolized as a death of one aspect of our being and a rebirth of that aspect within an expanded consciousness' (1990, p. 165). However, the transformations that occur in reality TV, although partaking of archetypical tropes revealed as thinly veiled sacred narratives of conversion, sacrifice and benediction, have little to do with expanding consciousness. In fact, if anything, the personal journeys of transformation towards an 'authentic' self-actualisation, 'the real me', might be seen as more akin to processes of entrenched, regressive consciousness.

Boyd and Rannells offer a thematic perspective on individuation, and one of their key themes is that of empowerment – visualised by those authors as occurring through a struggle to unite the ego's consciousness of its existing strengths with the inner powers of the Self. However, in such makeover programming where the path towards authentic self-actualisation is characterised by normalisation, such struggle may be seen as negated in favour of a more immediately gratifying outcome: melodrama. Not that melodrama is without its value – in fact, for Leslie Gardner (2011), melodrama is a collective archetype; and as such, is a way to forge an understanding of the inner world of emotion with the outer world of cultural expression, as a psychological experience. She writes that 'elements of melodrama conform to our inner hyperbolic imaginings of feeling, suffering, sacrifice and redemption. These elements participate at a deep level in the collective as complexes which seize us all' (Gardner, 2011, p. 153).

What is interesting to note about Totton's role in the final stages of the competition is that she, in having to compete exclusively with other women, takes on the symbolic character of what Luke Hockley identifies elsewhere in this collection in connection with similar fictional female characters as the 'male fantasy of the Female Warrior'. Additionally, despite her awareness of such imaginative investment – her audition testimony: 'If I'm backed into a corner, I'm obviously gonna . . . gonna defend myself, especially if I feel like I'm in the right' – she proves inadequate to the task, because the overwhelming burden of two such conflicting personality attributes (the healer, the warrior) brings the authenticity of her (newly self-actualised) identity into dispute. The level of performance required for Totton to carry this contradiction proves impossible to sustain, and cracks begin to appear in her groomed, carefully managed and professionalised persona as 'high-powered entrepreneur'.

This is fairly common in reality TV, as Bignell and Orlebar (2005, p. 116) suggest:

> In Reality TV, the key moments in individual programmes are when the performance of the contestant falls away. This seems to reveal the real person, since the audience is aware that the rest of the time the contestant is performing the self that they wish to project.

I would argue that, supplementary to this, the TV self that is constructed is a performed version of the self carefully managed through scripting or script-like narrative developments based upon genre conventions, as in the mounting tension and melodramatic criticism in the boardroom sequences in *The Apprentice*, Totton's carefully presented and often self-declared professionalism, etc. In addition, and more importantly, perhaps, this performed self is both reproduced and undermined through the media coverage of both the shows and the contestants themselves, as for example witnessed in the revelations about Totton's 'ordinary' personality beneath the veneer of eyelashes and 'mane' of hair, in her encounter with *Daily Telegraph* feature writer Judith Woods (2013).

Sugar-daddy melodrama: *The Apprentice* as 'a sanitized fairy tale of identity becoming'

In her article, 'Apprentice Winner Leah Totton says: "My Pout Makes Me Cringe – It's Just Terrible"', Woods seems to go through a personal journey of her own, a performed and knowing transformation in which she appears at first to detest Totton. The article is peppered with references to Greek mythology and even expressions acquired by archetypal psychology: 'Totton, who hails from Derry, used to date a footballer as well as being a straight-A student and a hottie. But that's not the source of my animus.' Which tempts the reader to assume that it might be; and: 'No wonder every week tuning into *The Apprentice* was like watching Icarus fall, burning from the sky.' Thus, even in the most oblique instances of Totton's narrative image, the contradictory burden of symbolic healer/warrior, supported through the archetypical journey from medical graduate to full-blown entrepreneur, is reinforced. The journey Woods undertakes through her own performative discourse here segues from sceptic jealousy and petty hatred to trusted confidant, full of sisterly benefaction. Indeed, it seems that she has been 'disarmed with charm'. That is, until towards the end of the article, where Woods seems to backtrack once again on her rehabilitated attitude towards Totton. This see-sawing between the outlining of Totton's overachievement, Woods's playful attempt to account for her faux jealousy, and her clear (politically driven) admiration for aspirational culture leads one to suspect, once again, the collective work of trickster energy here. Totton, a careful persona of blissful unawares, caring only for doing what is the professional thing to do – '"I don't see it as moving over to the dark side, I see it as medicalising the dark side and casting a light onto it," she replies smoothly' – herself betrays a sense of playfulness; at least, in the register portrayed by Woods. Once again, we find a narrative image of overdetermined signals. It is here that we need to add to the political side of the analysis, this time coming back to Millet's ground-breaking work in the politics of gender and sexuality. The following casts its own light on the exchange in Woods's article; and also to the deeper complex interchange between trickster energy and the patriarchal image. Millet (2000, p. 38) wrote that:

> One of the chief effects of class within patriarchy is to set one woman against another, in the past creating a lively antagonism between whore and matron, and in the present between career woman and housewife. One envies the other her 'security' and prestige, while the envied yearns beyond the confines

of respectability for what she takes to be the other's freedom, adventure, and contact with the great world. Through the multiple advantages of the double standard, the male participates in both worlds, empowered by his superior social and economic resources to play the estranged women against each other as rivals. One might also recognise subsidiary status categories among women: not only is virtue class, but beauty and age as well.

It seems strangely apt, not to mention salient, that Millet's words should strike such a chord with contemporary reality TV, and the culture that surrounds, informs, and is informed by it. Almost a play-by-play account of the final rounds of *The Apprentice*, the staged rivalry and performed roles within the unholy ménage of Sugar, Totton and Louisa Zissman (who has since gone on to further reality TV fame in the most recent series of *Celebrity Big Brother*), Millet's incisive reading of the byzantine social hierarchies existing between men and women (and particularly older men and younger women) is eerily accurate in psychological terms. We may even see a trace of a (more usually Freudian) familial psychology, whereby the younger women are, through their rivalry, invigorating the entrepreneurial potency of the older patriarch. Freud, in his famous book *Totem and Taboo*, wrote that 'Parents are said to remain young with their children, and this is, in fact, one of the most valuable psychic benefits which parents derive from their children' (1938, p. 33). If applied in this context, the image of the patriarch is a carrier of the goal of self-actualisation of the contestants in *The Apprentice*: it is through his ritualised blessing that they perish or flourish. Clearly, this image can also act as a spiritual beachhead from which personal journeys can embark, energised as it is, through its own vicarious journey of invigoration. The familial undertones are simply too tempting to ignore.

If, following Millet, patriarchy's chief institution is the family, and following Freud, parents live through the emotional lives of their children, then in the approval of a reality TV judge, invested with the psychological power of the patriarch (or, indeed, the arch-rival matriarch), surely their decisions have the potential to carry deep emotional weight for the participants. Although I do not wish to speculate here that this kind of power might be extended to the viewer (although others, such as Annette Hill have tentatively suggested that this might be the case), what does seem clear is that this potential to be taken seriously is given legitimacy through the narrative images of those who participate, as either judges or judged, in these shows. Indeed, it seems that audiences do play a part, vicariously, in the way such judgement lives on in the popular imagination. As Hill describes, 'Audiences frequently discuss the difference between performed selves and true selves in reality programming, speculating and judging the behaviour of ordinary people, comparing the motives and actions of people who choose to take part in a reality programme' (2005, p. 68). This overflow of discourse from text to water cooler, online and beyond into the narrative image of reality show contestants, has its own transformative aspect, where the ordinariness of the people under discussion is amplified beyond the sphere of the personal and into that of the celebrity persona. At the same time, this celebrity persona carries the weight of personal transformation, and the contestants themselves (real people, let us not forget) carry the pressure of maintaining an impression of this movement between ordinary and extraordinary, the highly personal and the highly synoptic.

It is here that the myth of an authentic self-actualisation in reality programming seems to take on a powerful narrative life of its own. As Bignell and Orlebar (2005, p. 115) suggest:

> Reality TV programmes claim a kind of realism by demonstrating how contestants attempt to keep up the facade of the persona they want to create, and yet reveal a kind of authenticity beneath this. Reality TV therefore borrows, perhaps surprisingly, some of the values attributed in drama to 'realistic' acting, and connects this to documentary's revelation of current social issues by means of telling personal stories.

Indeed, Gray (2008, pp. 54–5) develops this kind of approach to the masquerade through a discussion of the more traditionally Jungian notion of persona, as represented through the symbolic-imaginary (the represented and represent-able expression of identity through everyday language and creative artistic construction), stating that:

> During early life and young adulthood, the persona develops as a response to the demands and expectations of its collective and the world. It becomes a person's mode of being in the world. [. . .] The persona is a construct, a system of relations that produces the illusion of individual I-ness.

This constructed nature of persona is, to my mind, important in thinking about how the myth of personal transformation is reproduced through reality TV. The most important aspect of this is perhaps the performative, melodramatic version of personhood who ends up being shown as the 'real me' of the participants involved. The mode of being that reality programming encourages is a literalised, transformed version. In this way, such a version is able to bear some of the burden of aspiration, for which such emotional investment (on the part of the audience, vicariously, and on behalf of the other participants, whose reactions in constructively stressful situations are often little more than emotional outbursts) would surely weigh heavily on anyone. Of course, how anyone could live up to that burden of expectation is part of the mythology: if only *we* could learn to do so, we might attain happiness.

Conclusion

There are two important points to make in relation to Boyd and Rannells's observations in connection with these issues of living up to the demands and expectations of the collective and the world: first, coming from the rather classical Jungian position, they regard myths as having enormous potential in moving an individual towards change, by joining contemporary experiences with archetypes arising from the dialogue between inner and outer lives. Second, in connection with their own study of a sample of women who, having taken a women's studies course, had felt empowered through their encounter with and discussion of mythologies involving deities, these figures were over-represented by female deities or goddesses. This is entirely understandable (and probably desirable) given the context of the sample and the subject matter as for Boyd and Rannells such educational programmes, in common with many early second-wave feminist aspirations, sought to empower women through a meaningful reconnection with old myths, featuring long-forgotten 'deities' or god-like figures which express a sense of self way beyond the newer, supermodern transient myths of individualisation. Of course, in some Jungian scholarship, the figures of such psychic power are given tremendous significance. These are 'deities' which impart knowledge about how things are at a more spiritual, or at least, holistic level. The message is therefore quite clear: transformation of the self through a connection between inner and outer worlds is possible. However, there are a couple of contentions that ought to be raised here. The first is that such over-reliance on 'old myths' is counter to any project which would seek to deconstruct, or indeed dispel, the rather glamorous and seductive prospect of recapturing a lost sense of self, of purpose and of individual merit. To rely on 'deities' in such a way would be to ignore their status as a literalisation of myth and symbol. My second contention here is that the kinds of 'deities' encountered in a semiological sense in reality TV are over-represented by male authority figures presiding over the 'journeys' undertaken, and those matriarchal images existing in reality TV are nobbled through a reductive representation: reduced to the status of rival, or to that of the 'revelatory', simple one-dimensionality of intelligent beauty. Whether Sugar, Cowell or a male cosmetic surgeon, such reality TV patriarchs are hardly conducive to fostering the kinds of realisations experienced by the subjects of Boyd and Rannells's study.

As Heyes suggests in the opening epigraph, for makeover contestants, sometimes this is taken to extreme measures to the extent that physical and irreversible change needs to occur before the authentic inner self can be actualised and, importantly, witnessed. Both Brenda Weber (2009) and Heyes discuss these extreme changes in relation to makeover programmes specifically. Shows such as *Extreme Makeover*, *The Swan* and *Ten Years Younger* present impossible outcomes. These shows tell us 'sanitized fairy tale[s] of identity becoming, in which the makeover enables the recipient to achieve longstanding personal goals presented as intrinsic to her own individual authenticity' (Heyes, 2007, p. 21). It is this sanitisation process, perhaps more than anything, which expresses the artifice of the myth of personal transformation in reality programming. For, if the fairy tale of individuation is to be at all persuasively real, then surely it is a messy psychological business, and worlds away from Dr Leah's cleansing and enlightening medicalisation thesis? In this chapter, I have extended their observations to other reality TV programming featuring the trope of transformation, and the achievement of authentic self-actualisation. It is through the narrative of empowerment that the normalisation process is both justified and desired: participants of reality TV fit into the expectation of what it is they ought to become, instead of truly becoming individuated; and even then, perhaps, such deflection from 'authentic' development is a ruse, for in the end the participants of reality TV may well be little more than recipients for collective fantasies about transformations where the personal journey we undergo can make anything seem possible.

Notes

1 I am grateful to Luke Hockley for pointing out the relevance of these contradictions for analytical psychology, in personal correspondence.
2 www.bbc.co.uk/programmes/p018chfx

References

Augé, M. (1995). *Non-Places: Introduction to an Anthropology of Supermodernity* (trans. John Howe). London: Verso.
Bassil-Morozow, H. (2012). *The Trickster in Contemporary Film*. Hove: Routledge.
Bignell, J. and Orlebar, J. (2005). *The Television Handbook* (3rd edn). Abingdon: Routledge.
Boyd, R. D. and Rannells, J. S. (1990). 'Individuation of Women Through Their Encounters with Deity Images', *Harvest* 36: 164–74.
Byers, M. and Johnson, V. M. (eds) (2009). *The CSI Effect: Television, Crime, and Governance*. Plymouth: Lexington Books.
Casey, B., Casey, N., Calvert, B., French, L. and Lewis, J. (2002). *Television Studies: The Key Concepts*. London: Routledge.
Dover, C. and Hill, A. (2007). 'Mapping Genres: Broadcaster and Audience Perceptions of Makeover Television', in D. Heller (ed.), *Makeover Television: Realities Remodelled* (pp. 23–38). London: I. B. Tauris.
Dovey, J. (2000). *Freakshow: First Person Media and Factual Television*. London: Pluto Press.
Ellis, J. (1982). *Visible Fictions: Cinema, Television, Video*. London: Routledge & Kegan Paul.
Freud, S. (1938/1919). *Totem and Taboo*. Harmondsworth: Penguin Books.
Gardner, L. (2011). 'Gestures of Excess: An Exploratory Analysis of Melodrama as a Collective Archetype', in L. Hockley and L. Gardner (eds), *House: The Wounded Healer on Television* (pp. 152–68). Hove: Routledge.
Gray, F. (2008). *Jung, Irigaray, Individuation: Philosophy, Analytical Psychology and the Question of the Feminine*. Hove: Routledge.
Hauke, C. and Hockley, L. (eds) (2011). *Jung and Film II – The Return: Further Post-Jungian Takes on the Moving Image*. Hove: Routledge.
Heath, S. (1981). *Questions of Cinema*. Bloomington: Indiana University Press.
Heller, D. (ed.) (2007). *Makeover Television: Realities Remodelled*. London: I. B. Tauris.
Heyes, Cressida J. (2007). 'Cosmetic Surgery and the Televisual Makeover: A Foucauldian Feminist Reading', *Feminist Media Studies* 7(1): 17–32.
Hill, A. (2005). *Reality TV: Factual Entertainment and Television Audiences*. Abingdon: Routledge.
Jerslev, A. (2008). 'Cosmetic Surgery and Mediated Body Theatre: The Designable Body on the Makeover Programme *The Swan*', *New Review of Film and Television Studies* 6(3) (December): 323–41.
Kramer, L. (2009). 'Forensic Music: Channelling the Dead on Post-9/11 Television', in M. Byers and V. M. Johnson (eds), *The CSI Effect: Television, Crime, and Governance* (pp. 201–20). Plymouth: Lexington Books.

Lusted, D. (1986). 'The Glut of the Personality', in L. Masterman (ed.), *Television Mythologies: Stars, Shows and Signs* (2nd edn) (pp. 73–81). London: Comedia/MK Press.

Masterman, L. (ed.) (1986). *Television Mythologies: Stars, Shows and Signs* (2nd edn). London: Comedia/MK Press.

Miller, C. (2011). 'Twilight: Discourse Theory and Jung', in C. Hauke and L. Hockley (eds), *Jung and Film II – The Return: Further Post-Jungian Takes on the Moving Image* (pp. 185–205). Hove: Routledge.

Millet, K. (2000/1969). *Sexual Politics*. Chicago: University of Illinois Press.

Roscoe, J. and Hight, C. (2001). *Faking It: Mock-Documentary and the Subversion of Factuality*. Manchester: Manchester University Press.

Samuels, A. (2009). 'The Economic Psyche: From Inequality to Utopic Fantasy (and Back Again)'. Conference keynote, 'Psyche, Power, and Society', IAJS/Cardiff University, 12 July 2009.

Singh, G. (2011). 'Cinephilia; or, Looking for Meaningfulness in Encounters with Cinema', in C. Hauke and L. Hockley (eds), *Jung and Film II – The Return: Further Post-Jungian Takes on the Moving Image* (pp. 163–84). Hove: Routledge.

Singh, G. (2014). *Feeling Film: Affect and Authenticity in Popular Cinema*. Hove: Routledge.

Weber, B. (2009). *Makeover TV: Selfhood, Citizenship, and Celebrity*. Durham, NC: Duke University Press.

Woods, J. (2013). 'Apprentice Winner Leah Totton Says: "My Pout Makes Me Cringe – It's Just Terrible"', *Daily Telegraph*, 17 July. Available: www.telegraph.co.uk/culture/tvandradio/the-apprentice/10184750/Apprentice-winner-Leah-Totton-says-My-pout-makes-me-cringe-its-just-terrible.html (accessed 21 January 2014).

10

A DIFFICULT TASK

Sarah Lund and the crime of individuated happiness

Alec Charles

The most famous tales of that Danish fabulist Hans Christian Andersen speak of how an uncompromising quest for truth may project an individual towards an integrity of meaning and being. Thus Andersen suggests the moral exigency of the small child who sees through the delusions and hypocrisies of political society to declare that the Emperor is in fact naked (Andersen, 2009, p. 106), and shows how the often agonizing and alienating processes of coming into individual being offer problematic yet potentially transformative paths towards happiness. A princess is only recognized as 'a real princess' (and therefore becomes a real princess) by virtue of her sensitivity to the most minute phenomena of the world, a perspicacity which ensures that she is kept awake at night and made miserable by the presence of a pea beneath twenty layers of mattresses (Andersen, 2009, p. 32). A duckling 'slighted by every creature' and 'oppressed by a peculiar sadness' eventually – driven suicidally to risk the company of those who he believes will kill him – is transfigured into a being of 'happiness' and 'splendour' (2009, pp. 258–260). And, perhaps most famously, a 'melancholy' mermaid who lacks 'an immortal soul' but who would 'come up from the bottom of the sea and find out how our world looked' – who 'dreamed of happiness and of an immortal soul' – and yet who remains disconnected from the world and the love to which she aspires and who therefore fails in her existential quest to develop a soul. Andersen's mermaid in the end, unwilling to murder the object of her unrequited love, is transformed into an ethereal being who floats away on the air but who may one day through the reality of experience come into soulful being and 'take part in the eternal happiness of men' (Andersen, 2009, pp. 80–100). This contemporary and countryman of Kierkegaard hereby offers an early existentialism as a form of fairytale – though it may be noted that Kierkegaard had in 1838 complained that Andersen's work lacked philosophy (Fenger, 2003, p. 307).

The problematic moralization of contemporary crime fiction often seems to serve a similar psychological function to such folklorish stories. Swedish crime writer Johan Theorin's *The Asylum* (2012, p. 134) describes its own fairytale, one discovered in that novel's eponymous madhouse, the story of a princess who declares: 'I'm not unhappy, I just like *unhappiness*!' The fairytale princess's declaration offers the possibility that the acknowledgement of the inevitability of the absurdity of existence – and therefore the acceptance of a resultant state of unhappiness – might in itself afford the chance of some sort of individual happiness. This chapter will examine how this notion of existential, psychical or moral individuation is explored by another popular Scandinavian tale of crime.

Forbrydelsen (Danish Broadcasting Corporation, 2007–2012) – literally 'the crime' but translated into English as 'the killing' – was created by Søren Sveistrup and starred Sofie Gråbøl as the emotionally repressed detective Sarah Lund, who is one of the most celebrated figures of Nordic noir. Over the course of its three seasons *The Killing* grew so popular, not only in its native Denmark but even in countries (such as the UK) whose television audiences have traditionally baulked at subtitled fare, that it merited the production of an American remake.

So why have so many people watched *The Killing*? The answer is, of course, that it brought them pleasure: pleasure in the darkness of its aesthetic and of its philosophy. There is something oddly life-affirming in the bleakness of *The Killing* – in the idea that, despite its acknowledgement of the futility and meaninglessness of being, despite utter disillusionment, the struggle to remain true to oneself remains ennobling and may even afford some prospect of happiness. We see something similar in the Sisyphean existence envisaged, for example, by Albert Camus (1975, p. 111), a condition, however absurd, wherein 'we must imagine Sisyphus happy.'

Sofie Gråbøl has described Sarah Lund as isolated and unable to communicate yet somehow at peace *(The Making of the Killing*, High Rising Productions, 2011). Lund is alienated from her family and detached from her colleagues – yet somehow at one with her own existence. As Sofie Gråbøl has said – on the subject of the character's predilection for Faroe Islands sweaters (Frost, 2011): 'It tells of a person who doesn't use her sexuality [. . .] Lund's so sure of herself she doesn't have to wear a suit. She's at peace with herself.' Gråbøl's juxtaposition of sexuality and self-assurance (or individual integrity) points to a degree of psychical maturation. As Jung (1928, para. 112) suggests, while youth is for the most part focused upon instinctual sexuality, maturity opens the possibility of 'the development of individuality'. Lund's transcendence of sexual immaturity in this way anticipates her path towards individuation.

Søren Sveistrup advances a response to the absurdity of existence experienced by that other great Dane, Søren Kierkegaard, but unlike Kierkegaard Sveistrup's response does not require the impossible absurdity of religious faith. There seems some disconsolate consolation in Sveistrup's position. It offers a community of despair or of meaninglessness which may not lead towards hope but which may afford the possibility of meaning. That is the extent of the happiness that we may, without recourse to the illusion of external destiny, be permitted to expect. In the fourth episode of the first season of *The Killing*, Lund is asked whether she believes in fate. She responds that she believes that people control their own lives. She adds that her own life is good. For Lund a good life, a life lived well, is one which is self-determined.

An existential hero

On the face of it Sarah Lund might not appear the most obvious of heroes. Lund is not only an avatar of a late postmodern zeitgeist of existential incoherence, disruption and exclusion, but also a figure who demonstrates an unorthodox capacity for an individuated mode of happiness, unlikely and difficult though that happiness might be. Her problematic relationship with the society she inhabits results from that society's refusal to accept her struggles towards individuation. The notion of happiness may herein be seen as dependent upon definitions imposed by structures of societal power which label unorthodox modes of happiness as unhappiness and that pathologize the appearance of unhappiness.

Sarah Lund is almost psychically incapable of compromising her own sense of self, even at massive personal cost. It is this absurd faith in her own capacity for individuation (and the necessity of that individuation as the only possible path to happiness, regardless of external demands and constraints) which defines her heroism – and which therefore addresses, invokes, attracts and offers an incongruous mode of faith to contemporary audiences. She acts at once as a saviour and a scapegoat who performs and suffers the almost irreconcilable existential tensions experienced by her audience; she consoles against, and atones for, those impossibilities.

Fictional detectives tend to be loners, unorthodox certainly, sometimes even outcasts. Although Ruth Rendell's Wexford and Camilla Läckberg's Patrik Hedström may seem uncharacteristically homely sorts, the genre is littered with confirmed bachelors and spinsters (Holmes, Poirot, Marple, brothers Cadfael and William of Baskerville, Father Brown), often alcoholics or drug addicts: Morse, Rebus, Jimmy McNulty, Carrie Mathison, Gregory House. As such figures as Lord Peter Wimsey demonstrate, psychical normativity and social integration are hardly prerequisites for fiction's most enduring detectives. In Scandinavian crime fiction, the likes of Lisbeth Salander, Hanne Wilhelmsen, Kurt Wallander, Harry Hole, Joona Linna and Malin Fors bear similar stigmata (or badges) of mental illness and drug and alcohol addiction; in these characters the alienation of the fictional detective meets that curiously Scandinavian sense of absurdity, angst and alienation epitomized in Denmark, Sweden and Norway by such figures as Kierkegaard, Bergman and Munch, a bitterly cold Nordic existentialism – as if, as Henning Mankell (2008, p. 13) supposed, that region's 'bleak and blustery landscape had seemed to awaken [. . .] deepest anxieties'.

Susan Hill (2012, p. 194) has characterized Nordic noir as the work of 'dark Scandinavians' and there may be some validity in her scepticism as to that cultural industry's repackaging of what Diane Keaton in Woody Allen's *Manhattan* (1979) described as the fashionable pessimism of a stereotypically bleak Scandinavian perspective. Yet these fairytales for an age in which psychoanalysis and existentialism have already grown old unfold their heroes' desperate quests for meaning in ways which reflect contemporary anxieties as to the possible impossibility of happiness and which thereby offer profoundly problematic pleasures to their audiences, pleasures whose complexities and contradictions frustrate their commercial commodification.

Albert Camus (1983, p. 118) in the afterword to his novel *The Outsider* points out that his hero's defining crime – that which seals his exclusion – is not his act of murder but his refusal to subsume his sense of truth to insincere sentiment: 'In our society any man who doesn't cry at his mother's funeral is liable to be condemned to death [. . .] Meersault doesn't play the game [. . .] he refuses to lie'. The experience of Camus's Meersault is shared by Jo Nesbø's Harry Hole: 'After they had buried Harry's mother he had gone five days without feeling anything, other than that he ought to have felt something' (Nesbø, 2012, p. 206). Hole inhabits a world whose occupants 'were desperately hoping that things would cohere, have some meaning' (Nesbø, 2013, p. 239), yet that meaning constantly eludes them. Hole shares his rejection of such sentiment with another Nordic detective, Mons Kallentoft's Malin Fors – a figure who also cannot mourn the death of her own mother (Kallentoft, 2013, p. 27). Malin Fors demonstrates a typical sense of alienation: 'like you're trapped in an autumn river full of dirty torrential water and you've made up your mind to float off into the darkness' (Kallentoft, 2012, p. 21). A similar sense of detachment is witnessed in the vulnerable and indomitable figure of Anne Holt's Hanne Wilhelmsen (Holt, 2011, pp. 31–32):

> My relationship to other people is [. . .] more academic in its nature. I would prefer not to have anything to do with them at all, something that can easily be interpreted as a lack of interest. That is incorrect. People do interest me [. . .] It's having people close to me that I find difficult. I am interested in people, but I don't want people to be interested in me.

(This detachment might indeed, some might say, be intrinsic to the analytic situation.)

Sarah Lund recalls such figures, and also brings to mind Stieg Larsson's Lisbeth Salander and her 'astonishing lack of emotional involvement' (Larsson, 2008, p. 33); yet she lacks Salander's psychical excesses. Lund is much more real than the fantastical (and sometimes almost superhuman) Salander. Salander, for all her darkness and her detachedness, is – unlike Lund – clearly on a path towards redemption: she finally, literally, opens the door to let trust 'into her life again' (Larsson, 2010, p. 743). Lisbeth Salander is a fantasy, absurd perhaps, yet absurd in the sense of a Kierkegaardian faith in praternatural fate. If Salander approximates Kierkegaard's redemptive and redeemed figure of Abraham, then Lund is closer to Camus's Meersault or Sisyphus.

In the fifth episode of *The Killing*'s second season another Sisyphean figure, the embattled justice minister Thomas Buch, interrupts his own press conference convened to announce his government's counter-terrorism measures agreed with the right-wing People's Party. As he listens to the People's Party leader's invective against

Islam, Buch sees his own face reflected in a coffee pot on the table before him; this absurd distortion exposes the absurdity of the situation in which he has found himself: he stands up and announces to the assembled journalists that this situation cannot continue. Buch's act of moral non-conformity anticipates Lund's own more radical moral stand and her ultimate moral transgression that is to come.

Sarah and Søren

Sarah was, as Lund's countryman Søren Kierkegaard (2005, pp. 9–13, 17–19) reminds us in his meditation upon that man of infinite faith, Abraham's wife in the Book of Genesis; Sarah was also, as Kierkegaard (2005, p. 127) goes on to remind us, the name of the heroine and avatar of faith in another book of the Hebrew Bible (one considered apocryphal by Protestantism but recognized by Roman Catholicism), the Book of Tobit.

The eponymous killing that frames and foreshadows Sarah Lund's narrative is eventually shown to be her own act of murder. Lund, like Abraham, comes to commit a cold-blooded (yet morally inevitable) killing at the very end of the series' final season; she also thereby comes to sacrifice her relationship with her own son. Yet, unlike Abraham, she not only *comes to* do these things but actually *does* them. The hypothetical absurdity of the divine test of faith that Abraham undergoes is reified into the actual absurdity of Sarah Lund's experience.

As epitomized by the figure of Abraham, the 'knight of faith' – Kierkegaard (2005, p. 44) tells us – acts entirely 'on the strength of the absurd [. . .] he drains in infinite resignation the deep sorrow of existence, he knows the bliss of infinity, he has felt the pain of renouncing everything, whatever is most precious in the world'. In short, Kierkegaard (2005, p. 45) observes that this figure of faith 'resigned everything infinitely, and then took everything back on the strength of the absurd'.

But what if, like Sarah Lund, you live in a world of existential absurdity modelled not upon Kierkegaard's anchoring faith but upon a Sartrean acknowledgement of nothingness? 'If there were no eternal consciousness in a man', says Kierkegaard (2005, p. 14), 'if at the bottom of everything there were only a wild ferment, a power that twisting in dark passions produced everything great or inconsequential; if an unfathomable, insatiable emptiness lay hid beneath everything, what would life be but despair?' Sarah Lund's world is a realm of Kierkegaardian absurdity without the possibility of Kierkegaardian faith: it is therefore the kingdom of an infinite resignation that cannot be redeemed, it is a domain of despair.

Kierkegaard (2008, p. 27) supposed that 'he who says without pretence that he despairs is [. . .] a little nearer [. . .] being cured than all those [. . .] who do not regard themselves as being in despair'. Sarah Lund may thus be *a little nearer* to the cure, but only tantalizingly so; she does not have the possibility of actually attaining it. Yet, like Kierkegaard's knight of faith, she retains, in the uncompromising integrity of her position, the possibility of a strange kind of happiness in the awareness of infinity, even though, for Lund at least, that may be an infinity of resignation and despair. Bereft of that 'monstrous paradox' of faith – 'a paradox capable of making a murder into a holy act [. . .] a paradox which gives Isaac back to Abraham' (Kierkegaard, 2005, pp. 60–61) – all that remains to Sarah Lund is the stark absurdity of killing and irredeemable loss.

Kierkegaard (2005, p. 65) observes that for Abraham 'it is precisely the absurd that as the single individual he is higher than the universal'. Roland Barthes (1977, p. 134) witnesses a similarly transformative absurdity in the triumph of Abraham's grandson Jacob in his struggle with the angel. Again, the individual transcends the universal. Kierkegaard (2005, p. 78) adds that the fact that Abraham 'has, as the single individual, become higher than the universal' is the only thing that prevents him from being merely *a murderer*. In other words, the absurdity (the miracle) of faith would in the absence of that faith become fatally empty.

For Kierkegaard (2005, p. 82) it is 'only when the individual has exhausted himself in the infinite, that he reaches a point where faith can emerge'. But what if, at the end of this existential measuring up (this coming into being as an individual through facing up to the reality of existence, through an acceptance of the despair engendered by the individual's infinitesimality, through a recognition of that being as essentially nothingness), faith does not emerge? What if the miracle of the reversal of moral scale (the profane individual imbued with divine significance) does not in fact take place?

The 'knight of faith' is one who, for Kierkegaard (2005, p. 95), endures 'cosmic isolation' – s/he is 'absolutely nothing but the individual, without connections and complications'. Sarah Lund approaches that condition in her sacrifice of her relationships with friends, family and colleagues (just like Abraham's willingness to sacrifice his son) and ultimately in her sacrifice of her societal and professional position and values for the sake of a moral absolute manifest in her willingness to become a killer herself. Yet in the absence of a transcendent universality Lund's moral absolute is unredeeming. Her process of individuation lacks the essential factor of Kierkegaardian faith, namely that existential leap which brings one into a wholeness of being so that, in the absence of the external absolute of eternal law, all that remains is the individual's exhaustive exclusion from humanity, from human society and human law. This exclusion represents a solitary punishment which Kierkegaard equates with 'the punishment of law-breakers' insofar as 'the lovers of solitude are put into the same category as criminals' (Kierkegaard, 2008, p. 78).

This being-outside-ness is typical of a Sartrean notion of human consciousness: 'it is precisely because consciousness [. . .] is total emptiness (since the entire world is outside it) [. . .] that it can be considered as the absolute' (Sartre, 2003, p. 12). For those who recognize the absurdity of existence without the consolation of the absurdity of faith, the uncompromising nature of this process of individuation (of coming to terms with their being) is the extent of their potential for happiness. The possibility of happiness may then reside in the acknowledgement of the inevitability of despair, which is not the same thing as an acceptance of that inevitability. There seems something necessarily paradoxical and appropriately absurd in that acknowledgement.

Sofie's world

Sarah Lund's world is nightmarishly pedestrian. It is a world in which, though we may expect its rationalizations to come in the form of grand political conspiracy theories, we end up discovering that the true motivations behind the devastating crimes which Lund investigates are small, sordid and meaningless. It is a world in which everyone is suspected, in which every possible explanation is explored and yet it is one in which meaningless coincidences accrue to generate the semblance of patterns of illusory significance and magnitude. The massive societal scope of the twenty-hour epic that was the series' first season is in the end exposed as an exercise in the squalid and the mundane. Its byzantine complexity eventually gives way to banal simplicity.

The world of *The Killing* is ultimately incoherent. At the end of its first season the pointless little man revealed as the killer tells his own story, but his narrative contains neither truth nor reason, nor indeed consistency: it is merely his moral alibi, a deluded self-justification. His story is full of holes: he says himself that his crime could not have been predicted or therefore explained. His account does not make sense: it shifts between the three scenes of the crime (the flat, the forest, the house) without any sense of motivation, cause or even sequence. This incoherent narrative ends with another killing – the killing of the killer at the hands of the victim's father; that is the only logic, balance, justice or closure which Lund's world permits. There is no possibility of redemption, of breaking the cycle of meaningless violence; the only meaning lies in the inevitability of that violence, the deterministic nature of meaninglessness. Even the official narrative of the case is to be as incoherent as the murderer's version: as Lund's boss tells her, key facts will be struck from the record for the sake of political and professional expediency. There cannot be any further explanation about what happened because, as Lund's boss also points out, the killer died before he could be questioned. Nothing has been achieved and nothing redeemed or understood. The brilliant, honest, progressive and idealistic politician has become jaded, cynical and corrupt (exactly the same thing happens to another young politician during the course of the following season); the father of the victim has been goaded by the murderer into becoming a killer himself in an act which merely perpetuates the senseless violence; and Lund's own emotional life and professional career have been irretrievably damaged by her uncompromising quest for the truth (a quest which is never really satisfied). Yet Lund, unlike those other characters, has somehow remained true to herself. She retains her integrity not through faith but through her steadfast Sisyphean persistence.

In the third episode of *The Killing*'s first season, the parents of the murder victim visit a church to arrange their daughter's funeral. When the priest tells them that they can take comfort in the thought that she is in heaven the girl's mother asks what good this should do her. The priest admits that, though life lacks meaning, faith allows the possibility of hope. But *The Killing* presents a world – Lund's world, the world through Lund's eyes – in which there is no such hope; the death of a child does not hold the spiritual significance of an Abrahamic sacrifice to religious faith. The priest's Kierkegaardian call to faith as an absurdly transcendental antidote to the absurdity of meaninglessness is, for the grieving mother, merely empty cant. The world of *The Killing* is one which resists audience expectations of, and dramatic tendencies towards, redemption.

In the fifteenth episode of the first season another religious figure, the manager of a Christian hostel, tells the victim's father that there is some plan behind the pain and loss which shadow human experience. The father, however, again rejects this faith in divine fate: if there is anything that can give him hope, he says, then it is nothing at all Christian.

The universe of *The Killing* is a domain of late existentialist absurdity, a realm without God, without faith and therefore without meaning. A soldier driven out of his mind by the horrors of war tells another priest in the fifth episode of *The Killing*'s second season that he has never believed in God and that, though he would have liked to have had faith, he finds faith hard. Yet harder still is that most difficult task which Sveistrup sets for Lund: the determination to sustain the Sisyphean struggle towards truth without that faith in external meaning.

So lonely

Sarah Lund's moments of intuition have a quality of uncanny revelation: a quality manifest through the sudden stillness and fixedness of Sofie Gråbøl's performance – accompanied by a pair of simple yet haunting three-note leitmotifs on the piano – recalling a state described by Sweden's Lars Kepler (2013, p. 31) as the mental stillness that allows the detective to observe the scene of the crime. These moments are uncanny at once in the sense advanced by Freud (the revelation not only of what is unfamiliar but specifically of what is made un-private – in that sense of *unheimlich* – of that which was hidden but has been exposed; the recognition of what is under our very noses) and in a sense suggested by Heidegger: what Heidegger (2010, p. 182) characterizes as the 'uncanny feeling' of existential anxiety – an anxiety which Heidegger (2010, p. 181) sees as 'a mode of attunement' – an anxiety for being-in-the-world which simultaneously discloses the worldliness of the world. Thus intuition becomes a route towards individuation in a process which mediates between inner and outward being, one whose defamiliarizations offer competing possibilities for the development, consolidation and entrenchment of the self.

At such moments Lund's detachment from the noisy trivia of the world enables a focus upon its significant phenomena. Her alienation from quotidian existence or, in a sense of the uncanny advanced by Heidegger (2010, p. 182), her 'not-being-at-home' allows her with a sudden clarity to see and to understand the *things themselves*, the phenomena of the world. Lund's moments of deductive revelation represent oases of calm and distanciation, moments in which the noise of life – the hell of other people, as Sartre (1990, p. 223) supposed – suddenly recedes. These are moments of almost spiritual significance, moments that approach an existentialist nirvana. At these points she becomes detached even from those closest to her. In the first episode of the first series, as she experiences one such moment while on her mobile telephone to her boyfriend, she lowers the phone and his voice (along with all the rest of the noise of life) recedes from her consciousness.

It is ironic then that during a pivotal moment in the third season precisely the opposite happens; for once she finds herself distracted from her work by the sight of her son with his heavily pregnant girlfriend at a railway station. As a result Lund, while engaged in a kidnap ransom drop, misses the train that the kidnapper has told her to catch – an error which leads to catastrophic consequences. For once her emotional life takes precedence over her work: this incident offers a momentary counterpoint to the prevalent situation in which her work overwhelms all other aspects of her life as, for example, in the series' first season, when her obsession with the murder of a young woman devastates her family life, her personal and professional relationships and her career. It results in the death of a close colleague.

Lund's lack of faith in external structures of meaning leads to her exclusion of virtually all *external others*. Her former boyfriend points out to her in the sixth episode of the third season that she does not allow anyone into her life. Lund's emotional life is constantly subsumed to the consuming compulsion (the intellectual and moral imperative) of her professional pursuits. In the opening episode of the second season Lund – during a party celebrating her mother's engagement to be remarried and in one of her moments of alienated revelation – infers from a discarded plastic wrapper for a blank camcorder tape the fact that a murderer filmed his crime. In the sixth episode of that season, distracted by other professional concerns, she walks out of her mother's wedding reception, at which she is supposed to be acting as toastmaster – during her mother's speech – twice.

Lund is not great in groups or parties. In the very first episode of *The Killing* she misses her own leaving party. This not only anticipates her eventual failure to quit her job, but also reflects her desire to be apart from society. As her son tells her in the first season's fifth episode, she thus comes to seem interested only in the dead. Two episodes later her mother tells her that she has never let her boyfriend into her life. She says she just wants her daughter to be happy but fears that she will end up lonely. But Lund is not really listening to her mother: her attention is focused instead on a news story on television related to the murder she is investigating.

Sarah Lund sustains her possibility of happiness not through the consolation of love but through the uncompromising integrity of her moral identity. When, however, she fails to adhere to her own priorities – in that moment in the third series of *The Killing* in which she is distracted by the sight of her son and his pregnant girlfriend – her entire world view falls apart. It can only be by the most extreme reassertion of that perspective (an act of killing which casts her beyond human society) that Lund is eventually able to return to the integrity of herself for which she pays a high cost – the sacrifice of love itself.

In the second episode of the first season of *The Killing*, Lund's boss talks her through a list of the atrocities committed upon the murder victim (a slow drowning preceded by several hours of abuse which had included vaginal and anal rape) in an attempt to justify his demand that Lund remain on the case until it is solved. Lund, however, seems unmoved by this call upon her emotions; rather, it is when her boss points out that the dead girl had held a heart-shaped pendant tightly gripped in her hand that Lund's interest is stimulated (signalled by the recurrence of that musical leitmotif which accompanies her moments of revelation). It is this clue which draws her in: like Sherlock Holmes, her involvement is not emotional but intellectual, which is not to say that it is not a moral involvement as morality is clearly here a function of the intellect.

Jung observes there can be a discrepancy between intellect and feeling and he specifically notes that one 'must carefully exclude feeling [. . .] to satisfy the logical laws of thinking, so that the thought-process will not be disturbed by feeling' (Jung, 1928, para. 64). Lund's insulation of herself from others reflects her separation of thought and feeling. Sarah Lund is not simply introverted: her condition represents a desire for insulation rather than an imperative towards total isolation; a desire to be invisible to others is not the same as a pathological introspection. Jung (1928, para. 77) describes introversion as a 'retreat from the outside world' that, in extremis, 'drives a man into a state of dull brooding'. In this sense, Lund does not seem introverted so much as regressive. As Jung (1928) himself points out, regression is only vaguely analogous to introversion and it may be that regression as an emphasis upon the inner world of the subject's psyche in the promotion of psychical individuation may offer a better model for this fictional character type. Jung (1928, para. 75) contrasts regression with progression, before advancing a possible reconciliation of these two opposing positions:

> Progression as a continual process of adaptation to environmental conditions [. . .] enforces [. . .] the suppression of all those tendencies [. . .] which subserve individuation. Regression [. . .] as an adaptation to the conditions of the inner world, springs from the vital need to satisfy the demands of individuation. Man [. . .] can meet the demands of outer necessity in an ideal way only if he is also adapted to his own inner world, that is, if he is in harmony with himself. Conversely, he can only adapt to his inner world and achieve harmony with himself when he is adapted to his environmental conditions [. . .] the one or other function can be neglected only for a time. Progression and the adaptation resulting therefrom are a means to regression, to a manifestation of the inner world in the outer. In this way a new means is created for a changed mode of progression, bringing better adaptation to environmental conditions.

How then does Sarah Lund so resolutely appear to neglect her progressive function in favour of a regressive inner focus? An existentialist perspective subsumes this apparent paradox: if selfhood is not *a priori*, but is performed in response to (and as an effect of) experience of the external environment, Jung's juxtaposition of the inner and outer worlds seems somewhat moot. Or, rather, Jung's reconciliation of the progressive and regressive functions as interdependent aspects of the same processes of adaptation and harmonization seems less paradoxical than it is inevitable.

This reconciliation becomes inevitable insofar as the self and its environment are similarly interdependent. Thus these processes may promote not the adaptation and harmonization of inner and outer worlds as mutually exclusive conditions so much as the adaptation and harmonization of contradictory aspects of self/environment as an integrated phenomenon. The channelling of the external world performed by Lund's moments of deductive intuition appears to achieve precisely this integration.

Individuation and *Dasein*

Should we see Lund's apparent lack of human empathy as sociopathic? Not necessarily. She is hardly the first great fictional or televisual hero to exhibit such emotional distanciatian. Perhaps the most famous – and explicit – of these is the character of the half-Vulcan scientist Mr Spock, who first appeared in the original *Star Trek* television series in 1966. Zachary Quinto's reinterpretation of Spock, in J. J. Abrams's 2013 film *Star Trek: Into Darkness*, argues that the reason he suppresses his emotions is not that he does not care but precisely the opposite. We might therefore see Lund as a Spock-like figure, struggling – as Hockley (2001, p. 21) has elsewhere suggested of Spock – towards a reconciliation with himself. Spock is clearly not a sociopath; he does not lack empathy or moral conscience (quite the opposite: his moral conscience seems heightened) but promotes emotional balance and control. This then is not so much a matter of pathology as it is a process of psychical individuation.

Sarah Lund is at once dissolute and resolute, inwardly resolute in her public dissolution. This may give the appearance of self-destructiveness, but it is not perhaps that at all: it may be quite the opposite, namely a coming to selfhood through the dissolution of the former self and its relations with the world. Lund's insulation may be seen as part of a process of individuation: not as a state of psychical paralysis but as a progressive dynamic. Jung (1947/54, para. 432) emphatically distinguishes between acts of overweening egotism or solipsism and the process of individuation: 'individuation does not shut one out from the world, but gathers the world to oneself'. This is not, then, mere isolation but a process of being-in-the-world, one in which individual integrity is not extinguished by that integration: a revelatory *Dasein* which cuts through the banal noise of the quotidian, a process which for Heidegger (2010, p. 159) incidentally involves the rejection of the empty socialization of 'idle talk'.

In Heidegger's notion of human being as a continual process of coming into being, *being here* is essentially (that is, existentially) a process of *getting there*, yet (as Heidegger's *Being and Time* approaches Sartre's *Being and Nothingness*) it is also a matter of *going nowhere*. This is a particular absurd form of existential individuation. It is an individuation without essence and it is this in which the likes of Sarah Lund are caught between a mode of being-in-the-world as an experiential projection into the future and a recognition of that future as an endless nothingness. Yet to see this process of coming-into-being as stultifyingly vacuous is not to refute its value or its necessity.

Jung (1928, para. 111) argues that:

> Every advance in culture is [. . .] a coming to consciousness [. . .] an advance
> always begins with individuation, that is to say with the individual, conscious
> of his isolation, cutting a new path through hitherto untrodden territory. To
> do this he must first return to the fundamental facts of his own being, irre-
> spective of all authority and tradition, and allow himself to become conscious
> of his distinctiveness.

Jung sees this heroic process of individuation as essential to the progress of
civilization, and Sarah Lund comes to approximate the Jungian archetype of the
developing hero who undergoes 'an individuation process which is approaching
wholeness' (Jung, 1940/51, para. 281). Jung (1928, para. 112) emphasizes the cultural significance of this process: 'There are large numbers of people for whom the
development of individuality is the prime necessity, especially in a cultural epoch
like ours, which is literally flattened out [sic] by collective norms.' Such collective
norms seem ever the more prevalent in the postmodern world of Sarah Lund. As
Jung (1957, para. 535) stresses, 'ultimately everything depends on the quality of the
individual, but the fatally short-sighted habit of our age is to think only in terms
of large numbers and mass organizations'. The problem is that we tend to forget
that 'the individual human being' remains 'that infinitesimal unit on whom a world
depends' (Jung, 1957, para. 113).

Jung (1939, para. 490) glosses the term individuation as denoting 'the process by
which a person becomes [. . .] a separate, indivisible unity' – 'an open conflict and
an open collaboration' between conscious reason and 'the chaotic life of the unconscious' (Jung, 1939, para. 522). Sarah Lund mediates between the political heights
and the criminal depths of the psycho-social hierarchy, and discovers that, beyond
their finery and grime, the two may be virtually indistinguishable. *The Killing* (or,
for that matter, any detective narrative) represents the protagonist's internalization
and integration of external chaos and conflict, her dream of the revelation, rational-
ization and reconciliation of the superstructural and subversive forces within society
and the human psyche. These are the forces of law, order and structure, on the one
hand, and of atavistic violence and unregulated desire on the other – of, that is, the
archetypal and the instinctual, of *lumen* and of shadow, of civilized consciousness
and of the primordial unconscious. As such this dream represents a dramatization
of what Jung (1934/50; 1947/54, para. 400) would call an 'individuation process'.
This is a process performed by the protagonist on behalf of and for the sake of the
audience, a process of atonement whereby the social order consumes and gives
voice to, acknowledges and integrates its transgressives and transgressions – a process
which therefore comes to represent an act of *at-one-ment*.

The categorical imperative

Jungian individuation – like, for that matter, the universality of Jung's archetypes –
presupposes a certain essentialism (at least the gravitational pull of a symbological

system rather than a fixed point of literal alignment). If, however, coming-into-being is, in a Sartrean sense, an act of performance grounded upon an abyssal nothingness, then this process constantly and endlessly projects selfhood out of an entirely illusory sense of original authenticity. Lund's emphasis, however, upon an essential moral imperative affords her a sense of absolute authenticity and anchors her process of individuation against this existentialist disorientation – even at the point of her ultimate dissolution and alienation.

At the end of *The Killing*'s third and final season Sarah Lund's final act (the execution of a murderer whose guilt she cannot prove) represents a triumphant reconciliation of her intellectual and emotional aspects. It is simultaneously a resolutely intellectual and an uncompromisingly emotional act; it is an absolutely moral act which transcends (in that it at once completes and effaces) her professional authority and in her rejection of the law she *becomes* the law. She is both law and chaos at the same time. This final transgression, then, remains absolutely true: true to herself as an undiluted reflection and integration of the experiential conditions of her existence; it reflects the perseverance and preciseness for which the killer commends her shortly before she executes him. As a consequence of this act, she loses not only her defining professional status, but also her kinship status and specifically her status as mother and grandmother: it is implied she will never meet her newly born grandchild. While Denmark's prime minister collaborates in the cover-up of a murder on the grounds that he believes that it is for the good of the nation (at the end of the series' third season – as at the end of the second) Lund rejects a moral sophistry determined by external, objective and institutional forces. Though Jung (1957) warns that in contemporary society individual moral responsibility has been replaced by the policies of the state, and Bourdieu (1977, p. 79) suggests that, subsumed to the objective institutions of the state, the individual's 'actions [. . .] are the product of a modus operandi of which he is not the producer and has no conscious mastery', Lund desperately attempts to reassert the possibility of individual moral and psychical self-determination against all the evidence of existential determinism.

In that final act Sarah Lund appears an existentialist caught between Kierkegaard, Heidegger and Sartre: her leap of self-faith lacks the miraculous inversion permitted by religious faith and therefore projects her (whole yet still infinitesimally insignificant) into nothingness; her faith is not divinely absurd but humanly absurd and cannot therefore transcend the absurdity of human being. Yet her anchorless existentialism maintains a paradoxical grip upon the uncompromising essentialism of a Kantian assertion of the moral imperative. The kind of moral law which motivates and sustains Lund stands for Kant beyond such experiential flux insofar as any 'precept which is founded on principles of mere experience [. . .] can never be called a moral law' (Kant, 2005, p. 3).

Bishop (1999, p. 4) has shown how Jung's differentiation between synthetic and analytic modes of psychotherapy, a distinction based upon Kantian arguments, posited his own practice (unlike Freud's retrospective analysis) as offering a progressive synthesis which might 'deal with the trajectory of the neurosis' and which thereby 'looked forward to the future'. Yet, as Bishop (2008, p. 48) has pointed out, Kant's notion of synthesis required the empiricism of '*a posteriori* knowledge' rather than *a priori* essence. By contrast, Jung continued paradoxically to hang his syntheticism (a process to foster the dynamics of coming into being in the world) upon *a priori* structures. Jung (1912/17/26/43, para. 122) argued, for example, that 'the images or symbols of the collective unconscious yield their distinctive values only when subjected to a synthetic mode of treatment' yet suggested that such a mode might discover 'a definite entity in the collective unconscious' (Jung, 1912/17/26/43, para. 155), an archetypal entity as essential and pre-existing as it is psychologically definitive. Despite all his claims of forward-looking synthesis, Jung's remorseless recourse to such *a priori* principles recalls the 'Romantic yearning' which Bishop (2008, p. 1) witnesses in his interest in Kant's prioritization of 'intellectual intuition' as essentially valid.

Lund, like Jung, returns constantly to sets of essential principles and relies time and again upon intuitive processes which negate her own existential paradigm. The typically postmodern absurdity (the difficult task turned *impossibility*) of Lund's position is that she is, essentially, an essentialist in an existentialist universe, a universe, that is, which she sees through existentialist eyes. In order to navigate, to make sense of, this absurdity, she relies upon one essential and immutable precept of faith – not in her case a religious faith (nor indeed a faith in the institutions of society, politics or law), but a faith in an intellectual sense of absolute morality not determined by the contingencies of external experience but immanent to her individuated self. This represents her alternative to the orthodox pursuit of happiness.

Kant (2005, p. 35) argued that as 'the elements which belong to the notion of happiness are altogether empirical' it is inevitable that 'the notion of happiness is so indefinite that although every man wishes to attain it, yet he never can say definitely [. . .] what it is that he really wishes' and thus that 'the more a cultivated reason applies itself with deliberate purpose to the enjoyment of life and happiness, so much the more does the man fail of true satisfaction' (Kant, 2005, p. 11). Kant (2005, p. 12) therefore subsumes the ordinary pursuit of happiness to the self-validating quest for absolute moral and intellectual truth: 'our existence has a different and far nobler end, for which, and not for happiness, reason is properly intended [. . .] its true destination must be to produce a *will*'.

Kant (2005, p. 60) draws a clear distinction between morality as a categorical imperative and a mere sense of 'moral feeling' which he classes 'under that of happiness'. For Kant, the moral imperative is a matter of reason rather than of feeling; happiness by contrast is a matter of empirical or existential feeling rather than of essential and *a priori* reason. Negotiating between the essential and the existential, as between thought and feeling, Lund's process of individuation, which requires precisely this negotiation of contraries, replaces a conventional pursuit of happiness with a coming-into-being at once *in the world* and *in herself.*

A question of hermeneutics

Lund's relationships with men (from her distancing herself from her lover Bengt and her cold flirtation with the politician Troels Hartmann in the first season, through her nearly-but-not-quite romance with her police partner in the second, to her unresolved relationship with her former lover in the third) – her relationships with her mother and son – her relationships with her colleagues – all draw back from their points of climax. This emotional detachment is echoed in her relationship with her audience: she never quite gives herself to us, she remains ever distant, we can never quite grasp her, grasp who or how or why she is. In the second season's eighth episode, Lund begins to open up: she tells her detective partner about how she hid herself away after the death of her former partner the previous season, and how, after that death, the final result of the case (the detection of the killer) had seemed unimportant. Yet she cuts off that conversation; it never gets anywhere, nor does her relationship with her new partner. It eventually transpires that the person in whom she had chosen to confide was not after all the best candidate for confidant or soul-mate, when he is himself revealed as a serial killer – one whom later she kills. The communication of meaning is in this way never fully realized. We never really discover who Sarah Lund actually is. (And that is one reason why she remains so fascinating and attractive to us.)

The endless coming-towards-pleasure/meaning/being performed by Lund is also enacted by the structure and movement of the series itself: its remorseless processes of restructuration, its relentlessly slippery elaboration and re-ambiguation of its own plots. Indeed, there is something fundamentally existentialist about the way *The Killing* is made: the series is written and filmed in episodic sequence and the actors do not see the latest episode's script until they have completed filming the previous episode (cf. Kirby, 2012); thus they do not know the forthcoming revelations of the series (including the identity of the killer) while they are filming it – nor therefore do they fully understand their own motivations. The characters thereby lack motivational essence: they are entirely reactive, they are *all experience*. This seemed crucial to the series: Sofie Gråbøl has commented that her own performance was dynamized by this lack of knowledge (*The Making of the Killing*, 2011). In this way the series advances what Heidegger (2010, p. 42) would call 'the priority of *existentia* over *essentia*' as the characters come into being not through any preconceived essence but through the actors' ongoing experience of the drama: projecting the secrets of their characters into their futures, perpetually coming into being in the *Dasein* of an existential heremeneutic which is what Jung (1947/54, para. 352) himself would call 'a treasure-house, not indeed of anticipated, but of accumulated, life-experiences'.

Even *The Killing*'s restless camerawork seems constantly to be seeking an unattainable destination. It offers a visual metaphor for a process of coming-into-being (a metaphor composed not of solid substance but of fluid movement). That visual process is emphasized at the end of each episode as, rather than reaching a conclusion in a single climactic moment, the camera continues its relentless sweeping progress around the action in an orbit which projects its perspective perpetually into the future, one which never reaches a centre, an essence, a *telos*, a rest. The camera's restlessness, like Sarah Lund, seems symptomatic of a typically existentialist mix of *Dasein*, *Angst* and *ennui*: a hermeneutic unfolding which never quite reaches fruition – an ontological and epistemological foreplay, as 'null and endless' as Derrida's notion of textual pleasure as a 'threshold phenomenon' (Derrida, 1981, p. 58). The process of hermeneutic unfolding performed by *The Killing* is emphatically ambiguous and therefore endless; almost every episode centres on a revelation that leads the viewer and the detective to believe with virtually no shadow of doubt that so-and-so is the killer, only for that certainty to be overturned in the following episode. Thus, even at the end, in those season endings whose revelations remain unsatisfyingly banal, the process of coming-into-meaning never seems quite complete.

Sofie's choice

Despite the inevitability of the logic of faithlessness, most of us continue to believe in God, in love, because to do otherwise would be to cast ourselves adrift and eternally alone against the infinite and unmanageable flux, too vast to be negotiated, comprehended, imagined or envisioned. So we dream instead of that which we know cannot be in order to sustain a not-entirely-convincing illusion of happiness. There are a few, however, who choose to embrace the logic of despair, in the knowledge that the possibility of real happiness (however difficult, however practically impossible) is excluded by the maintenance of that illusion. This then is the soul-wrenching impossibility of Sarah Lund's ultimate moral choice.

Søren Sveistrup's television series *The Killing* offers us the possibility of happiness in a very different way from that proposed by his predecessor Søren Kierkegaard. Kierkegaard's hope for happiness is predicated upon the adoption of religious faith: the model he offers, that of Abraham, is of one who subsumes their individuality to a greater external meaning. By contrast, *The Killing*'s Sarah Lund discovers her only (slim) possibility of happiness in her individuation. Sveistrup's Lund represents a role model for how one might lead one's life without external faith; how one might seek to pursue happiness within the context of an acknowledgement of the absurdity of existence in a godless, meaningless universe. But can we really seek to live our lives like this? Is the Lund model any more viable than that, say, of Harry Hole, Lisbeth Salander, Carrie Mathison or Gregory House – or Camus's Meersault or Sartre's Antoine Roquentin for that matter? Are these really sustainable models for being? Or are these figures who soldier on despite having seen through the illusions and hypocrisies of everyday existence, mere fantasies themselves – illusory ideals of a paradoxically (even hypocritically) romantic myth of charismatic existentialism – more fairytales perpetuated by the mass culture industries?

Yet if we cannot really be expected to live our lives *in imitatio* of Sarah Lund, then what purpose does this avatar of individuation serve? How then can Lund bring us pleasure, or even the possibility of happiness? There are three possible ways which spring to mind: (1) Lund's fate serves as a warning against non-conformity and therefore a reassurance of happiness for the conformist mass audience (but if that were the case then why would we identify with her – why would audiences like her and root for her as much as they do?); (2) Lund represents for her audiences a wish fulfilment or aspirational identification (we would all like to be as true to ourselves as Lund; we find her charismatic and attractive; yet her heroism is clearly problematic, as is our idealization of that heroism); (3) her rejection of illusion and hypocrisy in her futile quest for intellectual and moral truth is recognizably and fundamentally human, yet her persistence and integrity in this quest are extraordinary and heroic, and although it leads towards loss, failure and sacrifice, that sacrifice is morally triumphant and is performed *on behalf of* all of us: it is the price for our possibility of happiness.

Sarah Lund is a fairytale seeker after happiness repackaged for the late postmodern age. She is, as such, something of a saviour figure, or at least a sacrifice which pays for our happiness. Yet her final flight into the night does not represent a triumphant transfiguration in itself: hers is a flight towards the frozen isolation of Iceland, clasping a photograph of the grandchild she will never meet. Lund is then, in the end, a Christ unrisen, a Christ bound into a Sisyphean, Sartrean hell. She is a godless Christ, a Christ who believes that she has been forsaken and yet struggles on; an Abraham who lacks faith and who nevertheless sacrifices his son. Her inner faith lies in her outer faithlessness (her public appearance of faithlessness and her lack of faith in externalities); her meaning resides in her absurdity. For her audiences to accept that paradox requires the most extraordinarily absurd act of faith. This cult of existential absurdity, this romanticization of meaninglessness, represents the greatest fairytale and requires the greatest, the most absurd leap of faith of them all.

References

CW = C.G. Jung, *The collected works of C.G. Jung*, eds H. Read, M. Fordham and G. Adler, trans. R.F.C. Hull (1953–79). London: Routledge.

Andersen, H.C. (2009). *The complete fairy tales*. Ware: Wordsworth Editions.

Barthes, R. (1977). *Image-music-text* (S. Heath, trans.). London: Fontana.

Bishop, P. (1999). Introduction. In P. Bishop (ed.), *Jung in contexts* (pp. 1–30). London: Routledge.

Bishop, P. (2008). *Analytical psychology and German classical aesthetics*. Hove: Routledge.

Bourdieu, P. (1977). *Outline of a theory of practice* (R. Nice, trans.). Cambridge: Cambridge University Press.

Camus, A. (1975). *The myth of Sisyphus* (J. O'Brien, trans.). Harmondsworth: Penguin.

Camus, A. (1983). *The outsider* (J. Laredo, trans.). Harmondsworth: Penguin.

Derrida, J. (1981). *Dissemination* (B. Johnson, trans.). London: Athlone.

Fenger, H. (2003). Kierkegaard: A Literary Approach. In J. Stewart (ed.), *Kierkegaard and his contemporaries* (pp. 301–318). Berlin: Walter de Gruyter.

Freud, S. (1985). *Art and literature* (J. Strachey, trans.). Harmondsworth: Penguin.

Frost, V. (2011, March 10). *The Killing*: Sarah Lund's Jumper Explained. *Guardian*.

Heidegger, M. (2010). *Being and time* (J. Stambaugh, trans.). Albany: State University of New York Press.

Hill, S. (2012). *A question of identity*. London: Random House.

Hockley, L. (2001). *Cinematic projections*. Luton: University of Luton Press.

Holt, A. (2011). *1222* (M. Delargy, trans.). London: Atlantic Books.

Jung, C.G. (1912/17/26/43). 'On the Psychology of the Unconscious'. In *CW*, vol. 7.

Jung, C. G. (1928). 'On Psychic Energy'. In *CW*, vol. 8.

Jung, C. G. (1934/50). 'A Study in the Process of Individuation'. In *CW*, vol. 9.

Jung, C. G. (1939). 'Conscious, Unconscious, and Individuation'. In *CW*, vol. 9i.

Jung, C. G. (1940/51). 'The Psychology of the Child Archetype'. In *CW*, vol. 9i.

Jung, C. G. (1947/54). 'On the Nature of the Psyche'. In *CW*, vol. 8.

Jung, C. G. (1957). 'The Undiscovered Self: Present and Future'. In *CW*, vol. 10.

Kallentoft, M. (2012). *Autumn killing* (N. Smith, trans.). London: Hodder.

Kallentoft, M. (2013). *Savage spring*. London: Hodder.

Kant, I. (2005). *Fundamental principles of the metaphysics of morals* (T. K. Abbott, trans.). New York: Dover.

Kepler, L. (2013). *The fire witness* (L. Wideburg, trans.). London: HarperCollins.

Kierkegaard, S. (2005). *Fear and trembling* (A. Hannay, trans.). London: Penguin.

Kierkegaard, S. (2008). *The sickness unto death* (A. Hannay, trans.). London: Penguin.

Kirby, E. (2012, April 28). *The Killing* and *Borgen*: Danish drama wins global fanbase. *BBC News*.

Larsson, S. (2008). *The girl with the dragon tattoo* (R. Keeland, trans.). London: Quercus.

Larsson, S. (2010). *The girl who kicked the hornet's nest* (R. Keeland, trans.). London: Quercus.

Mankell, H. (2008). *Firewall* (E. Segerberg, trans.). London: Vintage.

Nesbø, J. (2012). *The bat* (D. Bartlett, trans.). London: Harvill Secker.

Nesbø, J. (2013). *Police* (D. Bartlett, trans.). London: Harvill Secker.

Sartre, J.-P. (1990). *In camera* (S. Gilbert, trans.). London: Penguin.

Sartre, J.-P. (2000). *Nausea* (R. Baldick, trans.). London: Penguin.

Sartre, J.-P. (2003). *Being and nothingness* (H. Barnes, trans.). London: Routledge.

Theorin, J. (2012). *The asylum* (M. Delargy, trans.). London: Doubleday.

AUTHOR INDEX

SUBJECT INDEX

For Product Safety Concerns and Information please contact our EU
representative GPSR@taylorandfrancis.com
Taylor & Francis Verlag GmbH, Kaufingerstraße 24, 80331 München, Germany